PICKING BONES FROM ASH

PICKING BONES FROM ASH

Marie Mutsuki Mockett

Graywolf Press

This publication is made possible by funding provided in part by a grant from the Minnesota State Arts Board, through an appropriation by the Minnesota State Legislature, a grant from the National Endowment for the Arts, and private funders. Significant support has also been provided by Target; the McKnight Foundation; and other generous contributions from foundations, corporations, and individuals. To these organizations and individuals we offer our heartfelt thanks.

Published by Graywolf Press
250 Third Avenue North, Suite 600
Minneapolis, Minnesota 55401

www.graywolfpress.org

Published in the United States of America

ISBN 978-1-55597-541-8 (cloth)
ISBN 978-1-55597-576-0 (paper)

2 4 6 8 9 7 5 3 1

Library of Congress Control Number: 2010937514

Cover design: Kimberly Glyder Design

Cover photo: Ignacio Ayestaran, Getty Images

To my mother and father,
who taught me to join worlds together

*"When there are secrets, the flower exists;
but without secrets, the flower does not exist."*

ZEAMI, FROM *FŪSHIKADEN*
(TEACHINGS ON STYLE AND THE FLOWER)

PART ONE

CHAPTER 1

A Change in the Weather

Satomi
Kuma-ume, Japan, 1954

My mother always told me that there is only one way a woman can be truly safe in this world. And that is to be fiercely, inarguably, and masterfully talented.

This is different than being intelligent or even educated. The latter, she insisted, could get a girl into trouble, convincing her that she has the same power as men. Certainly the biggest mistake a woman could make was to rely on her beauty. Such a woman is destined to grow old and ugly very quickly because she is so much more disappointed by what she sees in the mirror than someone who is busy. "But when you are talented," she whispered to me late at night as we lay in our *futons*, "you are special. You will have troubles, but they won't be any of the ordinary ones."

In the beginning, we thought my talent was going to be music. Mother had an old out-of-tune piano that she kept in our small second-floor apartment and that I practiced on as a child. "It's such an ordinary piano," my mother lamented to the other ladies in town. "Nothing like the fine *koto* or *shamisen* I used to play. It's unfortunate because Satomi has talent. I know better than anyone else that talent must be developed when one is very young." My mother ran an *izakaya*, or pub, downstairs from our apartment, which meant that she was home most afternoons when I returned from school. It also restricted her social interactions with other women to the buying of vegetables or clothing from the shops during the day; she had no time for lunchtime get-togethers. In the evening, after I'd eaten my dinner and become consumed by homework, she was serving drinks to tipsy men and entertaining them with her wit.

"What," murmured the other women of the town, "does she mean when she says she knows that talent must be nurtured when one is young?"

"Witches," someone muttered, "must start training when they are young. Perhaps Satomi's mother is a witch."

"Witches are blind," another woman scoffed. "Satomi's mother can see."

"Well, she must be a geisha then," someone else said. "She became pregnant with her lover's child. He wouldn't leave his wife. And here we are with Satomi and her mother living in our town. Remember? They just showed up one day after the war ended."

"Satomi's mother *is* very beautiful."

"And accomplished."

"She isn't *that* beautiful."

After a moment, one of them added, "But her daughter *is* very talented."

Having decided that my mother was no less than a retired geisha, the other women gave her as wide a berth as possible, and kept an ear out for any gossip that involved the interaction of their husbands with a woman who had doubtless been trained since she was very small in the art of engaging a man in meaningful conversation.

I heard about all of this from Tomoko, who was my best friend until middle school. Tomoko often looked for ways to cheer me up because she knew how much it bothered me not to know my father's name. There were other children without mothers or fathers, and even some orphans who lived with their grandparents, but at least these children all knew who their parents had been. I only knew my mother. This ignorance hinted at a willful dismissal of social niceties in my personal history, and this past negligence was often enough reason for me not to be asked to parties or to be invited to walk home from school with the other girls. "But everyone thinks you are talented," Tomoko comforted me.

"I'd rather be pretty."

"*I* think you're pretty," said Tomoko of the little nose, slim hands and legs, and small round mouth. "In the long run, I suspect that being talented is going to matter more than being pretty."

My mother was not some geisha. But because we lived far north of sophisticated Tokyo or Kyoto, it was easy for her to maintain the illusion that she had once been connected to the old Japanese tradition of hospitality and art. This trick protected us for a long time. Women were nervous around her, and men saw her as some sort of ideal they should strive to impress and protect. The women knew how the men felt and it bothered them, but because there was never any definitive gossip linking my mother to one particular man, they mostly left her alone.

My mother was very particular and had a strong aesthetic sense that could at times be intimidating. Given a choice between two kinds of tea bowls—a gaudy and greenish *Kutani* teacup or a *wabi-sabi* style *Shino*—she would always choose the latter and couldn't understand anyone who would choose the former. She was rigorous in training me to see these differences too, every so often pulling out her small collection, amassed during and immediately after the war years, for our tutorials. I was allowed to touch the plates and bowls, except for one light-green-colored pot in the shape of a melon. "That one," she said to me, "is Korean. Maybe you can play with it when you are older."

To women she would say things like: "Did you see the *kimono* display in Kyōya's? Why would anyone with such cheap-looking *kimonos* even pretend to have a relationship to Kyoto?" Or, "Really, didn't you know that those bright *meisen* kimonos are considered unsophisticated now? It's a good idea to just cut them up and turn them into *futon* covers. *I* can show you how if you don't know."

With men she affected an alert, almost childlike expression, wide eyes taking in everything they said as though it was all, right down to the most inane reenactment of a day at work, the most interesting information she had ever heard. At the same time she kept her lips pursed in a little closed-mouth smile to make it clear that while she was good at listening, she would not disclose their secrets. When things became heated, as they did when a man was momentarily convinced that he should leave his wife for her, she knew how to deflect this kind of ardor with a lighthearted remark that would spare the man any embarrassment the next day when he was sober. "Nobata-san has done much better with his wife than he would ever do with me," she would smile, with no small hint of regret in her eyes. In the hazy morning that followed a night of drinking, the men remembered her as a beautiful if tragic figure who knew her place and thus was deserving of patronage the following evening for yet another round of *shōchu* to drink.

The *izakaya* was small, with perhaps enough room for eight people at the counter and ten more in the back. The wall behind the counter was stocked with a supply of liquor and glasses. There was also a small refrigerator, stuffed with vegetables, meat, and the frozen ingredients my mother needed to cook her specialties. She was a wizard at utilizing every single spare corner of that refrigerator. Even now, when I pack a suitcase, I feel ashamed that I am not similarly gifted.

Although she only had four small gas burners and a fish grill, my mother managed all the orders for beer, *sake*, *oden*, and *tempura*. Alone, she kept the place clean and tastefully decorated following a rustic theme befitting our mountain town, Kuma-ume. Here and there were muted patchwork wall hangings refashioned from our drab wartime clothes, dried flower arrangements, and mismatched glasses and blue-and-white teacups she'd rescued from various trash cans. It is a style that is very popular now but seemed elegantly eccentric at the time. It was a feminine enough place that men always bowed when they entered and wiped up any beer that they spilled, but not so oppressively frilly that they were afraid to get drunk and talk politics until the early morning.

I never did learn where she developed her sense of taste, because she never told me where she was born. Instead, she filled my head with stories about the moon princess who as a baby was discovered stuffed inside a fat bamboo stalk by a poor bamboo cutter. The baby grew up to be a beautiful and accomplished young lady who was ultimately reclaimed by the kingdom of the moon.

"One day the kingdom of the moon will come for you, and I will be rewarded for having cared for you all these years."

"If I'm your daughter, you must be a princess too," I said.

"That has to remain a secret." She sighed deeply. "You see, I resolved a long time ago not to be a princess, but to teach everything I ever learned at the palace to my daughter, so she could go and reclaim her rightful place."

It was a lovely fiction for a child to believe. Sometimes I ran around in the forests near our home looking for a stalk of bamboo large enough for a baby. I'd already seen how certain stalks could hold enough water to support a bouquet of lilies, and how the fattest trunks could reverberate like the rain when they were tapped with chopsticks.

We children were told that the woods were filled with *oni,* or demons, and that many of these monsters liked to kidnap and devour children. Some *oni* specialized in preying upon little boys. Some preferred girls. Many were indiscriminate. Every now and then a child who had once gone to school with a playful smile upon her face simply disappeared, dragged off, it was said, by the demons in the woods, and then we were all advised to avoid the woods for a good few weeks.

Although I wasn't immune to the potential terrors of the woods, I thought of nature as being my friend and believed that it would always protect me. I had names for the sparrows who ate *osenbei* crumbs from my window. In early spring, when the *yabutsubaki* wild camellias bloomed, I made necklaces from their flowers and little whistles with their dark brown seeds. When the other children chased me home from school, I could hide in the tall weeds while they ran past. In our hungriest days, my mother and I caught crickets and minnows by the river for dinner.

And then one day, when I was around ten years old, I carried a long stick into the forest and imagined myself to be a female *ninja.* I had recently learned from my mother's customer Mr. Nobata that the women in Japan were as capable of mastering those dark arts as the men. I had decided to approach the heart of the forest and find the fat stalk of bamboo from which I had been born. Perhaps there might be an altar there to mark the spot, or maybe the moon goddess's father would be waiting for me with a bag of treats. I was often hungry in those days, and I dreamed up elaborate scenarios in which the prize at the end would be plentiful food.

I ventured deeper into the woods than ever. Even the barking dogs and roaring trucks, the noises of the town that carried the farthest, grew dim. Soon all I heard was the playful rustle of bamboo leaves toying with each other. I thought I must be the first and only person to feel the breath of nature like this on her neck.

It was difficult terrain, for the bamboo stalks leaned against each other, inadvertently forming little huts that I had to break apart. I became aware of how much sound I created. A small deer picking her way delicately across a patch of fallen leaves could move more quietly, despite having four legs. Birds fluttered in between branches and I marveled at the reflexes that allowed them to dart so skillfully. I resolved to be noiseless. *Ninja,* it was said, could move through the woods without detection.

Suddenly I was overcome with cold, as though the woods had been invaded by fog. But the air was still clear, and high above the sun was shining. I began to feel an icy pressure upon my neck, and when I reached up to touch the space behind my head, I felt clammy tendrils intertwine with my fingers. I recoiled and, reluctantly, the cold let go of my hand, then gripped my wrist. The hand was attached to an even larger mass and I could feel its bulk using me as an anchor as it tugged its body through the trees. No sword of bamboo could protect me now.

I'd climbed a good way up the hill into the woods and it would take me some time, not to mention a great deal of noise, to retreat back to civilization. So I did the only sensible thing to do in these circumstances. I shook myself free of the moisture and crouched down low behind a particularly thick patch of bamboo. Cold air sailed overhead. My heart and brain frantically signaled each other. *Be afraid,* said one. *I'm panicking,* said the other. *Give this body as much blood and adrenaline as she can stand,* said the one. *I'm pumping as fast as I can,* came the reply.

There I sat, muscles taut, instincts at the ready, when in front of me, perhaps just ten meters away, I saw a figure. As it came closer, I realized that it was an old woman with a woven basket strapped to her back. She was tiny, even smaller than my mother, with coarse hair pinned to her head in a small knot. She wore faded bluish-gray clothing, the kind of thing worn by rice paddy workers, and her feet were bound by fat swathes of cloth that looked impossible to remove. I wondered if she slept with her shoes on.

She pulled what looked like a fat knife from the inside of her garment. The air inside my lungs screamed for release. I tensed, poised to flee. But then she did the oddest thing. She bent down and cleared a patch of bamboo leaves with her free hand. She sniffed at the dirt, like the deer I had seen perhaps not fifteen minutes before. With a deft movement, she cut at the earth, and when she stood up a moment later, I saw that she was holding a fat bamboo shoot. The knife was actually a spade. I smelled an aromatic scent and saw a few more triangular shoots, with their leafy, golden-brown covering, sticking out of her woven basket.

The old woman knelt back down and brushed leaves off the ground. The ground yielded a few more shoots. She stood, and adjusted the straps on her back, for the basket hung more heavily now. She took one tentative step, then another, and, bracing herself, continued on through the forest. I watched her until she rounded a clump of bamboo, and then she and the cold air were gone.

I forgot all about my quest to find the life-generating bamboo grove at the heart of the forest. Now food took precedence. Bamboo has a shallow but elaborate network of roots that cling to each other fiercely, like lovers. My mother had often told me how, during an earthquake, she'd once taken shelter in a grove. "The ground opened up and swallowed five men running through a rice paddy. But the roots I was standing on held firm," she said.

I examined the ground where the bamboo shoot lady had stood. She'd covered the disturbed earth with fallen leaves so there was little evidence that she'd passed through. No trace at all, in fact, save for the lingering scent of bamboo in the air. I pawed at the earth and uncovered a few smaller shoots she'd left behind. Perhaps she'd intended to return when they had grown larger, but I wasn't about to give her the chance.

I squatted most inelegantly to the ground and began to dig, to hack, to claw at the shoots, an effort that would have been much easier had I had a spade. Instead, I had to improvise with small rocks and with my fingers. At last the shoot was free. I repeated the process a few times until my pockets were stuffed, and then I flew down the hillside like a foreign aircraft descending on the town below, not at all concerned with who might hear me coming. I had the image of my mother's face before me; she would be beaming when I bombed her with bamboo shoots.

She was pleased. Very pleased. First she immersed the shoots in water with a little rice bran. This she cooked till the shoots were tender. Then she turned off the heat and left the pot overnight. The next day I helped her peel. How exciting it was to see the beautiful, blond flesh of bamboo appear. "When you care for something," she said to me, "it becomes beautiful. You see?"

She made three dishes. She cooked the bottom part of the shoots with chicken meat and served this to her customers at the *izakaya*. With the tips, the most delicate part of the shoots, she made a *sunomono* salad, with seaweed and *miso*. The middle part of the bamboo shoots she added to our daily rice pot, sprinkling in some *ginkgo* nuts I'd harvested the previous fall.

"I've gone to look for shoots at the edge of the woods," she said. "But everyone else gets there before I do. It's all this work I do. It doesn't leave me much free time."

"You have to go deep into the woods," I said. "*Very* deep."

She gave me a strange look. "What were you doing there? Who did you go with?"

"I went alone!" I protested. "I was looking for the bamboo where the moon princess was born."

She smiled then, and I could almost hear her thinking to herself that I was still just a little girl after all. "You must be careful. There are many strange people in the woods. Not to mention *onis*."

"I saw an old woman. She was carrying a basket on her back and picking shoots." I described how the woman had been dressed.

"Must have been your imagination." She smiled kindly. "No elderly woman would go tromping around in there on her own. And how would she get up into the hillside?"

"But I *saw* her."

"I haven't heard of people collecting bamboo shoots and wearing the outfit you describe since I was a little girl. And if there was a woman collecting that many shoots, surely she'd be trying to sell them in town."

"Maybe she is selling them now and you just don't know about it."

"I'd know about it if there were such a thing as an old woman selling delicacies that have been scarce ever since this stupid war ended." A black mood overcame her then and my mind's eye darkened with hers.

"Maybe it was a ghost," I said. "Or a god."

She liked this idea. "A god showed you the way to give us some food for dinner? That's a much better explanation. And much more likely too."

"Or maybe," I whispered with reverence, "the moon princess sent the bamboo shoot lady to me."

"We must," she whispered in kind, "thank the moon people for this generosity."

"It's a sign."

We looked out of the window and up at the sky at the same time. There was the deep, blue-black night filled with hundreds of silver knowing eyes and a moon as round as an *omanju*. I was happy in the fantasy of the moon people and pleased that my mother had so enjoyed my gift. But the moment didn't last long. My mother began to breathe quickly, and I could feel her eyes darting around as though searching the room for the answer to an unarticulated question. My attention fell down from the sky and back into the room with the one lightbulb fixed inside a paper lantern filling the kitchen with a weak yellow glow. My mother put down her chopsticks. Though I hadn't been prompted to do so, I put mine down as well. She took my fingers in her hands and examined them. "You have to be careful. You have a competition next week and you can't win if you hurt your fingers by digging up bamboo shoots."

"My hands are fine."

She pushed my hands away as though she had just borrowed them and was now returning them to me. "You have to remember that you aren't like everybody else. You are a very unique person."

"I am?"

"I've told you that many times," she said loftily. "I've met many, many people. Before you were born, when life was different, I used to know many people who are famous now. And you are smarter and even more talented than they are. Remember that." She nodded.

I remembered and I believed her.

I won the piano competition easily, and another one the following weekend in which I was awarded a photo album, which was very often the grand prize in those days. Due to labor laws, children weren't allowed to earn money, even from a contest. It was nearly always the same two dozen or so students and their parents from several neighboring towns who crowded together in an auditorium to slog through Mozart and Beethoven. By now I had half a dozen photo albums, which my mother stocked with pictures, my essays, and pressed wildflowers.

The weekend after I harvested bamboo shoots, I wore a pair of wool mittens my mother had knitted for me to keep my fingers warm. When it was my turn to play, I strode up to the piano, made eye contact with the judges, and bowed, counting to five as my mother had taught me. Two counts to go down, one to linger, and then two to come back up. My fingers slid easily through the first movement of the Mozart Sonata in A Minor, Köchel 310, despite the difficult left-hand passages. My picture appeared in the local paper the next day, with Tomoko's face just barely cropped out of one side, and my mother's face on the other. I still have the clipping. At the time, I felt very regal and important, every inch the heir to the throne of the moon people.

Tomoko had made it her mission to come to almost all my competitions. After I performed, she always came to the edge of the stage and solemnly handed me a bouquet of *nogiku* wild chrysanthemums in autumn and freesias in the spring. We bowed to each other in imitation of seventeenth century French courtiers we'd read about in history class. Thus I was able to prolong my time on stage by a good thirty seconds or so.

Flowers were something of a luxury in those days. Our town, Kuma-ume, was located along the Mogami River, just one of a series of small towns lost in northern Japan, barely subsisting after the war. But Tomoko's family owned a small chain of laundries in several neighboring towns, all the way to Yamadera, and was relatively well off. The family indulged their only daughter's childhood whim to be my champion, though they themselves were less inclined to cheer for me or to pose in my photos.

I had grown accustomed to winning, and my teacher, an elderly man named Mr. Kisahara who had sported a mustache since the Taisho era and studied music in Tokyo, was used to being the teacher of a prizewinning student. We knew most of the other music students in the area, and had cataloged their foibles. I also understood, from having spent time watching my mother in the bar, the valuable power of gossip. If I caught wind that Mariko, the goody-goody, was going to try to play Debussy in the next contest, Mr. Kisahara and I determined that I would play Ravel. If I learned that Satoshi, the technician, was going to play a Bach fugue, I played the same piece and vowed to be better.

So it was perhaps a bit surprising that my mother conspired to enter me in a new contest that would take place the following fall in the city of Akita, a good five hours away. This was the Tōhoku regional competition and included students from all the northern prefectures, including my own.

"Satomi has a false sense of her abilities," my mother said sternly to my teacher. "She needs a good competition to wake her up."

"We don't know the competitors," Mr. Kisahara retorted. "What should she play?"

"True competition," she replied coolly, "implies risk. Satomi needs to learn this."

We settled on two pieces. I chose Debussy's "Clair de Lune" (because it was about the moon). To complement this, my mother insisted I tackle the Beethoven *Moonlight* Sonata.

All summer I practiced my two pieces in secret. One day in October, when the maples had started to blush on the mountainsides, my mother and I watered the plants, giving extra care to the *hechima* vine just outside the entrance to the *izakaya*. In her clear and careful handwriting, my mother wrote a note, which she placed in the pub window, explaining that we would be out of town and that the business would be closed for three days. Of course everyone in town already knew why we were leaving, but she wrote that our absence was due to a "family situation." To anyone else she would have looked poised as she locked the door, but I knew she was wildly excited. Over the past few weeks as the competition date had grown closer, her shifting moods had settled into pure and radiant happiness. I would have traveled to a hundred competitions that year to keep her so steadily elated.

The competition came with a grand prize in each age category. The prize included a month's supply of Erubi fermented milk drink, a large bag of rice, a free toothbrush, and two tubes of toothpaste. It was by far the most ambitious bounty I'd ever tried to win.

Every trip I have taken since reminds me of that first journey. My mother, emboldened by our adventure and by our anonymity, spoke confidently about our plans to the little ladies who shared our seating area on the train. She had spent the last few days preparing a gorgeous *bento* lunch box for us to eat. A bed of rice was a blank canvas on which she had painted scenes from home: wild greens formed a bamboo forest, eggs cut into flowers bloomed in the foreground, little wisps of seaweed arched into the silhouettes of cranes flying off into a blushing sunset of pickles and sour plums.

The ladies on the train nodded with admiration as we ate. Whoever you are, they seemed to say, you must be special, wandering off into the world with such beautiful food, with all your youth and enthusiasm and talent.

"My daughter is the talented one. Piano."

I nodded.

"A musician? *Ah so.* Good luck," everyone said to me, bowing as they departed the train, for most ended their voyage before we did.

When we arrived in Akita, it was dusk, that uncertain time of day when gentle animals watch for predators and many flowers close their petals like fingers forming fists against the night air. Mother had found a little *ryokan* for us to stay in through the help of one of her customers. The building was old, a depressing place that had seen better times and seemed to know it; the windows clung to cobwebs and dust, and the dingy entryway refused to offer up any heat. I was so cold I clenched and unclenched my toes inside the faded blue slippers and tried to warm my feet. I was homesick for our little *yojōhan,* the four-and-a-half-*tatami*-mat room that my mother and I shared at home. And I didn't like the elderly woman who ran the place; she was hunchbacked and slow and stared at me. But my mother soon calmed me down.

"Did you see the fishpond in the entrance? And look at how each beam of wood in our room is from a different kind of tree. This was once a fine old inn."

"It feels haunted."

"Don't be ridiculous. Anyway, there's a surprise here that I know will cheer you up."

She was right. Like most traditional inns, the *ryokan* had a large communal bath: one for women and one for men. The water, unlike the water at the bathhouse we frequented at home, came from a hot spring. There were three pools, each lined with stones. My mother read the signs by each bath aloud to me. One of the springs was said to be good for the heart, one for the skin, and one for the joints. This last pool had the face of a demon made out of wood attached to the wall, with hot water spurting out of his nose.

"When I was a girl," my mother said wistfully, "my home had a hot spring bath. A real one. People used to say that was why all the girls in the family were so beautiful; we bathed in minerals."

"How many girls?" I asked quickly.

"Oh," she shrugged. "I'm from the moon, remember? My sisters were all the stars you see in the sky, and that's too many to count."

"You had hundreds of sisters?"

"Thousands. The moon people have large families."

My mother wanted to eat dinner in town at a noodle shop, but the proprietor of the inn informed us that our dinner was already under way.

"There must be a mistake," my mother said. "I reserved a room to sleep in, but no meals."

"The meals have already been paid for by a gentleman," the proprietor huffed.

I had heard from Tomoko, whose family often spent part of the summer and the winter in *ryokans*, that hotel meals were delicious and beautiful. "Can't we just eat here?" I whined.

"That will cause problems for us," my mother said to me in a low voice.

"Look, everything's going to go to waste if you don't eat it," the proprietor said.

So it was that at seven that evening, my mother and I sat in our *ryokan* room in our casual *yukata kimonos* that the inn had provided for us, newly bathed (again) and seated on *zabuton* pillows. As the kitchen staff served us, I sat up importantly, pretending that I was accustomed to eating this way at home every day. After a little pressure, my mother agreed to some plum wine, and she relaxed and came to enjoy the meal. I'm sure it was just the standard *ryokan* fare: fresh *sashimi* gleaming in blue-and-white porcelain plates, a medley of crab and shimp and clams in broth, seasoned rice bursting with mushrooms and chestnuts, and a dozen different pickles. I'm also sure that I've eaten many better meals since. But in my imagination, this meal has taken on the proportions of a feast that exists only at the table of the gods, for I remember that I was awed. There were people in this world, I realized, who ate like this every night. When I went to the moon, I would eat like this three times a day.

I was nervous in the morning. I hadn't yet seen the concert hall where we would play, and I hadn't been able to practice the previous day because we had been traveling. My mother and I had a bath before breakfast (rice balls she'd made at home before we left), and then again afterward.

"Keep your hands in the water," she instructed. "The minerals will make your fingers fly across the keys. This bath is famous for healing people's hands. Imagine what it will do for someone like you who is still young and healthy."

I changed into a white blouse and velvet magenta skirt with a dark red satin *azuki*-colored sash. My mother had designed and sewn the whole outfit with an adjustable waist and a fat hem that she had released over the years as I'd grown taller. She combed my hair and braided it carefully, then pinned the braids to the top of my head.

"My scalp hurts," I complained.

"The pain will go away," she snapped. "This stage will be grander than anything you've ever seen and I don't want you to look like some country girl who doesn't know how to behave in a nice place."

By age eleven I had been with my mother long enough to know that her moods would always be shifting like this, but I never did give up the hope that I would be able to control how she felt. And the fact was, I could alter her emotions, as I had done not so long ago with the bamboo shoots, or as I did every time I conquered another music competition. The problem was that these good moods never lasted. There was always some new indiscretion I accidentally committed that displeased her. One day I'd find the precise combination of independence, forthrightness, and humility to keep her perpetually smiling.

"You know I'm going to win, right?"

"I hope so." She gave my hair a good yank and stuffed another pin against my scalp. She sighed and I knew she was thinking about the expensive meal from the night before.

We mistakenly entered the auditorium through the front door of the hall. The room was shaped like a slice of orange, with a wide entrance at the back and a sloping wall and a narrow entrance at the front. The stage rose one and a half meters above the audience floor and was covered by a heavy red curtain. Judges were already sitting in the front rows, gossiping with each other. From behind the curtain I heard the sound of someone playing a few piano bars. She was playing lightly, just testing the keys and her fingers, but the chords were unmistakable. "Clair de Lune."

"May I help you?" a woman asked us.

"We are here for the competition." My mother's voice trembled uncharacteristically.

"Let me take you around to the back."

We walked along the side of the auditorium and up through a door. As we passed the wings of the stage, I caught sight of the girl who had been playing. She was still seated on the piano stool and looking up at two adults who murmured so low I couldn't hear what they were saying. The girl wore a long pink skirt with a curious white-and-lime-colored blouse. The material shimmered in the light and I realized that the little girl was wearing an expensive silk outfit. As I passed by, she turned her head just slightly and looked at me, nothing more than a curious glance, then re-directed her attention again.

But if she wasn't interested in me, I was certainly curious about her. For the girl was unmistakably wearing a *hanbok,* the outfit of a Korean.

I knew there were Koreans in Japan, but most hid their identities, dressing in Korean outfits only on weekends when they went to Korean school.

"There was a Korean girl," I whispered to my mother.

"Well, now you can say you participated in an international competition," she quipped.

Backstage we were introduced to the coordinator, an elderly woman with a mouth that looked like it had permanently puckered from eating one too many *umeboshi* sour plums. She explained to me that each student had a few minutes to warm up her fingers on the keyboard, and to practice walking the distance from the wings to the stage. After that, I would be assigned to a group and we would be sent to a large room to sit with all the other contestants. From here on out my mother was to sit in the audience and I would be alone.

I wanted to cry when I was parted from my mother, but one look at her serious face told me it was the wrong time to act in any way that might be construed as childish. After I tested the piano, I was led to the room where my group was waiting. There were twelve of us: seven other girls and four boys. And then the door opened and in came the Korean girl.

It occurred to me that the Korean girl had a role not unlike the one I had at school, someone who was obviously out of place and perhaps even a little bit scared. I thought about my friendship with Tomoko. I could be nice to the Korean girl and then everyone would compliment my kindness. But I couldn't bring myself to talk to her. She looked so unnecessarily haughty, with her nose in the air and the sleeves of her blouse puffed out like a bird promenading its plumage. I knew this look. I often adopted it myself on the playground when no one invited me to a game of volleyball and Tomoko was either home sick from school or off talking to a teacher, leaving me alone. Again I nearly rose to approach the Korean girl, but then I realized that no one in the room knew that I didn't have a father. To the other children, I just looked like some Japanese girl here for a piano competition.

"Is your family here?" I asked one of the other girls.

"Just my mother. My father had to work." Her voice trembled.

"My father had to work too." I sighed. "I wanted him to come and he wanted to come, but it's just my mother out there."

"I'm so nervous," the girl blurted out.

"Me too." I smiled. "I know I'd be less nervous if all my family were here."

"My grandparents are here," one of the boys said.

"You're so lucky!"

"I hate it when my family comes," spoke a sharp voice and we all turned at once to look at the Korean girl. I was surprised that she had no accent. "They all clap so loud and take pictures and it's really annoying."

I waited to see if anyone would say something to her. I thought of Tomoko and her bouquets. Then I turned my head and looked back at the first girl I had spoken to and said, "We can pretend our fathers are here, shall we? Now, if your father were here, what would he be wearing?"

Midway through the lineup, I knew for certain that I had a chance to win. My group had the right level of talent; good enough to be competitive, but not so good as to be unbeatable. One by one we were called to the stage until only the Korean girl and I remained in my group.

"Satomi Inoue," a woman's voice said.

Obediently I strode out across the sea that separated the wings of the stage and the piano. I paused in front of the piano seat, as I had been taught, eyed the judges (there were so many—nine in all), and bowed. Then I sat down and adjusted the seat until I felt it was just perfect and began.

I kept the tempo steady. Where we had decided it would be a nice effect to slow down, I *rallentandoed*. Where Mr. Kisahara had asked me to play with vigor, I pounded and frowned. I held the final chords a second longer than felt comfortable. Five seconds later, I began the *Moonlight* Sonata, carefully recreating that piece as Mr. Kisahara had imagined it should sound. I didn't miss any notes. When I finished, I rose and bowed, soaking in the applause. Then I strode off the stage.

People looked at me as I passed. Children stared. Some of the mothers smiled and nodded, but I hustled by impatiently.

"Very good." My mother squeezed my hand.

"Were you nervous?" I asked, patting my face with a handkerchief. Relief always made me sweat.

"No. Yes. No. Of course not! I knew you would be the best." Her good mood restored, I was able to relax at last.

The announcer had to call out the Korean girl's name several times before any of us could hear it, for the applause continued well after I had been seated. After that, people began to whisper to each other, filling the room with a rattling sound like the noise of pigeons in an abandoned building.

"Shinobu Kaneshiro." The Korean girl was using her Japanese name. She took to the stage, but, unlike me, she stood to the side of the piano and rested her hand on its body. She smiled and very slowly scanned the room, tilting her head from side to side as though each and every one of us were adorable. I groaned inwardly. What a calculated way to engage the audience! But it worked. People stopped talking and stared at her pearly smile instead. Our attention won, she sat down and began to play.

In her hands, the piano didn't sound like the same instrument the rest of us had touched. The music raced along, moonbeams fluttering on the surface of the water, daylight fading while Venus appeared, stars gaining confidence in the darkness till they shone.

When the Korean girl bowed, she was poised at first, then abruptly gave an endearing girlish smile so the gap in her teeth showed. The applause burst spontaneously from the audience and I thought of the hot spring bath back at the *ryokan,* and how the water simply burbled so naturally from out of the *oni*'s nose. The girl ran to the right of the stage and bowed, then nimbly skipped over to the other side of the stage and bowed again.

"Why don't they stop clapping?" my mother groaned.

Still the applause continued, until finally one of the competition workers came to get the little Korean girl off the stage so the next age group in the contest could begin.

We waited for a full two hours to learn the results. By then my carefully braided hair had come undone because I'd taken a nap. When I woke, I was hungry and my mother handed me some *onigiri* rice balls to eat, and then we went outside for a walk.

"You're going to win." Her voice was high and a little breathless. "I can feel it."

"Everyone wants the Korean girl to win," I replied.

My mother pursed her lips. "It was so annoying the way she just stayed on stage like that. Egotistical."

"She stayed because everyone kept clapping."

The judges announced the winners of the youngest category first. Some of the losers could not help but cry. When it was time for my age group, my mother held my hand, as she had at every contest we'd ever attended together. The third and second place winners were announced first: a boy and a girl. When my name was not called, I knew that I had really and truly lost for the first time in my life. The Korean girl, Shinobu, seemed to know that she would win. She was sitting on her father's lap, bouncing up and down and smiling excitedly and speaking with her parents in Korean and flirting with the judges, her enormous eyes fluttering like the bows in her hair, which flapped every time she turned her head.

"Our first place winner," said the man at the microphone, "in the children's fifth and sixth grade category is . . ."—he consulted a sheet of paper— "Satomi Inoue!"

I heard a crash like the ocean. People were clapping. My mother pushed me. "Go!" she exclaimed. "Go onto the stage!"

I was handed a recognition certificate and the basket of sundries, which were quite heavy when I held them all together. Later, my mother would keep the certificate in her *izakaya* behind the bar and up alongside the *sake* cups of our regular customers. Beside this would hang a photograph taken that afternoon. My eyes are focused on something just past the camera. To the casual observer I look dazed, a truly humble girl grateful that her talents had been recognized. I might be looking with awe at my mother, wondering how she knew to enter me into this contest, or gazing at the deciding judge who cast his vote in my favor. But each time I look at this picture, I remember what I was really seeing: the Korean girl, mouth erased of the playful smile, distaste on her face, politely clapping along with everyone else.

My mother told the *ryokan* proprietor of my triumph, and that night we feasted on an even more ostentatious meal than the previous evening as my mother recounted the story of my playing and declared me the most talented eleven-year-old in the north of Japan. The cook sent up two special dishes of shrimp and mushrooms, and the hunchback proprietor brought us a small bottle of *sake* to share, and then gave one to the other guests.

The next morning, I was wrestling again with an uncomfortable feeling, something bordering on recklessness combined with a strong need to be kind to someone. I begged my mother to buy us a box of Akita *omanju* to give to Tomoko as a present. My mother, usually so thrifty, allowed me to buy a box. She also let me buy a stuffed Akita dog toy. I was surprised to see her linger over a makeup stand in the department store by the train station. Eventually she talked herself into purchasing a cherry bark compact from Kakunodate.

"You did well," she said as we began the long journey home. "Several people came to talk to me about your playing. Important teachers."

"From Akita?"

"From Nagoya, Tokyo, and Osaka. Satomi, people recognize your talent and want to help you. They say you should enter a special school, just for music."

"Hmm," I said, and gazed out of the window at the sparse landscape of the north. Before us rose the mountains we'd have to cross to go home. I clutched my stuffed Akita dog and pretended to go to sleep. My mother carefully brushed my forehead with her cool hand, and, hypnotized by this soothing feeling, I soon fell asleep for real.

It was late in the afternoon when we arrived home and I had that horrible feeling that comes from having spent a day in naps, of resenting the sun as it slips down over the horizon. I dragged my feet, wanting to remain a traveler for just a few more seconds.

"*Tadaima!* We're home!" my mother called out to the dark doorway. This was what I always said when I arrived home from school, and it struck me as odd that she would announce herself this way to an empty house.

"*Ara.*" My mother was frowning.

The *hechima* plant that had been growing outside the entrance to the building was gone. Two days ago when we had left, swollen *hechima* gourds had dangled from vines clinging to a trellis my mother had woven from string she'd collected from various store packages. Every year my mother grew *hechima* like this. She used the vines to make special beauty water for her face and dried pulp from the gourds to scrub her dishes.

We knelt down by the rectangular pot and looked at the roots. They were snipped. Someone had come by and cut the vine back. I knew that my mother could make do with rags to wash her dishes. The beauty water was another matter. Someone had struck a deliberate blow to her vanity.

"But the *hechima* didn't do anything," she protested as she fingered the roots. "The poor gourds."

Dinner was a quiet, uncomfortable affair. My mother tried to cook something special, a whole fish she ran out and bought from the market to celebrate my success, but I knew she was distracted.

She said she wasn't hungry and insisted that I consume most of the fish, even though I was already full.

"We have to eat the whole fish tonight to celebrate your entire success. You see? Eating the whole fish means that you will become a whole person. That you will continue to succeed."

"Can you help me?"

"I'm full. But *you* have to eat until it's all gone."

For a time, we were allowed to forget about the mysterious fate of the *hechima* plant. When I went back to school, I was greeted as a hero. The teachers all knew that I had won the Tōhoku piano competition and that I had been scouted by teachers from the glamorous southern cities. No one knew about the Korean girl and I decided that it was best to pretend that I had deserved to win, that I was as good a piano player as everyone said. The local news station even came to interview me at school, and that evening I went to Tomoko's house and watched my grainy black-and-white portrait on the screen as I confidently told the reporter that I loved the piano and hoped to play in Paris one day. I did not yet understand that my accomplishment was not large enough to protect us forever, and I was somewhat surprised when, walking home from school a few weeks later, Tomoko came running behind me, her hair flying and skirt jumping up and down as she ran.

"*Chotto! Matte!*" she called out. Wait wait!

I stopped walking. "Hello," I said when she caught up with me. "Are you going home?"

She ignored the question. "I need to talk to you," she panted. "It's about your mother."

She had overheard her own mother speaking to some of the other ladies in town. All had complained that since my mother had no husband, it was only natural that she should try to find one. But was it necessary, the women asked, for my mother to behave as though all the men in town together could collectively function as her spouse? No fewer than seven men were known to have contributed money to the trip we had taken to Akita for my contest. And then there was the mysterious man who had paid for our elaborate dinner.

My mother had promised to pay back all the men, but still the women were unhappy. What did it suggest that my mother thought it appropriate even to have asked for such a favor?

One of the women—Tomoko's mother—suggested that perhaps my mother hadn't asked for the favor at all and that the men had simply volunteered, but this had been met with derision. Even if that were true, they said, my mother shouldn't have accepted the money and should have found a way to provide for me on her own. She would have known what scandals borrowing the money would bring, and she should have known better than to proceed.

"But look," Tomoko's mother had protested. "Satomi is clearly a talented girl. She deserves this kind of help, doesn't she?"

"Yes," the others had agreed at first. "But then it is only right that Satomi's mother turn to the community for help. It says something that she only turned to the men, doesn't it?"

Even though my mother had been making public rounds to return the money, damage had already been done. The women, long jealous of our unorthodox life and the unconcerned manner in which my mother had raised me, let out their many years of repressed anger. They spoke of things they could do: refuse to sell my mother vegetables, suddenly "run out" of fish in the markets, or, worse, order their husbands not to visit the *izakaya*.

Tomoko chattered on and on, waving her thin wrists as she spoke, clearly delighted to have procured this information and clearly proud of herself for sharing it with me. I could practically see the twin internal thoughts she had in a bubble over her head, like the captions that appear above cartoon characters. "Tomoko the good runs to the rescue of town outcast, Satomi. See how she hurried to share the news! Tomoko is such a good girl!"

"Why are you telling me this?" I screamed at Tomoko. "Those women are awful! It's not my fault I don't have a father, and anyway, we'll pay everyone back. So what's the point?" I was pretending to have known that we had borrowed money from all those men.

Tomoko was genuinely startled by my outburst. "I just thought you should know."

"Why?" I shouted. "So you can laugh at me?"

"I'm not laughing at you! I ran all the way here to tell you so you'd be prepared!"

"And then what? You'll go back and tell Matsumi and all your fancy friends how I cried about the news and you'll all talk about me like I'm some kind of charity case? Well, guess what. I don't care what you and everyone else says about my mother behind my back!"

"But . . . everyone admires *you,*" she sputtered. "That's part of the problem."

I grabbed her wrist and pulled her little perfect face up close to my nose. "Do you really think I care what any of you think about me?" I let go and Tomoko lost her balance and crumpled onto the dirt.

She was stunned and spent a moment examining her skirt, now soiled and in disarray. Then she saw that the fall had cut her knee. Emotion gathered in her face, like a gust of wind. "You *are* horrible!" she screamed. "Everyone's right! You need to learn some manners or you will never, ever have a happy life!"

I chased her as far as the edge of Mr. Nobata's rice paddy. I didn't really intend to catch her; I just wanted to scare her a little bit more. Then I stopped and screamed at her back, reminding her that children of wealthy parents, such as herself, were spoiled and would never know what it was like to develop magical powers as I had done.

An island of trees hovered in the middle of one of Mr. Nobata's rice paddies. Inside was a Shinto shrine so old and powerful that, it was said, no one would cut down the trees even to make way for more grain. When Tomoko had disappeared, I ran along the path to the island and climbed up the worn stone steps to the fox shrine, guarded by a *torii,* or gate, painted a fading red.

Here the air smelled green and wet. I huddled up against the shrine itself, just a small wooden box, and began to cry. I have always been a generous crier, unable to stop once I start, and I learned early to hide myself whenever I felt tears coming. I clung to the old wooden shrine, staining it dark gray with my tears, for a good hour, and when I was finished it was as though an infection had been drained from my blood and my body was now sapped of energy and resistance to anything more nature might send my way.

Like so many others in those days, my mother and I didn't have our own private bath. Instead, we relied on the local bathhouse. We usually went in the afternoon after school, washing and rinsing in the cleaning area before soaking in the large wooden tub inside the steamy building. We couldn't go in the evening since by then my mother was already serving drinks to the men in the bar.

That afternoon, when I went home after my fight with Tomoko, my mother seemed irritated and so I didn't tell her what had really happened. I lied and told her that I'd been kept after class by teachers who wanted to hear the story of my triumph in Akita just one more time. But nothing I said seemed to please her. She looked at my schoolwork and said that my handwriting was sloppy on my notes and that I should have scored higher on my geography quiz. In fact, she seemed increasingly agitated and finally I declared that I wanted to go to the bathhouse.

Now she wilted a little, as though suddenly aware of the bad mood she had been in, and its effect on me. "I might stay here," she said.

"Why? Do you have a cold?"

"No. I just . . . Oh, never mind. I'll go," she huffed, as though I were forcing her.

It didn't take long for me to find out then why she had wanted to avoid the bath. The minute we entered the changing area, the conversation between the other women preparing to bathe completely stopped.

Meanwhile, my mother peeled off her clothes with unusually brisk movements. I did the same.

"Excuse me," one of the women finally said, "this bath is not for *mura-hachibu.*"

My mother looked her straight in the eye. "Satomi and I are members of this town. You know that."

"Well, but you do live near the train station. By those bars. Technically, you aren't part of *central* Kuma-ume."

"Yes," agreed another woman. "Perhaps the next town over will not mind if you bathe there."

Just then, a woman opened the sliding door separating the changing area from the actual bath. I caught a glimpse of women relaxing in the hot pools. I yearned to be in there with them, completely warm and nearly weightless. And clean. Then the door shut and the woman stood in front of it, arms crossed meaningfully.

"Did you see that?" I asked my mother once we had dressed again and gone outside.

She had tears in her eyes. "I didn't think they would do that while you were here too."

"This morning . . . ?"

"The same thing."

The following day she went to the bath with me again as usual, and the women—a different group this time—once again prevented us from bathing. After that, my mother refused to go to the bath with me. "It's not that I care," she said. "I don't. But I can see that *you* care so it's better if you go alone."

Tomoko's mother invited us to come bathe at their home, and we did go once. But it was awkward. Tomoko and I weren't really close anymore, and there was Tomoko's mother speaking to us both with overeager enthusiasm, as though we were still best friends. We limped through the meeting halfheartedly, like bad actors in an even worse play. My mother resorted to other means after that. She sent me to the bathhouse by myself while she took a bus to the nearby temple, run by a famously compassionate priest and his mother. Every other day my mother assembled a small package of goods—*sake* or pickles she had made—and ventured to Empukuji for her bath.

But our problems didn't end with the bathhouse. When my mother went to the vegetable shops to buy food for dinner, doors closed before she could enter. It fell to me to go shopping after school. Then business slowed in the *izakaya*. Only the most loyal customers, the men without wives, came in to drink. I noticed that my mother cut her weekly orders of beer for the store and that our meals became even leaner.

"Are we going to have to close?" I asked timidly one night.

"Don't be ridiculous," my mother huffed. "Things won't stay bad like this forever."

But I wondered.

Of these things, though, the worst was the humiliation at the bath. For the very fact that others in the town thought we were unclean made me feel as though I was in fact dirty. During that period of my life, I began to inspect myself, my hair, the backs of my ears, and the bottom of my feet before I climbed into the water. I was doubtless cleaner than ever during this time, but you cannot endure such an active shunning without wondering if perhaps you have done something offensive after all.

"How long is this going to last?" I asked my mother one day.

"What?"

"You know."

"Satomi," she snapped. "I don't ever want you to ask that question again. If you ignore this treatment, it will go away like a bad dream. I expect you to be tougher than this."

She made fun of the townspeople behind their backs, calling them ignorant, like "ants who methodically dissect the same rice ball, when a nice *omanju* is sitting in plain view." At night, she told me she wasn't hungry and gave me the majority of the food. But as much as she insisted she didn't care about our treatment, I know that she did. Her playful mood all but disappeared, and no matter how well I did in school or in my lessons, she couldn't muster even the slightest words of praise.

Then, a few weeks into November, we had our first snowfall of that year. Overnight people in town began to wear quilted jackets made of indigo and stuffed with *wata* cotton or *mawata* silkworm fibers. Farmers wore straw snowshoes and snowboots into town. My mother put on a pair of heavy gloves and shoveled the snow off the entryway to her store.

"Satomi," she called to me. "I need your help. Go to the market and buy an extra dozen eggs, three large *daikon,* and some fish cake. Hurry."

I pulled on my boots and donned a thick jacket and strode out in the fading light to the nearest store.

That evening, a group of men, her old customers who'd been missing for so many weeks, burst into the shop demanding *sake* and *oden* to eat. "It's so cold!" they exclaimed.

"I just couldn't stand being cooped up with my wife for one more minute!" another declared.

My mother was all smiles. "What makes you think I'll serve you anything after the way you've ignored me?"

"Aw, come on. We weren't ignoring you. We thought of you every day! We missed you!"

She laughed and began to ladle boiled eggs and fish cake out of a pot of broth. The *izakaya* stayed open well past the hour I went to sleep, and I was only dimly aware of my mother slipping into the *futon* beside me, humming to herself. When I came home from school the following day, she greeted me with a girlish giggle. "I've been waiting for you! It's so cold. Let's go sit in the bath."

In the warm water, the women gathered in groups of twos and threes, and all said the same thing. It was so cold already, and not even December yet! Thank goodness for the bathhouse where we could all warm up.

And so our public humiliation had ended on account of a change in the weather.

CHAPTER 2

The Moon People

I will never know the extent to which our treatment by the other women in the town affected my mother and prompted her to do what happened next. She must already have been thinking about my future. She knew that if I were really going to be able to compete against that Korean girl and others like her, I was going to have to have better lessons.

Toward the end of winter, I noticed that my mother was eating very little again. She'd also taken to checking and rechecking the mirror and patting her flushed cheeks.

"Do you have a fever? Are you sick?" I asked her, point blank. Up until then, that was my greatest fear. I was terrified that my mother might catch tuberculosis or some equally insidious disease.

"No," she panted. "A little nauseous, maybe."

She was thirty years old. I thought of her as an old woman, but I've come to understand now that she was still young enough to have plenty of dreams, to want to see herself as a romantic prize.

At dinner one evening, not too long after the first cherry blossoms had released a froth of pink against the green of the mountains, she told me that she was tired of working at the bar. She wanted me to live in a house where I could have my own room. She wanted us to have our own bath.

We were moving.

She was going to get married.

Certainly the possibility had always loomed. She was good with men and more than a few had wanted to marry her. In the past she had always demurred because, she told me, marriage would get in the way of our plans, by which I understood her to mean that a man would greatly interfere with her ambitions for me.

Looking back now, I think that she felt her plans had become more complicated than she'd anticipated. She must have realized that the shunning could happen again the moment the women felt compelled to enforce their judgments on us.

A Mr. Horie came to her rescue. She said they'd been friends for some time, though how this could be true and I not know about it seemed a mystery. Then again, there were hours of the day when I didn't see her, when I was at school or at the piano teacher's house, or, as I was still prone to do, exploring the woods for treasures. She might have been meeting with Mr. Horie then. He ran a fishing business near Hachinohe, a city so far north it was inhospitable to bamboo. Many boats bearing the Horie name braved the Pacific waters each morning to snatch purses of *bonita* tuna, squid, crab, *sanma* mackerel, and other seafood to send to the markets in Tokyo. My mother told me that the house in Hachinohe had a natural hot spring for a bath. "It will be like we're in a *ryokan* every day," she said enthusiastically.

Mr. Horie had two daughters a few years older than me; their mother had died two years ago after an illness. He was willing to buy me a proper piano and pay for my lessons, but in return, he wanted and needed a wife.

I knew from the moment I met the Horie girls that they would have joined in with the women in Kuma-ume to shun us in the bathhouse. They had that quality that sends married men running from their wives and into the shelter of a bar or an *izakaya*. It was an ability to look at you reproachfully, as though they just *knew* that you had done something terrible, even if they knew nothing at all.

Chieko was the older of the two. She was fifteen when I arrived, and very pale, with long straight hair and a face that could have been pretty, my mother liked to whisper to me, if only she tried. She was a hard worker, studying to an almost abstemious, Zen-like degree. I had good grades too, but I would never punish myself in the extreme way that Chieko did, and I found it amusing that I was able to be so much better a student with so much less effort.

"You roll your eyes and move your body too much when you play,"

Chieko complained to me about two weeks after I had arrived at her house with my ragtag wardrobe of hand-me-downs carefully picked and coordinated by my mother.

"That's because I play with feeling."

"Have *you* lost your mother recently?" she asked me sharply. "Talk to me when that happens and then maybe you'll know something about the sincerity of feeling."

Mineko was thirteen, but determined to remain eight years old for as long as possible. She had a little lisp, which apparently people had made the mistake of telling her over the years was charming, and she liked to twist her body from side to side as she talked, as if she believed this made her girlishly appealing. She was constantly scribbling secret observations on little pieces of paper that she stuffed in crevices around the house. Then she spied on us to see who would find her notes.

My mother would uncover scraps of paper that read: "Today you looked at my mother's funeral portrait for an hour" or "I do not like *satoimo* sticky potatoes for dinner" or "Satomi should learn to line up the toilet slippers when she is done going to the bathroom." My mother would gather up the notes for Mr. Horie to read at dinner. He thought they were very funny.

To my surprise, my mother took to writing back on the notes and putting them where she had found them. In her lovely handwriting she would pen: "Your mother was very beautiful" or "I will try to give you extra fish cake instead" or "I will speak to Satomi about this." I wondered why my mother had fallen so naturally into this game. One night, looking up at the sky, I remembered. My mother had once lived in a house full of sisters.

Although Mineko was different from her sister, they were very close to each other. One of their favorite activities was to follow the daily *manga* that appeared in the newspapers. They would sit side by side and look at the drawings and make little comments about the stories and sigh and speculate on what might happen next.

Mineko herself was a fairly good artist. The first month that I was in that large house with its glossy black wood hallways and the kitchen with the bright-orange linoleum floor, Chieko quietly celebrated her sixteenth birthday. Mineko gave her sister a large hand-drawn portrait of their favorite *manga* character, a hero named Antares. That night, and for many nights after, both Mineko and Chieko refused to sleep until they'd kissed the portrait of Antares on the mouth and said good night to him. Over time, the lips on his penciled-in face grew darker and grayer, and I hated to think what kinds of germs were congregating on just that one part of the paper. But such, I suppose, is the power of a romantic idea. It goes without saying that I was never allowed to kiss Antares.

After that Mineko began to draw a lot. Instead of notes, she started leaving sketches around the house. I found one of her sketches in a glass cabinet. My mother had sent me to bring four glasses to the kitchen so we could refresh ourselves with *mugi-cha*. There in between the two yellow glasses was a piece of paper, hastily folded, the corners not lining up. I opened it.

The picture, while done in the hand of a child, was still quite good. There were two animals. A cat was admiring one particularly long eyelash in the mirror. The other animal, a badger, stood on its hind legs, eating a bunch of candies till its belly had become distended so it looked like a balloon. The drawing was a caricature of my mother and me.

I said nothing, just sat in the kitchen while my mother patiently poured the tea and tried to engage the girls in conversation. Cavorting with the enemy, I thought. I didn't have the chance to tell her about the note in private, for we no longer slept together. I'd been given my own room, a somewhat hastily converted storage chamber that had formerly held canned goods and an old wooden *tansu* chest and was now just large enough for a desk, a closet, and enough *tatami* space for a *futon* for one girl. I lay there at night and wondered what other secrets the house might hold.

As it happened, the secret observations were everywhere. The cracks in the floor whispered comments, windows yawned with insults, drawers squeaked with complaints. Always I was an awkward animal pounding away at the piano while the other girls in the pictures laughed at me or mimicked my sad, clumsy ways. My mother was sketched in exaggerated ballerina poses, or shown wearing a *tengu* mask with its red face and long nose while she was making powdered tea. She wore outrageous *kimonos* with the *obi* backward, or tottered around on high-heeled shoes like a flashy *oiran* prostitute. More than once I considered running away to our old apartment. My mother would come and find me and I would convince her that we could go on living there as we had before, with the bar downstairs to pay for my lessons and me hunting for vegetables during the day to supplement our diet. But I never did run away. I wasn't even really sure which way our old house lay.

Matters came to a head one day when I sat down to practice the piano and lifted the cover. For a moment, I froze. Then I screamed. There, wiggling its way across the black and white keys was a brown snake, very much alive and, to my mind, very hungry. I heard Mineko laughing as she raced past me on the wooden hallway in her mini pink socks, her long hair braided by Chieko just that morning into two elaborate plaits.

I ran after her.

Twin braids stuck out, like antlers, and I grasped them as you might take hold of the steering wheel on a bike, and turned them to the right. Her body obediently flipped over. We tussled just on the step by the entryway to the house. Our shoes and umbrellas and bikes were kept on the lower level, and I imagine that Mineko had been attempting to put on her shoes to run away from the house, knowing that I would make an effort to catch her. Had she made it out onto the street, the cars and pedestrians whizzing past would have stopped me in my tracks and I would have let her escape.

But she didn't make it that far. Instead, her body whipped to the right and she landed on her right hand—her drawing hand. I heard the sound of chalk crunching up against a chalkboard.

Her wrist never healed correctly, and she could never draw particularly well again, so in a way I suppose I accomplished my goal.

After a sullen period during which Mineko recuperated, she emerged from her cocoon to become a strangely older, more serious person who fluttered like a butterfly when she moved, smoothing the pleats of her skirt when she sat down and patting vainly at her hair. She was watchful and shadowy, and had taken to having intense conversations with her sister, who greeted her after the convalescence as though she'd just been waiting for Mineko to turn out like this, so adult and serious.

I was punished, of course. The worst thing my mother could think of was to take away the piano, but she wasn't about to ban the one thing that she said had prompted her to get married in the first place.

She couldn't forbid me to see friends because I didn't really have any. Instead she told me, with a pained, pale face, that for the next three months I was to take all my meals alone in my room. I was not to eat with her or with the girls. Worst of all, she would no longer bathe with me. She said this severely, while I cried, because already I was starting to feel that she didn't care for me as she once had. She told me that she thought we needed to do something to get the girls to like *us*. We had to be nicer, she said. Pay compliments. Act as a family. All these years I'd gone without a father and they'd gone without a mother, and now we had a chance to rectify these injustices. Wouldn't I like to have sisters? I should think about these things while I was waiting for the three-month sentence to pass.

The punishment confused me. This wasn't the mother who'd told me I was special, just biding my time, waiting for the moon people to appear and rescue me from an ordinary life. What a torture it was to sit alone in my room and to hear the muffled giggles that streamed out from the kitchen, where my mother and the others talked about school, about boys, about parties and college plans. Once I peeked into the front room and saw my mother, who loved to take old *kimonos* and turn them into handbags and blouses long before it became so trendy to do so, sitting next to Chieko, both of them sewing. They were whispering in quiet and confiding voices, pausing to examine each other's seams and stitches. The image stung. I'd thought my mother would grieve not to have me with her. Instead, she had replaced me.

In my room, I took to listening to a shortwave radio I'd found abandoned in a closet. It was capable of picking up a radio station from somewhere in Russia. In the evenings while my mother and her new family sat in the dining room, I turned on the radio and listened to choral music and orchestral music pouring out of the speaker. One day, I promised myself, I'd be far away in some exotic location Mineko and Chieko would envy, and I'd be responsible for making music just like this. My life would be richer and purer than theirs could ever be.

I started doing something else too. My mother had been so convinced I was to be a musician that it had never really occurred to me to try my hand at any of the other arts. But Mineko's sketching made me curious. One evening, listening to the chorus from *Khovanshchina,* I picked up a pencil and tried to draw a caricature of Mineko. First I made her a snail, but then I decided that even this animal was too sweet a creature for that horrible stepsister of mine. She was nothing more than a pile of dung. So I tried again. I drew a cat, prancing off from having just gone to the bathroom in a low bush, then drew a pile of waste. There was Mineko, her little precious mouth wailing how she was now nothing more than a pile of brown goo.

I rather liked my sketch and did several versions of it. Sometimes Mineko languished at the bottom of a toilet, her eyes trained to look up at a sky that she would never see. Sometimes, when I was feeling especially cruel, I simply drew an additional picture in which she and the rest of her dung-friends were silenced under a blanket of earth.

In my angriest days I liked to tell anyone who would listen that my mother had sacrificed my happiness for hers. This isn't entirely true, of course. When I won a scholarship at age fifteen to attend a high school in Sendai, a good five hours away by train, my mother urged me to go, insisting that this was the chance we had been waiting for. "You'll finally be around other artists," she said. Mr. Horie, who had become tolerant of me after I'd gone for a good year without maiming any more members of his family, agreed to pay for my schooling, and for the train rides home on holidays and long weekends. Occasionally he sent me some money himself with a note that said things like "Buy yourself a blouse" or "Go get some sheet music." I suppose he was kind in his way.

I did well in high school, and by my senior year, everyone knew I'd be going to the Tokyo University of the Arts, or Geidai, as it is commonly known. This is the most prestigious arts university in Japan, akin to Juilliard in America. My mother was ecstatic.

"You see?" she said to me one evening in the kitchen when the two of us were alone and peeling freshly picked *tsukushi* horsetail shoots. "You are finally becoming the person I knew you would."

She accompanied me on the overnight train trip from Hachinohe to Tokyo, a journey that invoked our voyage to Akita so many years ago.

"Do you remember," I said to her, "when you made me enter that competition? And afterward, the neighbors wouldn't let you take a bath."

"It was worth it," she said. "That competition gave you the confidence to be here today."

"Mother, did you *ask* the men to give you money? Or did they offer?"

She smiled. "Why, they offered, of course. I never had to ask." She set her hands primly in her lap. "It's a skill we women have. We know how to talk to people so an idea seems to have occurred to them, even if we are the ones who really suggested it. That's why we can do witchcraft and men cannot. But you, Satomi, I don't want you to ever have to rely on such

tricks to survive. I want your life to be more secure. Whatever happens to
me now, I know you will survive on your own talents. You won't need to
be like me, turning to men for help."

It was a strange speech and I did not fully understand it at the time.
"Do you ever wish you hadn't married Mr. Horie? That we could return to
life the way it was before?"

"Ha!" she laughed. "I know *you* do. Look, Satomi, you'll be able to
decide who or *if* you want to marry. But really, what choice did *I* have?
Anyway, I like those two girls. It's wonderful to be part of a family. I know
you don't understand."

"I would have protected us, even if you hadn't gotten married."

"That's the problem," she sighed. "You thought you could be a woman
and a man rolled up into one, and you couldn't at that age. Soon you'll be
old enough." She turned her head and gazed out the window.

We arrived at Ueno station early in the morning and, after a fitful night
of sleep on the train, were eager for a nap. I wanted to find a *ryokan* as we
had on our trip to Akita, but my mother disagreed. We would stay in a
business hotel near Ueno Park. When we arrived, we had to use a cramped
shower for bathing in lieu of a nice hot spring, then slept for a few hours.
When we woke, we each bought a *bento* lunch and ate in the park.

"Let's go for a walk," I said to her. "I want to see the Ginza."

"We'll need to take the subway for that."

"Don't you know how?" I asked, for I still believed she could do almost anything, and indeed, she navigated the maps and the fares and soon
we were standing in that fabled neighborhood, in front of the Mikimoto
storefront where girls with white gloves had just begun to remove strands
of pearls from the windows to put away for the evening. Nearby was a
small café selling Parisian pastries. Men stopped to look at my mother—
she was so beautiful—and I felt pride because she was *mine*.

"Let's eat cake," I said, steering her into Fujiya, where I ordered a mont
blanc because I'd once overheard someone describe it on a train. She ordered an éclair.

"Is the cream fresh?" she asked the waitress.

"It's been refrigerated."

"Yes, but is it *fresh*?"

"I will ask."

I smiled. Here we were in Tokyo and my mother knew how to behave with such dignity. Even here everyone deferred to her.

"Like this." She showed me how to hold my fork. "Mmm. Isn't it delicious?"

"Like the moon," I said.

Later we walked along the perimeter of the grounds of the imperial palace; the actual castle was buried deep within a forest of trees. We craned our necks to see past the palace walls, hoping for a glimpse of the emperor, but of course he was probably fast asleep already. Now it was night and taxis whizzed by and neon filled the sky. "I wish it was always this way," I sighed.

"When you are rich and famous, it will be," she said. "You can hire maids to look after Mr. Horie and Mineko and Chieko, and I can be with you." She said it like a challenge.

"So you *do* wish it could just be us."

She paused, then smiled at me a little sadly. "It's just us right now."

In the morning, she took me to the school, whose campus was made up of an impressive collection of very Western-looking brick buildings that dated from the Meiji period. Together we completed my registration and paperwork, all of which took longer than expected, and this meant she did not have time to get me settled into my living quarters.

"I will call you," she said as we said good-bye at the entrance to the dormitory.

"Can't you take the next train?"

She shook her head. "Mineko needs my help with some sewing." She touched my face. "Don't cry. You will come home at the end of the term."

I waved halfheartedly and turned so she would not see my tears.

The inside of the dorm was musty and smelled of rosin from violin bows, old *tatami* mats, and freshly laundered curtains. I pretended to sneeze and wipe my eyes from dust in case anyone saw me crying. Then I began to search for the room I would share with four other women. A familiar shape was sitting in the middle of the *tatami* floor when I slid open the door. The surprise was enough to stanch my tears.

"Hello." The girl turned to look at me. While I stared at her, she smiled and asked, "Are you still stealing competitions?" It was Shinobu, the Korean girl from the competition in Akita.

I set my bags down in the corner of the room. For the next four years, my roommates and I would move low wooden desks onto the floor to study. At night, we would put the desks away and pull *futons* out of a cupboard and unfurl them onto the floor. I would be alone only when I practiced the piano or went to the toilet.

"Are you still flirting with judges?" I asked.

"I can't help it if I am charming!"

"Where did you go to high school?"

"Kikuzato. My parents moved to Nagoya just for me."

"To make sure you could get into university in Tokyo."

"I've always known my future." She grinned. "That's why I never bother with fortune tellers."

We became friends. Our bond was partly inevitable, for we discovered early on in the semester that we were outsiders: Shinobu because she was Korean, and I because I was from the country. Most of the girls were from the major cities: Tokyo, Yokohama, Kyoto, Osaka. They were here at Geidai because their parents wanted polished daughters who would either capture the eye of wealthy and accomplished husbands, or who could go back to their fancy neighborhoods to teach music. To be from the countryside, as we were, was to be an outsider forever. "How," asked our roommate Sachiko, a soprano from the Ginza district of Tokyo, "did you even become interested in music?" We were in the large communal dining hall eating off heavy tables that had been there since the Meiji period.

"Everyone *likes* music," Shinobu said.

"Yes, but most people where you are from become farmers, don't they?"

I tried to set my chopsticks down carefully, but they clattered and one rolled and fell to the floor. In Japan, a single chopstick is a bad omen. "You think you know what the countryside is from posters you see in train stations, don't you? The world is not so well defined."

"Yes, but how did you even find a decent teacher?"

"There are teachers everywhere," I said.

"Yes, but the best teachers stay in the cities. They study here, like we are doing now, then go back to their neighborhoods to teach the next group of students. And if they do come from the countryside, they don't go *back*. So, how did you ever find a good enough teacher to get into Geidai?"

I put my palms on the table to anchor my weight and began to stand up, but Shinobu put her hand on my knee and kept me in place. I looked at her, furious that she would prevent me from engaging Sachiko, but was startled to see her smiling that enchanting smile she'd used on the judges years ago in Akita. It was like being caught in a strong stage light and I was momentarily hypnotized into inaction.

"What you say is true, of course. Satomi may not have had access to the best teachers. But that is also why students from the countryside, like her, are generally of a better caliber. It is only truly gifted musicians who come from the outside to end up at Geidai," she finished sweetly. "Satomi must be truly talented, or else she could never compete with you."

That evening, as we ambled through the hallway back to our dorm room, she pulled me aside and told me that I would need to learn to work on my temper if I were to succeed in college. Could I not see, she asked, that Sachiko was a very literal girl, always playing everything note perfect and angry at herself if she missed a finger in a chord? "We must feel sorry for her," Shinobu said. "It's a terrible thing in life to be a limited person."

"Is it true?" I asked impatiently.

"What?"

"That only the very talented students from the countryside end up at Geidai?"

She smiled. "They know that we will either fail miserably because we cannot adjust to their ways . . . because we get into fights"—she nodded meaningfully—"or that we will have something they can never have. They are afraid, Satomi."

The question of talent was widely discussed at Geidai. It was the magical secret ingredient that separated all of the students and because it could not be meted out, its existence was questioned, and sometimes argued like the life of the gods themselves. That Shinobu and I were strange and accomplished was taken for granted. But it remained to be seen whether or not we would be put in one camp or the other: the group of general students destined for careers in teaching, or that rare breed who might actually be artists.

While there was plenty of speculation among the girls on the subject of talent, the teachers were unwilling to give any of us their formal blessing. I found this resistance to be troubling.

"Your teachers have indulged you and let you play only what you wanted," my piano instructor Uchihara-sensei said to me. She was a tiny woman in her seventies, and age had made her more brittle than frail, like the fossilized twig of a tree. "If you intend to teach, you must be proficient in Bach."

"I don't intend to teach."

"Neither did I when I was your age. Do you think you are better than I am?"

I considered this. It was more that I sensed a certain limitation in her character. The world, I suspected, would never embrace her the way it would embrace me. "I'd like to play Rachmaninoff," I said. "I like the stories he tells. I'm going to be bored if I have to play even *more* Bach."

She studied me, her eyes tiny, cold and dark as if they had been pressed from coal. "Perhaps next year, if you pay attention to me and pass your exams."

Alone, I practiced my Bach preludes. In the company of my classmates, I studied music theory, art history, and literature. Outside, the cherry blossoms dissolved like sugar in the heavy rains of spring and a wave of fleshy green leaves exploded through Ueno Park, bringing the smell of nature in through my window. I worked my way through Uchihara-sensei's lessons. I tried to listen to her. But I began to study the Lento from Rachmaninoff's Piano Concerto no. 1 on my own. I indulged myself in the melodic lines, in the way the voices braided together like a conversation. I imagined my mother and me as we had been before her marriage, when we had lived in wild Kuma-ume.

In the dorm at night, I drew little sketches of Uchihara-sensei and me engaged in a lesson. I was usually a sad little pencil in the drawings, and Uchihara-sensei an eraser, struggling against a desire to rub out what I wrote, even as she tried to convince me to write even more on paper. One of my dormmates, Taki, was in the fine arts program and was studying portrait painting. She liked to wear a beret, as though she were in Paris, and I sometimes threw her into my cartoons as a little teacup with a cap on its head, admonishing us that our great battles were having no effect at all on the direction that art in Japan was now taking. I always drew Shinobu as a tattered novel, disinterestedly watching our antics from a bookshelf.

"You know," Taki said to me, as she looked over my shoulder while I sketched, "you are a pretty good artist, for someone so untrained."

"You are a pretty good artist too, for someone so untrained," I replied.

"Hey!"

"I'm just kidding. See?" I held out a sheet of paper and pointed out how the intelligent teacup had once again saved the life of the hapless pencil stuck inside a trash can.

At the end of the semester, each music student performed in the recital hall, located just above the school's administrative offices. The floor of the auditorium was weak, and even just one too many bodies on the second floor caused the ceiling over the offices to sag. It was not uncommon for some suit-attired woman to come marching in during a performance and demand that five people leave the audience, or risk collapsing the entire building.

"Come hear me play," I told the other students. "I'm going to have a surprise."

"You're going to finally collapse the building?" someone asked.

"Something much more interesting than that," I promised.

I did not even tell Shinobu what I intended to do. "Remember," she advised, "you must be smart about how you work with other people here."

"I know."

She frowned. "I'm not sure that you've taken my lectures to heart."

I was only somewhat disappointed when my mother phoned to say that she could not come to hear me play—Mineko needed her for some unspecified emergency—for the auditorium was full and two latecomers were turned away from the back of the room. I flexed my hands and prepared to play. I would show them an earthquake.

I dutifully fingered my way through Bach's Prelude no. 1 in C Major, as Uchihara-sensei had expected. But when it came time for me to perform the Mozart Piano Sonata no. 5, I stretched my fingers and began the Rachmaninoff instead. I had known, of course, that this would be a surprise. Uchihara-sensei would not be pleased that I had made a program switch, but my strategy was simply to play so well that Uchihara-sensei would have no choice but to allow me to work on more Rachmaninoff next semester. When I finished playing, I stood up to take a bow. No one clapped as they had after the Bach. The room was silent, girls glancing at each other, unsure of what to do.

I strode from one end of the stage to the other, bowing the way my mother had trained me. Still silence. Then I began to worry. Even if what I had done was unexpected, the audience should have been moved. Just a little. I searched for Shinobu and found her sitting in the middle, as she had promised she would be. I smiled at her and she flinched. I continued to smile, willing her to lift her hands, and finally she began to clap, the sole person in the room to do so. A moment later, Taki joined in, and then the room filled with the warm, appreciative applause I had expected. I smiled, triumphantly, and exited the stage where Uchihara-sensei was waiting for me in the wings.

"I'm sorry," I began, "it's just that I wanted you to know that I could . . ."

"Sloppy," she declared, before rattling off like an old crab.

I rolled my eyes. Of course I had done something rather unusual, but I certainly hadn't been sloppy. Eventually, the old woman would see this.

By the time I had gathered my things and made my way down into the audience area where Shinobu and Taki were waiting, most everyone else had left the auditorium, though I could still hear the excited rumble of gossiping voices tumbling down the stairs.

"I wish," Shinobu sighed, "that you had told me what you were going to do. I would have advised you to use the Rachmaninoff as an encore. Satomi, what if you aren't invited back next semester?"

"Of course I'll be invited back," I scoffed.

"They could fail you."

"But I didn't fail," I said. "The truth is the truth."

We began to wend our way toward the exit. "You know I admire your spirit." Shinobu shook her head. "I understand it, really. But now you've made Uchihara-sensei look bad. The other teachers will say that she cannot control you." Shinobu began then to detail a plan for how I was to extricate myself from the very grave situation that I was in. Her ideas involved writing letters and appealing to different teachers in the music department and much bowing, which she herself would coach me to do correctly. But I only half listened, for something had caught my eye. Rising out of one of the auditorium seats like a ghostly wisp of fog now materializing into human form was an older woman wearing a black felt cloche fitted close around her temples. I stopped walking. The woman was staring at me, and though I could not place where I might have met her, there was something familiar about her bearing.

She smiled, a slow, liquid expression that spread from her lips to her eyes and gave them warmth. I smiled back.

"They say that you are very daring," the lady said. Her voice, though notched with age, was confident and rich. It was a voice that had spoken of many things and without much fear through the years.

"Thank you."

"They say that what you have done is problematic."

I saw that she had a cane and as she began to shuffle at a slow but determined pace, I moved to help her. It hurt me to see someone who carried such an air of dignity about her moving with so much difficulty. But Shinobu gripped my wrist and kept me in place.

The older woman said, "The best students always know when they need a new teacher. And they also know when they no longer need any teacher at all." She pulled a small piece of paper out of her coat pocket with her free hand. "Call if you like." She smiled one more time, then bent her head to focus on her steps. We heard her slowly shuffling along and, out of respect for her age, waited for the sound to fade away before we too departed the hall.

"Who was that?" Taki finally asked.

I did not recognize the name and handed the sheet of paper over to Shinobu. "She wrote that my wrists are too stiff."

"It's Rie Sanada," Shinobu breathed.

"Who?"

"She left you her phone number."

"But you aren't supposed to take lessons off campus," Taki noted.

Shinobu tossed me a look and gave her head a barely perceptible shake. "No," she said. "We aren't." Then she linked her arms in ours and led us back to the dormitory.

All during the second semester of that first year, I'd looked forward to the train ride from Tokyo to Hachinohe for the New Year holiday. I knew it would be long and tiring, and then I'd have to deal with Mineko once I finally arrived at my destination, but I was looking forward to seeing the passengers and the scenery change. And indeed, once I started my journey home, I loved having the sense that I was someone with somewhere very, very far to go. It made me feel that my own story was particularly important again.

I sat in my most college-girl-looking outfit possible, a pleated skirt and a fitted sweater that I'd bought with money Mr. Horie had sent to me, and a dramatic pair of large gloves I'd found in Ameyoko, a flea market. The gloves, or rather the gauntlets, were leather, and therefore obviously imported from the West. People gave me a wide berth, though I was very happy to tell the one person who asked me where I had gotten those oversized things that I was a pianist, and that protecting my hands at all times was of utmost importance. The news spread throughout the train, and thereafter, when people walked past me to go to the bathroom or to look for the *bento* seller, they gave me little smiles, which I ignored, preferring to stare haughtily out the window.

At Hitachi station, there was the usual transfer of passengers and the new passengers avoided sitting next to me because of my gloves. I was surprised when a young man plopped down in the seat opposite me, grinning as though we'd met long ago and had finally been reunited. I snuck a look at him. He was handsome in that self-aware way, with round eyes and full lips and a straight nose. Immediately I didn't trust him. I always assumed that overconfident and good-looking boys thought they could get away with things, and planned to.

"Are you going to go boxing later today?" he asked me.

"Do I *look* like a boxer?" I asked.

"From what I understand, looks can be deceiving." He grinned at me. "You never know what kind of physical power even a little girl might have."

Who was he? Someone from Hachinohe who remembered how I had attacked Mineko? I scanned the car for other seats where I could move and be alone. But there were few. Most had little old ladies or drunk older men, and I wasn't entirely certain that moving next to them would stop me from having to have these kinds of inane conversations.

"These are gauntlets," I said, pronouncing the foreign word very slowly. *Gon-to-re-tto.*

"Are you expecting a sword fight with someone?" he persisted.

I hadn't anticipated that he would know how the gloves were originally used.

"I read a lot of English literature. Mostly in translation, of course, though I try to read the original too."

"In Hitachi?" I snorted.

"We have books in Hitachi," he said soberly. "And if you learned to read by going to school in Tokyo . . ."

I raised my eyebrows.

". . . at Keio University, then you would be able to read just about anywhere. Even in Hitachi. Anyway. It's not like *you're* from Tokyo either."

I liked this directness, even though it was intended to humble me a little. "No," I agreed. "I'm sorry. I play the piano. I'm trying to . . ."

"Protect your hands?"

"Yes," I lowered my head. "And I guess I thought if I wore something this strange, people would leave me alone on the train. I have this fear that I'm going to run into people I know."

"Why would that be a problem? I'm always happy to run into friends. I don't see them enough as it is."

I shrugged. "I'm supposed to be a genius. And I might not be."

"That's not what I hear."

I stiffened. "What do you hear, exactly, and from whom?"

He grinned. "My name is Masayoshi. I'm about to be your brother-in-law."

Chieko had married a year earlier, and now my mother was quite caught up in the preparations for Mineko's nuptials, even going so far as to come down to Tokyo to look at silks and see what went on at a Tokyo wedding banquet. This man, Masayoshi, was an attorney and the brother of Mineko's intended. He'd known in advance which train I'd be taking and had decided to try to catch the same one.

"Everyone said I'd know you right away, and it's true. You stand out." He smiled.

I squirmed a little. "I see."

"So, what's this about not being a genius?"

"I'm a good piano player. But sometimes I . . . people don't always like me. I'm not sure I'm going to be able to go on the concert circuit."

"Why not?"

I paused. "I don't know if anyone will let me," I said. "I'm a very expressive player. Isn't that what music is supposed to be? Emotional? But people don't always appreciate that." And then, perhaps because he was a stranger, or because he was more engaging and more open than most people, I began to tell him about college. Now that I was there, I felt as though something wasn't quite right. Masayoshi thought that perhaps it was all the distractions of Tokyo, the shops, the museums, the parties, but

I told him I didn't think this was the case. It was more that I'd counted on at last fitting in, but instead found myself a little bit bored and already hungry for life outside the university walls.

"What do you do with your spare time?" he asked.

What *did* I do with my spare time? I liked to doodle caricatures of people. I liked to take walks with Shinobu. I liked to look at people. I was always hoping I would find someone who was easy to talk to, but this rarely happened. "I think I waste a lot of time," I admitted.

"Me too!" He beamed. "Actually, I don't think that *you* actually waste time. Some people do. But what you call wasting time, the nobility would have considered *cultivation.*"

"Like studying the tea ceremony."

"Gazing at the moon and writing poems."

"Drawing."

"Speaking of which." And he pulled a slim folder out of his bag and showed me a watercolor of a temple flanked by green leaves. "I did these."

I examined the picture. "That's nice."

"My younger brother is the real artist," he continued, trying to sound modest. "He goes to your school. He's studying painting, not music."

"If he's the real thing, then what are you?"

"Just a hobbyist." He grinned, clearly pleased that I liked his work.

We were quiet for a few minutes, looking some more at the watercolor of the temple. I admitted that I liked to draw little pictures too, but demurred when he asked to see an example. "I'm not that kind of artist," I said.

"This is not my best, perhaps," he continued cheerfully, "but I liked the fact that I could use purple in the eaves."

"That *is* purple, isn't it?"

"I like unusual things," he said to me in a low voice. Something about the way he said this shook me and I felt half-afraid of him, even as I was also thrilled.

"You're a collector." I managed to keep my voice steady.

"Of unique experiences," he agreed. "Which is one reason I've been wanting to meet you."

Though it infuriated me, I found myself blushing. "Curious about the odd one in the family?"

"I said unique. Not odd." He nodded at the landscape outside the window. "Chinese mystics believed that you could tell the essence of every living thing. Some trees have good living energy. Some don't. You can tell by their shape."

"If I were a tree, then, what would I be?"

"Well, that's just it. Since you're unusual, it's hard to tell." He grinned. "But I do intend to find out."

I saw Masayoshi nearly every day. We explored Hachinohe together, me brazenly riding on the back of his bicycle as he struggled through the streets to take me to a hot spring. Once we took the bus all the way to the Misawa Air Base because I said I wanted to see some *gaijin*, or foreigners. We couldn't actually go onto the base itself, but settled for tea in a small coffee shop in town where the bus driver had told us we might see a few *gaijin* faces out and about running errands.

"There's one," I murmured.

"Where?" Masayoshi craned his neck.

"Don't be so obvious! But there. By the mailbox."

"I thought they were taller."

"This is like bird-watching."

Masayoshi turned to grin at me. "That's what I like about you, Satomi," he said. "You dive right into the world, and things just happen around you as a result. Time with you is always interesting."

I brushed the compliment aside. "What is someone as sophisticated as you doing in Hitachi anyway?"

"You make it sound like sophistication is a crime."

"In some periods of history it has been," I said.

"In the spirit of honesty, then, I'm as conflicted about sophistication as you are."

"*I'm* not conflicted." I laughed.

"Sure you are. I'll bet you tell all those fancy Tokyo girls just how much you love Hachinohe for the good seafood and the honest nature of the peasants. And when you meet someone from Tōhoku who looks lost in Tokyo, you're nice to them and give them directions. But then you come home to Hachinohe and you are bored and you like to wear your gauntlets and provoke gossip by hanging out with a junior attorney who lives in Hitachi."

"You just don't seem like an attorney. You seem better than that."

He blushed a little. "I wanted to study philosophy. But of course there is no money in scholarship."

"Well, you'll be rich some day. You'll make some girl happy."

"I don't want just *any* girl," he said to me, with great sincerity.

He had the ability, even though we were in Hachinohe, to ferret out the most Tokyo-like spots. So it was that we visited a little club on the water that played jazz. Every now and then, there was even a *gaijin* musician in the mix. There was always an energy to the way those foreigners played that we in Japan simply couldn't emulate.

Actually, by 1965, we were very aware of just how much we weren't like America at all. That country had come into our consciousness first with the bombs and then with benevolence, and then television. In those days I was as taken by the idea of Americans as everyone else. How confident they seemed. I was old enough now to know that there was no kingdom on the moon, though the powerful image of America made it feel to me as though there was something just about as potent as the moon, even if it was overseas and not in the sky.

Masayoshi told me that he wanted to travel as soon as possible. He was working as a low-level attorney in the Hitachi corporation, which he thought would one day lead to the opportunity to go overseas. He couldn't talk too openly about everything that the company was doing, but it partly involved the high-speed rail that had made its debut in time for the 1964 Olympics, which he promised would one day make it easy to travel from Tokyo to Hachinohe.

"Easy?" I laughed. "It'll always be the country up here."

"No," he said seriously, "I imagine that the world will become quite small one day. Already with airplanes it is so much easier to travel."

Our closeness wasn't lost on the rest of the family. Mineko, in her typical fashion, was jealous of my friendship with her fiancé's brother. She thought I was spending time with Masayoshi just to embarrass her. But she wouldn't talk to me about it directly. During family meals, she would look my mother in the eye and say things like, "People are going to wonder what kind of a girl I am, marrying into a family where the boy behaves this way."

"We're just friends," I grumbled.

Late one night, my mother intercepted me in the hallway and asked me to come and sit with her in the kitchen.

When we'd first moved here to Hachinohe, I'd been astounded by the size of the house. The orange-and-yellow linoleum had looked so modern to me. But now the house seemed a bit old. The floor had grown gray, despite repeated attempts to scrub it clean. The walls and the eaves seemed to have lost their crisp edges, the way a freshly pressed sheet becomes crumpled from use and exposure to too much mist. The atmosphere made me feel a little sad, and so I was already in a melancholy mood when she asked me to join her in a late-night snack of tangerines.

"You like this Masayoshi boy," she said.

"He's entertaining."

"Did you know," she said, "that he is engaged to someone else? A young woman from Nagoya."

I hadn't known. But I said, "So? It doesn't matter to me."

This seemed to relieve her a little bit. "I thought perhaps you were developing some serious feelings for him."

"Well. No," I said. "It's just that once I'm here, I'm always so bored. You know, it's tough being here after all the excitement in Tokyo."

"I always hoped you'd do something important with your life. Other than get married."

"*You* got married."

"It was too late for me to do anything else." She smiled thinly.

I asked Masayoshi about the Nagoya girl the first chance I got. "Oh, that's nothing," he said to me.

"Does *she* think it's nothing?"

"She's a friend."

"The same way I'm a friend?"

He considered this. "She and I have less to talk about."

I was flattered in spite of myself.

"I was always under the impression that you'd never want to get married." He said this very quietly.

"Do *you* want to get married?" I asked, my heart beating quite fiercely.

"Come on!" he grinned. "You know me better than that!"

By the end of the break I'd relayed the story of my first exam to Masayoshi, who had laughed heartily at my audacity, then begun a gentle campaign to convince me to return to school and to go see Rie Sanada while I was at it. I told my mother too—not about the exam, but about meeting the strange woman and her apparent offer to teach me.

"Rie Sanada. I've heard of her," my mother said. "Why don't you call her and see what happens?"

So I did. The day I returned to Tokyo, I called the mysterious woman from the dormitory pay phone, trying not to speak too loudly and keeping my phrases general enough that no one listening to me would know what I was trying to do.

"Thursday at four o'clock," I said into the mouthpiece. "Yes. I believe I can manage that."

I learned even more about Sanada-sensei, as I would soon call her, from Shinobu, who had found two of the older woman's vinyl recordings in her parents' library. We played them on the phonograph player that Shinobu had also brought with her, explaining away our habit to Taki and the other girls by saying that we wanted to listen to past masters for inspiration. The records had been made in the thirties, and from what Shinobu gathered, Sanada-sensei had once been poised for a major international career. In 1939 she had returned home to Japan, suffered through the war years, and nearly been felled by an illness. By the time she had recovered somewhat, she had been unable to recapture her earlier youthful success. Still, she was famous in Tokyo circles, and up until ten years ago had regularly performed with the NHK, or Japan Broadcasting Corporation, symphony.

I went to see her one fall day, with an envelope of money Mr. Horie had given me to use for "clothes" and "more sheet music." She lived in an ugly postwar building not too far from Ueno Park. It was difficult to reconcile this smog-stained concrete structure with the elegant woman I had met some weeks earlier, but when I tapped on her door and she let me into her apartment, it was as though I'd been transported into another world. The apartment was small: three rooms at the most, with a kitchen unabashedly blending into the living space. Despite the size, the apartment had an aura of romantic grandeur, as though I'd stepped into a painting by Renoir. She lived mostly western style, with fleshy rugs, pertly stuffed chairs, a small velvet sofa, and oil paintings framed in gilded wood. In the center of the room, shining like a pool of oil, was a baby grand piano. She watched me with quiet amusement as I took in the photos hanging in the hallway: there she was with various prime ministers, the emperor, and American actors whose faces I recognized, but whose names I did not know.

"It has been an interesting life," she said as if reading my thoughts.

"I listened to your recordings," I said. "They were very good."

"Do you know what they used to call me? Chop Suey. The English thought I sounded like an Asian person in a Western country. But to the Asians who knew better, I did not sound authentically Asian at all. I play much better now. Come sit down."

She gave me a pair of slippers to wear—one of the few Japanese concessions in her home—and sat beside me at the piano. Our afternoon was made up of neither Bach nor Mozart. Instead, she dazzled me with Tchaikovsky, Grieg, and Rachmaninoff. By the time she had moved on to her third piece, I could have sworn we were sitting in a thick forest, with a canopy of moss and mist and large exotic birds with suspicious eyes peering down at us from the branches.

And then, abruptly, she stopped. "I can't play for as long as I used to." She rubbed her hands.

"It was beautiful."

"I prefer the Eastern Europeans. I have a theory that because they are closer to us geographically, we Japanese can understand them better. I can never focus myself as well when I play Bach, for example. Now you try. How about that prelude you performed for your exams?"

I had made it through a few bars when she stopped me. "Do you see how you are playing? Like this?" She played the same bars, keeping her wrists unnaturally stiff. "No movement. Until now," she continued, confidently, "you have been taught to play pieces. You don't know anything about the piano, and until you understand that, you won't really be able to tell all those stories you have locked away in your heart. Now watch."

She taught me her secret. I was to play the Bach prelude very slowly. As each finger hit a note, I was to adjust my wrist to center with that one note. I was to do this every day, a few hours at a time, and to return the following week. "I will have a cup of tea for you when you come. And some sweets. Students are always hungry. Now you'd better go before poor Uchihara-sensei tries to find you."

I reached into my purse to pull out my wallet.

"Not this week," Sanada-sensei said. "After all, you hardly played."

I was not in the habit of listening to people very much at that stage of my life, but Sanada sensei's playing had captured my attention. I found her exercise a strange way to practice and yet I listened to what she said, spending hours in the practice room on my own, preparing for lessons for both sets of teachers. Day after day I continued to practice, and soon it was time for my first official lesson.

This time Sanada-sensei did not play at all. She asked me to begin the Bach prelude, watching to see that as I struck each note, I carefully re-centered my wrists as she had asked me to do. When I finished she smiled and said, "You actually practiced."

"Yes."

"Now try again. Faster. Like this." She set her metronome. I obliged. "Faster," she commanded. "Again." So I played the prelude over and over, at faster tempos, until we reached a speed that was entirely impractical. To my surprise, I saw that my arms and hands flowed easily through the piece, as though the music were suddenly free to wash through me, as though it were originating from somewhere in my body other than my hands.

"Muscle memory," she explained, when she saw the look of surprise on my face. "You must see the ballet students at school? They start each day with pliés and *tendus* to train their bodies for related steps. Their bodies remember these poses. We musicians must learn to do the same." She sighed. "It is a shame how little this is taught."

I looked at my hands, feeling for a moment as though she had replaced my old fingers with these new ones. "That's it?"

"Essentially," she said. "Although, if you are going to go overseas, the way that I did, you must learn to hear music differently. Must learn to play it differently. They won't respond to your current sense of musicianship. We forget," she sighed, "that Mozart and Beethoven are part of *their* culture. Not ours. When they hear us play, we sound to them the way that we do when we speak English. We have an accent. It will take work to understand this and go beyond it. I can help you and I will."

My lessons with Sanada-sensei would save me in Tokyo and make it possible for me to behave with all the outward contrition that Shinobu had advised me to employ. I apologized on my knees to Uchihara-sensei. I wrote letters to the music department promising that I would not pull any stunts again during my exams. I would accept a low grade and promised to play the Mozart in my next recital. I would not assume that I knew better than my teacher.

Except, of course, that I did.

CHAPTER 3

Scattered Petals

Masayoshi came down to see me in Tokyo quite often after Mineko's wedding. The girls in the dormitory took to calling him my boyfriend, and after a while I gave up protesting and let them believe this was the case. There were more jazz clubs in Tokyo than anywhere else in Japan, and he was always researching which show to go to together. He brought me little luxuries: hand-embroidered handkerchiefs, an elaborate fruit basket I shared with my dormmates, tea imported from England. Even though he'd never been out of Japan, I couldn't help but think of him as a cosmopolitan person who knew the secrets of the world. He kept up with the latest things and took me to see them, so the city of Tokyo quite literally blossomed before me. This went on until the middle of my second year.

It is easy to assume when you get along so easily with someone that you know who he really is, that you can see into his heart. I accepted that Masayoshi wanted to be a lawyer, a man of the world, a patron of the arts. I also began to accept that our friendship would simply continue as we grew older. After all, we never really argued.

Although, I suppose there was that one strange conversation we had when he came to see me on a Saturday in March toward the start of my second year. There wasn't anything particularly unusual about that weekend. People were glad that spring had arrived, but they weren't out picnicking and celebrating *hanami,* or cherry blossom viewing, the way they had been just two weeks before, when the flowers were blooming at their fullest.

53

Now the sidewalks were covered with fallen petals. Riding the bus through the city, I often saw a swirl of pink froth overtake the windshield so the driver had to turn on the wipers. I would arrive at the dorm with petals on my clothes and in my hair. In some ways, I found this part of the cherry blossom season, when everything was falling and fading with such abandon, even more beautiful than when the trees were at their peak.

We were walking through Ueno Park when Masayoshi turned to me and asked, "Do you think you will really become a concert pianist?"

"Of course."

He stopped walking. "Really?"

No one had ever asked me this before.

"Sanada-sensei says that I am an *interesting* player. I can *move* people."

He grinned. "I believe that."

"Of course, the teachers at Geidai are more concerned that I learn the correct repertory so I can go back home and teach young kids how to play the right pieces so maybe *they* one day will go to Geidai. Uchida-sensei doesn't care at all about the *beauty* of music."

"So, instead of giving up music or changing how you play, you'd rather change your audience."

"Yes."

"You're going to leave Japan."

"I didn't say that."

"But that's the logical conclusion."

The conversation was starting to annoy me and I tried to change the subject by drawing attention to a funny-looking bird I had spotted in a cherry tree. But Masayoshi persisted.

"I think it would make more sense to do something else with your life, something that fits your personality better, rather than deciding that everyone else is wrong and you are right and if you just move you'll find people who will bend to your wishes."

"Who said anything about bending?" I said. "I've always known I was going to be a musician, Masayoshi."

"You know," he said gently, "if you don't become a musician, it doesn't necessarily mean that you've failed."

"Don't be ridiculous. I'll never give up the piano."

"Not for anything?"

"Not that I can think of."

We stopped at Uguisutei, a small café, for a nice cup of green tea and Uguisudango, white, green, and red bean sweets. Then Masayoshi said, "Sometimes, I think about giving up law."

"Why?" I was taken aback.

"It's very hard, Satomi," he said seriously. "Many hours. Lots of competition."

"That's what it takes to build a new Japan, isn't it?"

"What happens once we have our new Japan, Satomi? What do people do then?"

"You enjoy it." I exploded. "I don't know what you are trying to say. If this is the kind of philosopher you were going to become, then I think it's a good thing you became a lawyer instead. It's ridiculous wondering 'what if' all the time."

At this he bowed and apologized. "Of course," he said. "It was a silly train of thought. Please excuse me." But his contrition was so formal that I felt unsettled the rest of the afternoon.

During dinner, I told Shinobu about our fight, leaning my face close to hers over my tray of food in an effort to create privacy.

"Satomi," she said seriously, "have you ever considered that he might be in love with you?"

"Masayoshi?" I scoffed. "But . . . that's ridiculous. He's just a friend. Like you. I only know him because his brother married my stepsister."

"I don't think a friend brings presents all the time the way that he does. And he's always trying extra hard to find things for the two of you to do that you will like. And . . ."

I cut her off. "Please don't ever say anything like that to me again. Masayoshi. In love." I picked at my bowl of rice. "Disgusting."

"I know you don't *like* the idea, Satomi. But if he is in love with you, don't you think you should consider his feelings?"

"And do what?"

She pursed her lips. "Maybe let him know somehow that you don't love him, or spend less time with him."

"I . . . he . . . when did you become such an expert in *men*?" Even as I said this, I knew the answer. Shinobu had started dating someone. He was, importantly, Japanese. He was also, unfortunately, married. But Shinobu insisted that they were in love and that being a mistress to a wealthy man wasn't the worst thing in the world because she'd always have time for the piano and wouldn't be saddled with laundry and housework.

Fortunately, the next time we met, Masayoshi didn't even mention our awkward conversation. He just smiled when he saw me and immediately started laughing at a story I told him involving Sachiko, the stuck-up soprano from the Ginza. I was relieved to be in his company again, to be the "interesting" person he so admired. We continued to spend time together on the weekends and during the holidays when I was home in Hachinohe.

In the middle of my second year of college, however, Masayoshi began to act a little bit strange again. It all started when his father had a small stroke around the same time that I was caught up in preparing for the annual *Messiah* concert. Every year, students of Tokyo University of the Arts got together to put on a performance of this Christmas tradition. The piano students were made to sing the choral parts with the voice students. Instrumentalists played in the orchestra. Ostensibly, the whole point of the concert was to help raise money for orphans in Japan, just as Handel's initial performance had been to help provide for the poor.

I'd now had four semesters at Geidai in which I hadn't upset Uchihara-sensei, but had in fact been praised as one of the most promising students. The transformation, they said, was fortunate because I'd come close to being expelled. Now I felt confident in my place at the school, so I decided to give voice to the frustrations of piano students participating in the *Messiah* concert. I complained that we were not at all accustomed to having to share the stage with anyone. We did not want to be put in the back row of our voice groups just because we were not singers. We wanted a chance to audition to stand in front.

The teachers, who were always happy to indulge our competitive desires, agreed. When they posted the seating chart, I found myself ranked above Sachiko. She and her friends were incensed and demanded that I give up my spot on the risers.

While this was going on, Masayoshi was still coming to visit me every weekend, even though his father was ill. I tried to entertain him the same way I always had, by telling him stories about people at school and what I had experienced during the week.

"Sachiko," I said to Masayoshi at one point, "doesn't even have good pitch. That's what happens when you learn to sing without playing an instrument very well. You never really develop a good sense of intonation."

Day after day the drama intensified. Someone put broken glass in my *futon,* which Shinobu discovered just before I climbed in to sleep. I retaliated by stealing one of Sachiko's music books and gluing all the pages together. Shinobu did not approve of these antics, but continued to support and defend me, stalwartly informing Sachiko that I had simply had the better audition. The singers turned away from me with disgust in the cafeteria, a childish bit of drama that I was happy to reenact for Masayoshi when we met. The pianists started to urge me to change my major from piano to voice. To my delight, I found that I had become something of a leader.

Finally, one day, Masayoshi burst out in anger. "Do you have any idea how egotistical you are? I mean, this *Messiah* concert is supposed to benefit orphans. And here you are obsessed with your rank and how superior you are to everyone else!"

I was shocked. We walked along silently while I absorbed his criticism.

"You may think," I began gently, "that we are all quiet and pretty girls engaged in the beautiful world of art. But we are not. School encourages us to compete with each other. I've been fighting with other girls my entire life."

"I'm beginning to think that the whole reason you became a musician in the first place is just so you can compete against all these girls you claim to dislike so much." He began to talk about an uncle who lived in Kyoto, whom he believed had become a painter out of pure love for the art. "That's why you should do music. Because you love it. Not because you think it makes you better than other people."

"Competition is what makes art great," I insisted. "If we all just did what we felt like, there would be many mediocre musicians and artists."

"That's an elitist attitude," he shot back. "It's naive too. Haven't you ever noticed that museum exhibitions always show off things that belonged to rich people? I mean, what about poor people?"

"I was poor and my mother still managed to make our lives beautiful."

"Your mother is an extraordinary woman," he said seriously. "But most people don't get to spend their days stuck in a university practicing scales or trying to win competitions, Satomi. Most people have jobs like I do.

Art should be something that we can enjoy and that makes our lives more human. It shouldn't be about all this childish backstabbing."

"What are you talking about?" I screamed back at him. "Your whole job is about competition. Aren't you always going on and on about how Hitachi is devoted to getting Japan to be as powerful as possible as soon as possible?"

"That's different."

"No it's not," I insisted. "You can't start an argument with me, then expect me not to say something back to you when you are wrong. If you weren't an elitist person," I challenged, "you would have studied philosophy, or opened a little bar somewhere so workmen could relax after a long day. You wouldn't be buying me tea and handkerchiefs and bragging about beating the Americans one day through economics."

For two weeks, I heard nothing from him.

Then one afternoon I was in my dorm room with Shinobu, drinking a cup of tea, when I heard the phone ring. "It's your boyfriend!" a trio of sopranos stuck their heads into the doorway and squealed.

It was a quick call. He told me that he had some extra work to do and that he would need to cancel our plans to go to the zoo. I said that I understood and tried to devote my newly gained free time to practicing. The truth is that I sat in a practice room and read a book, tapping out a few passages on a keyboard whenever someone passed by. Masayoshi canceled the next weekend. And after that, he simply stopped calling.

Once or twice I called him and even tried to send a few lighthearted postcards. But he didn't respond.

"Where's your boyfriend?" Sachiko and her friends chortled.

"I told you," I said evenly, "he's not my boyfriend."

"They must have had a fight," Sachiko cooed. "How tragic. Like Puccini. Would you consider killing yourself? In Puccini operas, the soprano always dies."

I picked up a book and hurled it across the room, and the girls all ducked. After that, they stopped teasing me.

Once or twice, Shinobu tried to talk to me about Masayoshi. "Satomi...," she began.

But I knew what she wanted to tell me. "Don't," I said. "It's a ridiculous idea."

When I went home to visit my mother during the next holiday, she casually let it slip that Masayoshi had quit his job as an attorney and had gone to study Buddhism. He was engaged to a girl whose family owned a temple.

"Buddhism!" I exploded. "What is he doing that for?"

"He is thinking of becoming a priest," she said, quite seriously.

"Why?"

"I think it has something to do with his family. His father had a stroke, you know. And even though he is doing much better, Masayoshi took it very hard."

"But . . ."

"You don't know, Satomi," she said to me gently, "what it is like to see your family in jeopardy. It can change you."

You're my family, I thought. I've had to watch you change. Instead I said, "But he can't change *that* much. No one changes *that* much. He told me he wanted to be an attorney so he could see the world. Go to La Scala."

She lowered her head. "Masayoshi is doing what he must to help his father. The family is very vulnerable right now. I imagine Masayoshi feels he is helping everyone somehow."

Still this made no sense to me. I could imagine Masayoshi taking up painting with greater earnestness, or asking for a transfer to go live in Europe. When people receive a shock, they sometimes have the extra energy to do the things they have always wanted to do but have put off. Still, I couldn't understand how he would suddenly give up his job to study Buddhism.

I had something of an answer a couple of years later. I was visiting my mother again during the last school break I would have before graduation. Mineko was at the house with her two small children, and my mother was busy acting as grandmother. She sat on the floor with them and played with a small wooden top, the traditional kind that you can still find for sale in countryside tourist towns. The top was made of wood and painted with red and green stripes. You pulled a string, then released the top on the ground. Midway through its spinning cycle, if it was handled correctly, the top would flip over and spin on its reverse end. The older girl could make the top spin easily, but the littler girl had difficulty releasing the top so it landed on the ground and spun. My mother was showing her how to do this by holding the little girl's hands with her own. I couldn't help but feel some reproach in the way that she did this, as though she were silently telegraphing to me that should I have children of my own, she'd be willing to lavish them with the same care. This was confusing because I'd always been under the impression that my mother did not want me to follow a domestic path.

I must have sighed deeply because Mineko turned to me and blinked rapidly a few times. "She'll get it eventually. They aren't born knowing how to do everything, you know." She was talking about her children and the spinning top.

"No. Of course not," I said.

"Children take patience." She smoothed her skirt and took a sip of tea, the silence giving weight to her words, making it clear that she had meant to insult me.

"Satomi-san is very talented and very busy and it is understandable she doesn't have the patience to deal with small children," Mineko said matter-of-factly. The way she said it, she might have been talking to herself, or to an invisible audience about me.

"That's probably true," I muttered.

"Yes," Mineko continued lightly. "It's one of the reasons why Mother didn't think it was a good idea for you to marry Masayoshi. With time, of course, he'll understand that. Actually, I imagine he's understood it already."

Ara! My mother exclaimed. The littler girl was clapping. Her top had finally spun correctly and the older girl was looking uncertain, not sure if she should cheer her little sister for having learned to do something correctly, or if she should feel threatened that a skill over which she once held dominance was now being learned by someone much younger.

"Excuse me?" I said.

Mineko put a hand to her mouth and her eyes opened wide, like the greedy mouths of *koi* seeking food just beyond the surface of a pond. "You knew, though, didn't you? I hope I didn't say something I shouldn't have." She continued to babble, with false nervousness, that she hoped she hadn't offended anyone.

I was confused. "I knew *what*, Mineko? Speak *clearly*."

But she wouldn't say anything more because at that moment the two little girls had begun to fight over the top and who was going to spin it next. My mother looked on in alarm, raising her voice just slightly and unable to prevent the wrestling match. Mineko, called to duty, jumped up from the sofa where we had been sitting and grabbed each girl roughly by the shoulder, separating them and reminding them that they were to play nicely with each other and to love each other as sisters.

I asked my mother about Masayoshi the next opportunity that we had to be alone, which was in the bath. My mother had relaxed into the water, her hair pinned up against her scalp. Her face was flushed and pink and she looked youthful.

"*Okāsan*." Mother. "Did Masayoshi ask you if he could marry me?"

For a little while I thought perhaps she hadn't heard me, or that we were going to pretend that she hadn't heard me. She began to kick her legs in the water in a rapid bicycling motion, working out her joints, which, she had confided at breakfast, were beginning to stiffen. "You don't really want to get married."

"But did he ask you?"

"Satomi," she sighed, "you are far too talented a girl to just go off and get married. We've discussed this."

"But . . ."

She fixed her eyes on mine and said, "You have a tendency to react to the moment, without thinking of the future. Remember Mineko? Of course that was partly my fault. If you'd had a more secure childhood, you wouldn't feel the need to fight everyone around you, like an alley cat afraid that each meal might be its last. But, honestly, what kind of happiness would you have in ten years if you married Masayoshi? He is a more conventional person than you realize. He's fascinated by you for now, but that kind of attraction doesn't make a really good match in the long run."

"And you know so much about good matches."

She raised her eyebrows. "I found us a good home, didn't I?"

"You found *yourself* a good home."

"Satomi," she said. "Of course this is your home. You could have settled in here a lot more easily if you'd behaved differently."

"You never asked me if I wanted you to marry Mr. Horie."

She shook her head. "I made some mistakes when you were small. I spoiled you. I let you think you were an adult before you were one and let you throw tantrums for far too long."

This wasn't the response I had expected. "Ever since you got here, you've been so different, Mother. You act like Mineko and Chieko are much more your daughters than I am."

"They *are* my daughters."

I tried a different tactic. "You sent me away to school. You never sent them away."

My mother sighed and her breath disturbed the steam on top of the bathwater so that it fluttered. And then in a voice that sounded tired, as though she had repeated this point many times, she said, "You are *talented,* Satomi. They are nice girls, but they are ordinary. You should know this by now."

"But . . ."

"One day perhaps you will all be friends. That is my hope." She began to ask me about my plans now that my final year of school had started. She had all but forgotten the original reason for our conversation, which was Masayoshi and his marriage proposal about which I had heard nothing, and she was carrying on instead about my other future, the one in which I finally fulfilled my promise as Japan's next great contribution to the world of Western music. She wanted to know what path I had sketched out with my teachers. Try as I might to steer the conversation back in the direction of Masayoshi, she would have none of it. I realize now that in her persistent way she saw Masayoshi as a distraction, the main reason why I hadn't already debuted with the NHK symphony, and that now that she had gotten rid of him, I could focus on my purpose again.

"Will you play in concert halls?" she asked.

"I don't know," I said, sulking.

"What are the other girls doing?"

"Getting married. Teaching."

"Well, I suppose it's my fault too," she said out loud, as though finishing up the tail end of another conversation, one that had taken place in her head. "Perhaps what you say is true. If I had paid more attention to you when you were a teenager, you'd be further along in your studies."

"Maybe I never really had that much talent in the first place."

"Nonsense. Remember the story about the moon princess . . ."

"That was just a story."

She looked as though I had slapped her. "Of course it was just a story. It was the only way that you as a young child could understand what I saw in you." She paused. "The only other option for you now is to marry someone whom Mr. Horie and I think is suitable for you. Or, for a time, you could come work in the business."

"*Fishing?*"

"Hasn't it paid for your schooling so far?"

The very thought of working down by the wharf where I would doubtless need to get up early in the morning and wear a pair of rubber boots and tromp around in cold saltwater and fish blood disgusted me. "There is one thing," I said. "You remember Rie Sanada? She says that I would benefit from studying in Europe. She wants me to audition for school in Paris."

"Oh?" My mother raised her eyebrows.

I chose my words carefully. "She says that I have a passionate nature and that I would do better in Europe. She lived there for several years before coming back to Japan. I remind her of the French musicians. She says that Japan isn't going to be able to teach me everything I need to know and that if I am going to perform before an international audience, I have to, well, 'lose my accent.'"

My mother settled back into the water again and I waited to see if my words would have an effect. "Of course," she finally said. "Japan didn't invent classical music. The Europeans did. It shouldn't be expected that you would learn to play truly great music here in Japan."

I thought of the jazz musicians that Masayoshi and I had gone to hear. "I wonder if we will ever play as well as they do."

She laughed. "Eventually we'll play better than they do. And so *you* must be part of the new wave of artists who truly master Western classical music and come back to Japan to show us how to do it correctly. *Sah.*" She stood up out of the water and began to walk across the tiled floor of the tub to the steps. She gripped the railing with one hand and held a small white towel over her breasts with the other. Slowly she began to climb out and I looked at her figure, still so girlish. How could she have changed so much, but still look so young?

"Masayoshi . . . ," I began, but she waved her hand at me.

"You'll see him from time to time because he is family. But he's changed the path of his life. You must continue on the one that you started."

Sanada-sensei and I continued my Thursday lessons, working and reworking the repertory I would use to audition for the École Normale in Paris.

But one afternoon when she let me in, she surprised me by asking me to sit at a table by the window. As we made small talk, she served me a small meal of bread, soup, and sardines.

"You have to learn to eat soup with a spoon," she said. "That's what they do."

"I'm not going to play today?" The sudden barrage of eating utensils and the formality of so many cups and plates intimidated me.

"I think we are all done with lessons," she said. "Don't you?"

"I still have my last exam. And I have to record my audition tape."

"You're ready for all that."

"You'll be there for the exam?"

"Of course. I suppose I'll have to see if there is anyone else with any talent I can take on. Mostly, it's been so disappointing listening to those children." She sighed.

I watched her cut her sardines in half and followed suit.

"Do you have any questions?" she asked.

I spent a minute chewing and swallowing my food before I asked, "What if I get there and I'm not good enough?"

"Not even a question anymore." She smiled kindly. "I know for a fact that all the teachers at Geidai think you are ready to go overseas and that your ability would be wasted here. They find you an overly emotional player, of course. Rather baroque. So while no one is going to help you with the NHK symphony, they do support your application to go overseas. Satomi, it's really up to you now and up to your will. Many things can happen to a young woman to derail her. I should know."

"War," I said. "Bad health."

"A broken heart," she replied, darkly, and I wondered to whom she referred.

"But you still played."

"Yes. Because the piano is my first love." She watched me intently and set her fork down on a plate. "You are wondering if you will be happy."

"Yes."

"It's a question with you, isn't it? Will music be enough for passionate Satomi? Will it make you feel secure, even? I don't know. It has been my focus. You will find out if it is yours."

I passed my exams easily and was admitted to school in Paris just as Sanada-sensei had foreseen. Though I was elated to have accomplished something so few Japanese students had even dared try, I was also deeply uneasy.

"I'll miss you," I bawled to Shinobu. As I have said, I can be a terrible crier once I begin. That day I was a geyser of tears and she dutifully handed me Masayoshi's handkerchiefs one after another while I sobbed. "Who will rescue me when I am in trouble?"

"Don't get into trouble," Shinobu said sensibly.

"Why don't you come with me?"

She shook her head. "He says we're going to have a baby, which means my children will be half Japanese. It's an opportunity for me."

"But you're a better pianist than I am!"

"Maybe I was once, Satomi. But not since you've studied with Sanada-sensei. And also," she sighed. "It's just not as important to me as it is to you. I realize this now."

About a week before I left to go to Paris, I saw Masayoshi once more. I was home packing when I heard the front door slide open and felt the walls tremble with pressure. We had visitors. I stiffened, waiting for the moment when my mother would call me to come out of my small room and to help prepare tea and sweets, but the call never came. I just sat there in my room, looking at the plastic-wrapped packages my mother had moved into my room. Clearly she was intent on turning my room into a storage area once I had permanently left the house.

I heard low murmurs through the wall and then laughter. The cadence was familiar and I decided that it must be Mineko here again for a visit with her two small brats. I lay down on my bed and began to read a magazine I'd picked up from the grocery store. Its pages were filled with glossy photos of ordinary Americans having fun at something called a diner and at the beach, and I wondered at the way their polished cheeks seemed to glow even through paper, how the men looked at the girls with such protective kindness in their eyes.

My musician's ears heard the low rumble of a serious voice making a comment in the other room. It wasn't the voice of Mineko's husband, but someone else's.

I slid out of my room, trying to be quiet so I could escape back to solitude if necessary. I walked across the floor, picking the beams that did not squeak and whose positions I'd memorized since childhood. Then I knelt and looked through a hole in the *shoji* door separating the main room from the hallway. It was Masayoshi sitting at a table with his back to me. He'd shaved his head, but I would have recognized him anywhere, what with the straight shoulders and the gentle swoop of his neck, a private place, like an inner room in a house that few people ever see.

"Satomi?" My mother's gaze shifted to the far side of the room where I was hiding.

I tried to enter the room as noiselessly as possible to give the impression that I hadn't been hiding all that time, but that I had been on my way in to see them. "Mother," I purred. "Would you and your guests like a fresh change of tea leaves?" I made sure my eyes did not once brush his face.

My manners surprised my mother. "Thank you."

I threw out the old leaves into a strainer that rested on top of a bucket by the back door. I boiled water on the stove, then set about carefully measuring fresh tea leaves into the teapot. The tea was from Uji, famous for its manicured hedges, rich soil, and the ladies dressed in indigo-colored clothing and straw hats, who had picked the young leaves to make this *sencha,* the first crop of the year. It was my mother's favorite kind of tea.

I heard a noise. Masayoshi had excused himself from the front room and was carrying in several plates. I knew he was doing this just as an excuse to see me; we'd need plates again when my mother decided to serve her guests something else to eat. But by bringing the dishes into the kitchen he was giving the impression of being a helpful guest while coming up with an excuse to see me alone. No one followed him and I knew that they knew exactly what he intended.

"Well." I tried to sound lighthearted. "I leave you alone for a couple of years and you lose your hair."

He blushed and ran his hand over his scalp. "Actually, this is considered kind of long. I have to get it shaved again soon."

The teakettle was whistling and I turned off the gas and let the water sit for a few seconds to make sure it was the perfect temperature for tea. Then I began to pour the steaming water over the leaves. They unfurled at the touch of the hot liquid, like little fists relaxing at last. In a few minutes, the tea would be ready. If I waited too long, my mother would complain that I had made the tea too strong. So, quickly, I said, "If you wanted to get married you could have just asked me."

He didn't seem to know quite how to respond, which infuriated me.

"Ah. Is that so?" he said.

I frowned. "You can't come in here looking for an excuse to talk to me, and when I finally bring up what you want to talk about, just stutter like that."

"Excuse me."

I waited.

"You always were very blunt. I used to wonder if maybe you didn't grow up in Japan. If maybe your father was a foreigner," he said.

"Could have been. No one knows who my father was. I'm not even sure anymore that my mother does."

"Well, either way. I'll bet you will do very well overseas. I hear that the foreigners are much more direct than we are."

"Let's hope so," I muttered.

"Satomi . . . ," he began.

I waited a few seconds then turned to take the tea back into the front room. It wouldn't have made much difference if I'd continued standing there. I know how men's minds work. Masayoshi probably told himself that if I'd been able to give him just a few more seconds, he would have come up with the words to ask me to forgive him. He took my quickness as evidence that he had been right after all to just let our friendship go. But this is silly. It is very easy to convince yourself that you have done something correctly if you never really pay attention to what else you might have done in the first place. What kind of person, I asked myself as I slid open the *shoji* door to the front room with one hand while carrying the tea carefully into the *tatami*-lined room with the other, doesn't speak up for himself? I saw my mother give me a probing look, the pressure of her gaze feeling a little bit like the weight of her hand stroking my forehead when I had been a child and had a fever. But I didn't look at her. I simply knelt down and held the teapot over the table, giving it a few swirls before I offered our guests an additional cupful to drink.

Then I excused myself and went out to the entrance of the house. I put on my shoes and went for a long walk, all the way down to the water. When I came back, several hours later, the guests had gone. And if I half hoped that there would be a letter for me, some little scribbled note asking for my forgiveness, I was disappointed. No such missive was waiting for me. There was only my mother sewing a button on one of her golf shirts and listening to the broadcast of a live symphony orchestra coming from Tokyo and dreaming, no doubt, that I would be piped to her in similar fashion one day.

I sat by myself in my room and looked at all the objects I had collected over the years. There were scale books and étude books and photos and old certificates from music contests. In the closet were my old recital dresses and skirts whose hems my mother had let out numerous times as I had grown. I looked over my record collection and chose an old album, Rubinstein playing études by Chopin, and I listened to the delicate, impressionistic notes stream into my room. I thought how wonderful it was for Chopin to have created such lovely music that we were still listening to and of the many girls who had gone through Geidai University struggling to play these same notes. It was a cool evening and I opened my window. Leaves stirred just beyond the glass and I smelled the ocean air riding up the street and past my window. I thought of how fine it would be to do something grand, to create something that others would listen to and care for long after I had gone. The thought made me sad and determined all at once. I was certain at that moment that I could do something important in the world if only I were to focus and if only I were given the chance.

There is one more thing. That same day I went for a walk, venturing down to an old noodle shop by the fish market. Masayoshi and I had gone there on our first evening out together when we had met so many years ago on the train. I ordered some noodles and slurped them up, listening to old fishermen talking. I'd finished eating and was just thinking about leaving when I saw a *gaijin*, a stranger, wander in.

He looked just like someone I would see inside the pages of a magazine. In fact, he could have been one of the models selling chocolates or have been James Dean himself. My eye wasn't yet trained to see the difference between various Caucasian faces.

The man ordered a beer and fumbled through a few phrases of Japanese. *"Udon kudasai?"*

The counter staff explained that there was no *udon* available, and when the *gaijin* didn't understand what was happening, the waiter spoke at an even louder decibel. Finally, the foreigner pointed to my nearly empty bowl. *"Udon,"* he insisted.

"Soba da yo!" the waiter countered.

"Excuse me?" *Ex-ecue-zu-me.* My heart was beating very rapidly, but I managed to get the words out. "This is *soba*. It is brown. It is not white."

There was a moment of stunned silence, as if I were a mute statue suddenly brought to life and now chatting.

"Ah. *Soba* then," the *gaijin* said and nodded to me with gratitude. I exchanged a few words with the waiter. Perhaps it was best to give the foreigner some *tempura-soba*. I'd heard that foreigners liked fried food and he might balk at something like fish cake that didn't exist in America. Plus, why waste the delicious fish cake on someone who would not appreciate it? The waiter agreed.

"Where are you from?" I asked the man slowly.

"America." He beamed.

"Next week," I informed him, "I will go to Paris." America. Paris. They didn't seem as though they could be that far apart.

"Ah!" He nodded. "To travel?"

"For school." I told him, haltingly, the name of my school. He babbled back to me, but this discussion was now far beyond a simple one involving the correct ordering of food and establishing which countries we were from. So I smiled at him as he spoke. He had a bright and active energy around him, though there was something in his speech that made it sound as though, at times, he were talking about himself, then making fun of himself for talking about himself before returning to whatever it was he wanted to tell me in the first place. He often paused to smile and, as I could feel that this was what he expected from me, I smiled back, sometimes clapping my hand over my mouth when I felt he believed he had said something funny.

At last he said to me, "What is your name?"

"Satomi," I said. "Satomi Horie." I collected myself. "What is your name?"

"Timothy. Timothy Snowden."

We shook hands, an unusual and uncomfortable sensation for me, but this was what people from that part of the world did. The noodle chef and the patrons in the restaurant watched, quiet and even a little shocked. I smiled, as though I were accustomed to greeting people in this way. But I didn't want the men to get the wrong impression of me altogether, so I hurried out of the shop and went home. That evening, I tried my hand at drawing a caricature of the man in the noodle shop. At first I made his nose too long and his ears too large. Then I crossed out the cartoon and tried to draw again, this time sketching the face of Timothy Snowden, the most handsome man I had ever met.

CHAPTER 4

A Double Life

Satomi
Paris, 1966

I lived in the 14th arrondissement at the very top of a curlicued prewar building with a view of the Eiffel Tower. My room, and all the others on my floor, had once been inhabited by servants and I occasionally consoled my lonely self by imagining that I was a character in *La Bohème*. To reach my room, I either climbed six flights of stairs from the lobby or took the elevator to a family apartment on the third floor where a set of stairs led from the kitchen to the top level. The father of the family, Professor Montmartin, taught at the École Normale and was an aquaintance of one of Sanada-sensei's friends. Professor Montmartin was also my main instructor and gave me additional lessons in the apartment. Initially, this had seemed like an additional piece of good luck.

In the morning, the Montmartin family was out of the house and I practiced the piano in the living room. In the afternoons, I went to class. At noon the entire family came home for lunch and I ate with them. In the beginning, I couldn't understand anything they said. I just sat in the dining room and tried to finish all the unfamiliar dishes with nothing to drink but a glass of wine. Professor Montmartin had a quintessentially handsome Parisian face: straight nose and lips that fell in a pucker when they were at rest. His wife was slim, with bright blue eyes and dark hair, and she smiled so much it was impossible to tell when she was really happy or if her mouth were merely frozen in this position. They had two children, a boy, Patrice, and a girl, Madeleine, ages sixteen and fourteen, respectively.

Whenever I tried to say anything in French, the girl and the boy were quick to correct me, while the mother gave me a half smile before turning her attention back to her children. They both took piano lessons from their father, but they were clearly without talent and were completely insensitive to the emotional stories told in the sonatas and partitas they practiced.

And so, apparently, was I.

In our very first meeting, the professor said to me, *"Mais, où est la passion?"*

I played my most recent pieces: Beethoven and Debussy. But these earnest efforts brought little more than a tolerant smirk to his lips.

"Vous n'avez pas d'émotion?" He looked at me accusingly.

I was, in his eyes, a player without any heart, a girl whose blood was asleep. Now and then he would shake his head and mutter, *"Les asiennes."* This came as something of a shock to me, the pianist whom everyone at Geidai had considered so emotional as to be frightening. In Paris, I couldn't communicate what I was feeling at all. It is the job of the artist to stimulate the audience, however large, however small, he would say. But nothing I did, not even my very appearance, moved him. It was as Sanada-sensei had said it would be: I played with an accent.

Professor Montmartin's method to induce proper emotion from me was to shout. At unexpected moments he slammed down the piano lid and I had to quickly withdraw my hands from the keys or risk a broken finger. Sometimes he would throw my books on the floor and insist I pick them up. Other times he was eerily, dangerously sweet, coming so close to my face I could smell traces of coffee and, on some days, wine. Once he even kissed my cheek and I screamed and refused to play for the rest of the day. We Japanese do not invade anyone's space like this. To this day I am frustrated with the inability of a Western person to notice how much space he occupies on a crowded subway or bus.

I did what anyone would have done under these circumstances. I started smoking.

Outside of my lessons when I was shaking from having been so humiliated, I took to wearing a pair of large sunglasses and stabbing at the air with a cigarette in my hand. I visualized the day when I would light a cigarette in our sessions together and casually pass the burning stub over his right hand and grind it down. Instead, I affected a look that I thought would convey I was far from unfeeling. I'd clench my jaw and show him I was strong. I refused to cry before him, saving any tears for my bath at night. Alone in my room, I drew little caricatures, Mineko style, fashioning the temperamental professor as a lone volcano crushing a field of daisies.

I was homesick and lonely. At first, Shinobu sent me letters, and I looked forward to the thin blue aerogrammes that arrived from her every few weeks. But abruptly, she stopped writing to me and my pleas to her for more correspondence went unanswered. I wondered what I had done. My mother wrote to me, but letters cannot indefinitely sustain a person in the physical world. I took to counting out a few coins every day to buy myself a cup of coffee at a café, La Coupole, sipping it so slowly it always grew cold while I alternated between staring at the pedestrians and trying to do my music theory homework in a language I barely understood.

Fortunately, I became friendly with a singer from the Netherlands who was also taking music theory classes. His name was Theo and he was Indonesian, but his family had been living in Amsterdam for a good decade or so and he spoke decent French. Theo took pity on me. I wasn't embarrassed to speak in front of him, and in his presence my language abilities blossomed, for we spoke both in English and in French. When I became tired of one language, he switched to another and I began to gain a little confidence. Even the arrogant Montmartin children noticed at dinner one night that I was no longer mute in their native tongue. *"Qu'est-ce qui c'est passé?"* they asked, as though I had managed the impossible.

It was through Theo that I met Timothy again. Theo had become friendly with a group of expats whose most recent venture consisted of a trilingual production of Shakespeare's *The Tempest*. Theo was to play Ariel, the spirit messenger.

"Classical music is dead." Theo yawned. "I never realized that until I came here. All those arias. Symphonies. They are nothing but museum pieces."

"Great art is universal," I replied.

"Well, fine." He shrugged in a most un-Asian manner, which reminded me of the difference in our respective upbringings. "But I'd rather be part of the great art that's going on *now*. It's easy to participate in things from the past, when all the critical choices have already been made. It takes a genius to be part of the art movements that will be famous in the future."

I was invited to a cast party.

"You must come," Theo begged. "It'll be good for you."

The party was to be held in a home half an hour outside Paris. The owner was an Eastern European noble who had fled to Paris just as the iron curtain had fallen across Europe. The family had sunk all their savings into an old château that had once belonged to the keeper of Louis XIII's hunt. Much of the building could not be heated because there wasn't enough money.

I sat with Theo and his boyfriend in the back of a small car as we sped across the dark night road to this mythical castle, which had grown turrets and a moat in my imagination. But as the car began to slow, I saw a rather plain-looking two-story building, manned by a small family living in a gatehouse, their faces just barely concealing a look of suspicion as our headlights flashed on the garden grounds. A white deer, a white horse, and a white dog trotted by.

"The count," Theo explained to me, "loves white animals."

The first thing I remember seeing inside was a staircase leading up to the bedrooms, and over this, a large framed and hand-drawn family tree, with little photographs inserted whenever someone of importance sprouted up along the branches. There were pictures of bishops, kings, and princes. Another version of the family tree, written in black cursive, was propped up on an old wooden music stand in the entry.

I followed Theo to the living room. He was nursing his throat with a cashmere scarf while he was waving one hand to indicate that, yes, he would like a glass of wine. Dusty red velvet curtains that would have looked more at home in a theater separated the entry from the formal foyer. Later I learned that the man everyone referred to as "the count" was an opera devotee and that he had befriended a set designer who had procured the drapes for him wholesale and hung them in lieu of doors. The drawing room, in fact, looked like an opera set. Arms of ferns tangled around old marble columns and windowsills. There were paintings of subjects I'd seen in the Louvre: women with windswept hair standing on battlefields, portraits of important men in dark suits, and landscapes in moody green. All the paintings were dirty from the smoke of candles and incense the count kept on various brass holders. The count apparently had no housekeeper, for the dirty house was filled with dust that gave the air a magical, silvery glow.

Here and there little groups of partygoers stood or sat draped over baronial chairs and chaises whose silk covers had long ago started to fray. Blink once and the walls looked pleasant and decorative, covered with the usual wallpaper design of flowers and birds. Blink again and all I saw were more dead animals, the obsession of the bloodthirsty French, eaters of meat. The château had once belonged to the keeper of the hunt, and the wallpaper— actually a hand-painted pattern—depicted geese on platters, boars rooting around in the woods, and dogs chasing foxes.

A fireplace roared away. The count had asked that his guests bring something personal to burn. I had chosen one of my sonata books, which just that day Professor Montmartin had hurled across the room when I had failed to employ staccato adequately. Theo was throwing away an old cashmere scarf from a former lover. The two of us dumped our unwanted things at the same time. Someone else had brought a more useful gift— firewood—and this sat in a bucket on the floor, waiting to be put to use.

I immediately spotted the count standing in the center of the room with two young women and two men. He was pale and puffy and wore a black velvet suit. He had the longest natural eyelashes I've ever seen on a man or a woman, and when he blinked, his entire body bobbed, so he gave the impression of floating on water.

"I'll introduce you," Theo said.

"No, no." I was too shy.

After pleading with me a bit, Theo went to speak to the count alone. I nibbled on a canapé and wondered what to do next. Theo was good at parties. He circulated among the Europeans, exhibiting his most Ariel-like persona, dancing and whirling as though at any minute he might fly away, and they applauded and admired him for this lightness of being. I, as usual, was silent. I was shy and uncomfortable in French and English; the few times I tried to say something funny, I was met with blank stares.

"If only people knew," Theo sighed, "how silly you really are."

I wandered out to the courtyard, which looked like a medieval abbey, what with a tower of a dozen fused candles oozing wax onto the cobble-stone patio. I saw a group of men and one woman wearing a long red shawl. They were smoking. I threw my stub to the ground and lit a new cigarette. I heard a rumble, and the white horse with another woman on its back came barreling toward us out of the darkness. This woman murmured something in the horse's ear, and the beast slowed to a stop and she hopped off. Almost immediately, one of the men put out his cigarette, patted the horse on the neck, then jumped on and rode off. The galloping sound faded. Then I knew that the gardens were very large.

"It's the nobles," someone said in English.

I looked up. A white man was talking to me.

"They all learned to ride when they were kids. When their parents thought they were still going to inherit the earth. Now they're poor but they still have all those upper-class habits. Bet they still take tea every day, only they have to make it themselves."

I stared. The man had a relentless, rich smile that showered me like a beam of light.

"I know you," the man said to me.

"Yes," I breathed.

"Where are you from?"

"Japan."

"Ah." He nodded and seemed to think, slowly sipping his wine. "That little dive in northern Japan."

"My name is Satomi."

"I'm . . ."

"Timothy Snowden," I said.

By this point my English had improved sufficiently that I could under-stand him much better than at our initial meeting. He said he'd come to France on business, then he laughed at himself as though he'd said something funny. Instinctively I felt at ease and knew immediately that he would never laugh at me. Timothy said that he was originally from Cali-fornia but had since dropped out of college. He was "seeing the world." He had met a man through mutual friends at a party in San Francisco who said he was collecting porcelain from Japan and China, and one thing led to another and Timothy had become a courier. He'd just taken a ship-ment to San Francisco and decided to spend his money on a visit to an ex-girlfriend in Paris.

Had I heard of her? Priscilla from Italy? She usually hung with this crowd. Most expats in Europe had heard of her. Other Californians were busy celebrating the beauty of blonds, but he had a penchant for girls with dark hair and olive skin. In fact—he squinted—there was something vaguely Mediterranean about me. That must be why he'd remembered me in the first place. I'd stood out. "I kept asking myself for a few days after meeting you: 'What's her story?'"

I told him that my music professor considered me so shy and retiring that I was incapable of playing Western music with emotion. I told him that my professor suspected I wasn't even capable of feeling things the way a human being was supposed to.

"Let me get this straight." Timothy frowned. "According to this professor, you don't feel things, and that makes it okay for him to insult you. I think it's the other way around. He's the one with bad social skills," he finished kindly, eyes twinkling.

The attention unnerved me and I tried to change the direction of the conversation, asking how Timothy had liked Japan. He followed my lead easily. He had fallen in love with my country, he declared. Everything we did was a little act of art, from the way women neatly hung up laundry to dry on carefully designed circular hangers, to the plastic and wax food replicas in restaurant windows, to the tremendous care given to our rice paddies. What the professor considered a lack of emotion, he saw as a concern to get things just right. The world would be better off, he declared loftily, if everyone were dedicated to caring so much. On the other hand, it must sometimes be exhausting living under that pressure to make things so perfect. Once again, I didn't know how to respond to this unsolicited gesture of sympathy.

"Do you think you will ever want to return to Japan?" I asked.

"Oh, definitely." He wanted to go back to look for more antiques, but the language barrier had been difficult. He needed to either find a partner or start studying himself. The answer to what to do and how to do it would come to him. He was still young, only thirty, and in this new age, youth could be prolonged. He was sure that I with my worldliness and artist's sensitivity would understand what he was talking about.

I pretended that I did.

I asked him about his travels and he told me stories of sleeping in a tent in a ruined Scottish castle while it rained, of visiting the Keukenhof gardens in the Netherlands when the first tulips began to bloom, of submitting himself to a massage in Constantinople, of renting a car and driving through Yugoslavia, and then taking a ferry boat to Libya, where he had seen the most gorgeous Roman ruins I could ever imagine. Forget Italy, he said. Libya was the place to be. He'd stayed in people's houses, winking at them that he was a Canadian and not an American and they'd winked back.

As he talked, I could not help but wonder what it would be like to drift from country to country, as though following a map and the promise of an adventure were in and of themselves sufficient goals for living. The very idea was at once intriguing because of the storyteller it had turned Timothy into, and also unsettling. What, I wondered, would my mother make of a person so without ambition for himself and for his family, and yet who was clearly intelligent and capable of accomplishing so much?

At the end of the party he told me that he would be in Paris for a few more days and that, if I was interested, he wouldn't mind spending some more time with me. The beautiful Priscilla had fled to her homeland with a young Italian, heir to a textile mill, and he would be by himself drifting from museum to café.

"We should hang out," he said. "You probably know Paris much better than I do."

"I have a lot of work," I said. "I don't know."

I was conflicted about men in those days. Outwardly I liked to appear as though I didn't care about them at all. At the same time, I secretly thought of their attention as something important to gain. Women, those herdlike creatures, were so easy to win over. Just be thoughtlessly nice like my childhood friend Tomoko and women loved you. Men were much harder to please. Men were always seeking a woman who was smart and engaging and capable. What greater reward than to be seen as interesting in their eyes? To be interesting, I believed, was a quality women could not understand.

"It isn't healthy to work all the time." Timothy shook his head with concern. "Even you have to alternate work with play. It's better for the imagination."

I conceded that I would be happy to show Timothy the parts of Paris that I knew. Then, because I didn't want to seem too eager, I told him he could find me in the 14th arrondissement. I practiced in the morning, had class until three, then generally did my homework with Theo at La Coupole. If Timothy wanted to, he could find me there.

I was tense for the next few days, like the shortest, tightest string on a piano. Sitting in the window of the café, I often strained my gaze past the immediate stream of pedestrians to see who else might soon glide past the large glass windows. Theo noticed. "You're already in love with him."

"With who?" I took a puff of my cigarette.

Three days later, he appeared, sidling in through the doors and grinning almost apologetically as if he'd meant to arrive two days earlier. Theo eyed him up and down. I tried to appear disinterested. "Oh. Hello."

"Sorry. I've been a little tied up."

"Priscilla?" Theo asked.

"From Italy?" I said.

"She's back there now," Timothy said. "Never to return. Until her honeymoon, anyway." He sat down.

Theo turned to me and began to talk again about our homework. "You ought to at least try to understand why Debussy sounds so different to you, Satomi. He was one of many composers working on avoiding a cycle of fifths as a way to build a score."

"Hmm."

"You need to be able to look at this and see where Debussy was moving chords around for color or for an actual key change."

Timothy leaned in close to my face. "Can you help me get a cup of coffee? They won't understand my accent." Warmth passed from his body to mine and though I had been slightly chilled sitting so close to the window, I felt a fever in my stomach.

"American?"

He blinked. "No. The French kind. But with milk."

"*Garçon,*" I called. "*Un café au lait.*"

"*Olé!*" Timothy smiled.

Theo groaned audibly.

"So, you two meet here every day and do homework like this," Timothy said.

"She needs the help," Theo explained.

"It's true. I do."

"What about . . . Paris? *Bateau mouche?* The Seine?"

"No time," I said.

"You have your life all planned out."

"I have always had a plan."

His mouth, that elastic arch of a line, stretched into a broad smile of glee. "And did your plans include me?"

It wasn't long before I stopped going to class, to my café sessions with Theo, and to the apartment to practice, though I still met with Professor Montmartin. Time was better spent with Timothy, who didn't laugh at my English and who spoke even less French than I did. He was also grateful that I could act as interpreter, even with my handicapped *r*'s and *l*'s. *"Comment? Comment?"* the French asked me when I stumbled over their words.

"Try saying it again. Slower," Timothy suggested.

Timothy's encouragement and attention made me feel stronger. I was reminded of that time in my life when I had lived just with my mother, and her love for me had been enough to convince me that the moon people actually existed and that I belonged in their kingdom. When Professor Montmartin gave me my weekly lesson and criticized me, I stood up and stalked out of the apartment. I could see how stunned he was when I did this, and the next time we met, he checked his temper.

"See, you need me," Timothy said when I reported on Professor Montmartin's change in behavior.

It was true. It was not enough for me to want to express something. I needed Timothy, as I had once needed my mother, to help me unleash all that I felt I could do.

One night, not a week after we'd met, we walked along the Right Bank of the Seine, willows sweeping the waves, the moon high and bright and the boats churning through the water. Timothy leaned over and kissed me.

It was my first kiss. Masayoshi and I hadn't so much as held hands. Kissing was something people in Paris did all the time, whether they were married or not. Certainly I'd learned to endure the cheek kissing that accompanied a greeting. But this was my first real kiss.

When it ended, I could feel Timothy studying me, waiting, with typical concern, to see how I would react to this new experience. I wasn't too sure what to do. So he kissed me again, and gradually it became easier for me to kiss him back. Little by little, I found that I enjoyed it.

"I'd like to go back to your place tonight, if that's okay," he whispered while he held my hand tightly.

"My apartment?"

"Nothing has to happen." He smiled reassuringly. "I'll just miss you tomorrow morning, unless I wake up next to you."

I liked the idea of waking up with him, of finally not feeling quite so alone in Paris.

"Anyway," he murmured, "I'm falling in love with you. So you don't have to worry about that."

At the time, I didn't completely understand what he meant—why would I be worrying? I wasn't worried. I was a little startled, but mostly I was pleased. I liked the changes in my life that Timothy had brought. It felt completely natural when, a few days later, he moved out of the small pension where he'd been staying and came to live with me. We kept his presence secret from the Montmartins. He used the community toilet and shower on the sixth floor. At night we climbed up the staircase from the lobby and soon I eschewed going into the Montmartin apartment altogether, except for lessons.

Timothy had a philosophy of life. I'd never met anyone outside of Masayoshi who had a theory of how the whole world worked, as though it were something you could study, know, and master.

"We can go anywhere. Do you know how hard it was for all those Victorians to get to Japan from England? We're so lucky. I think we were meant to take advantage of the jet age. We're free, Satomi. Freer than our parents, even. We can see the world."

"It isn't always better to travel. The French are a very rude people. Maybe it was better when I was home, believing that this was a beautiful place with beautiful people."

"You're going about it all wrong, Satomi. You can't travel and expect to find nirvana out there. You go and you find the best things about a country and you make that part of yourself. Then you move on. My guess? This is the first generation of humans that will actually attain enlightenment because we will be exposed to the greatest number of things."

"You want to be a Buddha?" I was teasing him, but he took me seriously.

"It's the only religion that really tells people how to be holy. Christianity just makes you feel bad all the time. The Buddhists are life affirming."

I thought about Masayoshi. "I don't know," I said. "We are very Buddhist in Japan. Plenty of Buddhists are unhappy."

He ignored me. "I wasn't ready to understand the Buddha back in Japan," he said. "I still need to travel more before I can go back and really hear what people there have to tell me." He smiled. "Maybe you'll help. I mean, you already have."

"Me?"

"Sure." He continued to grin. "You're a very calm person, Satomi."

I told him that I didn't feel calm. Certainly no one in my family would describe me as calm. I was considered rather terrible. Temperamental, in fact.

"This is why it's important to travel. If your family saw more of the world, they'd see how self-possessed you are in contrast to most of the human population."

"What do your parents say about your travels?"

"They think it's a phase."

"A what?"

"You know. A phase."

I looked up this term in my small Kodansha dictionary. The word *phase* in Japanese had several translations, mostly to do with the stages of the moon, or with the development of the mind from child to adult. By Timothy's age, though, had he been Japanese, he would have been expected to be an adult. What kind of a phase was he in?

"What do you do all day, when I'm in class?" I asked.

"I read. I sleep. I dream."

"Don't you get bored?"

"The imagination is never boring."

"But," I insisted, "you cannot just dream for the rest of your life."

I was hurt when he laughed at me, and he tried to explain it away, something about how serious I was all the time. Then he said that he would show me one of his hobbies the next time I had a free day and wasn't playing the piano for the professor.

The next Saturday we went to a small museum known as the Musée Guimet, which housed a number of important Japanese and Chinese antiques. He spent a lot of time looking at the porcelain in particular. He said he was studying. When I asked him what he meant by that, he took me next to the Louvre and asked me to look at a number of Dutch still lifes and portraits from the sixteenth century.

"What do you see?" he asked.

I pointed out the usual European fascination with dead animals and skulls and fanciful clothing.

"What else?"

The closer I looked, the more I began to see something quite odd in all the portraits. Something very, very strange.

"All these rich men," I said. "They all have . . . Chinese bowls."

"Bingo!" Timothy grinned.

The Netherlands had been an economic powerhouse in the fifteenth and sixteenth centuries, and had actively traded with China during its powerful Ming dynasty. Well-to-do Dutchmen had been very likely to own a Ming porcelain collection and to pose for their formal portraits displaying these blue-and-white wonders as evidence of their wealth. Time and again, amid the plump wives cushioned by lace and the fat pheasant dinners in the background, were these Chinese dishes.

"Know anything about porcelain?" Timothy asked me.

I told him about my mother's love of Arita and our small pieces at home in Hachinohe.

He held my hands. "I'm thinking of going to Amsterdam in a couple of days. Lots of flea markets."

"You're *leaving*?"

He nodded. "This guy in San Francisco—he's hard to get to unless you have an 'in.' Theoretically, I'm just a courier. But I tried to make it sound like I knew what I was doing. The collector said he'd buy anything from me that I found. Of course, it has to be the real thing and not some nineteenth-century copy."

"That sounds really interesting," I said. This was a loose translation of the Japanese phrase *omoshiroi desune,* which means roughly the same thing. It was a handy phrase at home, something to say to fill up empty space in a conversation, and I couldn't break the habit of using it in the West. Timothy was still holding my hands and I turned my face to the side, not wanting to show him how upset I was that he would be leaving.

"I'll bet," he said slowly, "that you know more than I do."

"Of course I know about antiques in Japan. It's my culture."

"Can you tell the difference between Korean and Chinese?"

"Can't *you*?" I turned back and smiled at him.

He grinned. "I could pick you out of a crowd." When I didn't say anything, he continued in a soft voice. "Look, I'm telling you that I wouldn't mind more of your company, if you'll come along."

I left a note for the Montmartins that I had been called back to Japan on a family emergency. Home was so far away and the language barrier such a problem, I doubted the professor would ever think to call to make sure that I was actually in Hachinohe. I could just imagine what would happen if he were to actually pick up the phone and hear my mother's polite, purely Japanese voice on the other end of the line. If he didn't hang up out of frustration, I knew she would hang up out of embarrassment.

I had thought we would be taking the train, which was what most of the other students did in Paris when they went somewhere. But Timothy had a small car, a Peugeot, which he said he'd bought some months earlier and driven all over Europe and planned to drive until it died.

Amsterdam surprised me by how much it was and was not like Paris. The coffee was different, each cup coming with a small side of sweetened milk. The breakfasts were larger and included ham and cheese. There was also a very welcome surprise: *rijsttafel,* an Indonesian specialty. While the spices in the *rijsttafel* weren't at all what I had grown up with in Japan, it was a relief to eat a meal with rice instead of bread.

Over the years, I've followed the antiques news enough to know that the world of collecting has become increasingly difficult. There are now entire factories devoted to churning out false paintings and statues, with increasingly complicated techniques used to make sure that glazes look real and that the fake ladies of the T'ang dynasty bend in just the appropriate manner and that their makeup is in place, but not so perfect as to raise suspicion among connoisseurs.

What I mean to say is that I don't know if I would be of any use to someone like Timothy today. But back then, in the late sixties, all I had to do was to look at a piece of porcelain and tell him if I thought it was old or if it was new. If a plate resembled something my mother might have used to serve food, we shouldn't buy it. If it looked like something she would have kept in a wooden box and covered in silk, or like something I'd seen in the Tokyo National Museum, then we should purchase it immediately.

Timothy and I developed a code, like baseball players. A cough meant we should move on. If I put my hand over my mouth and smiled, it meant that there was something in the stall for us to look at. One finger meant early Ming. Two meant the middle period. And so on. It was fun, this game playing. And the traveling was fun too.

I sometimes had to remind myself that the Dutch were not on display for me to watch and enjoy. Amsterdam was a real city, as real as Tokyo. But everything was so different, and so interesting, it was difficult not to feel as though I had fallen into a storybook and was watching characters come to life. This is the difference between traveling to a foreign country and trying to live in one, as I was doing in Paris. Countries, like people, are at their most beautiful when you visit them briefly and allow them to enchant you over a short period of time.

Timothy was always offering to buy me something: a vintage pin, a used scarf, an old hat. I demurred out of politeness and, frankly, my Japanese sense of not wanting to buy something that was once worn by a smelly European. One afternoon, however, I could not resist a little leather jacket we found for sale on the street. It was soft and brown, with a fringe on the sleeves and across the back like something an American Indian might wear. I felt at home in it, not because I thought of myself as a Native American, but because the jacket made me feel conspicuously from another country. It emphasized and made no excuses for my foreign face.

Timothy bought me a one-way train ticket back to Paris with a promise to be in touch soon. He had "business" to do alone. He said he was worried leaving me by myself in Paris, but I calmly explained that I would be fine on my own. In a way, I was relieved to see him go. With Masayoshi, I had always had to worry what my mother or stepsisters would say. Timothy and I were complete strangers with no expectations on our relationship and I feared I was becoming a bit too accustomed to this kind of independence. Once or twice, I even said something to Timothy about my feelings.

"We can't just travel like this forever."

"Says who?" He stroked my hair. "All those rules you have in your head. Illusions."

But I kept hearing the voice of my mother telling me that what I was doing was not what she had dreamed of for me. I should go back to Paris and resume my studies.

How surprised was I then when a yawning, sick emptiness flared open inside my stomach as the train pulled away from Amsterdam. Without Timothy in Paris, I would have to think seriously about my future. Was I really going to graduate from the École Normale as previously planned? Should I go back to Japan a failure? The questions were so serious and so large. Why was I having them now? It was true that I had been away from home for a long time now, and perhaps this had left me open to influence. But I'd been on my own before and not wavered from trying to be a musician. It wasn't that I didn't want to play music—not exactly. I still had that longing to do something important with my life, to feel the world embrace me with all its love. But I had discovered there were ways to capture this feeling that didn't involve pianos and teachers and audiences. I was hungry to know more of the world.

I wanted Timothy to come back.

When I returned to my Paris room, I found a wad of mail shoved under the door. Most were postcards from my mother. She had a cold. Nothing to worry about. Mineko's children were growing. Buried in a comment about changing autumn colors was the fact that Masayoshi's son had celebrated his third birthday. I thought that any feelings I might have had for him had long since changed with the seasons. You can't imagine what *I've* been doing, I replied, mentally, to all the postcards.

I only told Theo where I had been. He said, "I don't want you to be in some *Madama Butterfly* opera, waiting for this man to come back to you."

"He'll come back."

"Men are fickle creatures. Don't you know your operas? I don't want you to waste any energy on this American."

I told Theo that I was just fine and not the least bit heartbroken. But privately, I did wonder if I would ever see Timothy again.

I was nervous that the Montmartins might suspect I hadn't been to Japan at all. Instead, they misread my watchfulness as worry over my mother. Grief even. The time I had spent with Timothy acting as his interpreter had strengthened my language abilities. The family was surprised by how my "trip to Japan" had actually helped my fluency. While they were no more interested in me than before, the children, at least, did not pick on my French quite so much.

My trip with Timothy also had the curious effect of improving my piano playing. I was nervous when I first sat down to play. But Professor Montmartin merely nodded: *"Bon."* There were no more tantrums. He no longer questioned my ability to emote. He began to talk, instead, about which pieces I should play for my first jury, and which competitions I should enter.

To the professor, I looked like a girl who'd suddenly come into her own as an artist. This was the goal my mother had been after for so many years. If she had suddenly come to Paris, she would have been proud of the result.

Late at night I sat in my apartment and looked out over the city. On clear evenings, the gold moon shone bright against the blue-black sky. I thought about my mother's stories about the mythical moon kingdom. I thought to myself that this life in Europe was most likely the closest I would ever come to being in a foreign place capable of bestowing magic on my life. How easy it was to lead a double life when you traveled abroad. Timothy had said he craved enlightenment. I craved the power I'd felt while we were traveling in Amsterdam, the sureness of knowing that I was a complete stranger with a special gift in an enchanted land.

CHAPTER 5

Where Unseen Things Are Hidden

I tried to fold myself back into the ordered world I'd lived in before meeting Timothy. But my imagination wandered and I could not stop craving something grander and more elusive from the world. Music, suddenly, was not sufficient.

But what to do?

I remembered Timothy's subtle and mocking question: "Did you plan on me?" he had asked.

Throughout the fall, I struggled to concentrate. Mostly I was able to hide my inner battles and occasionally was able to convince myself that I still planned to play the piano until I was old and arthritic like Sanada-sensei. There were plenty of nights, though, when my sleep was interrupted by a dream involving Timothy, and I sat up in a sweat, wondering if he would come back, or if that adventurous path in my life had forever been abolished. I would need to learn to curb this craving. Fall turned to winter, and winter to spring, and still he did not come.

Is anything worse than a broken heart? Once again, I was lonely in Paris. To anesthetize myself, I tried to empty out my feelings in music. Professor Montmartin was impressed. Soon, he said, it would be time for me to enter competitions and he expected that I had a good chance of placing. The news should have made me happy, but I found that it left me feeling profoundly empty. I wrote to my mother: could she come visit me? She sent back a card explaining that she still had her cold, but that I should not worry. One day, she promised, we would be together.

Then one day that spring, I was walking home from class when I heard a voice behind me murmur in English. "Don't you drink coffee anymore?"

I tried to appear impassive. "I do not need help with my homework anymore. So I do not go to La Coupole with Theo."

"You know everything there is to know about music theory?"

"No one knows everything about music theory."

Timothy smiled broadly and opened up his blazer. Peeking out of the inside pocket was a fat wad of French francs. He closed the jacket and continued smiling. A few people had seen this bold display of money and their attention unsettled me. Plus, Timothy appeared to have changed somewhat. He harbored a new confidence that seemed slightly alarming but also, if I were to be honest, attractive.

"Your commission, Satomi," Timothy murmured quietly. "Don't you want it?"

"It looks like lot of money," I breathed.

"Not that much. Minus your train ticket. Minus the plane ticket."

"Plane?"

"To Japan," he said. "The collector bought almost everything we picked out in Amsterdam. Not a fake in the bunch. Those were his exact words. You made me look good."

"I am happy for you." I turned away and began to walk briskly. For a moment I heard only my footsteps, but then I heard his shoes slapping the pavement as he ran behind me.

"Aren't you happy to see me? Because *I'm* happy to see you!"

"Five months," my voice caught.

"Baby."

But I pulled my hand away and my tears streaked across my temples as I ran.

"Hey. Satomi!"

I would not be distracted by this man again. Just recently, I'd come to feel relieved that he was gone from my life and that I could focus on my music as my mother had asked me to. "You," I screamed, "are a bad person! You make promises. But you are sloppy. You live in phases!"

At this, he pulled me into an embrace and I, still so lonely, so determined, relented.

I led Timothy up the stairs to my little garret and made him a cup of tea on my hot plate. I prepared a plate of cookies I had bought the day before and kept on the windowsill to try to keep cool. He counted out my commission. It was the first time I had ever earned money.

"We leave in two days, in case you were wondering."

"I didn't say that I was going with you."

"But you will." He grinned. "It's lonely sleeping by yourself at night."

I turned away from him.

"I *know* you've been alone," he said softly. "I didn't like it very much either."

"Where were you?"

"I got sidetracked," he said, bowing his head. "Look, I went to a party and got caught up with some people who were into some shit. Took awhile for the police to figure out who did what."

"Police!"

"That's why I didn't say anything to you right away. I didn't want you to worry. I came as soon as I could."

"I have to prepare for my juries," I replied stiffly.

"You told the professor you were going to Japan last time. This time you'll be telling him the truth."

"I cannot fail my mother."

"*Cannot fail,*" he mimicked. "Jesus. You sound biblical."

No matter how many years have gone by, I have never managed to sound casual and natural in English. I am aware of my stiffness, of my complete lack of the jocularity that oozes so naturally from American mouths. Still, the teasing rankled me.

"You have never made fun of my speech before," I said.

"It's only a few days, Satomi. Easy cash. Anyway, isn't travel romantic?"

At the sound of the word *romantic,* my body hardened. At the same time, the idea of an adventure together intrigued me. "Yes, travel will be romantic, and then you will leave again for Priscilla, or someone else."

He came up behind me. "I'm not going anywhere. I would have come back even if it weren't for the antiques I know we are going to find together."

I was silent.

"We go to Japan, I deliver the stuff to the collector in San Francisco, and you come back for your juries."

"And then?"

"Then I promise I'll come back to you. And then I won't go away again unless you go with me."

If one's speaking voice can acquire an accent while one is overseas, I felt that my body had acquired nearly the same thing. I did not realize it in France, but I now moved with a boldness and intention that I had not possessed as a young student. Not surprisingly, I was annoyed by the slowness with which everyone else moved in Japan and by the shyness of the other women my age. I hated the way they paused in front of vending machines, pretending to be unsure of what they wanted to drink. When they really were unsure of what they wanted to drink, why, I was all the more annoyed. How hard is it to decide whether you want tea, or Coke, or juice?

Timothy had planned for us to go to Kyoto and Nara and, if there was time, the village surrounding Lake Biwa. To me these towns had existed only in textbooks and in *samurai* movies; I'd never actually expected that I would visit Kyoto itself and see the temples and the shrines.

I learned then just how adaptable a person Timothy was, perhaps even more adaptable than I was. He'd already traveled so much by the time we went to Japan together he understood very quickly that to be comfortable here, he would have to behave differently. And learn he did, keeping his arms close to his body, checking to make sure that no one was behind him when he shifted his weight on a train, and pointing at things with his entire hand instead of his index finger. Years later, I realized just how competent a traveler Timothy had been when I observed other foreigners wandering around Japan, never quite adjusting to our rules or to our rhythms. He was a remarkably fluid person, though I never stopped feeling concerned when he wandered off by himself and I feared he was lost. It was only much later that I would learn what he was actually doing in those moments.

The best stores were in little towns where some eccentric elderly man had a house stuffed with plates or statues or odd things that he knew were "old," but whose purpose and value he might not understand. My very favorite thing we found in those weeks was a large red-and-white dish with a swirling pattern and some green turtles.

I suppose I was also on edge during that trip because I had a deep fear that we would see someone I knew. Actually, it was fear mixed with hope.

I'd been so homesick and lonely in Paris and now I was in my homeland, which I hadn't expected to see for many months yet. It felt like cheating. And yet, I longed to see someone I knew. Several times a day I flinched at the sight of an elderly face I was sure looked like our old neighbor, or a priest I thought might be Masayoshi. Once I even thought I saw Shinobu. I knew the chances of encountering an acquaintance were slim. Who among my family or my school friends would be wandering around these small towns near Kyoto?

Timothy urged me to call my mother. The call would be cheaper from here than from Europe, and as long as I made sure no other Japanese person burst in on my call, she'd never know which country I was phoning from, but would be pleased that I had contacted her. My guilt would be eased.

I disagreed. I thought she'd be angry that I was wasting money on a call that had no specific purpose, but Timothy was adamant that phone calls didn't require a specific reason. I could just call because I felt like it. I could tell her that I was homesick and that I missed her. So, armed with a handful of change, I found a bright-green phone in a train station.

The phone seemed to ring a long time before someone answered. The voice on the other end caught me by surprise.

"Chieko?"

"So. You finally decided to call." She sounded almost pleased with herself as she said this and her tone of voice alarmed me. Had she, or someone we both knew, seen me?

I decided to play it cool. "I have to be quick. This is expensive, you know."

"You've had the letter for at least two weeks."

My heart was suddenly possessed by an allegro tempo. I took a deep breath to calm my blood, but my body wouldn't cooperate. "Letter?"

"Look, she died a month ago. We couldn't wait for you. We had to have the funeral. If you come back now you can make the forty-nine-day memorial."

"*You* could have called!" I was shouting.

"No one here speaks French. And anyway, what took you so long to read your mail?"

I remembered the postcard I'd found from my mother on the floor of my room. *I've had a cold.*

I told Chieko I would be there the following day.

"That fast?" Now she sounded nervous.

"Don't worry if you haven't managed to clean up the house, Chieko. Housekeeping never was your strength." I said this just to be mean. Chieko had always been a model housekeeper.

"I didn't mean . . ."

"Yes, that *fast*," I hissed. "The modern world is a very *fast* and *complicated* place, but I doubt that someone like you would understand." I slammed down the phone.

Rice paddies bled into bamboo forests, and the jangle of the railway crossing alarm swelled and faded with the same Doppler effect that blurred the notes of honking cars. The familiar landscape rushed by. I saw the same faces on the train from Tokyo to Hachinohe that I'd seen since I was a college student, and I took on the same poised posture I'd always assumed on the way home: the talented girl just visiting the countryside for a mandatory reason after a spell in the sophisticated city where she belonged. I knew that my mother would not be there in the house waiting for me. But surely everything else would be the same. The countryside never changed. I, with all my experiences, was the only person to be different this year than last.

I had asked Timothy to wait for me at the hotel while I went home. I didn't want to include him in my family problems. I certainly would not be in a frame of mind to help him adjust to what would surely be a culturally confusing situation for him.

I understood what Chieko had told me on the phone; my mother was dead and I would never see her again. But I was anxious and in a hurry, as though by arriving there as soon as possible, I might see my mother one more time, or might hear her tell me she was sorry not to have had time alone together. Just the two of us. It was illogical. The funeral and cremation had passed, but I rushed through every part of my journey as much as I could.

I took a cab from the station to the house. No one came to the door to greet me. When I turned on the light, I saw that the entrance was stuffed full of aging flower bouquets, and a few new ones that had come in the past few days. I touched a card. "From the Hachinohe Golf Club," it read. In the middle of the bouquets, seated on the ledge was the reproachful portrait of my mother. It wasn't a photograph I recognized. It looked like it had been blown up from a smaller picture, perhaps from a group portrait, for it was blurry, as though she were peering out at me through a fog.

I put on a pair of slippers. *"Tadaima!* I'm home."

I passed through several curtains of beads to the front room. The television was on, and I turned it off because no one was watching. I went into my room and reached for the light-switch cord dangling from the ceiling. When the light snapped on, it took me a moment to get my bearings.

Most of the room was covered with white sheets. On one side, where I normally unfolded my *futon,* someone had stacked a series of boxes, two deep and three high. I lifted the cover of one and found that it contained toilet paper. My closets were filled with clothes I didn't recognize, but from the dark, dour look of their tailoring, I guessed the skirts and blouses belonged to Chieko. Only my glass case of dolls remained untouched, though it appeared to me that two or three were missing. I set my luggage down and retreated back into the main wing of the house to look for something to eat.

The refrigerator was empty. The family, I guessed, had gone out to a restaurant to eat and left the door unlocked in case I showed up. I opened the freezer. My mother had always cooked too much and put leftovers away in here.

I found a plastic container with a strip of paper taped on it. "Seasoned rice," it said. My mother would have made it in the fall. It was now April. Suddenly I didn't care if the rice would be bad, or how old it was. It was something she had touched and I tore open the container and dumped the contents into a pan, then added a little water so it wouldn't burn while I heated it on the stove.

I ate the entire containerful. I didn't want Mineko or anyone else to eat the rice. If they'd ignored it all these weeks, then they couldn't have appreciated how good it was in the first place. I thought about the previous fall and how my mother would have bought the *ginkgo* nuts and the mushrooms from the market herself, and eyed her collection of spoons as she measured out the seasoning. But I wasn't going to cry. I wasn't about to get myself into such an emotional predicament.

Instead, I wondered how it would be best for Mineko to find me. Probably she expected me to wander around in my room, angry that I had been displaced. I thought about this for a few minutes and then decided to enjoy the *kakenagashi,* the natural hot spring water in the bathtub.

An hour later, when I finally heard the door squeal open and heard the high-pitched voices of Mineko's spoiled children, I had grown prunish and red from sitting in the water for so long. But the steam had the effect of hiding how swollen my eyes had become from crying.

"There you are," she said, standing in the doorway of the bathroom.

"Didn't it occur to you to knock?" I asked.

"It's my house." She shrugged.

"Nice house," I said.

"We're leaving early in the morning for Akita for the memorial. So, if you don't mind, I need to let the children take their baths so they can go to bed."

"Why Akita?"

"That's where Masayoshi and his wife have their temple." She just barely emphasized the word *wife*.

"Of course. About my room," I began.

"Yes?"

"Are you expecting me to sleep there?"

"There isn't anywhere else for you to sleep, is there?" She smiled faintly. "I'm sure you'll manage. You're good at managing. You learned to very early in life."

Masayoshi had done very well for himself. He was that somewhat rare thing among the Buddhist priests, a handsome, educated man who could have gone to join the successful ranks of Japan's salarymen, but wanted instead to oversee the journey of the souls of the deceased to the afterlife. It wasn't surprising that he had been such a desirable marriage candidate among the many temple families whose boys were turning away from the chosen family profession, or even worse, had borne only girls.

Masayoshi had been promised all kinds of things: a nice house in Yokohama if he chose a two-hundred-year-old temple in need of a new roof, a Mercedes if he moved to Kyūshū, a spare room for his mother if he went to Hiroshima. All that time I'd been in school, Masayoshi had been entertaining marriage requests. I thought to myself that I was lucky to have been away from my stepsisters, oblivious to the gossip that surrounded Masayoshi's daily maneuvers. I could just imagine how Mineko and Chieko would have gone over and over each of the offers, declaring how rich Masayoshi was going to be, what with his management skills and a temple already so well endowed with cash. It would have driven me insane to listen to such banal conversation.

In the end, he'd chosen a temple just a few hours from Akita. It was located in the mountains, on the other side of Japan's northern tip, in a place so rustic and remote I burst out laughing at first when Mineko told me how far we would have to go for the memorial service. The Masayoshi I knew, the one who had loved jazz and museums and English handkerchiefs, never would have elected to live somewhere so provincial, but Mineko scolded me and told me that Masayoshi had liked the family he had married into and that the temple had an intriguing past, something about a noble who had been sent to live there in exile during the Edo period, and who had quietly put together a *hondo* filled with very old sculptures. It was a beautiful place, and many historical records mentioned it; *shoguns* and emperors had taken refuge there during the wars, and the Japan Rail company was always encouraging visitors to go to see the treasures, but because it was so far out of the way, only the most die-hard art lovers and pilgrims ever went.

"Masayoshi wouldn't want some place like they have in Nara or Kyoto," Mineko sniffed. "He doesn't want to have a tourist attraction."

"What's the point of having all those sculptures," I said, "if no one comes to see them?"

"People go to see them," Mineko replied. "But only people who are willing to make the effort. People who *care*."

We had to take a zigzag path of trains to reach the temple. This was before the days when someone finally got smart and put in a bullet train that would go from Morioka to Akita and make the trip across the mountains easier. Instead, we had to go via a series of little one-track routes, pausing in a station to let another train pass on a specially built "overtaking lane" before continuing on. Then we stood out in the cold to pick up a different train that would lumber off in a new direction. The process repeated itself. We bought terrible *bento* lunches, so unlike the delicious food my mother had prepared for our trips, and ate them inside the train cars in silence.

There wasn't much to look at, either. Just mountains tiered with trees and bamboo and above that, clouds in a moody sky. So we went from station to station—my stepsisters, their husbands and children, Mr. Horie, and I—sitting on the velveteen seats, not speaking, and watching the landscape pass. How much more rugged and jade-colored was Tōhoku than

France. Chieko was carrying my mother's remains in a purple *furoshiki*, a square piece of cloth she'd wrapped snug around the box, the corners sticking up like little rabbit ears.

I had missed my mother's cremation and so had not been present when Mineko, Chieko, and the rest of their family had stood around her still-hot remains to remove her bones from the ash. They would have used chopsticks to do this, carefully culling only the most essential parts of her body and placing them in an urn, which was then set inside a box.

It was out of the question that I would carry the box. From the moment I had arrived home, it had been made clear to me that I was a poor excuse for a daughter. I'd arrived too late to sit with my mother as she lay dying, though, they liked to tell me, she had asked over and over again if I had been called. Each time the front door had slid open and she had heard the sound of someone climbing onto the landing and putting on a pair of slippers, she'd asked if it was me. Worse, she sometimes woke up just as someone was walking away and she'd called out, wondering if I'd come home while she was sleeping, and that because she'd been so preoccupied by a dream that she'd missed me.

When they told me this—repeatedly—I was enraged, but only on the inside. Anger burned like a fever in my chest and my eyelids seared my pupils. On the outside, though, I would not let them see how I felt, would not cede to them that kind of control.

Chieko came and sat next to me on the train, the box of bones neatly between her hands. "There is something we must discuss," she said to me. She rocked back and forth with the train movements and the box rocked with her. I could not take my eyes off it.

"Yes?"

"There is not enough money for you to continue living in France."

I could hear the *goton-goton* of the train as it passed over the tracks. My heart matched the rhythm of the sound, and then my pulse increased until we were out of sync. Modern music, I thought to myself.

"Satomi?" she said. "Did you hear me?"

"Yes."

"I know this seems unfair . . . ," she began.

"I said I heard you."

"Your mother didn't know she was going to die. Things happened quickly."

I said this next part very carefully. "Standard inheritance laws say that money is to be divided equally among the surviving children."

"There are debts," she replied curtly. "The golf club membership. Money she forwarded to you in France. We have a lot to pay."

"Let me guess. There is just enough money left over from the debts for you, your sister, and your father to keep the house."

"Something like that."

"Her porcelain collection?"

"We've already sold it to a dealer in Tokyo."

I was shocked. After all these years, I had never once touched the Korean melon pot.

"You had no right. Those were *our* things."

"She was *our* mother," Chieko countered. She pursed her lips. "No matter what you may think of me, I wouldn't deliberately cut you out of your mother's will."

"You mean, your husband mishandled the family business when he took it over after your father's stroke. And now there is no money for me. It's all just been an accident."

I could feel her seething. "It's true that we've had a difficult year. And my husband isn't as talented a fisherman as my father was."

We both looked over at Mr. Horie. He was drooling and Chieko was wiping his mouth with a handkerchief.

"My room in the house . . . ," I began.

She shrugged. "You can always visit, I suppose. Though Mineko will be moving in with her family and there won't be much room anymore. If you want my advice, I think you should consider getting married. That's what my sister and I did. And look at us. We have our own families. *We* don't have to struggle with this question of where to go."

Masayoshi was waiting for us at the train station when we finally arrived. He had two cabs lined up to take us to a small *ryokan* where we would spend the evening before going to the memorial service in the morning. The few times I started to catch his eye he looked away, and I felt myself veer from disappointment to anger. How polite we were all being at this forty-ninth-day memorial. I had been so restrained since going home. Now, seeing his face, and remembering our days together, I felt as though my body were being suddenly flushed with emotion, as when you wake up from a particularly magical dream to find yourself returned to the real world. I was being pulled back into being Japanese, and I didn't want to resume my role. I found myself missing France and the emotional outbursts that would not at all be out of place there.

I have been in love since I met you, I wanted to say to Masayoshi. *I would bet anything that you haven't felt any love at all since you got married.*

The *ryokan* was located on a hillside and the hostess promised us that we would have a view of the ocean. I was to share a room with the women. Mineko had originally arranged that she and her husband and their children would occupy one room and Chieko's family another. My unexpected arrival had uprooted these plans.

"We're going to have to sleep separately from our husbands," she huffed.

"I can just stay in my own room," I offered.

"Can you afford it?" Mineko smiled. "I thought not."

That night we all piled into the main dining room, wearing our *yukatas,* pajama-style *kimonos,* as though we were just out on a family trip to the spa and had come out of the water newly revived from the inn's mineral baths. The decor was meant to suggest old-fashioned northern Japan, with a big hearth in the middle of the floor where the cooks would occasionally prepare a boiling pot of food. Near the entrance sat a thick wood sled that would have been used during the Meiji era in the middle of a snowstorm.

A large cod had been filleted into *sashimi,* its skeleton and head preserved and pinned so it appeared to be twisting out of a bed of seaweed and scallops and shrimp. There was no meat, of course, because we were here for a memorial. A part of me was relieved not to be confronted with the pungent food smells of France, and another part of me thought how provincial this all was, as though by eschewing meat we were going to negate the fact that my mother was dead.

Masayoshi stayed with us while we ate, sitting on the opposite side of the long table where we had congregated. He pretended not to notice as Mineko's and Chieko's husbands first turned salmon-colored then scarlet from numerous glasses of beer. A waitress murmured sympathetically to Chieko that she, too, had recently lost her mother and that it was the kind of event for which there was no preparation. Chieko cooed back her thanks.

At this I rose up from the table and announced my intention to retire to bed. Everyone stopped talking for a moment. *You are in Japan,* I heard a disembodied voice say. *You must continue to sit here until everyone else has finished eating and then you must follow them, like a lowly caste member in a royal procession.*

No way, I retorted. *I've lived in France, traveled to Holland, eaten raw meat, and visited a château. I don't have to sit here. Japan may still be here,* I said to myself, *but that doesn't mean that I am completely in Japan, or that I will necessarily stay here forever.*

I left the table and stopped in the hotel hallway to use the green plastic public phone to call Timothy and let him know where I was and that I intended to return to Tokyo soon. Then I went to the room. When Mineko and Chieko came back hours later, I pretended to be asleep, and when one of them inadvertently stumbled over my feet, I groaned, as though deeply disturbed.

I had a fitful night. I dreamed of my mother, who was not dead. She was ill, but waiting for me to come home to see her, which I did. In the years to come, I would dream this often and, as I did that morning, I would wake to disappointment and a new day without her.

We traveled by two taxis to the temple, Chieko holding my mother's bones on her lap the way I'd seen Grace Kelly hold on to her handbag in a movie. She looked both serious and coy, and she thanked the taxi driver for his sympathy.

The memorial service would not take place for an hour, and we were expected to wait in an adjoining meeting hall where we would eat another meatless lunch after the service ended. It had grown unexpectedly hot and I was melting in my hand-me-down black wool skirt. The memorial hall had a kitchen with a small refrigerator and I helped myself to a Fanta to cool down. Then I went for a walk. At first I could hear the footsteps of some of the children following me, so I darted in between trees, tombstones, and boulders trying to lose them. I wasn't prepared to be indulgent of Mineko's offspring. Not today.

I ventured further and further into the temple grounds, my mood temporarily lifted by how beautiful everything was. Over the centuries, the gardeners had clearly kept the original lines of the garden. I loved how the moss-covered rocks, dripping with condensation, formed a natural path through the bamboo.

I remembered visiting the woods so many years ago, and how I had found bamboo shoots for my mother. The memory brought a tear to my eye and my vision blurred. When it cleared again, I saw a strange figure standing in the bamboo grove.

It was a *gaijin,* a white man.

He was standing beside a small waterfall. Alongside this were old stone carvings of what I guessed were Buddhist deities. I didn't look closely. I was too startled by the man's presence. He was wearing Buddhist robes, but because he was so tall the robes didn't cover his ankles, and his wrists stuck out from the sleeves. He looked as out of place as a husband wearing his wife's apron in the kitchen.

"Oh. Hello!" he said in English. Then he began the labored process of trying to speak in Japanese. When my ears could not take any more—I had the same tight-throat feeling I get when I hear a soprano sing off-key—I put him out of his misery.

"Maybe my English is better."

"You speak English?"   .

"And French," I sighed.

"Why? I mean, how?"

"I wanted to."

"It's that simple?"

"Of course!"

"I suppose it is. Your accent's a bit thick. But I can understand you."

I began to walk around in the grotto, pretending to examine the stone carvings. They were simple, one of Fudō Myō and another of what looked like a Shinto god. Both had been beaten by the rain, so only the suggestion of carved lines appeared, as though they'd just been pressed out of the stone. The effect was eerie, but I wasn't about to let some Westerner think I was nervous.

"Aren't you a little bit curious?" he asked.

"Curious?"

"About what I'm doing here. Usually you Japanese girls squeal or want to take my picture."

"I am more interested in the stone sculpture."

"Oh. Oh yes. Well, that's why I'm here too."

"Who told you about stone sculpture?"

"Yamagata-sensei. The priest. I'm studying with him."

"You are a priest?"

"Actually, I'm an anthropologist. Or studying to be one. Came to Japan to do research. Yamagata-sensei roped me into this outfit. I think he finds it amusing. He's here at the temple for a memorial. I came to watch and participate. Some girls lost their mother." He looked at my black skirt and blouse. "Oh. I'm sorry." He gave a quick bow, which made me laugh. He was so tall, he looked like an ostrich dipping its head to counteract the effort that went into picking up one foot.

The man's name was François and he said he was from England.

"François is a French name," I said.

"Be that as it may, I am English."

"But you must speak French," I insisted. "I speak French better than English. Could we . . ."

"I'm English," he repeated, and not in an altogether friendly tone.

He had a camera and snapped some photos of the stone sculptures to add to his file on Japanese art. Then we went back down to the temple together.

"Have you seen the interior? The sculptures?" he asked.

I told him that I hadn't.

"I spent a week photographing Nara and Kyoto. But there are many more sculptures all over Japan that are just as impressive. Take Muryojuji temple, for example. It's breathtaking."

I went back down to the temple with my new *gaijin* friend. The children had exhausted themselves looking for me behind trees and had retired underneath the temple, which was built on stilts that left a good two feet or so under its belly where a small person could hide or play in the dirt. One by one the children came out and marveled at the giant blond-haired man. Actually, François wasn't blond at all. I know this now, having spent enough time in Europe and America. But a few days in Japan were enough to readjust my eyes, and because his hair looked so light in comparison to everyone else's, he looked blond to me.

The children parted before us, like fronds of grass in a field making way for the wind.

"Aren't they charming? I adore the little people in this country." François sighed, reaching out to pat their heads as though they were delicate flower buds.

Mineko, with a mother's sixth sense, came out of the memorial hall wearing her husband's shoes. She hadn't taken the time to wrestle with her ugly pumps. Her mouth twisted into an expression of unabashed horror. Like a shadow, Chieko appeared beside her and mirrored this expression of shock. I was pleased. With François there, I had the feeling that I wasn't quite in Japan, but somewhere else where I wouldn't be expected to follow all the little rules and the niceties.

I invited François into the memorial hall for a drink. He said he didn't trust himself to drink beer, though he enjoyed it, and so I gave him an orange Fanta and tried to interest him in talking to the children. I offered to translate. They were curious, as children are, and I indulged their questions while Mineko fidgeted in the background.

François wanted to look at the temple with me so I asked the children if they wanted to come, and though Mineko told them not to go, we all went in together.

It was a large structure, rectangular in shape, with a high roof whose hips plunged down at a precarious angle before its eaves gently fanned out like the tail of a phoenix. The front doors of the *hondo,* or main hall, slid open with some difficulty, as both the door panels and the grooves on which they rested were made of wood and had grown temperamental with age. When we stepped inside, the children grew hushed, immediately in awe of what they saw.

The hall was covered with enough *tatami* mats to hold a crowd of several hundred, and a dozen stacks of square-shaped *zabuton* pillows. From the high ceiling hung a golden chandelier dripping with lotuses and wheels, and around this on the rafters were painted celestial beings playing various musical instruments. At the very back of the room was the altar, which was set up like a small theater with various statues posed in stances of protection or meditation on a black lacquer stage. Buddhas held up their hands to ward off fear. Fudō Myō brandished his sword and scowled at illusion. A Guanyin lovingly cradled a lotus flower. And in the very center was a large crate, perhaps two meters high, which I gathered would contain a very big Buddha that, for reasons I did not know, was not on display today.

In front of the box was an even smaller stair-step altar. My mother's bones were sitting here, divided into two discreet containers. There was one rectangular container, the size of an ice cream tub, wrapped in purple cloth, and a tiny red box beside this that contained her Adam's apple.

Masayoshi must have arranged these earlier in the day when I'd been out for my walk.

"There's more," François said. "Come on." He made a small motion with his head, the way Westerners do, that I knew by now meant I was to follow him. He went around to a door, which opened up to a room behind the altar. The room was filled with statues, with objects and paintings. The children followed close behind.

I circled around each object. Nothing was locked in a glass case. As full of treasures as Masayoshi's temple was, it was also just a little northern temple meant to serve locals. Nothing that art scholars visited all that regularly. Nothing here had been cataloged. And yet even I, with my mother's training in antiques and basic education that consisted of trips to the Tokyo National Museum with Masayoshi, knew that I was looking at a room full of priceless objects.

François continued on into yet another antechamber, but I hesitated. This new room smelled like the old prewar houses of Kuma-ume, the town my mother and I had lived in before moving to Hachinohe. The ceiling was low, even for me, and I gathered that the room had been built for a time when people were even shorter than they were today. It didn't feel like a room for the public, but something that only priests would enter.

"I think I will go back," I said.

"Wait." François faded into one of the darker corners of the room. "This is the best part."

He was standing in the shadows, surrounded by strange objects. I peered into the room. The walls were lined with shelves, each four levels high and shaped like a cubbyhole. Inside each slot was a box wrapped in cloth. Many were white, and some were wrapped in brocade.

"This is not a place for visitors," I said.

He ignored me. "I find it beautiful myself that the Japanese take such good care of their ancestors' bones. Much better than the out-of-sight-out-of-mind nonsense in the West."

He was looking at a cubbyhole with a small statue inside. I looked and saw a carving of *kannon* with numerous arms all reaching out to aid lost souls. I touched one of her hands.

"We bury our bones," I said, even though I was looking at plenty of evidence to the contrary.

"According to the *roshi* I work with," François said, "that doesn't always happen. At least not right away. Maybe there's been a frost and it's inconvenient to bury the bones. Or maybe someone doesn't have the money to bury remains."

"Then the bones come to stay in here?" I asked.

"Yes."

I didn't like standing in this room with so many bones rattling in their urns. I wondered whose had been forgotten, and who was too poor to be buried in the earth. And I certainly didn't like that this *gaijin* I hardly knew had brought me here and was now telling me things about my own culture.

"I'm going back out. The memorial will start soon."

"Is it time already?" he asked, following me back out. I wondered what he had seen in me to make him think that I would be interested in looking into the heart of this temple where things that were intended to be unseen lay hidden.

I remember the memorial as a bloom of incense, a flock of priests in cobalt-blue-and-saffron silk robes, and unrepentant tears. Up until Masayoshi's first recitation of the *sutras,* during which the guest priests pounded skull-shaped drums and rang brass chimes, we had all been sitting quietly on the floor, the men with their legs crossed and the women on their knees, and my mother's small box of bones perched up high beneath the golden Buddha's gaze. When Masayoshi began to chant, it struck us all that she was really dead. There is such a thing in life as a final parting. This is the sadness, I thought, that strikes all people. All around the world as we age, we realize with greater clarity that we will one day part from each other, and from the things we love the most. Children are unhinged from parents, never to be children again.

First Mineko choked on a tear. Then she deftly pulled a handkerchief out of her purse and began to mop her face. I saw her husband crying too, though he sat stolidly while water poured down his face. The tears spread, as though we were all linked together by an aqueduct for a deluge of water that only sprang when grief called it forth. The children moved me the most. They sensed the sadness in the room the way you might feel the pressure of a typhoon as it begins to descend on a town in the late summer. They wept wildly, half-afraid at how the adults in their lives had been transformed into flailing, undependable creatures and conscious that they too would one day die.

Over and over Masayoshi shouted at evil spirits, warning them to stay away from my mother's newly born soul. He cried in *kiai*, shouting nonsensical but frightening syllables so loudly that even I was startled. Sometimes he attacked the first part of the word, letting it trail off at the end. Other times he started softly, then raised his voice half a pitch. I had never before nor have I since heard this sound so many times in a row. I know that he was doing this to fix in our minds that my mother had truly gone—and to let her soul know she was dead and it was time for her to leave all of us—and that this is the custom. But the needless repetition felt like a torture to me. Every time he cried out, I thought back over the past few years of my life, pictures fluttering into my mind's eye like the slats of a fan, each with a different image, closing slowly. There were our early years together, my stubbornness at the piano, her endless faith in my special qualities, the time I had spent wandering around Europe, and even now in Japan while she had been dying.

I hadn't expected Masayoshi to call us up to say a few words to my mother's bones. Mineko pulled a piece of paper out of her pocket. It was a speech she'd prepared. But I, as the flesh and blood daughter, was asked to speak immediately after Mr. Horie, who, since his stroke, could only mumble a few words. Everyone looked at me to see what I would do.

I held onto Masayoshi's arm as he escorted me from the floor to the altar. He had not touched me in a long time. Alone, I stood in front of the altar and stared at my mother's bones. On either side of the altar was a priest, both waiting for me to speak. I caught sight of François, off to the side, and he nodded at me.

What should I say? What one final speech would I make to my mother?

I cleared my throat. Parted my lips.

Then I thought about the fact that we would have a memorial for her on Ohigan, the two times of the year when the boundaries between the spirit world and the living would be thin enough to permit her return. She'd return every year during Obon. And then there would be the memorials to commemorate her death. Each time, I'd have the chance to say another speech to her. Would Mineko and her family be with us each time?

I began to grow hot. I turned my head, looking for Masayoshi. He stepped forward and took my hand. "You can say whatever you are feeling."

"Masayoshi . . . ," I began.

"Just anything."

But I didn't then nor do I now ever want to share all that I was feeling with the people in that room. I know that there are some who grow weak with grief, and who believe that mourning has the power to dissolve all the divisions we feel in daily life. I could feel what everyone wanted from me. They wanted a display of regret that I hadn't been there when she'd died. As sorry as I was about that, I could feel something else from them, a desire that I express something greater than grief. They wanted an acknowledgment that they were right and I was wrong, and this I could not give them.

I don't know in what way they felt they were actually superior to me, as I hadn't really done anything so terrible, nothing beyond that incident all those years ago when I'd broken Mineko's arm. Wasn't she the one who always persisted in reviving this past incarnation of me to my face, as if always to remind me of who I had been when I was thirteen? People always say that it is best at funerals and memorials to remember the people who have died as you want to remember them. What I wanted was to remember the years long ago before my mother had gotten married to Mr. Horie and invited all these other people into our lives.

I made up my mind then and there what I would do. I looked up at her bones and said, quickly, "Mother. Thank you." Then I sat back down, this time without Masayoshi's help in navigating the temple.

I felt much better having done things this way. The sick feeling I'd had was gone. The world around me didn't quiver as though I were underwater. I felt clear and confident now that I knew what would happen.

The rest of the family was very, very quiet. I looked at Chieko, expecting her to speak next. It was her turn to speak, after all. She and Mineko were staring at me, their mouths open like *koi* searching for nonexistent food on a pond's surface. I nodded in the direction of the altar to urge one of them to get up and start speaking. After a few tense minutes, Chieko finally rose up from her seat and began to read from a letter she had prepared.

"I wouldn't worry," François said to me at the after-memorial lunch, which, as had the dinner the previous night, contained no meat. "I didn't know what to say when my mother died either."

"I had things to say." Why was he trying to make excuses for me? It wasn't as if I needed some sort of justification for the way I had chosen to act during the memorial. "Just not in front of everyone."

He had taken it upon himself to sit next to me, apparently unaware that there was a proper order in which we should all sit. Technically, as the closest living blood relative to my mother, I should have been sitting at the end of the table, next to Masayoshi, who was seated at the head. But I had been placed in a subservient position to Mineko and Chieko. Perhaps they had done this to keep me away from Masayoshi. Or maybe they had done this to try to assert themselves as her true daughters. Whatever the case, I was annoyed, and so when I saw the priests lurking around waiting to take their place at the table, I ignored them and made it clear that François was not going to move, thereby displacing one of Mineko's children to the other end of the table. I could tell that everyone was perturbed, but no one dared say anything. This is the kind of effect a foreigner can have on a group of Japanese.

That day, I met Masayoshi's wife. I was disappointed that she was pretty. When she came to serve me a cup of *sake,* she murmured under her breath how pleased she was to meet me. She lifted her face after bowing, and in it I saw no jealousy, only a concern that I would like her and treat her with courtesy. I suddenly felt years older and more sophisticated than she would ever be. I shot a glace at Masayoshi, who was pretending not to watch our exchange.

I bowed back to her. "What a pleasure," I said with as much sincerity as I could muster, "to finally meet you too. This is a lovely temple. I'm very impressed."

"Oh!" She blushed. "I'm just a country person and this is a country temple."

"Everyone knows that what you have here isn't the usual country temple." I smiled back at her. She was a simpleton. No threat to me. It would be fun to befriend her. Mineko and Chieko would not expect this.

She bowed her head and blushed a deeper shade of pink.

"Anyway," I confided, "I live in Paris now, but you know, I grew up in the rice paddies of Japan. So, really, I'm just a country person too."

Her eyes smiled and she glanced around the room at my adopted sisters, a look of sheer happiness on her face, and they looked back with disappointment.

Then she moved on down the table, serving the other guests.

"What was that all about?" François asked me.

"She's the wife of the head priest."

"Yes, I gathered. But there was something . . ."

"Just a friendly conversation," I replied. "Wouldn't you like a drink?"

"At a memorial?"

"Didn't anyone tell you that we Japanese like to get drunk even on serious occasions? We are not puritans." I smiled meaningfully.

"That's true," he said quietly. "I've learned that you are not."

I stood up and went into the kitchen and got out another *sake* cup for François. I brought this back to him and filled it. Safe in the cocoon of cavorting with a foreigner, I toasted the safe journey of my mother's soul to nirvana.

Later, when François had excused himself and left to call a taxi, I went to the bathroom. I could hear women whispering outside while they waited for their turn at the toilet. Someone declared: "It must be all that time abroad."

"She hasn't been gone that long," Mineko hissed back. "She's *always* been strange."

When I came out of the bathroom, I avoided meeting their eyes. I knew that what they wanted was for me to cry. Instead, I lifted up my head and strode outside.

I decided to go out for a walk. I went in the direction opposite to the one I had taken earlier in the day, humming to myself. The stone path ended on a cliff overlooking the valley floor and I stood there looking at the rice paddies. Below, some farmers were planting seedlings by hand. The women wore sunbonnets with wide brims that covered their faces like oversized rose petals. The oldest among them were hunched at the back, even when they attempted to stand up straight.

One person could change this afternoon: Masayoshi. He could come and speak to me. He could tell me that he'd made a mistake and that he never should have listened to my mother. He would offer to help me now. He would not just leave me to my stepsisters.

But he did not come and my longing to speak with him turned into great disappointment at his cowardice.

The farmers had finished planting rice in the paddies and were now sitting on the bank sharing a thermos. I envied them, for it had to be much

better to be down there than up here on the hillside with a house full of
grieving people.

I thought of my room in Hachinohe. The boxes against the wall. My
toys, now fingered by Mineko's children.

It occurred to me that I was as alone as I would ever be.

What was going to happen to me? Wasn't I too old to be an orphan?

"Hello," said a voice.

It wasn't Masayoshi, but a child.

"Hello," I said. When he didn't say anything more, I asked, "How old
are you?"

He flexed his palm, then, looking sheepish, folded down his thumb
so only four fingers remained in the air.

"And who are you?" I asked.

"I live here," he answered frankly.

"Here?"

"My father's the priest."

"Oh." I nodded.

The child was watching me with tremendous curiosity. He had unusually round eyes, and as he searched my face his pupils seemed to dilate and
I felt drawn in by them. "Are you a child or an adult?" he asked me, quite
seriously.

"What?"

"You seem like an adult. But you seem like a child too."

"Did your father put you up to this?"

"You aren't sitting inside doing boring grown-up talk."

"That's true."

"You look like you've been out playing."

"I have. I *have.*"

"Only children play."

I knelt down till I was facing him at eye level. "What is your name?"

"Akira."

"Akira-kun." Little Akira. "Tell me, Akira. Is there a way that I can become a child again? I mean, completely a child?"

He furrowed his brow. He pursed his lips. I thought to myself that I
loved this little boy. How like and unlike his father he was! How different
from Mineko and Chieko's brats. "You have to pray," he said.

"Pray?"

"Every day. Like I do. At the *hotokesama*."

"I don't have a family altar."

"Everyone has a *hotokesama*," he said.

"Well, but I don't."

"Didn't your father buy one for your house?"

"No," I said. "You see, I don't have a father. I was actually . . ." I hesitated. "I was born inside a big piece of bamboo. My mother found me there. I don't have a father."

"Well, that's what's wrong." He nodded as though he had easily uncovered the source of all my woes. "If you had a father, he would have made sure your house had a *hotokesama*." He looked at me kindly. "You can use ours while you are here."

He led me by the hand to the house. Under his protection, we passed by Chieko and Mineko, who watched with no small awe that a child had been able to tame the temperamental Satomi into submission.

The shrine was typical. It sat in a specially designed recessed area of the house. It was shaped like a large black cabinet whose doors were left open during the day but closed at night. Inside, gilded steps representing levels of paradise rose to the top where the Buddha sat, one hand raised, palm flat against the air: "Have no fear."

Akira dragged a *zabuton* pillow across the floor. His movements reminded me of his efficient mother, someone who knew instinctively how to care for guests and make them feel at home. Just as quickly he reminded me of his father, with the careful, concentrating way he lit a candle, then took a slim stick of incense from a vase and handed it to me. I lit the incense and waved it around until the flame had subsided to just a glow at the very tip of the stick. Then I placed it in the ash. Akira picked up a little mallet and rang the bowl-shaped gong inside the altar. While the sound carried in waves throughout the shrine, I closed my eyes and tried to organize my scrambled thoughts into a prayer.

A few minutes later, I took the *zabuton* to a corner of the room and put my head on it. Very quickly I fell into a dreamless sleep. When I woke up an hour and a half later, I felt clear-minded. The house was empty: Akira had gone and the guests were somewhere else on the temple grounds. I put my shoes on by the entrance to the house and crept along to the temple.

There, in the middle of the altar, were my mother's bones, still wrapped in the purple *furoshiki*. It was quiet and I sat down on the floor in front

the ashes. "Finally, we are alone," I whispered to her. What would she
say to me if she could speak? She would tell me I was talented. A daughter of the moon kingdom. And what else? Would she tell me she had always loved me more than anyone else on this earth? "I have always loved you," I said.

Briefly, I wondered where everyone else was, then realized they must be up at the burial plot, reading *sutras* and giving incense. In a few weeks, when it was even warmer, Masayoshi would bring my mother's bones. *And then,* I thought, *they will always have you.* How unfair life could be.

I remembered my mother's early advice that talent would keep me safe. It was up to me, I thought then, to protect what ought to be mine in the first place. I stood up from the floor and prepared to leave Masayoshi's temple.

I didn't go back to the house in Hachinohe, but bought a ticket from Akita to Tokyo, spending a grueling night on numerous trains with my bags. I called Timothy to tell him I was on my way and would see him in the morning, phoned a cab, and left.

"You'll be there?" My voice was shaking.

"Right here." A pause. "Satomi? Is everything . . . ?"

"My mother is dead. I don't . . . there's not much . . ."

"We'll take care of it," he soothed. "Just get here and we'll take care of everything."

Hours later I was in another taxi on my way to the hotel in Tokyo where Timothy had agreed to meet me. I didn't want the man at the front desk to see all my luggage so I hovered outside the door, waiting until he went to the back office to get something for a customer. Then I pulled the key that I had taken with me out of my pocket, snuck inside, and took the elevator up to our room.

I struggled with my bags, then kicked open the door of the cheap business hotel with my foot as though I were an American. Timothy was not there. All of his belongings, his bags, our boxes of dishes, were gone. I looked for a note.

I thought that perhaps I had the wrong room. That must be it. He'd changed rooms without telling me. I did my best to remake the crumpled bed and fold the used towels. Hoisting my packages on my shoulders, I went downstairs to speak to the man at the front desk. He was young, like me, reflexively polite and reserved, no doubt working part time while he went to some sort of school. I asked him if he knew what had happened to the foreigner who had been staying upstairs in room 517.

"Ah." The young man bowed. "It's you. Our guest."

"Last time I checked, I was myself, yes."

"It's a delicate matter."

"If something has happened . . . ," I quavered.

"The fact is, the truth is . . ." He hesitated. "The *gaijin* was taken by the police this morning." He held out a note.

"Police!"

"Before he left, he told us that you were coming." He checked his books. "The room had been paid for in advance for a week. We assumed that you knew."

"Well, I didn't." I took the note over to the sofa in the lobby and began to read.

But the man at the front desk continued speaking to me. "*Anoh*. I need to give you the room key. There is a new room."

"Thank you," I said.

"I need the old key. Also," the young man said, "we have your things in the back."

"Things?"

"The luggage."

"I'll be right there," I said. Then I unfolded the paper.

On the surface, the note didn't reveal too much. Timothy told me who had come for him and where he was being held. He didn't say why. I'd heard about this kind of thing, how foreigners would be singled out for some crime, and certainly I knew how relentless the wheels of justice were in Japan. The police would have arrested him only because they were convinced of his guilt, and all the questioning they did now would serve the purpose of extracting a confession, not clarification.

Bag by bag, I carried everything upstairs to the new room and once I was alone collapsed onto the bed.

I was exhausted, but I did not want to give in to fatigue and grief. Not yet. My flight from the temple had done a good job of keeping my tears at bay and I wanted to find—had counted on finding—Timothy and having another reason to keep moving. How could my flight have led to this dead end?

I would not cry.

I would *not* cry.

I had to do something.

Thinking was painful. I stood up and began to inspect the contents of Timothy's bags. The police had obviously upended everything, for the packing paper we had used to carefully package the contents had been disturbed. But everything was still here.

I paused. If I sat here and just wallowed, I'd have to give myself over to the seduction of grief, to Timothy's disappearance and the loss of Paris. I had to *act*. I lit a cigarette.

I looked inside the bags again. There were Timothy's clothes, his shoes, paperback novels, and address book. I found his razor and underwear. I took a few changes of the latter and put them in a bag. Then I took my purse, locked the door, and went downstairs to make a few calls.

PART TWO

CHAPTER 6

True Nature

Rumi
San Francisco, 1980

I loved Charlie, even though he was missing an arm, a leg, and most of his hair. Eventually, we were able to take care of these flaws. But he would always retain his sharp white teeth and remain an unabashed scowler.

My father, François, brought Charlie home one winter and gave me the task of coming up with a name. We spent many evenings studying pictures of figures similar to Charlie, sketching his missing features on sheets of loose paper. "Isn't it a pleasure to communicate with the past like this?" my father said to me. "Centuries ago, an artist pondered the same questions you and I are considering now."

"What's that?" I pointed.

"I'm making a nimbus. It's like a halo. All good Buddhist deities are surrounded by fire. You know. Some people just seem brighter than others."

At night, after François and I had finished our work, I took the clothes off my dolls and dressed and redressed Charlie. I particularly liked to see him in the outfit from my Madame Alexander Russian Courtier doll, which my father's girlfriend, Sondra, had given to me in an effort to win me over and convince my father to marry her. (It hadn't worked so far.)

Once we had carved the missing pieces out of wood and attached them to his body, Charlie was magnificent. His scarlet skin glowed, and his face took on a cast of pleasure. He stood up straighter. His jaw tensed into a

119

ferocious scowl, and his wild hair echoed the flames of the nimbus that rustled behind him.

"Now everyone will see Charlie's true nature." My father beamed.

A few days later, François changed his mind and removed the lasso that had rested in Charlie's right hand, and though he later told me it pained him to do so, he darkened some of the paint on the nimbus.

"We have done our job too well, Rumi," he said. "These days people appreciate perfection, but they will not expect perfection from our friend."

This is my first clear memory of entering into my father's world. After Charlie, I understood that my father was a collector, restorer, and dealer all in one. The objects in our San Francisco home had not been selected by an interior decorator; they had been fashioned hundreds of years ago by artisans in China, Korea, and Japan. In this delicate atmosphere, I grew up to be a child everyone considered too serious and too bookish.

"Your daughter doesn't like to play with the other children," teachers complained.

I explained to François that it was the other children who didn't want to play with me.

"Well," he sniffed. "Can those other children tell the difference between peach bloom glaze and oxblood? I doubt it. I much prefer you *this* way." And for a long time, his was the only approval I needed.

I came home one day to find François surrounded by boxes lined with foam and dark-blue velvet. Sondra was with him, wearing an ankle-length skirt, the ends of her hair resting in the small of her back. Between my father and her there had been some kind of argument, for the air was thick beyond the usual tension that accompanies the frustrating act of packing.

"Do you *have* to sell Charlie, too?" I asked.

"We need the money, Rumi."

"The Buddha said it's not good to get too attached." Sondra sighed.

"I was thinking of a compromise. A way to prolong saying good-bye," François said. "How would you like to come to New York with me?"

Sondra said pointedly, "She's going to miss school." Sondra had looked after me last year when François had gone to New York for Asia Week, an annual event in which dealers from around the world convened to present their finest Asian antiquities to the public.

My father shrugged. "I'll get her assignments for the week. We'll do them at night. Or on the plane."

"Won't this be disruptive? To her budding social life?" Sondra asked, a little too hopefully.

"The decision isn't really yours," my father said.

"I'm *François'* responsibility," I clarified.

"A woman's first trip to New York should be made with a man who loves her," my father said to me, "so she will carry that first impression with her forever."

Sondra looked at one of the boxes containing a jade bird. "Lucky duck. Traveling in style."

We stayed in a hotel near Times Square, in a room that had a small, rigid bed and a window facing an airshaft. As soon as we arrived, my father hung up our clothes in the bathroom and turned on the shower so the steam would relieve his suits and my dresses of wrinkles. "Who needs a valet?" He smiled, pleased with himself. Then he unpacked the sandwiches Sondra had made, and we had our dinner and went to sleep.

In the morning, we took the bus to the New York City Armory, which housed Asia Week. I explored this labyrinth of good taste and high insurance premiums, admiring the English dealers who set up their booths with moody lighting. The Southeast Asian stalls, with their Hindu gods posing in flagrant sexual acts, disturbed me. A severe white woman, who wore a *cheongsam* and kept two *shi-tzus* with her, barked, "Don't touch. Anything," when I knelt down to pet the dogs. Charlie's exotic looks made him a hit with New Yorkers. "Like a demon!" they declared. But Charlie was also an expensive piece—the price determined largely by his age and impressive condition—and few people made serious inquiries.

Late in the afternoon on that first day, a Buddhist emerged from the parade to hover at the edge of our little booth. I was usually irritated by Buddhists, who were in plentiful supply in California; Sondra had recently joined a Pure Land sect. There was something precious about these men and women, as though in their fascination with another culture they had first become lost, then smug about their altered condition.

The man saw me staring at him, and his smile came upon me, broad and bright. "I knew your mother, Satomi." He had a tenor voice and the flat accent of a California native accustomed to a great deal of sunshine. "You have her eyes."

"François?" I called.

My father turned and inhaled sharply. "Timothy Snowden."

"You know that I prefer Snowden-roshi now." The man winked, releasing me from the taut intimacy of his smile.

"Rumi, Snowden-roshi is an old friend of mine who has recently become an influential Buddhist priest."

"Extreme conditions often force men to choose to become something they wouldn't have chosen otherwise."

"Yes," my father agreed, fidgeting. "I didn't originally mean to be an art dealer."

A pause.

"How's business?" Snowden-roshi continued, a little more brightly.

"Good, good." My father nodded.

Snowden-roshi swept past us and began to inspect our wares. "I was hoping you could help me. I'm looking for a statue for the main hall of my temple in Los Angeles."

"Buddha? Bodhisattva?" François recovered his composure and assumed his favorite posture, the expert.

"What I'd really like," he looked at my father, "is something old. Something made at a time in history when artists knew how to help the devoted focus during meditation. Something with a compassionate face. Like a Guanyin. Or a . . . *kannon.*"

"You're really better off with something new," my father said. "Nice, big, and shiny. Most people don't know how to appreciate art unless it has some flash."

"Tell me about the Fudō." Snowden-roshi gestured toward Charlie.

My father steered Snowden-roshi toward a corner of our display station, away from Charlie. A customer came into our area and began peering through a glass case to look at a row of *netsuke,* and my attention was diverted. Through furtive looks, I was able to see my father and Snowden-roshi speaking to each other, their hips cocked elegantly to one side like courtiers in a medieval painting, a hand every now and then adding urgency to a point.

The parade of sprightly, self-assured New Yorkers continued to churn through Asia Week. This perpetual motion extended to the street, where adults went in and out of shops and restaurants, busily weaving the taxing but alluring fabric of sophistication. I had hoped, after our first day in New York, that I, too, would participate in this tantalizing world. Instead, when our work was done, we went to a Korean deli across the street from the hotel and filled two plastic containers with food from a buffet—pasta, salad, fruit, and *sushi*. The stoic Korean lady at the cash register did a double take as she compared my features to my Caucasian father's. "Here," she said, handing me two pieces of Lindt chocolate.

Later, as we ate in our hotel room, I asked, "Who was that man?"

"Which man?"

"The Buddhist man."

"Time for you to do your homework."

"You *know* who I'm talking about."

"Snowden-roshi is an old acquaintance. I doubt we'll see him again."

"He said he knew my mother."

"Homework. *Now.*" François began to line up my books on the bed. Then, to soften his earlier severity, he said, "I'll help you." I was rather surprised to see just how quickly we could progress through the assignments together; a day's worth of lesson material could easily be finished in an hour.

"I'm sorry," he said when we were finished, "for that earlier bit of discomfort. But we are having a grand adventure together, and I don't want anything unpleasant to spoil it."

He hugged me, and I gave him one of my pieces of chocolate.

In the morning, I was sent on a mission.

"There is a piece of jade here, incorrectly marked as Ch'ing when it is Sung. Can you find it?" François asked.

I tried. I pored over every glass case, searching for the misidentified piece.

But I let him down. "I'll give you a clue. You are looking for a cow. But hurry. Some Chinese are already onto its value."

I looked for groups of Chinese gathered around a jade cow. You would think that this combination of elements would be rare, but the cow happens to be one of the most frequently carved figures across dynasties. Three men gazed at a glass case at Jade Phoenix of Ann Arbor and admired . . . a cow. A woman with horn-rimmed glasses and an ankle-length skirt of red crushed velvet sniffed at Suzi Wong of Long's offerings, which included . . .

a cow. The bovines were everywhere, at St. Mark's Kyber Pass, at Xia Xiu Ltd., at Cardeiro Connoisseurs. I went back to my father empty-handed.

He was disappointed. He left me alone in our stall for a few minutes, and when he returned, he held out his hands. "Cardeiro," he said. In the palm of his hand, it was clear to me that this sleepy, serene cow could be nothing other than Sung. "You must learn to see things out of context, Rumi. Like me," he said proudly. "Over time you too will learn to recognize what is right and what is wrong. Then you will be a true connoisseur."

Charlie, though popular, was not considered to be the most impressive sculpture in the show. That honor went to a slab of marble: an entire tomb wall depicting men wearing kerchiefs and carrying flaming pots while grapevines twined around them.

My father and the other dealers gossiped endlessly about this piece.

"Is it real?"

"Must be from central Asia," my father said, "with that weird blending of Eastern and Western iconography."

"Ah! You must be right."

"How did they get it?" everyone asked.

We had our answer late on the third day.

Despite my father's insistence that Snowden-roshi would not be back, he did return with several men and women—all Buddhists—who had come to Asia Week hoping to see the face of Buddha.

"What are you doing here with these people? They don't even care if they are dealing with Heian or Edo," François whispered.

"What does it matter"—Snowden-roshi shook his head—"as long as a piece of art does what its creator intended and moves the viewer?"

"It's dangerous," François said, "to be moved by bad art. Think of Hitler. Corporate boardrooms."

The air hissed with a collective "shh." The police had arrived with five men in black suits and two Chinese officials. They made their way to the back of the room where the tomb sculpture was sitting. François dropped his papers and hurried toward Charlie. I had seen him behave this frantically and protectively only once, when an earthquake had struck the shop.

We were all quiet, trying to listen. The word *stolen* flew around our stalls, and we held it at bay, afraid it might be contagious. Two dealers were guided out in handcuffs.

"Careful. Don't hurt it," one of the dealers begged as the strange tomb wall was wheeled out on a flatbed by the police.

"Let that be a lesson to you," François said to me later, "never to be too conspicuous."

On the last day of the show, Snowden-roshi arrived with an older couple. The man had an aura of disinterested vagueness, but the woman had made every effort to ensure that she would spring to the foreground of any setting. She wasn't very tall, but she was extremely thin and swayed back and forth, a cobra rising out of a basket, undulating, eyes alert. It was April, and she was wearing a bright-red coat that matched her scarlet wig. She removed the coat with her husband's help and displayed her clavicle, ornamented with entwined amulets in ivory, coral, and a great deal of gold.

"This is Mrs. Mack," Snowden-roshi said to my father. "And her husband."

"Mr. and Mrs. Mack," my father bowed. "François des Rochers."

Mrs. Mack drifted between the cases. She asked many questions and even tried, at one point, to get my father to sell her a piece of jade marked with a red sticker, which meant that it had already been sold. Finally, she came to rest in front of Charlie.

"Look familiar?" Snowden-roshi asked.

At first, Charlie and Mrs. Mack did look very similar, with their unnaturally red coloring highlighted by bits of gold and black.

"How old is he?" she asked.

"Kamakura," my father said. "You can tell just by looking. Stylistically, there is no other period he could be from."

"He's in *very* good condition." She began to peruse our catalog.

"Obviously he was well cared for in the past." My father smiled.

"*Minor repairs?*" She quoted the text describing Charlie's condition.

"The paint has dulled with age," my father said smoothly. "And you can see he's missing one of his weapons. But otherwise, he's intact."

Mrs. Mack knelt down to the floor and stretched out her palms toward Charlie's feet. "Yes," she said. "I can feel something from him."

Behind her, my father rolled his eyes.

We arranged to ship all the unsold pieces from our collection back to California and, after much discussion, moved Charlie into our hotel room.

François instructed Sondra to call my school and tell them I was still sick. Then we turned our attention to Mrs. Mack.

"We'll go to lunch. Where are you staying?" Mrs. Mack asked. "I'll send my driver to get you."

"The Plaza," François smiled, "but Rumi and I have morning engagements. It's best if we meet *you*."

I hoped that this invitation to lunch would, at last, result in the chance to eat something other than food-by-the-pint. My hopes were only partly realized when François persuaded Mrs. Mack to eat in the cafeteria of the Metropolitan Museum of Art. "One should be inspired by great works when one is contemplating an acquisition," he said.

We spent the afternoon wandering through the Met. In the Asia wing, vacant compared to the foot traffic that passed by the impressionist and modern paintings, we marveled over a display of embroidered *Nō kimonos*. A Japanese businessman examined the contents of the cases with an expression of deep attention and a clenching jaw that belied his discontent.

"You see?" my father whispered to Mrs. Mack. "*There* is the kind of customer who, in perhaps ten years, will do everything he can to bring Japanese treasures back to his own country. China will follow. I have always maintained that the Chinese aren't really communists. They are born merchants. And once their wealth begins to flower, they will want to reclaim their history."

"I know all about merchants," Mrs. Mack said. "You've heard of my father?"

"Airplanes, was it?"

"Steel, to be exact. Which they used on the airplanes. Classic story. He worked all the time and was hardly home."

"But you must feel some pride seeing his name connected to this museum."

"He donated money to avoid paying taxes, Mr. des Rochers. I would like a little more out of life. You understand, I'm trying to connect with *him*. With the Buddha."

"Do you meditate?"

"Every day. But I find I need a focal point. The three Buddhas at home haven't been sufficient. Snowden-roshi suggested I find something more unique to help me."

While François, Mrs. Mack, Snowden-roshi, and the vague Mr. Mack circled the halls and floors of the museum, I took in the dizzying displays of Egyptian tomb paintings and Greek statues. I wondered at the forces that had conspired to bring these varied treasures into one location.

"It is so sad to see these things here, instead of home in Athens where they belong," Mrs. Mack sighed.

"Modern Greeks have little genetic connection to the Greeks of Pericles' kingdom," my father said.

"You think it is all right for wealthy nations to steal art?"

"I think art belongs with the people who will appreciate it the most at any given point in history."

When we passed through the African section of the museum, François said, "It'll be years before anyone notices that this stuff is missing from their country."

I looked at the dark, angular heads of ebony statues and thought briefly of the hands that had made them, wondering if the artists were mourning the loss of their creations.

Unbeknownst to us, Mrs. Mack had asked her usual dealer to take a secret look at Charlie while he had been on display, and this dealer, no doubt concerned that my father was horning in on a favorite—not to mention wealthy—customer, had phoned Mrs. Mack to say he suspected Charlie was a fake.

"My dealer said we should test the hand," she said.

François was horrified. "And *cripple* him?"

"I just want to be sure." Mrs. Mack stiffened. "It is *my* money I would be spending."

I could not tell if François' display of inner struggle was real or fabricated, but he finally said, "If you wish, we can take a sample of wood from the Fudō's base and perform a carbon 14 test. However, I want you to realize that we will, in effect, be defacing a statue that has already survived hundreds of years of natural disasters and wars." He waited for these words to sink in and have an effect before he added, softly, "But I will be happy to pay for the cost of the test, if that would put your mind at ease."

That evening, when we returned to the hotel, we found Snowden-roshi waiting for us. He helped two Australian girls, just arrived from the airport, with their bags, then turned to say hello.

"How did you find us?" François asked.

"The old-fashioned way. It's not too hard to follow people in New York."

He nodded toward a paper bag in my father's hands. "Why don't you let me take you out?"

"We've already purchased our dinner."

"I all but guarantee you a sale, and you won't eat with me?" Snowden-roshi took the bag from François' hands and gave it to a homeless man sitting with his back against the hotel wall. Then we took a cab to a Japanese restaurant in the Village. A large Buddha, made of ice, sat underneath a red lamp, while red rose petals floated around him in a pool of water.

Snowden-roshi gently placed his hand on the wrist of our cocktail waitress. "Can you tell me who's here tonight, honey?" he asked.

She blushed and whispered the names of a few actors and other people I did not recognize before drifting away to retrieve a bottle of *sake*.

"Buddha is making you a wealthy man," François observed.

"Buddha didn't believe in self-deprivation."

"Making up for lost time?"

Snowden-roshi smiled. "Believe me, François, I know how to enjoy myself. That hasn't changed." He leaned forward. "But we both know that if all this disappeared tomorrow, I'd be the best equipped of all of us to deal with such a loss."

There was a fat silence between them and I wanted to puncture it. "How come you knew my mother?" I asked.

The cocktail waitress returned, and we sat silently as she explained that our rare bottle of *sake* had been cured inside an ice cave north of Sapporo, and that the cups were cut from a bamboo forest just north of Kyoto.

"We generally don't discuss Satomi," François said, after the cocktail waitress had left. "Anyway, Rumi doesn't remember anything."

"Not at all?" Snowden-roshi looked at me.

Over the years, I had recalled vague impressions of someone I had earlier assumed to be my mother. A smell like baby ferns. A tanned wrist peeling an orange. Someone rolling down a hill beside me. But François had long ago insisted that these memories were not of my mother but culled from stories, poems he had read to me when I was younger.

"Your parents met through me. In Japan. At a social event."

"Years ago," François added.

"Your father was already in the business of identifying beautiful things." Snowden-roshi's eyes narrowed. "Even if those things belonged to other people."

"If I remember correctly, I was also good at lending you a helping hand when you needed it."

Snowden-roshi relaxed a little. "Yes. You did the best you could under the circumstances. I do know that."

"And here you are now, torturing me with the company of this silly rich woman who has fastened onto Buddhism as an alternative therapy for her breast cancer."

"She's not a bad person."

"I didn't say she was bad. I said she was silly. First she's not interested in money, then she won't make a purchase till she knows its value. A true connoisseur would never behave this way."

"She's *rich.*" Snowden-roshi smiled.

"The Chinese say that wealth only lasts for four generations. After that, a family is like an overripe fruit. Too sweet. Good for nothing but birds and other scavengers."

"That is what I love about New York," Snowden-roshi sighed. "You can see that fruit forming before your eyes. The first generation in a family makes money. Learns to smoke cigars and play golf. Their children hope to hold on to their legacy. Then *their* children stumble upon irony and think themselves clever and superior. So *aware.* This goes on until you reach the decadent generation—like Mrs. Mack—the final flowering of a family's genetic potential."

"And here you are, ready to harvest their riches."

The waitress returned with a glass of pear juice, and all of a sudden the men were again conscious of my presence.

François said to me, "You must not become a silly creature like Mrs. Mack, relying on other people to tell you what is valuable and what is not."

"Yes, François."

"Remember, the most important thing in life," François continued feverishly, "is to be able to see things as they really are."

"Why, François," Snowden-roshi all but purred. "Aren't we both basically saying the same thing?"

François and Snowden-roshi drank and drank and leaned back in their chairs, as though trying to escape a magnetic force pinning them to the table. My father became sick. Snowden-roshi took a cab with us to the hotel, then hoisted François over his shoulders and, as he walked brazenly into the lobby, said to the night clerk, "Nothing to worry about. Just a little too much fun."

In the hotel room, Snowden-roshi helped my father onto the bed. "In a way, it's good this has happened. Gives us a minute alone together. So to speak," he added, as François gurgled. "It's a shame. Your father could be a great art dealer with his eye for beauty." He parted the venetian blinds and winced at the restricted view. "How old are you?"

"Eleven."

"Still a girl then." He frowned. "Never mind. Your father will owe me a favor for this sale. This won't be the last time we meet." He put his hand on my cheek, and I trembled. "I wouldn't hurt you." He spoke sharply.

"No." I hoped this was true.

"Is François kind to you? Do you like to study all these art objects?"

"Yes." I was too nervous to say otherwise.

"Your mother loved them too. She was very talented."

I couldn't contain myself. "Was she pretty?"

His eyes softened. "Very. Very pretty. As you are." He sighed. "I loved your mother very much. I always meant to find her eventually. I never really expected I might be too late. When we are young, we don't know that we eventually run out of time." Then the look in his eyes sharpened again. "At least there is you."

About a dozen labs in the United States perform carbon 14 dating for a fee. Most are affiliated with universities, which Mrs. Mack distrusted after having flunked out of Yale Law School. We wrapped approximately five milligrams of Charlie's base in aluminum foil and sent it to be read by an accelerator mass spectrometer at Chrono Labs in Cambridge, Massachusetts. Because Mrs. Mack refused to pay for expedited service—as did François—we would return to California to wait out the dating verdict, with the promise to ship Charlie overnight and insured if the test came back favorable.

"Why does it matter if something is old?" I said to François. "If it's pretty and you like it, shouldn't that be enough?"

"Some people say that as long as you like something, that's enough reason to buy. Those people who believe in the power of positive thinking, for example." He patted his head, still stung by a hangover.

"What if you are wrong? What if Charlie wasn't made in the Kamakura period?"

"I'm not wrong. I can see the age in his face."

"Would you still like Charlie if he turned out to be fake?"

"He's not."

"But if he were?"

"I would be very disappointed. In myself and in him." François paused. "Do you know who Charlie is in the Buddhist canon?"

"He looks like a demon."

"Yes. That's a very Western interpretation." He sighed. "Charlie, or Fudō, looks angry because he hates illusions. He gets mad at all the little demons running around the world who make us sick and stupid. That's the wonderful thing about Asia. So much angry art. People like to think that Buddhism is about inner calm. The truth is, sometimes it is necessary to be angry. Intolerant."

The day before we returned to California, François took me to a small store in Chinatown, where we bought a large white scarf with a print of bougainvilleas. Then we took the subway to Saks Fifth Avenue, where François spent a long time selecting a box of chocolates. At the gift-wrapping counter he said, "I'm sending this to a client in Japan. You know how they are over there."

The girl behind the counter smiled and wrapped the chocolates in a gift box. Later, at the hotel, François carefully unpacked the chocolates, folded the scarf, and placed it inside the box from Saks.

When we got back to California, we presented the gifts to Sondra, who gushed over our generosity, immediately ate a chocolate, and wrapped up her hair with the scarf. "Was it wonderful? New York?"

I looked at François. "I had oysters for breakfast. Every day."

"And the hotel?" she asked. "The man who answered the phone when I called had an accent."

"There was a doorman," I said, thinking of the man who had stood outside the restaurant when we had eaten with Snowden-roshi. "He wore white gloves. And someone ironed our clothes each morning."

"What do you call him?" François prompted.

"A valet," I replied.

Mrs. Mack told my father on the phone that she had always known Charlie to be a Kamakura piece. She was glad that the carbon 14 dating and the lab in Massachusetts had agreed with her. The check was in the mail, and she would expect Charlie at her apartment as soon as my father had deposited the funds.

I made a small and completely ineffectual attempt to keep Charlie in our house.

I said, "What if Mrs. Mack notices that one of Charlie's feet is different from the other?"

"If she couldn't tell that Charlie was Kamakura just by looking, then she doesn't have the proper faculties to see him clearly for what he is. If she can't really see, then how on earth can she tell where the repairs are?"

"Aren't we lying?" I asked bluntly.

"*You* helped fix him, too. We're in this together, you know." He shrugged. "Anyway, *if* she ever notices that Charlie has been repaired, which I highly doubt, I can always claim that *I* had nothing to do with it."

Things were chilly between us until the check came a few days later. Then we packed Charlie in a wooden crate, with plenty of soft padding— Styrofoam and paper—to protect him on his journey as he scowled his way across the United States. When I came home from school, he was gone, and François insisted on taking me out for a steak to celebrate.

For a while, I liked to look at the picture of Charlie on the cover of our catalog and glower at him. He would always grimace back. I liked the fact that our true natures were known to each other, that our ferocious exteriors concealed a hope that all true things could be known in time.

CHAPTER 7

Love Material

People can live their lives with a tiny bit of hidden truth tucked away in a corner of the brain. It can trip up behavior over and over again, only to be revealed in full when an accident forces it out, like a splinter in your toe that has kept you limping for years and only exposes itself when you fall.

Before my visit to New York, I expected people to tell me the truth and I expected objects to tell me the truth too. If a painting looked like it was done in the seventeenth century, I assumed that it was. After New York, François began to teach me that recognizing the truth was a far trickier endeavor than I had thought.

"Don't you see," my father said to me, "how the ink is too black? The faces too flat? The lines not dynamic?" When he talked to me like this, my eyes and my brain connected more tightly, and the world was suddenly in sharper focus. It was an awesome power he had, the ability to stand on the other side of a secret and powerful lens. I longed to be on the other side of that lens with him.

My wish came true around my thirteenth birthday. Only it didn't come to me as I expected it would.

"I got a tip that several retired generals are holding garage sales today," François explained to me on a drive south from San Francisco to the wealthy community of Pebble Beach. "High-ranking military people are always a good source for antiques since they get to live in conquered countries long before we civilians are able to visit."

There was nothing truly valuable at the first two houses. The third was an enormous Spanish-style mansion with white stucco, chocolate trim, and a garden of ferns. In the distance, I heard the whack of men hitting golf balls, while cypress trees drooped under the weight of a porous blanket of moss.

"Rumi. Come here," François said. He had found a collection of gongs mixed in with several sets of weights and a dusty exercise bike. "One of these belonged to the Ch'ing emperor," he whispered. I tested gong after gong. Waves of sound overlapped each other. Finally I struck one of the last remaining gongs. Shimmering silver flooded the garage, colliding with windows and the electrical wiring. The walls buzzed. When the tight, higher waves of the sound died down, the cavernous lower register continued on, pinning my ankles to the floor.

"That's it," I said, and to this day, when I look at a fake, it strikes me as if it were a wrong note in a song.

It isn't just musical instruments that have a voice. This is what most people don't understand. They look at a vase or a statue and see something static. I hear the way the robes of a Japanese wooden warrior god cut through the air, and the sound tells me if the statue was crafted during the dramatic Kamakura period, or later. I watch porcelain bowls open their mouths, like a school of fish in a pond, and hear them sing in clear or cloudy notes.

I learned to hear how different objects speak with the same voice if they were crafted around the same time. By the time I was twenty, I understood that the squabbling of the Warring States era carried over from a chaotic frieze of warriors and chariots decorating a metal flagpole to a clay half-dragon-half-lion, the kind of fanciful creature that can only come to life when a country is in chaos. An Edo print of a town scene, sharp with detail and color, came from the same period as a Buddha carved in haste, his allure forgotten as people turned their attention away from the temples to the streets.

"Now you can see clearly," my father said to me.

"Actually," I said, "the objects talk to me."

He thought I was joking. "Objects don't talk."

"They do to me."

"Whatever you have to believe." He shrugged. "Whatever it takes for you to realize your potential."

My relationship with objects developed in secret. Over time, I became almost as good at identifying art as my father. He was proud and liked to place piece after piece before me as a test. Secretly, I would wait until the object opened up its heart and told me its story. Out loud I would justify my discovery using the language and terms of which my father approved.

I was just a teenager when he brought me out from the back of the store where I was shyly researching and cataloging our inventory, to demonstrate my abilities to some dealer acquaintances, in town for the San Francisco Arts of Pacific Asia show.

"Pull out your treasures, gentlemen," he said, "and let's see how she does."

Peter Brockman from Chicago put on a pair of white gloves he'd kept tucked in his pocket. He untied twin strings wrapped around a cylindrical scroll and unfurled the paper on the glass countertop. I went over to inspect the sheet.

It was quiet, with only the sound of men breathing. I put on my own pair of white gloves and held the scroll open myself, running my eyes across its lines and shading. I could feel my father beside me, all anticipation and nerves. If I succeeded, his standing would be enhanced in the eyes of these men.

I waited for the painting to speak to me. It was a standard composition of a little hut on a sparsely wooded island in the foreground, separated from distant hills by a large body of water. I focused on the trees, on the way their roots gripped the earth. The roots should have been full of tension, like claws gripping a shoulder. But these roots were flat and almost floating against the dirt. There was no sound at all. Then my eyes slid over the slick, frictionless surface of the paper.

"Mid-twentieth-century copy of Ni Tsan," I said. "The paper is all wrong and the brushstrokes too timid."

"Aha!" François exclaimed.

"And this?" Another man I didn't recognize held out a small metal object.

"Archaistic door handle. The lines are too stylized to really be Han. There's no . . . life."

"You see," my father smiled. "She's quite bright."

At dinner that evening, which I cooked, I basked in not only his attention but also that of his colleagues. When my classmates at school picked on me the next day for failing to understand the punch line of a joke concerning a pencil sharpener, I comforted myself with the knowledge that at home there was someone much smarter and stronger than they were, someone who understood me and who would always render their criticisms unnecessary.

So it went, François and I living and working together in the dark-green Victorian house, whose goggled windows were bordered with chiseled lattices and scrolls. I graduated early from college, UC Berkeley, and became his partner. We divided business duties. I spent time at the university library doing research; he met with clients and went on buying trips to augment our stock.

I always spent the evening with my father. I loved walking home from the bus stop in the fog and looking at our house and marveling how it loomed over Pine Street in Pacific Heights like a majestically carved ship anchored in the fog. François had had the good fortune to buy our house in the seventies, when housing prices were low and the goodness of California still something of a secret. Over the years, the building had increased exponentially in value, and François swore we could never move. Around us, old Victorians were one by one converted by youthful couples into monuments to yuppie glory: pink and purple palaces, red and coral estates. Our house remained as it always had been, slightly disheveled, enigmatic, a creaking reminder of a time when California was synonymous with restless beatniks in search of poetry and truth.

I turned and looked inside the window of the first floor, which housed our shop, Silk Road Antiques. How I loved its ramshackle, exotic beauty! Just one peek through the doors revealed a jumble of contents—here an edge of a painting, there a chair, and there again a glimpse of the corner of a blood-red porcelain bowl. It all reminded me of a glass greenhouse swollen with tropical flowers.

I passed through the heavy double glass doors to the back of the shop and François' office, with a small library of glossy-spined books and two wooden filing cabinets. On one wall, a white-and-indigo *noren* curtain displayed a design of dragonflies caught in a basket. Hidden behind this was a door, which opened to a staircase that led up to the kitchen of our house. The library and living room, which was nearly overrun with books and magazines, were on the same floor, and beside them was a dining room furnished with a rich saffron-and-mustard-colored rug from Turkey and a brooding table from China. Upstairs, on the third floor, were several additional rooms, one of which belonged to me.

Sondra left my father not too long after we had returned from the New York trip. I never really knew what set her off. I simply came home from school one day to find her in tears, bags packed and apologizing to me over and over again that she just "had to follow her intuition" and that she "couldn't take it anymore." One day, she insisted, I would understand. From then on, it was just François and me.

So it would have stayed, had it not been for an unexpected visitor one afternoon not long after my twenty-first birthday.

I came home after my usual Sunday trip to the library with a bag full of photocopies and books. I opened up the dark-green door to our shop and made my way through to the back where I could see my father's foot sticking out through the entrance to his office.

There, seated on a Ch'ing dynasty *huang-li* chair beside my father, was Snowden-roshi.

He was still very fair with pale, pure skin that blended easily into his light hair, cut short in the manner of a priest's. This paleness only offset his blue eyes. When they held still and took me in, as they did now, I felt a gentle pressure as though two snowflakes had landed on my skin.

"Darling," my father stood up and kissed me. "We have a visitor."

"I hope you don't mind too much," Snowden-roshi recrossed his ankles. "I was in the area and suddenly realized how much I wanted to see you."

"Of course we don't mind," my father replied. "We can cook an extra crab and you can join us for dinner."

We exchanged pleasantries.

François commandeered Snowden-roshi's shoulder and steered him around the store, lustily pointing out the Chang Dai-Chien paintings on the wall. I kept expecting Snowden-roshi to speak to me, but he didn't. Still, I was keenly aware of him and how he glided noiselessly over the wooden floor, long fingers cradling a bowl or tracing a line of paint across a dish.

"Rumi," François said, "let's show Snowden-roshi how much your powers have improved."

We went to the back-room office, and François pulled back a silk cloth to reveal a four-panel Japanese screen.

The screen was a Zen-style landscape, a valley town tucked in between bulbous, cerebral mountain peaks. The artist had rendered the entire scene with black ink on paper, varying the pressure of his brush. Here the mountains were stormy, there the air was clear. The detail of a bridge leapt out starkly in one spot, while tall, mysterious peaks receded into infinitely lighter shades of gray.

"Rumi has the brightest eye of anyone I know." François smiled. Then he looked at me. "There's one correction I had to make. Can you find it?"

I studied the screen, looking for a spot where the gray did not recede seamlessly, or where the artist's brush seemed to have been momentarily possessed by another hand. "It's a warm black," I said.

My father nodded eagerly. "The artist wanted you to feel introspective. But he did not want you to be left cold."

"Mmm."

I could hear my father breathing, and could feel Snowden-roshi's eyes searching the screen, trying to see as I did.

A small patch of paper near the middle spine did not have the same sheen as the rest of the screen and interrupted the whispering voice of the ink. But my father's work had been steady, blending in well with the rest of the piece. "You did a good job matching the color and the strokes."

"Yes." My father nodded. "It was as though the original artist and I were briefly speaking the same language. It was a joy to repair. A conversation in mist and mountains. Can you give me a date?"

"Seventeenth century. Early."

"That's my girl." He nodded proudly and I beamed. "It should go for a good price. There's a gentleman who lives not far from here who has asked me several times to ring him when I come across just such a piece. Now, let's see. I have something over here."

He placed a Chinese box in my hands.

I undid the ivory clasp and looked inside. Nestled in the satin pillow was a piece of jade in the shape of a cicada. I put the box down on his desk.

"You don't like it?" François was incredulous.

"Funerary objects make me . . ."

"*Funerary objects*," he interrupted. "Good lord, you sound like a college textbook! The cicada is a magical creature. The Chinese believed it could impart immortality."

"Doesn't it bother you that this was stuck in the mouth of some dead person?" I asked.

"It could have gone in other orifices."

"François."

He picked up the cicada with his bare hands. "See how beautifully it is carved?" He took my hand, uncurled my fingers, and placed the little amulet in my palm. Then he rolled the cicada over with his thumb and forefinger.

"It's beautiful," I finally admitted.

"A date, Rumi?"

I gazed into the cicada's eyes and could hear it humming, an archaic orchestra that sounded like the wind and reeds. "Han."

"Ah. Have a look again."

"Han," I repeated.

My father was frowning. "No, I don't think so . . ."

I racked my mind for technical information. "Aventurine in the cracks. So it was polished with quartz, not a modern tool." The words tumbled out of my mouth.

François took the cicada from me and inspected it intently with a small collapsible magnifying glass he kept in his pocket.

"Hmm." He put away the glass and slipped the cicada back into its box. Then he nodded and said, "About two thousand years old, is our Mr. Bug. Think of everything that has happened in all that time," he said softly.

"Empires." Snowden-roshi nodded, glancing quickly in my direction.

"Men's fortunes." My father beamed, clapping his friend on the shoulder.

I stood in place, smiling nervously at them both.

We locked the shop, set the alarm, and passed through the *noren* to the staircase. In the kitchen on the second floor, François wrangled the crabs into boiling water while I made a salad. I was grateful for this domestic distraction. I didn't fully comprehend what had happened a moment ago with the Han jade. What was more, I feared François' reaction to my not responding the way he'd wanted me to. And yet, I'd been *right*. He had been wrong.

Fortunately, the conversation burbled along in a polite and banal fashion with Snowden-roshi at the helm. He told us about his impending move from Los Angeles for a new job at the Stillness Zen Center in San Francisco. We laughed over a terrible pun Snowden-roshi made about mistaking the term *tao* for Dow. After a couple of hours had gone by, we retired to the living room. Snowden-roshi stretched his legs and walked around, looking at the objects in our personal collection.

"You have an altar," he said to my father, inspecting the makeshift structure: a Chinese table with a small Edo-period Buddha, incense burner, and candles.

"Yes."

"Do you give incense every day?"

"No."

"I would have expected a picture of Satomi," Snowden-roshi said softly.

"As I said, we aren't Japanese."

"But she was." Now I felt the cool and insistent probing of his blue eyes on me. "You've grown, Rumi." He smiled. "You're quite accomplished now."

I blushed.

"Connoisseurship is like learning to play a musical instrument. Start training young and the mind is flexible enough to develop a true instinct." My father said this proudly.

"Some of my parishioners go to Japan and report that they simply feel at home once they land there. An intensive Buddhist study—a very old tradition, mind you—prepared them for the unique beauty of Japan."

"American Buddhism is not at *all* like the Japanese version," François retorted. "The Japanese turn to Buddhism for clearly defined services— funerals, for example. Americans think that Buddhism is some sort of alternative approach to living."

"It *is* an alternative." Snowden-roshi twirled his wineglass slowly with his fingers.

"Yes, but that automatically gives it a meaning here that it didn't have in its homeland."

"I think it's a wonderful way for people to naturally appreciate something that might otherwise seem foreign." Snowden-roshi smiled and turned to me. "What do you think, Rumi? Do you enjoy Japan?"

"I've never been."

Snowden-roshi stared. "Surely you have plans to go?"

I looked at François. "I . . . I don't have any plans," I said.

"What a pity. Here you are immersed in all these things which . . . ," he hesitated for just a moment, "*with* which you have a personal connection.

I should think you'd be a little bit curious." He took a long drink of wine and pretended to need several minutes to inhale its perfume.

"I rely on Rumi to run the business when I'm away," François declared cheerfully. "*I'm* the traveler in the family, you see."

"Aha." Snowden-roshi nodded, giving me a curious look as if to say, so that's how it is.

That evening, before we all went to bed, I spoke to François and apologized for having embarrassed him over the cicada.

"Not at all," he waved his hand and smiled. "It's natural, I suppose, that I make a mistake every once in a while. Lucky for me that the piece turned out to be more valuable rather than less. It would have been worse if you had identified the screen, for example, as a fake."

I smiled back at him, relieved that all was right again.

In the morning, Snowden-roshi invited us to a party. A number of potential donors for the Stillness Center were meeting at the Lorenzi Winery in Napa Valley and Snowden-roshi thought we might like to go. François demurred because of a scheduling conflict, and I was about to refuse the offer out of habit when Snowden-roshi made a special plea for me to accompany him.

"You'll meet interesting people. And I'd much rather go to the party with an attractive young woman than all by myself." He grinned.

"I'm not very good at parties."

Lightning quick, his features changed. He dropped the seductive smile and became businesslike. "Think of it as work, then. You'll have the opportunity to scout out potential clients." Snowden-roshi looked at my father. "You did say that you needed to build the business a bit more. Improve your cash flow."

"Yes, but it's François who does that. Not me," I explained.

"She has to learn to deal with the public if she's going to take over your business one day," Snowden-roshi protested to my father. "I understand why you want to protect her, but you can't keep spoiling her like this."

"I'm not spoiled . . ."

"She's just very shy, Timothy," François said.

Snowden-roshi shook his head. "It's our job to help her out of her shyness."

"*Your* job?" I asked.

"I'd appreciate it, François, if you would let me take Rumi."

There was a silence, and then my father surprised me. "We could always use extra money, Rumi." He nodded. "Why don't you try your hand at finding us some clients?"

Later that day I found Snowden-roshi flipping through the clothes in my closet. When nothing he saw impressed him, he went out, returning a few hours later with a bag from a small boutique in which was folded a lovely dress made of blue silk, nipped at the waist, and with little cap sleeves.

"It's expensive," I protested to my father.

"I think you should at least see if it fits."

So I changed. When I didn't come out of the bedroom immediately, my father and Snowden-roshi insisted on coming in to take a look.

"I knew it!" Snowden-roshi declared.

"You look lovely, my dear," my father said. Then he whispered, "The man is loaded. Let him buy it for you if he wants to."

We drove to Napa in the late afternoon. The sun kissed the hills, which were covered with a soft down of aging golden grass. In Snowden-roshi's little black sports car, we crossed the Carneros region, with its neat rows of grapes gently tracing the outline of hills, over to the wide mouth of the Napa Valley stretching open to welcome us to the land of modern-day Dionysians. Here majestic wineries had been crafted out of a romantic architectural imagination—a château, an asymmetrical mix of rectangles, a Spanish villa. We followed a small road into the eastern hills, winding between vineyards marked for Zinfandel and Cabernet, the leaves of the grapevines filtering the light till it took on an emerald hue. We parked beside a stucco building perched on a bluff. Snowden-roshi held my hand to help me cross a cobblestone path, which led through an iron gate to a wide balcony. The valley stretched below us, bordered by low, sleepy hills to the west. Hawks scanned the valley floor for prey. The wind rushed past our ears, as even and soothing as the sound of the ocean.

This was the Lorenzi Winery, one of the grand originals, started by two Sicilian brothers in the twenties and purchased and renamed in the seventies by Dr. Phillip Lorenzi. His wines had won prizes in Paris and were served in the finest restaurants in San Francisco and Los Angeles.

At Snowden-roshi's urging, I accepted a glass of wine and soon all my thoughts were tinted with rose. The catering staff whirled through the party on the balcony like finely tuned gears in a machine, bearing hors d'oeuvres on silver trays. I tasted caviar, delicate egg rolls stuffed with morels, and tender shrimp. The guests were all a lot older than I. They were educated and wealthy, judging by their alert eyes and relaxed physiques, the expression of people expecting to get their way in life without too much trouble. My new dress covered me like a talismanic shield, and I felt young and elegant.

"How nice to meet you," Dr. Lorenzi said to me. He was wiry and tan, a northern Californian of the golf- and tennis-playing variety, and his wife was equally lean and muscular, with white teeth in a wolfish grin.

"What a pretty dress. What a pretty girl," Mrs. Lorenzi purred.

"She's lovely, isn't she?" Snowden-roshi beamed. "The perfect blending of East and West." There was the flattery again, and I squirmed inside, wondering what I would be expected to provide to continue receiving it.

Dr. Lorenzi began to drone on and on about how he'd grown wealthy first as a surgeon and then as a Napa Valley vintner, and how, now that he had exhausted the possibilities of accumulating physical possessions, he wished to do something truly great for humanity. He wished to touch the souls of men. He wanted to help spread the teachings of Buddha.

Snowden-roshi clapped him on the shoulder, and the two men drifted off into business talk.

"How do you know Snowden-roshi?" Mrs. Lorenzi asked, eyeing me over the edge of her glass goblet as she luxuriated in a gulp of wine.

"He's an old friend of my father's."

"Oh. Then you're not . . . ?" She wagged her index finger back and forth. Her demeanor changed and she grasped my forearm girlishly, drawing me into a walk that circled the perimeter of the balcony. "No one knows anything about his romantic history. It's infuriating."

"Ah."

"There are always these rumors. I mean, you look at him and there's something a little sad in his eyes, isn't there? Not surprising given his history, but still." She stopped moving. We were at the other end of the party, but situated so we had a clear and discreet view of Snowden-roshi and Dr. Lorenzi still deep in conversation. "They say he has a broken heart."

Together we watched Snowden-roshi, a man in his theater, speaking earnestly with Dr. Lorenzi while the sun caught his robes and his hands.

All around, women and men admired him, just as we were doing. It occurred to me that perhaps he had brought me here because he had wanted me to see him this way.

Mrs. Lorenzi clasped my hand with the self-assurance of one who is accustomed to drawing strangers into her confidence within moments of meeting. She nodded at Snowden-roshi. "You'll tell me, though, if you hear anything."

"Yes. Of course," I lied.

The sun slipped down behind the western mountains, and the valley began to grow cold. The euphoria from the wine and the amber evening light faded, leaving me with a heavy nostalgia. I wanted another glass of wine to try to recapture my earlier mood, but Snowden-roshi took my hands and steered me inside a hall with rust-colored Mexican tiles and stucco walls. He seated me toward the front, where a small stage had been erected. "You aren't used to drinking," he cautioned. "You must learn to hydrate," and he handed me a glass of water. Then he left me to sit alone. I drank slowly, taking in the enormous canvases covering the walls. They depicted scenes from the history of California—Native Americans in Yosemite, the valley in 1890 devoid of grapes, and pioneers engaging in a picnic by the sea. The isolation I had often felt at parties crept over me.

Now the partygoers threaded into the remaining seats behind me, and Snowden-roshi took the stage. He thanked the guests and his hosts. He wanted to talk about the ancient Greeks, from whom we had inherited much of our political and cultural system. These wise men had understood that a man's life was filled with two things—*mythos* and *logos*. "*Mythos*," Snowden-roshi declared, "is all that is sacred. It is the intuitive, spiritual side of life and can only be expressed and experienced through ritual, meditation, and art. *Mythos* anchored ancient people. It gave them a way to express joy, sadness, and pain. But it did not try to explain the world literally, only how we were meant to perceive it."

Causal, rational explanation was the realm of *logos*. Snowden-roshi believed that the ancient civilizations had been wise in keeping *mythos* and *logos* separate. Terrible things happened, he declared, if people sought practical solutions in *mythos* or tried to find emotional shelter in *logos*. Our own world was fractured because we had an imbalance between the two.

The air pulsed as the pupils of his eyes contracted and expanded, like little whirlpools. A blue vein pressed out against his forehead. Behind me, the audience seemed to breathe as one.

"We can see this now," Snowden-roshi continued, "with science trying to explain away the mysteries of the soul, and religion trying to explain all the origins of the universe." Those of us who were Elect—those of us in this room—had a duty to take our fractured selves and heal. This was the beauty of Buddhism, he continued. It didn't judge. It didn't frighten people into pretending to be pious. It merely asked that all humans engage in knowing themselves, and in practicing compassion and kindness.

The Indians had supported their temples through self-sufficiency. The Chinese had begged. The Japanese had performed social services. The American Buddhist temple would need to find a new way, one that mixed a free-market system with compassion. Snowden-roshi was certain that the donors there that evening would give generously. And then he announced the evening's highlight, a performance troupe from San Francisco, here to put on a classical Nō play. This was the kind of thing the aristocrats of medieval Japan had enjoyed.

The lights dimmed, and a group of musicians dressed in blue *happi* coats and pantaloons silently took the stage. They began to play. It was an eerie sound, just this side of music, a shade away from reeds rustling in the wind or shrill birds exclaiming in midflight. A man climbed the stairs leading to the stage and introduced himself both as the narrator of the story and as a character in the play, a Buddhist priest. He recalled a beautiful woman he had once met while crossing a river in the Japanese Alps. As he reminisced, a new character crept out of his memory and onto the stage. I felt my face grow both hot and cold.

She was wearing a Nō mask of the archetype of a beautiful woman. The mask was white, the lips scarlet and slightly parted, and the nose sloped elegantly between her high cheekbones. She waved the sleeves of her heavy orange-and-gold robes and swept the golden fan in her right hand through the air. Again and again she lifted her white feet and stomped to articulate a note, and the room spun with her dizzying, hypnotic dance.

The priest, too, was entranced by the young woman's dancing, but slowly grew alarmed. As she danced, the woman wailed that she had once loved a man, but he had betrayed her and now she was doomed to roam the earth as a ghost. Then the beautiful woman turned around slowly, so we could see only her back, and put a white sheet over her head. When she removed the sheet, her glossy locks had been replaced with matted, coarse hair. A minute later she turned around to face us and the mask of the beautiful woman was gone, and in its place was the face of a demon.

Shrill, eerie notes accumulated like falling water and pooled together into a thick and frightening atmosphere. The demon bit her sleeves and lurched to a stop in front of me. I peered up into her face, all bulging eyes, protruding teeth, and skin as scarlet as an angry red wound. She rattled her fan inches from my nose and put her hands on her hips and rocked backward, shaking her head in a way that mocked me. She staggered from foot to foot, then pointed the fan at my face. She ran to another corner of the stage, only to return to me again and again, as though I were to blame for her condition. I rose out of my seat, but Snowden-roshi put a hand on my shoulder and forced me to sit.

The priest cried out to Buddha and waved his rosary with ecstatic energy. Finally the music lulled like an ebbing tide, and the invisible strings tying the audience to the drama relaxed. The demon began to retreat. In the end we were left with nothing but the priest standing at the edge of the stage.

It was dark when we left. The valley was cold and I shivered until the heat came on in the car. I was feeling pensive and wanted to be left alone with my thoughts, but Snowden-roshi was in the mood to talk.

"Did you enjoy that?" He glanced at me out of the corner of his eye. "I thought you might like to see how some of those antiques you deal with are actually used. The masks, for instance."

"It was impressive," I said quietly.

"You were very charming with people tonight," he continued lightly. "I was proud of you. Some of these guests will visit the shop just to see you. If I'm there, I'll help with the sales. If not, you'll have to manage."

"Why are you here? I mean, really?"

He feigned surprise. "Haven't we had a nice time together?"

"You want something."

He studied me, almost with an expression of amusement. "You're not what you seem, are you? You can be surprisingly direct for someone under her father's thumb the way you are."

"People often confuse shyness with weakness."

He nodded and seemed to be thinking. "It's just *karma*. I hope to help you here and there. Your mother would have liked that. She wouldn't have wanted you to grow up never leaving François' house."

I smiled. "I'm spoiled."

"*You* I have no problem with. Your father, on the other hand . . ."

"He loves me."

"He's overprotective. No one else will tell you, so I will." He relaxed. "What's he trying to protect you from, I wonder?"

We fell silent. The conversation had not gone in the direction I'd anticipated, so I changed the subject. "What was she like?"

"Beautiful," he said. "Inspiring because she was beautiful. She hated to be bad at anything that she did." He paused. "I was in love with her, you know. We all were."

"We?"

"Small band of expats. It was the seventies."

"Am I like her?"

"I don't know yet," he said honestly. We were quiet for a moment, and then he asked, "Do you happen to know exactly where she is buried?"

"No."

"I wouldn't mind knowing," he said, "if you find out. We could offer some prayers for her. I'd like to take her some flowers, but François says her grave is in Japan."

This was news to me. "It is?"

Snowden-roshi continued. "Do you know what the Japanese believe about the dead? They say that you must pour water over their tombstones so their souls don't stay thirsty. Isn't that lovely? And there are all these complex things you have to do. Special *sutras* you have to read every so often to keep their souls chugging along toward rebirth. Oh well." He shrugged. "I imagine someone is praying for her somewhere in Japan."

Back in my room, I hung up the dress to let it air. I opened the window, and the cool evening breeze slid beside me, bringing in the scent of the ocean. From the dress I could smell something else, a faint reminder of dust and wine and incense.

All at once, I studied the dress again. I realized that it hid all my flaws— my small chest and long waist. I thought about all the times I had passed

Snowden-roshi in the hallway, or sat across from him at dinner. He already knew exactly what my arms and legs and breasts were like, and he had considered all these things before choosing an outfit for me.

Now the glamour of the evening didn't feel so pleasurable. I felt vulnerable. The old uneasiness I'd felt about Snowden-roshi since he'd returned to us reasserted itself in my gut. He wanted something from me. I, raised to always know the answer to a challenge, felt uneasily at sea.

That night I could hear Snowden-roshi in the guest bedroom, the springs of the old mattress complaining against his weight, and when I thought of him by himself, whirling in the sheets, I, too, squirmed inside my bed. Further down the hall, my father tossed in his sleep. The entire house seemed to complain. First one beam groaned, and then another and another, like the bones of a spine passing along stress. The creaking followed me into sleep, where I dreamed that I was a passenger on an old wooden boat.

Then, as dreams do, this scene delivered me to a new one, and I dreamed I was sleeping in a Japanese-style room.

The fibers of the lime-colored *tatami* floor undulated, reflecting the moonlight as it quivered through an open window. An actor stepped into view, wearing the Nō mask of a woman. She was dressed in a brilliant red-and-silver kimono. As the woman turned her back to me, her thick black hair suddenly grew coarse and matted and I became frightened in anticipation of seeing her face again.

I saw her nose first, sharp and curved like a meat hook. Her chin pointed down at the ground in a V, and her cheekbones drew up high against her ears. Vermilion eyes flashed. She put a hand through the window and motioned to me to come closer. The floor in the room tilted, and I was sliding down toward the window.

A voice called my name. "Rumi," it said softly. A woman's voice, just roused from sleeping. The mask fell. Through the open hole where her face had been, I saw a backdrop of whirling cherry petals carried by the wind. The hair and the kimono collapsed to the ground, mere actor's props without a body.

When I woke up, I was shivering. The curtains over the open bedroom window heaved.

I closed the window and looked around my room. Gray moonlight hung over the furniture in my bedroom, a blanket of ash from an adolescent Pompeii. I flicked on the lamp on my nightstand and the ash dissolved. Objects echoed with longing and romance. On one corner of the wall, François had hung my report cards, a wedge-shaped army of A's marching along like stocky sergeants.

I heard a sound, as light as a kernel of rice falling from a table onto a tile floor. The air grew cooler. Scratching traveled the length of the wall. Tiny fingers picked at the paint, looking for a point of entry through the wood. Then the sound faded, leaving me alone.

I felt a little the way you do on the first full day of autumn, when the air has permanently shifted from sultry to cool and the atmosphere has grown so tense the leaves on deciduous trees all fall in fear. Something, I knew, had come for me.

CHAPTER 8

The Ghost

Now the objects clamored for my attention. When François handed me a new Ch'ing dynasty vase or a Japanese *suzuribako* lacquer writing box, I didn't need to wait for them to speak. They called to me the moment they were unwrapped: gilded voices, cool sopranos, rasping coughs. My environment was a cacophony of dynasties, textures, and sounds.

My father began to notice that something was amiss. He brought home a damaged screen of waterfowl and willow trees that he had found at a garage sale in the Oakland Hills, convinced that it was from the Muromachi period. But I knew it was a much later copy, perhaps even as late as 1900.

"No, Rumi." He smiled at me, tolerantly. "See the way the water splashes against this rock? The lines are elastic."

"The forger was talented."

"Forger? You've become so suspicious lately. It's affecting your judgment."

I made him take the back of the screen apart. Even when he found that the original painting was backed with newspaper dated 1897, he still could not believe that the screen hadn't been completed three hundred years before. "But it looks . . . right."

"Didn't I tell you?"

He shot me an accusatory glance, as though I had magically transformed the screen from the undervalued one he had purchased to the relatively common piece lying here now.

The following evening, Snowden-roshi, exhausted from another interview in which he had expounded on the superiority of Buddhism, came for dinner with a group of friends. This had become something of a habit since the party in Napa Valley. He liked to come to the shop at the end of the day with some of his followers who were looking for small Buddhas and *mandalas*. After they made a purchase, we would invite them for dinner, and François and I would scurry to expand our dinners to accommodate the guests.

Before we ate, François placed a so-called Chinese Neolithic pot in front of these guests and they admired the whirling, primitive pattern painted on the belly.

"Isn't that a copy?" I said. "Ch'ing dynasty. They liked to mimic pieces from the past."

"Rumi." My father's eyes danced with irritation. "Please."

"No, I'm sure." I disappeared into the office. Ten minutes later, I returned to the dining room while everyone else was eating and placed a monograph on the table in front of my father. I opened it to a page with an old black-and-white photograph from an archaeological dig in China where the very same pot had been unearthed alongside some statuettes from the thirteenth century. "You can see," I said. "The paint is faded in the same places. It's the same pot."

I could feel Snowden-roshi watching me, his mouth bent in a slight smile of amusement.

My father carefully set his napkin down on the table but I could see his fingers trembling when he picked up the book. "How . . . interesting." His vocal cords were drawn tight.

Later that evening, he came to see me in my room.

"What are you trying to do?"

"What do you mean?"

"You want to embarrass me publicly."

"You were *wrong*."

"And you thought it was appropriate to find fault with me in front of everyone else?"

"I . . ."

"These people came to us as customers, and you stood there in front of them, insisting that I made an error. Do you have any idea what kind of an impression you made? You even ignored them at dinnertime. I didn't force you to eat with us because I have always indulged you in your little moods. But add it all up together, Rumi, and I'm deeply disappointed. Embarrassed on your behalf."

"I . . ."

"I don't understand this self-righteousness. It speaks to some deeper problem between us. You behave as though I have offended you and you want to retaliate by humiliating me in public. I cannot imagine what I have done to you to deserve this treatment."

I shook my head.

"Disagree with me if you want, but do it in private." With that, he slammed my door shut.

The following evening, we ate dinner in separate rooms.

As a child, I had always feared his disappointment. Now I discovered that his anger at me was an even worse thing. How could I make it right? Perhaps I was wrong to speak up when I saw him make a mistake. Perhaps my unusual relationship with objects was flawed. Alone, I ate my plate of grilled fish and vegetables and wondered what I could do to restore our earlier harmony.

For a few days, I tried to ignore the voices of the objects. When François issued a judgment about a painting or a scroll, I agreed on principle. But the objects would not leave me alone. They demanded attention, voices echoing against the ceiling of the store, like the flapping of birds inside a bell tower. They were gentle but insistent, saying to me that I was right when my father was wrong. My conviction would not die. The more certainty I developed, the more mistakes I saw him making. I began to wonder. All these years, I'd assumed that he was the one with the superior eye, and that my reliance on the way that objects spoke to me was a handicap.

At night, I continued to hear the woman's voice. She seemed to come from deep within the house. She knew my name and liked to say it while I was falling asleep. She said very little else, though I gathered that whoever she was, she felt lost or trapped. "Find me. Find me," I once heard her whisper. I didn't know at first where she wanted me to look. I'd get up and drift through the hallway half-asleep until I would wake up, startled to find myself out of bed. I would return to my room, but a few days later I'd just repeat the process.

"François," I said at work after we'd gone a few days without arguing and had resumed taking our meals together.

"Hmm?"

"Did you lose something?"

He gave me a strange look. "What do you mean?"

"Maybe there is an object missing?"

Slowly he shook his head. "From the catalog?"

That must be it. "If you don't mind, I'm going to spend a few days doing inventory."

He pushed his glasses back against his brow. "Rumi, what's troubling you?"

For the first time in my life, I discovered that I had the ability to hide what I was thinking. "I just think I would feel better if I could keep things in a little better order."

He hesitated, then nodded. "Whatever you need to do, my dear."

I knew that if there was something lost or hidden in the house, there was only one logical spot to look. For our home had a place for hidden things, a room within a room.

My father had told me this when I was thirteen. "Consider it a challenge," he said. "See if you can find it."

There were clues over the next few days.

In the living room, my father began to sing a French folk song he must have learned as a child. He carried a glass of wine and disappeared around the corner into the bathroom, and the sound of his voice traveled through the books on Chinese porcelain. The singing stopped and my father came back into the hallway with me.

"Did you like my song?" he asked.

"Yes," I said. I stared at the bookshelf.

"A little song about a genie in a cave," he said. "Sort of like Aladdin. You remember how he freed the genie?"

I took a sheet of paper from my room and drew a long rectangle standing on its end. I labeled the bottom length "books." On the right-hand side, I wrote "bathroom door." I put in a horizontal line, effectively slicing the rectangle in half and creating two squares. In the top square, I wrote "bathroom." I labeled the left-most line of the entire rectangle "outside."

There was a square room on the bottom that remained unaccounted for. The secret room.

I got up and walked around the corner to a portion of wall. Here my father had hung up a scroll of a Chinese tiger. Below this was a small wood table holding an orchid and, beside this, a bench. I had always avoided this corner of the house. As a rule, I liked paintings of animals, but this tiger had always frightened me. "His eyes are always going to follow you," my father had teased when he had first hung up the painting. I dragged the small table and orchid off to the side. Then I pulled a chair up next to the painting, climbed on top, and unhooked the painting from the wall. Still standing on the chair, I began to roll up the hanging scroll until I was sure it would not touch the ground when I descended. Then I carried it over to the dining room table and set it down on the white lace tablecloth.

"Aha!" my father exclaimed.

I had not heard him come into the hallway. "It has to be here," I said.

"What does?"

"The doorway." The wall looked just like any other wall in our house, covered with panels of chocolate-colored wood. I ran my fingers along the seams.

"You won't get it open that way," my father said impatiently. He set his wine glass down on a side table, then pressed a corner of one of the panels. Nothing happened. He pushed harder. Still nothing. "It must be stuck. Well, I couldn't expect you to get it open if it was just going to be stuck like that," he said, as though the fact that I had not succeeded in prying open the wall required an excuse. "It must be all the moisture in the air. Things become so wet in this climate." He rolled up the sleeve of his shirt and pounded the wall. It popped open with a comical *boing.* I smelled musty air. "There you go," my father beamed at me. "Your Aladdin's cave. And I am your genie. Look!" He whipped a flashlight out of his pocket, turned it on, and pointed it at a suit of armor. "Tell me the insignia."

I sniffed and stepped into the room, floorboards creaking under my weight.

"Come on. Insignia."

"Imperial."

"Now, how much should we charge?"

I shook my head. A newspaper cost a dollar. A full tank of gas cost twenty. Beyond that I had no sense of numbers.

"It's all good and well for you to know the difference between lacquer and wood. But you're going to have to learn how much to charge people," he said.

"Why?"

He was genuinely surprised. "Why, if you are going to be an art dealer, Rumi, these are the kinds of things you have to know."

So it was that I now turned to the secret room under the premise of conducting inventory. I removed the tiger painting, popped open the false wall, and flipped on the light. Here, crammed from floor to ceiling, were hundreds of wooden boxes. While François was downstairs working, I spent the next hour or so opening boxes and crates, some stamped with the Chinese symbol for export and others unmarked, checking their contents against the catalog. Nothing.

Then I wondered: What if the object wasn't exactly lost, but purposely hidden? I dug deep into the inventory, past the front rows of jades and pots, back toward the paintings and sculptures François said we would need to house for several years before they could be sold. Still nothing.

By late afternoon I was exhausted, and I settled back against two crates to rest. The secret room had no windows, and I was dependent on the overhead light and my flashlight to see anything. I turned the flashlight off and closed my eyes. When I opened them a moment later, a glimmer like the underside of a minnow caught my eye. It was one of our Japanese mirrors. I shifted my focus to the metal surface and picked it up. There it was: my face. I could see angles and lines. Slim eyes that were almost, but not completely, Asian. High forehead. Dimples. An aquiline nose inherited from François.

I had spent many hours looking at my face, partly from disappointment and the secret hope that I might suddenly become beautiful—Snowden-roshi had said that my mother was beautiful all those years ago—but also out of curiosity. If I could dissect my face into its discrete parts, I could attribute certain features to my father and assume that the remainder belonged to my mother. She would not have had my chin. She would not have had my hair, which was too light in color and texture to be Japanese.

Her eyes would have been brown. Her nose would have been smaller, and less obtrusive.

I imagined this second, separate face beside my own. She would have been young when she had been with François. She must have had thick, straight hair, which had fused with François' to give me mine. There was her round face, and her large eyes—unusually large for someone Japanese—which smiled when the rest of her face smiled as it did now. I smiled back. We both had the same strong teeth. In subtle ways we looked the same—the way our mouths were shaped and connected to our cheeks.

Dust rose from the boxes. I sneezed and sent a spray of water on the mirror's face. I wiped it dry with my sleeve, and when I looked at the mirror again, the woman's face—my mother's face—moved.

I looked to the side. There, gazing at me, was a woman. Her hair was unbound and hung heavily as though wet. Her brow furrowed with pain, and her white lips parted to reveal a row of tiny teeth. There was a vacant, hungry expression in her eyes, the look of someone who has not eaten for many, many days but has instead been overtaken by hallucinations. Her face was pale and luminous, like the moon, and the flesh of her neck pure white and translucent like a lychee.

I heard a wail. A low, throaty throb trembled up in pitch. The sound wound up my spine, climbing in a chromatic scale, a shivering finger of rising ivy.

And then she was behind me. She must be standing right behind me. I whirled around.

"Rumi," she said.

I saw the tail end of her kimono disappear around a stack of crates and when I followed her, I found myself alone in the entry to the secret room.

The figure had disappeared.

"Mother?" I called.

Over the years I had asked my father many times about my mother. François told me that while she had loved me very much, she had grown quite ill and died shortly after my birth. "But I will always be your father and your mother," he would say.

When I started high school I went through a brief phase when I demanded to know precisely what had happened. My father always responded with some variation of the following: "I can certainly understand a child's desire to know about her mother, but it has been so long. And anyway, you did not know her."

"At least tell me what she was like," I persisted.

My father would launch into one of his characteristically enigmatic speeches. "You know the Japanese sun goddess Amaterasu? She was born out of her father's eye. Sort of like the Greek goddess Athena, except *she* was born out of her father's head. Goddesses who don't have mothers end up becoming warriors. They are very cunning and smart. Like Brünnhilde in Nordic mythology."

"And this has exactly *what* to do with me?"

"If you are a goddess and you are only going to have one parent, it's best to have a father. All the goddesses who only have a mother end up silly. I've done you a favor."

"You've done me a *favor*?"

"Well, the fates have," he interjected quickly, "in giving you a father who dotes on you and appeals to your intelligence instead of teaching you the insipid hobbies that most of your female schoolmates have learned from their socialite mothers. If it weren't for me, who knows what would have become of you? Playing tennis and tanning, or screaming 'Woo-hoo!' over absolutely nothing of importance. By growing up with me, you've learned to do something useful with your life. And that's far better than turning you into a woman every man will idolize, isn't it?"

Now I heard voices: François, Snowden-roshi, and others. They were climbing up the staircase from the shop and into the house. After our last dinner together when I had not helped entertain our guests at all, I knew I would be expected to help prepare a meal, to sit with them while we ate. Somewhat still in a daze, I hastily repacked the secret room, shut the door, and replaced the tiger painting.

François was waiting for me when I turned around. "Oh, good," he whispered. "I don't want that open when guests are here."

"I heard you coming."

"And how's the inventory?"

"Messy."

He was going to ask me questions, but Snowden-roshi appeared just then with a bouquet of red and yellow roses for me. Behind him someone turned on the hallway and dining room lights, and abruptly the house was flooded with gold light.

"A young woman can never have too many flowers," he said, and I thought to myself how easy it seemed to be for men to have ideas as to what a young woman should or should not have.

Though I had intended to be a better hostess this time around, I ended up keeping mostly to myself that evening, making a large pasta dish and salad, while François found a couple of bottles of wine that had been languishing above the refrigerator. I was rattled from my experiences in the secret room, but my job as host precluded any self-indulgent panic attack. There were ten of us that night, including Dr. and Mrs. Lorenzi, who had come looking for a Zen ink painting to put in their living room. François had managed to talk them into buying the black-and-white screen, which he'd repaired just a few weeks earlier. I could tell that the extra cash had made François ecstatic. He was gallant and funny all evening, punctuating Snowden-roshi's stories with tales of his own. The priest told us how he'd gone for a pilgrimage like Bashō, walking from Solvang to Santa Barbara, and François recounted a time he'd escaped from China with a dozen pieces of jade sewn in his pants. Snowden-roshi had slept under oak trees, met with gentle Mexican farmers who had recognized him as a kind of monk, and given impromptu lectures about Buddhism to tourists gathered at wineries. François had been tested by an old antique dealer in Xian, who had placed three dishes on a table and been delighted when my father had chosen the "correct" one.

Later, we drifted off to separate conversations and Mrs. Lorenzi pulled me aside to chat. "You two are so cute," Mrs. Lorenzi cooed. "He's never brought *me* flowers."

I kept my voice cool, but amused. "You misunderstand."

"My dear, these things are never a secret. People always know."

When the evening was nearly over and the guests mostly departed, I wrapped myself up in an old horsehair blanket we kept folded over a corner of the sofa and stepped out onto the deck, which was through the kitchen. From here I had a view of a small garden and the backs of other similarly shaped houses. A black cat with a white bib paused under a lamp and looked at me before flying into a genesta bush. Off in the distance, I could see Coit Tower winking at me, and beyond this the glittering lights of the East Bay. I shivered, then turned around and looked into the sky. The cauldron of the ocean had whipped up a fierce plume of gray fog, and the moisture was now bearing down upon the city. Soon the contours of buildings and trees would be lost in the mist.

"You're not cold?"

"A little."

Snowden-roshi came to stand beside me. "Did you have a good evening?"

I drew the blanket more closely around me. "Do you remember when you asked me where my mother was buried?"

"Yes."

"Why did you want to know?"

"I told you. I thought it would be nice to take her some incense."

"I want the real reason."

He leaned against the deck railing. "Your father has a difficult time discussing what happened to her. What happened to her remains. Where she is buried. What he did with her things."

"Supposedly it's too painful."

He cleared his throat. "You know him best, Rumi. You know if there is something he is hiding." He moved very close to me now. I smelled something sweet and musty, like fruit and wine and smoke all at once. "You've remembered something, haven't you?"

"It's not a memory exactly."

"Then what?"

"It's like something stepped out of a nightmare."

"Something terrible."

"Something frightening, anyway."

"A feeling?"

"A person. In pain."

"Who?"

"A woman."

"Who?"

"I think it's my mother. And I'm supposed to help her. And I don't know how! I don't know how!" To my horror, I was crying. He drew me closer to him and held me, but only a part of me was able to calm down. Now everything smelled like incense.

"You must remember, Rumi," he said softly. "You must remember everything. Then I will help you."

Late at night, when everyone was asleep, I went back into the secret room by myself with a flashlight. I aimed this at the seams in the walls, searching for a crack. I tapped the walls, listening for a change in depth where a second secret room might be located. I'd seen plenty of puzzle boxes. I knew how my father thought, and I ought to be able to find whatever was hidden in this room. Try as I might, though, the walls yielded nothing.

In frustration I paced the floor, and the boards heaved and groaned. Heaved and groaned. I stopped and pointed the flashlight at the floor. One of the boards didn't match the others. I hadn't noticed it before; the floor had never been all that interesting to me compared to the objects in this room. Now it occurred to me that the grain of wood on one of the panels had a different rhythm than all the others. I knelt down and tapped one end of the board, and then the other. Abruptly it flipped up, forming a kind of handle. I pulled this up, and a portion of the floor came free. Underneath was a compartment several feet long, occupied by a wooden box. A secret room within a secret room. I took off the lid, removed a thin layer of tissue, and looked inside.

She was a thousand-armed *kannon*, a Buddhist goddess so named not because she actually had a thousand arms (she only had about forty), but because each arm was said to reach the beings of twenty-five worlds. Multiply the number of arms times the number of worlds, and the *kannon* had the power of a thousand hands. Each of her hands carried a different object: a tower, a mirror, a rope. All were instruments that she, the goddess of mercy, would use to rescue beings in pain.

I pulled her out of the box and set her on the floor. Then I focused on her movements and her voice. The room took on the smell of wood and rain. I tried to listen to her, the way I had always listened to antiques. I waited to hear how her robes moved, or how her hair fell across her shoulders. But she was still.

I examined her face. Her broad, intelligent forehead bore a crown of eleven smaller heads on top of her hair. Her eyes were squinting as eyes do when you smile, but her mouth was only slightly puckered. Her head was bent at the neck, as though she were about to add her comments to a conversation while preparing to shift her weight and stand up. She was small, perhaps only two feet high, so beautiful I sensed at once that she must have been carved by a master—maybe even the Kamakura genius Unkei.

As I was thinking this to myself, the shadows of the *kannon*'s face abruptly deepened. The corners of her mouth drew up, and her lips lengthened. "I've never seen anything like you before," I said.

"I would like to go home," she said politely.

"Well." I smiled. "You live here now."

Her eyes crinkled again. "I want to go home."

"*This* is your home," I said.

"No it's not," she insisted. "I want you to take me home."

A light shone in her eyes and she smiled. Then a white shadow gathered around her body, drew up into a muscular fist, and, like a bird taking flight, flew up and away.

I sat there for a long time, thinking over what I had seen. Though I tried to talk to the statue, she would not speak to me again.

In the morning, I took the statue downstairs into the shop. François was already there alone, dusting the shelves and the glass countertops. He gave a start when he saw me holding the *kannon*. It took him a moment to recover his composure. Then he asked, "What do you have there?"

"Something is wrong with this statue."

"Another copy?" he asked glibly.

"Not that kind of problem." I set the *kannon* down on a cabinet. "She was under the floorboards of the secret room."

I watched him pour himself a cup of coffee. His hands did not tremble. "What an odd hiding place."

"Where did she come from?"

"Some junk sale, I think. I don't remember." He walked over to the kitchen table and sat down. "However did you find her?"

"I heard her. The way I hear everything."

He gave me a rueful look. "Now, really, Rumi."

"It's the truth. I heard her and found her last night."

He shrugged. "Maybe it's time to put her up for sale then. It's been long enough." He took a sip of his coffee, watching me carefully to see what I would do next.

"You said that you don't remember exactly where she came from. But you remember *when* you bought her?"

"Not exactly. I just assume I hid her to let enough time pass. You know we do that with other pieces."

"Why isn't she in the catalog?"

He shrugged. "I'd forgotten about her."

"But you think she came from a junk sale."

"I assume."

"You don't remember?"

"You know that sometimes I have to keep things hidden from public view."

"But why would you hide something from *me*?"

"For the simple fact," he said smoothly, "that I'd forgotten all about it."

"But you remember how long you've had her."

He exhaled, long and deep. "Rumi. What is this all about?"

I felt that anything I said now might lead me into a trap. But I couldn't stop myself from talking. "I don't understand why you never told me about the statue. I think you've been lying to me. We both know you can be a very good liar."

Now he was angry. At last I felt the full brunt of his self-righteousness. "You!" He pointed at me. "I have given you more than most parents give their children. You will never know what it is to not have a job or a skill! And you act as though I have done all these things for you out of some secret plan to lie to you!"

"You just did."

"This isn't you, Rumi. Who put these ideas in your head? Tell me. What is going on! Who has spoken to you?"

I'm ashamed to admit it now, but I began to cry. "It's not . . . I don't . . ."

"You knew when you told me that you wanted to do inventory that you were looking for something, didn't you? How did you know you were looking for something? Who told you to look for this?" His rage was a physical thing, his voice thrusting across the table. I shook, as if an earthquake had gripped the floor beneath my feet.

I told him everything that I could remember, starting with the party in Napa Valley, my strange dream, the voices, the ghost. Everything. I felt agitated when I was done talking, but he looked surprisingly at ease.

In an increasingly calm voice, he asked me questions, which I answered, often repeating parts he claimed not to undestand.

"What did Snowden-roshi say to you about your mother?"

"That he loved her."

"And tell me again about the Nō play."

"The woman was a ghost with a broken heart."

"And that night you had a bad dream in which you saw a ghost."

"Yes."

"My dear, you know how high-strung you are." Now he smiled at me and drummed a countertop lightly with his fingertips. "Don't you see," he said, "what has happened?"

I did not.

"Snowden-roshi is a very charismatic man, Rumi. He's very, very good at getting people to see what he wants them to. How else does a man convert so many people to Buddhism?"

"He was so nice to me, François. But it made me nervous."

He sighed. "It was wrong of me to send you off to the party. I can see now that this was a mistake. I am very sorry to have put you in such a vulnerable situation. I know how sensitive and imaginative you are."

Because he'd known the priest before he'd become such a fixture among the wealthy and powerful, François was immune to Snowden-roshi's charisma and could therefore help me recognize what had happened. I with my tendency to befriend objects and imbue them with a story had simply let the power of suggestion carry me away. The drama at the vineyard had planted the idea of a ghostly woman, my mother, in my mind, and I'd gone about conjuring her up. Could I see that now?

"But I found this statue."

"So? You may well have seen me hide it when you were a child." He went on to say that I should not be ashamed of a weak moment. Plenty of people would allow someone else to think for them. He would take care of me now as he always had. The statue would be sold, and my contact with Snowden-roshi limited. Our days would once again be calm and ordered.

For a time, things did seem to go back to the way they had been. Snowden-roshi completed his move from Los Angeles, and moved into his new quarters at the Stillness Center. The statue disappeared and when I checked the floorboards in the secret room, I found it empty. The *kannon* was gone and I wondered if we could go back to the way things had been before.

Then one night a few months later, I had my answer. I woke up drenched in sweat from a nightmare whose details I did not completely remember. Moonlight sliced the curtains and struck my bedroom floor at acute angles. In the night, the colors of my room had been stripped down to shades of black, white, and blue. Silver objects pierced through the dull navy glow—a doorknob, a pair of earrings, the glint of a tin picture frame. Shadows blossomed in the corners, a meadow of tiny black-and-white fists ripe for harvest.

The air grew thick and cold, as though I had been wrapped in a chilled velvet blanket. I heard the brush of footsteps. I sat up, my body suspended by invisible arms. "Rumi," a voice whispered near my ear. "Rumi," it said again. It was a woman's voice, accented and absent of diphthongs. The first syllable came out past the top of her palate, with the *r* a cross between an *r* and an *l*. The second syllable echoed through the apartment. "Rumi-*mi*." The sounds collided and chased each other away.

It was the sound I had waited to hear all my life.

"Mother?" I asked.

The invisible arms directed me out of the bed and I began to follow the footsteps out into the hallway. The same force that had churned the air into such a thick consistency had also coaxed the threads of the hallway carpet to grow. They were now knee-high, and I staggered through this swamp a step at a time. Instinctively, I put my hand out against the wall to push my body along. The surface was icy and slick like the frozen flesh of a melon. My fingers yielded to the cold and grew stiff, and soon I could no longer feel the wall at all.

"Rumi-*mi-mi*," the voiced bounced around me. *"Me me me."*

"I'm coming." My breath collected into silver halos.

Even as my feet stuck to the cold floorboards in the living room, I felt a heat of pride blossom in my stomach and stretch out into my limbs. I knew that the cold could not hurt me. I would be triumphant.

A chandelier of sharp stars illuminated the living room. "Rumi," the voice called from behind. I turned my head.

"Where are you?"

The two candles on the altar flared.

"Haaaaa." Cold air exhaled against the back of my neck.

"What are you trying to tell me?" Wind circled through the room, disturbing the candles. They fluttered violently, butterflies trapped in a place.

Then there was something wrong with the candles. There was too much smoke and it was all thick and black. I could not control it. My eyes watered. Corners of objects blurred.

New sounds pierced the wind. Reeds whistled high and sharp. Drums throbbed through the floorboards as though the very room I stood in was the chamber of a heart. And soaring above these sounds, the crisp, metallic cry of crickets and birds. A sound just this side of music. The reedy, nasal twang of the animals swelled, as though their lungs had expanded, and suddenly the sound became a chorus of pipes hugging the shifting contours of a tune. The shape of the music twisted through the room, running like a brook, wrapping around my ankles, upsetting my balance.

"Wait. Please slow down," I said.

The music ran and ran through the room, and the shapes on the altar blurred and shifted, like high-speed film. The Buddha became a living man, then a woman, then a figure with three heads, then a man again. The gong became a light, a cluster of fireflies, a tree in blossom. The walls of the living room dissolved.

I was sweating. No, I was dancing. Spinning and jumping.

Something lay against my neck. Something solid, and coiled, like a rope. I looked at my right shoulder. A long black plait of hair hung over my collarbone and dangled against my breast. Then the plait moved, retreating like a snake across my neck and down my back.

The music stopped. I turned around. It was so quiet. Peaceful and cold. I was on a hill. No—a tiny planet. Darkness dripped over my head and down past my feet. And then, just above my line of vision, I saw the pale, luminescent ripple of a sail. I looked up.

A woman contemplated me, head tilted to the side. Her feet were hidden inside the folds of a long white *kimono* whose thin edges flapped frantically like a moth trapped against the walls of a tin box. I could see her hands desperately clutching the frayed edges of her sleeves and collar. I had the impression that if she did not hold the robe in place, it would fly away and the rest of her would disappear as well, as though this white garment was the only thing anchoring her to one spot.

Her dark, unruly hair spewed out in all directions like black ink run amok on a piece of white paper. In the first few seconds when we looked at each other, I saw her eyes flicker with curiosity. She leaned forward and peered at me with the cold dignity of a satellite sent down to inspect the earth. She was beautiful, with a small, round face, a tiny mouth, and tiny, delicate teeth. I began to weep. When my eyes were free of tears, I saw that she had grown older—more gaunt and haggard—as though those few seconds of expressing her personality had exhausted her. Would I, too, look like this one day? One of her hands loosened its grip from the folds of her kimono. The tissue trembled and parted, revealing the sharp point of her collarbone. She reached out to me, then her hand drifted off to the side, palm open.

She swayed overhead, and I heard a sound like wood creaking. I swiveled around, keeping the ghost in view, even as she moved around in a circle. She seemed to be enjoying the entertainment, having fun leading me around like this. I remained as focused as I could, watching her. After a while, she drifted down to my level, perhaps only a few feet away. And I began to find that I wasn't scared of her. Not exactly. In awe perhaps, but not afraid.

"Come on," I whispered. "What do you have to show me?"

She seemed to understand, and her face took on a look of deep sorrow. She drifted through the house. I followed her to the front door, where she disappeared.

I cursed, mashed my feet into a pair of slippers, and went outside. For a moment, I couldn't see. It was so dark outside. Then my eyes adjusted. I saw the ghost, half a block away, blending into the moss of an oak tree. I ran after her.

It was a serene time to be awake. The clubs and nighttime partiers had gone home. The homeless people in Golden Gate Park were starting to retreat to the trees to sleep. The only roar coming from the city streets was that of the ocean, kneading away at the beaches and embankments. Far off in the distance I could hear the foghorn warning boats off shallow ground, and the sound fused with another tone, a version of the high, reedy music I'd heard in the living room.

The ghost flew ahead of me, like a sail on a ship. I was so focused on her, I barely noticed the effort it took to climb up and down the angled streets. It was as though I, too, were flying with her. I swept by cars parked like dominoes ready for toppling, side by side and at a tilt. The bodegas in the Mission were shuttered, though occasionally I passed an open window rasping the refrain of a Mexican song, desperate in its longing for home. In these quiet and silver hours, the Victorians were less colorful, their plumage muted, as though, like electric birds in some imaginary tropical forest, they had toned down their feathers while they slept.

Every now and then a vehicle—a taxi or a cop car—glided along. But no one stopped to talk to me. I had the sense that the city was sleeping, all the bodies breathing in and out in the same pace, just like the ocean pulsing evenly from far across the Pacific till it met the land. A great feeling of peace came over me as I scaled the hills, first up, then down, then up again.

At last the ghost stopped moving. I realized that I had entered the Sunset District. We were closer to the ocean here, and already I could see the horizon begin to lighten, the first feathers of light sprouting in patches of pink and coral on the eastern hills.

The ghost was hovering over a brick building that looked very much out of place against the modest rows of two-story Victorians that were so common in this part of the city. As the sun rose, it caught the corner of a brass plate tacked beside a door.

"The San Francisco Stillness Zen Center."

I shot a look back up at the ghost. She seemed to smile at me, and then she melted into the roof of the structure. The sun was really rising now, heating up the particles in the air, turning the brick building from gray to bronze. As if on cue, I heard the sound of men and women chanting. Still dressed in my nightgown, I pushed open the door and went inside.

I knew something of the history of the Stillness Center from neighborhood gossip and news programs. A group of Japanese Americans had bought the four-story brick structure in the thirties. It had originally been built to serve as an institutional facility for single Jewish women, and this accounted for its many dorm rooms, the kitchen, inner courtyard, and assembly hall; the latter was now used by Buddhist students as a meditation center.

Large arched windows gave the entire structure a sunny disposition. The inside smelled of fresh white paint. As I wended my way through the corridors, I saw dozens of students, some whose faces were familiar. But there were many more I had never seen before. All were moving slowly and thoughtfully in one direction. I followed them to a set of double doors flung open to reveal the meditation room.

It was a fairly plain space, spare, but filled with people seated on small square mats. They were chanting. I was so overcome from the long walk, the sound of these voices, and the sudden rush I felt from the sun, that I almost forgot the reason I was here. In the presence of so many living people, I felt as though the ghost were from some strange nightmare and I'd followed it until morning and sanity had descended on me.

A young man met me just inside the door and placed a finger to his lips, then knelt down to retrieve a meditation mat from a stack he had beside him. He held the mat out to me and I took it from him and began to thread my way through the meditators, looking for a small spot for myself. I found a place at the back and settled down, marveling that my nightgown really didn't look all that out of place amid these men and women wearing robes in gray and brown.

On the far end of the room was an elevated podium, perhaps two feet off the ground. Half a dozen men and one woman were seated there, their eyes closed, their mouths moving in time to the *sutra*. In the very center of this group sat a man, his lips fixed in a half smile, even while he chanted. His pale face and self-assured quietness struck a nerve deep within my body.

It was Snowden-roshi.

Light streamed in from the tall windows, nearly flush to the ceiling. I looked up and saw a tall wooden case before me. I hadn't seen it when I'd first looked into the room because I'd approached the hall from the side and thus had apprehended the case only at an angle. But now I had a full view of its contents. In the top shelf was some kind of black-and-white document, written in Japanese.

And below this, rooted in place as though she'd always been there, was the *kannon*.

An invisible being sucked out the air from the space directly in front of me. I tilted forward and felt a cold breath press against my forehead. I could feel one of the *kannon*'s thousand arms reaching out to save me. The sun, now bursting through the windows, highlighted her nimbus as though it were rising specifically for her.

"What are you doing there?" I whispered to her.

But she was caught behind the glass and I couldn't hear what she said. I started to feel ill and began to breathe out of rhythm with the rest of the group. Then I was perspiring, breaking into a cold sweat. I stood up suddenly, knocking into the man seated in front of me. He turned to see who had struck him, thus disturbing the woman to his left. A small sea of heads broke their concentration and turned to look at us. Others followed suit. By the time Snowden-roshi opened his eyes to see what had dampened the enthusiasm of his followers, I had regained my composure. I left the mat where it was on the floor and strode out into the middle of the temple to face him.

He said, "Good morning. You know, we always welcome beginners." He realized who I was and seemed momentarily to lose his composure. Then he nodded at me as though we were complicit in some joke the others in the room would only now understand. He stood up, went over to the case, and pulled the *kannon* out with one hand, beckoning me with the other to come stand beside him.

"I would have come to you eventually, you know. But I am glad you are here." He turned the figure over gingerly, so I saw the underside of her base. There was a panel here, which he twisted and removed. Then he shook the statue, and a small red box fell into the palm of his hand. He handed the box and panel to me. I opened the box and started at the sight of a small piece of bone inside. Next, I examined the piece of wood. There in the center was a stamp. I could just make out the faded characters: Muryojuji temple.

"The thing is, Rumi, I can't go to Japan," Snowden-roshi said quietly, "But you, Rumi, you can go."

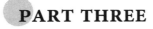

PART THREE

CHAPTER 9

To the Moon

Satomi
Tokyo, 1968

The Japanese criminal justice system has a conviction rate of nearly 100 percent. This is because we are a thorough people and only the guilty are ever arrested. No one I knew had ever been in trouble with the law before, and I couldn't help but think that Timothy must have done something very wrong or the police wouldn't have come for him in the first place. I'd gone to a foreign country and had the self-control not to do anything illegal. Even when the French had picked on me, I had at least behaved with dignity.

Eventually I calmed down enough to realize that Timothy was dependent on me as his liaison. I would need to put some of my Japanese outrage aside. In the afternoon, after I had tried and failed to reach someone helpful on the phone, I bought a cheap skirt, matched it to a blouse, and went to the precinct where Timothy was being held. I asked for a meeting. Impossible, I was told. Prisoners weren't allowed to receive guests as though they were dignitaries languishing in a state-sponsored hotel. I protested that Timothy was a foreigner and barely able to communicate even his basic needs in Japanese. Most likely there had been a misunderstanding, which he wouldn't be able to clarify without the aid of an interpreter. Not to worry, I was told. Timothy's attorney had secured an interpreter.

His attorney?

"Yes," said the man in the blue suit behind the glass window. "Of course we got in touch with his attorney once we had a name."

I caught myself before I blabbed that Timothy wouldn't and couldn't have an attorney in Japan because he wasn't familiar enough with the country or its language to have these kinds of contacts. I thanked the man for his help and quickly left the police station, my thoughts tumbling over each other as I struggled to understand what had happened.

Of course, Timothy *had* been to Japan before and it was certainly possible that there were things about him that I didn't know. Over the months that we'd spent together I'd learned something about his habits and his temperament. Despite the easy, laissez-faire quality he liked to project, there was a side to him that was secretive and contained, just as I too hid much of my own personal history.

So, perhaps he did have an attorney. Maybe it did occur to him to contact someone other than me. But whom did he know?

I wandered back to the hotel, where a new desk clerk gave me a wary look. "You have a visitor," he said, nodding at the lobby behind me.

I turned around. There, hidden behind a plant so large I had not seen him when I'd first walked in, was François, the *gaijin* from the memorial. He rose and came to stand beside me, looking a little remorseful, even as he was smiling in an effort to look friendly.

"Hello, Satomi. Can we go somewhere to talk?"

"François. What . . . ?" I began.

"It's about Timothy," he said gravely.

I turned on my heel, dropped my key off at the front desk, and led François outside and down the street to a cheap restaurant serving curry and beer.

François and Timothy had known each other for a long time. They had first met in the United States, where François had been doing something called a "gap year," and discovered that they both had a vague interest in "the East." Over time, they'd managed to focus their interests on Japan and Buddhism. They'd kept in touch over the years through letters and the occasional phone call. Now François was studying for a doctorate at a British university and had come to Japan to do some fieldwork in anthropology. Recently he'd moved away from studying Japanese rituals and become interested in the actual ritual objects, which, he said with a smile, was another way of saying that he'd finally come around to understanding Timothy's interest in antiques. They'd begun meeting quite regularly in Japan when Timothy had been over on buying trips and François had been visiting temples to study the *mudras* of various statues and the artifacts that priests used while chanting and conducting ceremonies.

François had heard Timothy speak of me so often that he'd become intrigued. In all the years that he'd known Timothy, François hadn't heard about a single woman who'd been able to pin down his fascination for such a long time. Art dealers weren't known for their long attention spans. They liked to find beautiful pieces, sell them, and then move on. And yet here I was, the girl whom so many other women would like to have been, accompanying the very charming Timothy Snowden in Paris, then Amsterdam, and now Japan. François had become curious.

"So," I said slowly, "it was not an accident that you came to Muryojuji temple."

"Well, that's just it," François sighed. "It was meant to seem like an accident. I assumed I'd meet you again at some later date and I'd go through the motions of being amazed to have met you before." I was interested to learn that Timothy had apparently been somewhat possessive of me. He'd rejected François' offer to come to Kyoto to meet us both. Then Timothy had let it slip on the phone that I was rushing off to Hachinohe and next to Muryojuji temple for a memorial service. "I wasn't that far away," François said. He had seized the moment and decided to come to Muryojuji temple himself, playing his *gaijin* card and hoping that his odd appearance, Buddhist robes and all, would be reason enough for him not to be shooed off the property.

He'd reported on the meeting to Timothy, who'd responded as François had predicted: anger, amusement, admiration. They were, after all, friends, but male friends, which meant they were rivals and always jockeying to see who was in a superior position. I was glad to hear that Timothy was annoyed at François for peering into my life at such a personal and critical moment. "I told him he was being silly," François said. "I think I did you a favor, cheering you up when it was so obvious that your family wasn't helping you out at all. I thought he should be grateful."

It had seemed something of a coincidence at the time to find another foreigner wandering at the temple during the memorial. But I'd taken it as a sign that I was different, perhaps even better than the rest of my family, and that this was why fate had conspired to send François to me that day. It was true that his presence had been enough of a distraction to keep me going through the most grueling moments of that ordeal.

"What kind of person," I said, "spies on someone else on the saddest day of her life?"

"Oh, a word like *spying* makes me sound so cold war. I was just curious. But no need to feel self-conscious. You were fine. Really. Intense in your emotions. I was charmed."

I twisted the tissue-thin napkin on the table. "I am not self-conscious."

"Of course you are. Everyone is. But the fact is that we are all always being watched, judged, evaluated. At least I've come clean about it." He fidgeted, like a small child who had misbehaved and hoped to get back in the good graces of a parent.

"I want to talk about Timothy. Did you find him an attorney?"

"Actually, Timothy had the police contact me. I told them I was his attorney. Not exactly true, but technically the police will only contact an attorney, so he pretended I was his guy. I called the embassy, and they set up a translator, and a real attorney. And here we are."

"Do you know why he is in prison?"

"Drug charges. Something about getting caught in Roppongi with marijuana."

"*Gaijin* ghetto," I muttered.

"Seems he was bored while you were away." François grinned. Then he reached out to touch my shoulder, and the waitstaff in the restaurant looked over in alarm. I was hyperventilating.

"Breathe," he said. "Slower."

I tried to catch my breath, to force myself to breathe evenly. I felt my head grow light, watched as the contours of the objects on the table faded. Drugs. I knew that the Japanese legal system would have little tolerance for what Timothy considered a minor indulgence akin to a glass of wine. They would punish him harshly. Now everything began to bleed together, before turning white. I swallowed one deep mouthful of air. And then another. The world, in all its hard and ugly colorful reality, reasserted itself. "What do we do?"

"We?" François smiled. "And here I was ready to convince you that you need my help."

I shrugged so his hand came off my shoulder. "What do we do for Timothy?"

"We have to wait," he said. "Look. This is going to take some time, even if Timothy is found innocent, which he won't be. You know what the conviction rate is in Japan. When he's found guilty, he'll be stuck here for quite a while, if they don't deport him."

"We had . . . plans," I said.

"Yes, I know."

"Do you?"

"Yes! Timothy told me. You had plans to sell a number of items to some *collector*. Do you know where he is?"

I bit my lip. "No."

"You're a terrible liar, Satomi."

"I'm not lying," I opened my eyes wide, till they watered. Then I dabbed away the tears and continued. "I don't know exactly what he planned to do. It is true that we bought things together. But, as you can hear, my accent is very thick," I said demurely. "I make many mistakes in English."

"Your English sounds fine."

"Timothy conducts the business. I am just a . . . helper." I tried to affect a look of self-deprecation.

At this, François sat back in his seat and looked at me, tapping his fingers together. I swallowed my beer slowly to give myself time to think. François' demeanor alerted me. He wasn't exactly like my old piano professor in Paris, but there was something professorial about him, a desire to provoke and to instruct and fascination at the thought that I could be guided to understand something new. I think this is the first inkling I had that François, while he was a foreigner like Timothy, was a very different person. I'm the first to admit it can be hard to tell the difference between the faces of Westerners. Even today it's tempting for me to think that foreigners will all be one of two things: graceful and kind, or crude. That afternoon I knew that I was being tested by a very intelligent person. If I wanted to maintain any kind of autonomy, I would have to be discreet and cautious.

"I am tired," I said. "I will go back to the hotel."

"Of course." Then his face softened and the air between us changed for a moment, the way fog lifts and temporarily provides a view of a previously hidden landscape. "We haven't exactly gotten off to a good start. I know that, Satomi. But let me tell you something. I am a much better connoisseur than Timothy. He has energy and charm and all that, as you know, but he doesn't really know the dynasties or how to authenticate anything. If you would consider working with me, I think you'd find that I am a more equal partner. We might even have fun building a little business together."

Timothy was held for twenty-three days, the maximum amount of time someone could remain in prison until appearing before a judge. Those twenty-three days were a strange period.

I have heard stories of women who collapse from grief, abandoning themselves to mourning, taking to bed and crying. I had no such time to indulge my emotions, for I had, quite frankly, encountered a crisis even larger than grief. I was without a place to call home.

Often I was seized with anxiety and completely unable to sleep. I sat in the hotel room and looked out the window at pedestrians going about their daily lives: to work, to the store, to school. I couldn't imagine a time when my life would ever be ordered enough again for me to be engaged in such routine and calm behavior. Instead, waves of emotion possessed and destabilized me. Occasionally I thought about running away with all the merchandise in the middle of the night when François was sleeping. But really, where would I go?

Masayoshi. Why hadn't Masayoshi seen my predicament and come to help me? Was he so deferential to custom that he expected me to do as my stepsisters wished? I couldn't very well return to France since the Horie family had made it clear they would not fund my studies. Sanada-sensei had said that the piano was her first love, but I felt no similar attachment calling me back to my previous life. It was as though my pride in my past successes had simply evaporated in light of all that had happened in the past few days.

I had loved my mother. I did not love the piano.

If I stayed in Japan and went to the house in Hachinohe, I'd have to scratch out a living until I was married off to a man Mineko and Chieko deemed suitable for me, and who knew the kind of person they would pick? I couldn't very well look up Shinobu and throw myself on her mercy; my problems were too vast for my practical friend to handle now that she was busy with a baby, and anyway, I had not heard from her in months. The only other alternative I could think of was to stay in Tokyo, get some service job, and find a little room to rent. And then what?

When I was feeling particularly angry, I enacted scenes in my mind in which I scolded my mother for dying, or successfully pulled Mineko's hair so hard that she hit her head on the pavement and never recovered. How completely useless to have only broken her hand all those years ago.

The entire time I thought about these things, waking, sleeping, smoking, barely eating, there was François hovering nearby, asking if I was okay, asking if there was something he could do for me. His energy never flagged. He brought me beer and *sake* and urged me to drink. He told me that Timothy's case was probably not very good, but that he would be there to support me no matter what happened.

And every now and then, he asked if I was certain I did not know where the collector lived.

After two weeks of waiting, I went through Timothy's things, making sure that François was taking a nap in his own room and would not come by for one of his impromptu visits. I found Timothy's small black leather book with names and numbers written inside. The writing was childish and hasty and often hard for me to make out. Then, as now, I could only read English easily if the letters were carefully printed. I sat at the desk of the hotel room with a blank sheet of paper, a pen, and a cigarette resting in an ashtray. I went through the book very carefully.

I deduced that any phone number that began with 415 was for someone in San Francisco. For a couple of hours, I struggled to decipher the whorls and angles that made up Timothy's brand of English. There were quite a few women's names on my list. I crossed these out. Only five men remained.

I scratched out a hasty script to follow. To be honest, I was terrified to make a phone call in English. To this day, I hate the phone, even if I am certain the other person is Japanese. A phone does not transmit the image of a young woman bowing out of embarrassment. I smoked a couple of cigarettes to fortify myself and then I calculated the time difference.

No one answered at the first two numbers.

A young man answered at the third. He was difficult for me to understand and I hung up the phone without continuing the conversation. Then

I dialed the fourth number. The minute I heard that curt, almost English voice, I knew I had my man.

"Hello. My name is Satomi Horie. I am in Tokyo. I am calling the collector."

He made some jokes about a tax collector and something about parking tickets. When he finished rambling on, I started again.

"I am friend of Timothy Snowden. I have antiques to sell to you."

"You *hyaboo*?" he roared with laughter. "*Hyboo anoo teekoo*. You guys will never learn to stop adding those extra syllables, will you? Can't even imagine a universe where a consonant isn't connected to a vowel."

I persisted. "One is very nice Korean bowl. Also I have plate."

"Not getting it, are you, girl? Listen. I don't know how you got this phone number. I'm not surprised that Timothy is sampling local cuisine while he's in Japan. Hope he tipped you fair and square. Maybe he didn't. Maybe he didn't have enough cash and you and your bosses got angry and he handed you this phone number and told you it was worth a million yen. Maybe you stole it from his pocket. Who knows? Point is, I don't care. Get it? I come to Japan, I have friends who give me the kind of thing you have for sale. They know I like your nice long backs and short little legs and flat asses. But you let *them* take care of me."

"Antique . . . ," I began again.

"No more, little *anoo teekoo*. Tell your *yakuza* friends the American says no, a word you might consider adding to that convoluted language of yours. I have friends, by the way. You call again and I'll have them find you. Understand?"

I hung up the phone. The man was thousands of miles away, yet I shook as though he were staring at me through the window. It was times like this that I hated being Japanese. I could drape myself in shame so quickly, and it was an intractable garment to cast off. I took a shower, felt dirty, then took another. I thought of the mineral baths I'd enjoyed with my mother. I needed one of those, yet here I was stuck in Tokyo with bags of useless merchandise and a collector who would not speak to me.

After twenty-three days, we learned that Timothy had been found guilty and that he would be spending two years in jail. He was being moved immediately to a prison outside Tokyo. The attorney who came to see us briefly said that in time Timothy would probably be able to send and re-ceive mail, but that visits would always be out of the question. So it was that François and I found ourselves again sitting in the curry restaurant and discussing our next move.

"What will you do now?" he asked.

"I don't know."

"I could still help you."

I employed my Japanese *shirankao,* my *I don't know* face, to keep him from reading what I was thinking.

"You aren't the sort of woman who sits idly by wondering what to do with her life, or waiting for someone to rescue her," François declared. "You are the kind of woman who can't help but look for a way out of a trap. The same way a cat does."

"You know my mother has just died." I lowered my eyelids.

"I find the demure damsel-in-distress routine fascinating, and you are quite good at it." François smiled. "But you mustn't think I'm going to be as easy to persuade as some of the other men you've met. Like that priest, for example, who is clearly still in love with you."

My *shirankao* became harder to keep in place. "Who?"

"The priest who performed the ceremony. Couldn't keep his eyes off you. I see that you know what I'm talking about."

I thought again of Masayoshi in his temple, of the house in Hachinohe, and then of Timothy. I studied François' face, watched his bemused ex-pression fade to a blank canvas so it was hard for me to read him, like a room whose light is slowly turned off so you cannot see the corners where the ceiling meets the walls.

I said, "Timothy will be in prison for two years. Even if he is sent to an American territory to finish his sentence, he will have to go to Guam, not to America. It will take him a long time to go home."

"Yes.

"He is my partner." I hesitated. "Actually, he is my employee. My trans-lator. I need him to sell merchandise. Now he will be busy for a long time and I still need a translator."

François brightened. In a patient voice he asked, "And who will you sell these things to?"

"The collector."

"And where is the collector?'"

I smoothed my skirt. "San Francisco."

We did not have the collector's name. Timothy's notebook included only a phone number. François tried to call again from Japan, but this time no one answered. "I think," he said, "that we should just go to San Francisco."

"It's far."

"Not as far as it used to be."

I glanced outside. How comforting it was to see signs in Japanese instead of French. Even though I'd already decided that my future here was going to be somewhat limited, I felt extremely reluctant to leave the place I associated with my mother, with Masayoshi, with university life—in short, with everything that had at one point been important to me. Grief will play tricks on you. If I left Japan, then my mother would truly be dead. If I stayed here in the hotel room, I'd forever be close to the moment when I'd learned she was dead, which was almost like going back in time to a period when she had been alive and my direction in life had been clear.

"Look," François said, "you already know that leaving Japan doesn't mean you won't ever come back."

"If I leave," I said, "things might change."

"Everything is always changing, whether we want it to or not. Staying here won't bring your mother back to life, or get Timothy out of jail. But if we find the collector and sell off these antiques, then we'll both have more than we have right now. And how could that be anything but positive in the long run?" He was happy to leave Japan and abandon his academic career, which he said wasn't amounting to much in the first place. He saw helping me to sell off the antiques as an opportunity, a chance to change his fortune. He promised, out of deference to his friendship with Timothy, to treat me respectfully and equally.

François tried to call the collector as soon as we arrived in San Francisco, but he was abruptly cut off. When he tried to call back, the line was busy. A day later, the line had been disconnected.

"The problem," François said to me, "is that we need an introduction. I will take care of that."

"What about me?"

He smiled. "If I were you, I'd play tourist. Go see the Golden Gate Bridge."

Haight-Ashbury. Don't worry. I'll take care of everything else." It might take more than a few months to get an introduction, but he would make certain that we survived. We wouldn't be wealthy for a while, but the wonderful thing about California and its climate was that it was possible to be poor and still live comfortably. We would live north of San Francisco in a van in a town called Bolinas. While I acclimated to the United States, he would dedicate himself to selling a few of the smaller pieces and to building what he called "connections."

I suppose that in other circumstances, I might have enjoyed San Francisco. When I look at photos of it now, or when I see it on television programs or movies, it strikes me as a colorful, decorative town with rich sunlight and eccentric characters. I should have been happy in such a place. If Timothy had been with me, I might have found a way to enjoy its easygoing culture.

Instead, I found it to be an unruly city, and far too cheerful for its own good. In California, people seemed to believe that anything actually was possible and anything imagined could be turned into reality. Flying saucers. Rock-and-roll superstardom. Finding a mysterious collector in the unfamiliar world of Asian art connoisseurship among Westerners.

I wasn't happy; I was scared. What if we didn't find the collector? What would happen to us then? "You must have some faith, Satomi," François would say, "in me if in nothing else." I told him that I didn't know what he meant. Having faith, as far as I could see, meant waiting and waiting for something to happen while I did practically nothing to ensure that it would actually come about. This seemed like a ridiculous way to conduct one's life. None of my successes had ever been won on the basis of this thing called faith.

I got a job. I humiliated myself by working at a vegetable shop in the Inner Richmond neighborhood near Golden Gate Park. The job paid me half in cash and half in vegetables. While I rang up bags of carrots and beans, François claimed to be out making "connections" and observing the few other dealers who had already set up shop in town. Some days he returned home not having made a sale, but having bought an additional piece of inventory, often with the money I had made, so I needed to work even more to pay for gas and our other expenses.

"How can we ever make any money if you just spend what I earn?" I asked him.

"Be patient," he said. "One day all this excess inventory will be worth something. I promise you. I didn't bring you to America so you would end up in a vegetable shop."

But his unpredictability made me nervous. "Please," I said. "Just find the collector."

To be fair, I knew that he was working. He kept notes. He listed all the antique stores and the names of the owners and their family members. Every now and then, one of them would buy our smaller dishes. The Butterfield auction house, a very small establishment, held monthly sales of antiques that François attended in order to learn who the major dealers might be. He bought men coffee and drinks.

"You are still spending more money than we are earning," I said.

"Just be patient." He smiled at me.

He often came back to the van with a little bouquet of flowers or some little gift he thought I would like. I was usually annoyed when he did this because it meant he had once again spent money on something that we did not need. He would laugh and say, "I do intend to make you like me, Satomi. So don't expect me to give up." I often felt that uncomfortable feeling of expectation between us, as though he wanted something from me and was waiting for me to understand what it was. I always shied away from this strange, tense energy. I realize now that we were engaged in a kind of courtship, but at the time, I was too frightened about my circumstances and the future to understand what was happening.

One night, when I thought I could no longer bear living in America in this fashion, and when I thought I might have to humble myself even further by going back to Japan and asking Mineko for help, François came home elated.

"I have the name of the collector."

San Francisco's wealthy group lived in a neighborhood known as Nob Hill. Buildings, businesses, and universities were named after these people: Getty, Packard, Stanford. Our collector's name was Brice. He was descended from an old oil family and lived with his wife and children. To the public, he was a man who donated to the opera and attended his children's sports games. To the antique dealers, he was a man whose hunger for Asian antiques was as notorious as his thirst for Oriental women. The newspapers didn't dare acknowledge this side to his life; he sat on all of their boards. But the dealers knew of his activities and didn't care. To the dealers, he was simply the big fish, the top prize to catch. Everyone wanted him as a client.

"We need an introduction," François told me. "He's a strange, paranoid person and he won't deal with strangers."

About a week later, François said, "What we really need is high-quality photos of the best pieces."

A week after that, we had our invitation.

I still remember going into the collector's home. My eye was drawn not to the glass case filled with porcelains and the Renaissance tapestries hanging in the entryway, but to the large glass window in the living room framing a clear blue sky, Alcatraz, and an enormous tanker bearing a Japanese flag.

The collector himself was surprisingly short—at least a foot shorter than François. He was wiry and tan and had a full head of white, curly hair, something I'd never seen before. He was also very alert and kept his head tilted up, as though he were sniffing the air like a dog searching for an unfamiliar scent.

It was a quick meeting, all over in half an hour. The collector spoke mostly to François, though he made plenty of references to me.

"There are many forms of connoisseurship," he said to François. "I see we share the same taste in certain things."

François grinned. "Isn't she a treasure though?"

"I've sampled many women in Japan." The collector nodded. "Back in the day, the government had programs for men like me. Pity they've ended. But you've found yourself a companion anyway."

"For now," François said in a way that indicated I might be for sale too.

The collector bought almost all the dishes, then asked if we had anything else.

"Some sculptures," François said.

"No, no." The collector shook his head. "Sculpture's not my thing right now. Tell me something. What are you going to do with the big fat check I'm about to write?"

"Oh." François pursed his lips and pretended to think. "Buy more inventory, I suppose. Start a proper business."

"Good. I like to make investments. A word of advice, however."

"Please." François nodded.

"Anything you have that might be hot, you keep locked away for a decade or so. Understand? Only bring it out when it's off Interpol's radar. In the meantime, you'll call me when you have something legal and special?" He took out his checkbook. "And to whom shall I make this out? I don't do cash."

"François des Rochers," François answered smoothly.

"I would like 70 percent," I said to François later when we were alone.

He grinned. "And they say the Japanese aren't direct. Look, we only sold those pieces because I could speak English without an accent and charm everyone into thinking that I actually knew what I was talking about."

"We made a sale," I said slowly, "because I had collected all those objects and I knew what they were."

His eyes twinkled. "I'll give you 10 percent. After all, the check was made out to me. You want any more, you'll have to work for it."

"We should share."

"Sure we should. But then you'll tear out of here on the first plane you can catch and I'll never see you again and that would make me sad. On a practical note, I have a business to get started and I need your help. You can quit smelling like vegetables, get cleaned up, and assist me for a while. Once we've earned a little more money, we'll talk percentages that are more partnership-like." He grinned.

I seethed. Did he have any idea what it had been like for me to be working in that vegetable shop while he wandered around San Francisco, doing who knew what and pretending to have an important job? I'd debased myself more than he knew. My mother, had she been alive, would never have allowed me to work in such a filthy place, and now he was adding insult to injury and refusing to pay me money that he damned well knew I deserved.

He listened, patiently, and occasionally made little comments like: "But the thing is, Satomi, we have no contract. You have no legal basis to get any money from me." And then there was: "How will Timothy feel once he learns you left him in Japan and went off to make the money on your own?" And even: "You know you're not even legal in this country." As I cried and cried, unleashing all the emotion I had stored since my mother's death, François remained almost impassive, countering each of my pleas like this, refusing over and over again to give me any more cash.

Eventually I grew exhausted from my outpouring of emotion and sat down, too tired to cry and thinking over the events of the past year. Would I have taken the money and run away as François predicted? I might have. But it also wasn't as though I had any place that I really wanted to go. I didn't want to go back to Japan, and what would I do in Europe now that I had abandoned my music career?

I heard François moving around nearby. "Look at this." He pulled a large photograph out of an envelope. "I'm thinking I could fix the damage."

I turned around to see a photograph of a six-panel screen. Though my eyes were swollen by now, I still strained to see the photograph. It was an amusing scene in which beaky-nosed foreigners with big hats sat in ships hoping to trade with Japanese standing on a gilded shore. Gold-colored clouds blossomed around both parties, a shape mirrored in the swelling water cradling the boats. In a corner, where one screen panel ended and another started, there was a large tear.

"I think I could paint what's missing," he said, pulling out a few pieces of loose paper from the same envelope. "Have a look."

They were sketches, proposed repairs for the missing corner of the screen. I looked back and forth from the painting to François' work. At the time, it seemed like a daring thing to do: copying the hand of a master, for the undamaged part of the screen was most certainly beautiful.

"This looks like it is from the eighteenth century," I sniffed.

"Early seventeenth," François replied quickly. "The *shoguns* had thrown foreigners out by 1639."

I snuck a look at him. His expression was quite serious and I thought to myself that if he were always this sincere and knowledgeable, I might have been able to like him from the very start.

"Maybe it is a copy," I suggested, more to test him than anything else.

"A copy? By the eighteenth century, no one could do faces quite like the ones you see here. No, this is a very good seventeenth-century screen and I think that we could sell it for a good profit if I could just fix the missing corner."

I took a pencil off the little table we used for eating and for work and drew in a few lines on François' drawing. "It would be better," I said, "if the water had a curve like this." I added a few more lines. "And you are right that there should be a plume here where the water hits the rock. But not so fancy. You don't want to draw attention to the missing corner. What I have done is more what you would call 'stylized.'"

He took the piece of paper from me and grinned. "The most difficult part will be matching colors. Finding the right paint. I'll have to befriend a museum curator next."

"I think," I said slowly, "that you will be able to do this."

He glanced at me sideways. "So you have finally developed some faith in me."

I didn't say anything right away. I just stood up and began to look through our tiny refrigerator for some ingredients to make dinner. François, for once, did not press me, though I could feel him beaming even when my back was turned to him. It was only after we had eaten—grilled fish, rice, *miso* soup—that I said to him, "I could help you."

"Yes," he agreed. "You could. Maybe you'll even start to like it here. Maybe you'll even like me as much as I like you."

So I stayed. I have no one to blame but myself. No one forced me. Certainly not François. I could have left even without the money, but again— where could I go? I occasionally saw young women my age from Japan and Korea on the streets of San Francisco, and they had a bruised look about them, like one of those vegetables I'd learned to pick out and throw away for having been handled one too many times at the market where I had worked as a cashier. I was aware that I could be like them, that I did have even further to fall. Would that happen to me? Might leaving be even worse?

"You promise to pay me?" I asked François.

"Of course." He smiled. "But we must be fair."

Not too long after that we received our first letter from Timothy. I'd been writing regularly, but each letter had been returned to me unopened. I had initially kept my letter writing a secret from François, but he'd come home one day when I hadn't expected him and had intercepted the mail. In a patient voice, he said, "It will be awhile before he is out of prison, Satomi."

"I still want to try to write to him."

"Of course."

Then a month went by and my most recent letter hadn't come back to me. Once again I held out hope that Timothy would be able to read the letter himself, and I was rewarded one day when a thin aerogramme came to our new address in the Marina District of San Francisco, postmarked from

Japan. Finally, the elaborate Japanese legal system had allowed my last letter to reach its intended reader, and Timothy, recently awarded rights to
pen and paper, had written back.

Mostly he wrote of his experiences in prison during his first year. In
the beginning he had been forced to stand in a room with no chair and
not quite enough room to lie down. On the few occasions that he'd tried to
sit on the floor, a guard had come in and hoisted him to his feet. When he
wanted to urinate, he was given a plastic cup. After ten days he was trans-
ferred outside of Tokyo to Chiba, a nearby village, and given a room with
a small cot. At night the light was left on in his cell and when he tried to
cover his eyes to sleep, a guard would scream at him until he removed his
arm from his eyes.

He told me that he became friendly with the other prisoners in cells
near his and that they prayed together. One man was from the Philippines
and had come to Japan to work as a gardener but had overstayed his visa.
Another man, a Korean, was accused of raping his neighbor's daughter.
Timothy taught them the fragments of the Lord's Prayer that he remembered, and they taught him to chant Buddhist *sutras*. Through the bars
of his cell, Timothy mimicked the lotus position that the Korean showed
him, and learned how to meditate.

I wrote back, asking if he was eating enough and telling him that I had
come to America with "luggage" and that I hoped he didn't mind that I
had sold his "clothes" at a garage sale. He told me about the powers he was
commanding, how he was able to remain calm when the guards beat him
for failing, again, to sign his confession, and how much weight he was losing on his prison diet. "The Korean," he wrote, "tells me that Buddhist
priests in training eat practically the same thing. I'm basically doing the
whole Buddhist boot camp, and if I can just focus on that, I'll quit thinking of this as a level of hell and more like an experience." I wrote to tell him
of life in San Francisco, how the city turned pink in the morning and evening, unlike any other place I'd ever seen in my life. I asked if there was
some place I should visit that he could imagine, some place we could both
be, where we could pretend to be together.

He told me how if he concentrated hard enough on his prison walls, he
could see a *mandala* emerge from the cracks in the concrete.

For one brief, wry moment I allowed myself to see the humor in having
loved two men who'd turned to Buddhism. Then I was just annoyed by the

self-righteous tone he'd adopted. He asked no questions of me in any of his letters. He didn't want to know how I liked living in America, he didn't express any regret that my mother had died, and he didn't even comment about the sale of his "clothes." All his letters were simply about himself.

François found Timothy's letters amusing. "It is true," he said, "that this description of prison is an awful lot like the monastery." François told me how he himself had arrived in Japan determined to become the first Western man ever to survive the Buddhist training at the famed monastery of Eiheiji temple as part of his fieldwork. He wouldn't be like the last applicant, an American, who'd been carried out on a stretcher, emaciated. He was going to become a full-fledged priest. He'd stood outside the temple gates, all six foot three of him, and begged for entrance alongside other hopeful initiates. Though the priests inside had ignored him even longer than they'd ignored the other waiting men outside, they'd eventually let him in, giving him a bowl of *miso* soup to drink and a bowl of rice to eat. Then he'd begun his days trying to sit *zazen,* or meditation, and cringing each time he'd been hit on the back with a bamboo stick.

He'd left the temple after two months because a visiting priest named Yamagata-roshi had come by for a visit and, in broken English, had said, "There must be another way to experience religion."

And then, he said so sincerely that I almost believed him, he'd gone to Muryojuji temple and seen a girl so unusual, he'd fallen in love with her in an instant. Love, he said, was a much better way to be close to any of the many gods roaming the planet. It was a shame that Timothy had never learned this, or if he had, that he'd been able to forget the lesson so quickly.

Timothy's letters continued to come to us, though they were always filled with philosophy and I learned to skim their contents. I suppose I never completely gave up hope that he would show some curiosity about my situation, but mostly I accepted that he had changed in some fundamental way and that he was no longer as interested in me as he had been. Then they came at increasingly wider intervals until they stopped coming at all. It was only much, much later when I'd returned to Japan that I thought over those letters again and wondered if he had worded them so strangely because he was in prison and was subject to extreme censorship.

We drifted along, François and I, growing the business and delighting when we made a sale.

"Congratulations, Satomi," he said, holding out a fistful of cash. "I'll tell you what. If you let me kiss you, I'll give you an extra 10 percent."

"No."

"One kiss."

"No," I said. "Just work. We just work."

Work we did. I kept track of all the pieces, drawing little sketches in notebooks and leaving the descriptions for François to write in by hand. I was responsible for reading signatures and seals, though he was studying *kanji* characters and making some progress with his language abilities. Even now I must admit that he was a very good connoisseur. I was frankly a little bit surprised that a Westerner could know so much about Asian art, know more than I did, in fact.

I was able to enjoy the work. My favorite thing of all was when we found a slightly damaged piece that needed our collective imaginations in order to be repaired. It felt like a game to me. Each wounded sculpture, each defaced painting required a different solution, and it was fun to sit together sketching out solutions on paper.

But the thing I enjoyed the most, the thing that made me happiest, was to see my pile of money grow.

I kept my cash in two places. Since I was, as François had pointed out, an illegal immigrant, I could not open a bank account. I kept most of my money on the dresser in a box. François knew about this stash and he used some of it when we moved from a rented apartment to a house. These were all in François' name because I had yet to apply for a green card, as he did, or citizenship. Every now and then François would propose that we get married so I would not have any legal problems, but I always demurred. I could not see the point of marrying someone I did not love.

I had a second pile of cash—much smaller, but always growing—that I squirreled away in a paper bag I kept at the bottom of my supply of sanitary napkins. François did not know where I hid the cash and, if he was inclined to go looking for it, he would most likely not think to look there. It was on this pile of money that all my hopes rested. If I were ever to leave America, it would be because I'd finally earned enough in my little brown bag.

Eventually, François and I became intimate. At the time it seemed an abrupt transition in our relationship, but I see now how naturally it developed, an outgrowth of the way we celebrated our successes together, how really we had no one to turn to but each other when we made a particularly good sale. Plus, I was lonely in San Francisco and made few friends. Men often wanted to talk to me, but I rarely wanted to talk to them, and it frustrated me that I could not go out for a cup of coffee or a smoke without some teenager sidling up beside me and attempting to start a conversation. It was much easier to go out in the evening if François was present and people naturally assumed we were a couple. Drunk on wine one night, I let him kiss me and he gave me an extra hundred dollars. Things progressed from there. From time to time I even enjoyed myself. Certainly I became accustomed enough to it not to mind.

I became pregnant. I found out the usual way. I felt a sensation vaguely akin to cramping in my abdomen and told myself that my period was on its way, just a little bit delayed. A week later I started to feel nauseous and weak, and when I threw up three mornings in a row, François insisted on taking me to the doctor. François' reaction, when he learned of my condition, confused me.

"Why, that's wonderful." He grasped both my hands and the doctor, a man, beamed at us.

François threw himself into impending fatherhood, signing us up for Lamaze classes and dictating my diet. He told our few acquaintances that he knew (knew!) that Lamaze would keep me from feeling any pain during childbirth. He bragged about my stoic nature. Sometimes I caught him saying things to someone on the phone, some mysterious person he spoke to at odd hours of the night. "Well," I once heard him say, "if it's a girl, then I'll be raising two women. I rather like that idea." When he brought up marriage again, I used a line I'd once heard a hippie say: "Why do you have to define everything?" And he'd laughed and beamed and hugged me and declared that I was a very modern girl, and not at all the kind of stereotypical Asian people were always accusing me of being. "If only people knew," he laughed.

The baby grew. I know that for many women this is an exciting thing. They cannot wait to make contact with the life growing inside them. Certainly the baby was trying to make contact with me. I would dream about her—I knew very quickly that I was going to have a girl. I could feel her thoughts intertwining with mine and I would wake up angry. My dreams, my thoughts, my fantasies did not need the interjection of this other voice. Though it was just a very small baby in the beginning, already its personality was quite clear. She wasn't at all like me, but more like my mother. She would be the kind of child who observed the world with a calculating brain. One day, after observing the bipedal monsters around her, she would simply stand up and walk. She would grow up looking into my heart and knowing that I wasn't sure if I loved her or not. She would know that I had fallen into the life I was leading now and that I had not deliberately chosen it.

Pregnancy can make women emotional and I was no exception. All the things that had seemed so foreign about America now frustrated me. I wanted my rice and *miso* soup every night, not just once a week as François had agreed to when we'd first decided what to eat and how to eat it. I wanted elderly people to stand up and give me a seat on the bus. I wanted to hear children's songs in Japanese and not the kind of rock and roll that filled up the lessons on *Sesame Street,* where puppets with large noses lived in trash cans and fought with each other until the humans intervened. I wanted to know where I would take my child on her third, fifth, and seventh birthdays. Home. I wanted home. Desperately. When I mentioned this to François, he suggested I go to a Japanese American Buddhist temple to look for guidance.

I was unprepared for my reaction when I met with my countrymen, for the sound of so many Japanese voices immediately caused me to burst into tears. Once upon a time I had lived in a country where I had effortlessly understood the language, regardless of dialect or class. Then sentences had washed past my ears like river currents supporting a water bird in her natural habitat. I had grown accustomed to living in America, where absolutely everything was an effort due to its strangeness. I had almost forgotten that there was once a place where I might have been unhappy or frustrated, but where I had always felt at ease.

For a time, I liked visiting the Japanese immigrants and hearing them talk. They were full of advice for the coming baby, what to feed her, what to teach her. Eventually, though, I grew frustrated with them. Most were peasant class, uneducated fishermen and gardeners who knew nothing of antiques or classical music.

What I really wanted was my mother.

I wondered if she had become pregnant with me in a similar fashion, if she had been just as terrified. If so, I understood even less why she had been so willing to escape into the domesticity of the Horie household, why she'd been all too happy to pick up golfing and lunches as though she'd always been destined to be a housewife with three daughters to raise. If it had just been the two of us, we would have managed. She could have come to Paris with me, or moved to Tokyo while I'd been in school. There would have been no neglected afternoon cold that evolved into pneumonia, no large house in Hachinohe filled with debts no doubt accumulated by overeager adopted daughters who had deluded themselves into thinking that their family deserved a better lifestyle than they could afford.

I do not like to remember the birth of the baby, whom we named Rumi, or of the days that followed. Fortunately I have been able to put much of it out of my mind. I do remember that I was physically the most uncomfortable that I have ever been. My skin had been stretched, the weight I had gained from pregnancy did not disappear, and I felt as bloated and heavy as the *umi bozu*, or sea monster, with its fat body and bald head that I now like to draw to frighten small children. What would they say if I told them that my scariest monsters are inspired by what I saw when I looked in a mirror during those terrifying days?

I was dutiful about feeding Rumi. She was always hungry, and I began to wonder how my life had been reduced to being nothing more than a food dispenser. I waited for the moment when everything in my world would feel right and I would be happy to be here with François, when I would be happy to be a mother and to have this little baby, to be in this story that was my life. The moment refused to come. I waited for it. Prayed for it. I sat in a chair by the window and watched the sky turn dark, then watched the sun rise again. I cried and I slept. It was more frightening to me to hold the baby than it was to hold a ten-thousand-dollar piece of porcelain. I might drop her. I might accidentally snap that soft neck. I wouldn't mean to drop her, but it could happen. I would never be forgiven.

All of the melancholy I had felt while I was pregnant now coalesced into one unbearable burden: the baby. I could not give her back, could not set her down for a day or two while I collected my thoughts and decided whether or not I wanted to be a mother. Well, that was just it. I had to be a mother. I didn't like not having a choice. So I'd put her down and go for a walk, and François would find her unattended and he'd scold me.

From the moment the baby was born, François adored her. Almost instantly after her birth, his face took on a different cast that is difficult to describe. He looked . . . satisfied. I did not understand how someone could change so suddenly, and become so contented. It was eerie. Watching him, I knew that he could never understand my frustration, my longing to go home. We'd come such a long way, he declared, and now we were a family. Things were as they were supposed to be. Couldn't I feel just how right it was to have Rumi in our lives? He knew how hard it had been to adjust to living in San Francisco, but why was I having so much trouble *now*?

"Don't you realize," he declared, "how much I love you?"

I didn't realize. At the time, I couldn't even believe him. I searched for a way to respond, but all I ever managed to relay was that I was deeply tired. At this he would relent for a while before growing angry again when I neglected the baby once more.

These were my lowest days. How had I come to this? A girl from Japan full of talent—of passion, Sanada-sensei had said—now living an unremarkable life in America. Worst of all, I couldn't muster the energy to change my circumstances. I was like one of our neighbor's cars that coughed and gurgled in the driveway, but whose engine never managed to catch fire. I wondered if all the rest of my days were going to be the same. So aimless.

And then one day while I was staring out the window, I saw a woman, stooped over, with a basket on her back. She was elderly, perhaps around eighty, but carried her head with dignity, like a dancer. She turned, seemed to see me, and smiled as though we shared a secret before shuffling on and out of sight. I thought of the old woman I'd seen in the bamboo forest so many years ago and of Sanada-sensei and my mother too.

At that moment, I felt split in two. There was the Satomi leaving the baby by the window and going to her room. She removed the brown bag filled with money from her drawer. Why had she been saving all this money if not to give herself some kind of choice?

This Satomi looked at the clock and calculated that François would be home in just a few minutes. She hurried to go out for a walk, knowing that this time she would never return. The other Satomi watched, horrified, but also fascinated that such a choice could be made. She allowed herself to be carried along, fairly certain François would find the baby, just as he always had. But by then the first Satomi would be far away where he could not find her.

PART FOUR

CHAPTER 10

Snow Devils

Rumi
Tokyo, 1991

An hour before my plane landed, a peak of white snow punctured the dual layers of mist and earth. The cabin came to life, and half a dozen people, mostly Japanese men, pulled out their cameras. "Fuji-san!" someone exclaimed. We circled around the mountain, then began to press down against the sky, and rice paddies and little roads with bright blue trucks and slate-roofed houses came into view. I thought of all the little hand scrolls I'd seen over the years. It was as though one of them had come to life, its images growing exponentially until I had fallen down into this landscape I knew so well from pictures and books.

However, the actual land of Japan was quite different from the one I knew from my studies of art. Very quickly, I realized how little conversational Japanese I actually understood. In the terminal, I listened to a recording, first in incomprehensible Japanese, then in studied English, advise me to keep track of my belongings. I exchanged some dollars for *yen,* then boarded a train bound for Tokyo's city center. Through a green-tinted window, I watched bamboo forests and rice paddies, brown in winter, give way to the spread of buildings capped by halos of neon and inscribed with one-word messages: Glico, Seiko, Panasonic. It started to rain, and a cheerful, high-pitched female voice announced that we would soon be making a brief stop.

At Shinjuku station the blond and brown heads of American travelers disappeared into the tide of subway riders and taxicab seekers. I was alone, the heterogeneity of my fellow world travelers diffused by the population of Tokyo.

It was nearly eight in the evening when I reached the hotel. The man at the desk greeted me with a bow and proceeded to walk me through registration. He handed me an envelope containing a note whose English letters had been written with extra courtesy and attention.

A Ms. Shizuka would be coming to see me at eleven o'clock the following morning. She would meet me after breakfast.

A porter carried my things up via an elevator to a sterile room on the fourteenth floor. After he left, I opened the curtains and peered out over the neon horizon. A low spread of buildings swelled and crested to a tidal wave of skyscrapers in the distance. Unlike San Francisco with its centralized downtown, Tokyo was a city in which tall buildings sprouted from a number of neighborhoods, where helicopters winged from district to district across a red sky.

I closed the shades and sat down on the bed. Everything was cold and new and I longed for the green hills of California, for the gentle lapping of the fog in and out of our neighborhood. As so many travelers have before me, I turned on the television and went to sleep.

Seventeen hours behind me, San Francisco whirled slowly, emerging into the dawn of the day I was now leaving.

At eleven the next morning I went down to the hotel lobby and found Ms. Shizuka waiting for me. She was rail thin and elegant, with tiny wrists and slim fingers. She wore an immaculate navy blue suit with a restrictive little blouse that gathered around her throat, and the skin on her face was flawless. Standing in front of her, I felt unkempt and sloppy. It was as though she had mastered all the secrets of the material world. Not even an atom would be out of place in her orbit.

Ms. Shizuka bowed, then extended her hand timidly, as if testing the air between us. We shook hands, then sat down on two large armchairs.

"How was your flight?"

"Fine," I said. "Long. Your English is very good."

She smiled. "Twelve years at the International School here in Tokyo. I went to UCLA for college. Would you like coffee?" She motioned to a hotel attendant.

"Yes please," I said.

While we waited for our refreshments, she reached inside a small briefcase and pulled out a long envelope.

"So, I am here," she said in a formal tone of voice, "because my law firm was contacted by Mr. Sumiyoshi in America. I believe he represents Timothy Snowden?"

"That's right," I said. "Timothy Snowden is a friend of the family. He used to know my mother."

"Our firm was unable to locate any records related to your mother, Satomi Horie. There was such a person at one point, but she has simply disappeared. This is unusual in Japan. We keep good records of all our citizens." She frowned.

"You don't know how she died or where she was buried or anything?" I sank into my chair.

"No. However, we did follow up on the Muryojuji temple connection for you." Now she extracted documents from the envelope. 'The first was a pamphlet. "The Handa family, who live at the temple, have requested that you come to see them."

Our coffee arrived, and while we took a few sips, I examined the brochure. On the cover was some *kanji* lettering, a picture of what looked like a large cabinet with two doors on hinges, and roman letters at the bottom that read "Muryojuji Temple." The cabinet housed a national treasure, a sculpture put on view only once a year. The temple was out of the way, but well known among art devotees for its collection of statues, donated by a pious, not to mention wealthy, *shogun* some three hundred years ago.

"Why do they want to see me?" I asked. "And who are they exactly?"

"It isn't entirely clear," she said. "Masayoshi Handa, the head of the family, is related by marriage to your mother. When we asked for an explanation as to what happened to her, he would not tell us. He only said he wanted to meet you."

She handed me a small map and a train ticket. I would need to take the bullet train from Ueno station to Morioka, then change to another bullet train that would cross the mountains and go all the way over to Akita, in the northwest corner of the main island. The entire trip would take around four hours but she thought I would be comfortable, and she had reserved my seat in the First Class Green car.

"Maybe you have some questions," she said.

"Will anyone speak English?"

"They said they would arrange for an interpreter."

"And if I go see this Handa family, I'll find out what happened to my mother?"

She swallowed. "I am afraid that I do not know. I only . . ."

"I know, I know." I sighed. "You only know that they want to see me."

She smiled, a momentary look of indulgence crossing her face. "You are a *gaijin*. A foreigner. You have a kind of pass in our country. People will, how do you say, cut you some slack?"

"I can get away with asking more questions than you can."

Ms. Shizuka's face relaxed into an intimate, confiding expression. "Aomori Prefecture, where you are going, is a strange place. They have an unusual sense of humor. Many things happen there that do not happen in Tokyo."

"What do you mean?"

"People have been kidnapped by the North Koreans. The Russians used to steal women. That is why all demons in the north have large noses. And there are also many more ghosts in Aomori Prefecture than in Tokyo." She said this with complete sincerity. "It is a shame you must travel there."

"I'll be careful." I tried not to laugh.

"Your train leaves in one hour. We must get going." Then she smiled, as though pleased by her ability to use another English idiom correctly.

The bullet train, that marvel of Japanese postwar engineering, awoke the child in me. For a time, I forgot that I was nervous and that I'd never been far from San Francisco, let alone out of the United States. I walked the full length of the train, end to end, and examinied the toilets, the vending machines, the speedometer. The conductor and attendants echoed the formal dress of the Tokyo hotel clerk, Ms. Shizuka, and the *bento*-box seller from the train station. All had worn navy blue and white, and bowed to me each time I passed. What an *organized* country, I thought.

The landscape fluttered between city and country. Clouds gathered on the horizon, and the sky grew gray, then white. Moisture slapped the windows. The rice paddies, covered by aged stubble close to Tokyo, grew a coat of frost. I spotted cars traveling in the opposite direction with mounds of snow on their roofs, a harbinger of the territory we would enter.

Each time we raced into a particularly long tunnel I felt pressure in my ears, as the tense air struggled to make space for the train. As we emerged, the landscape seemed to grow darker.

Two hours into the trip, the bullet train made an uncharacteristic hic-cup. A young man in a business suit reading a comic book jerked up his head. Older ladies whispered in the hushed sounds of the worried. After a few minutes, a voice came over the loudspeaker, but I couldn't under-stand a thing it said. An English voice assured me that we would soon reach Morioka station, and that passengers should change here to go to Akita. But the fidgety manners of my fellow travelers told me that they knew more than the robotic woman. Or perhaps it was the paranoia of a jet-lagged mind and my unwillingness to trust the pre-prepared bi-lingual signs around the country. In any case, I gathered my bags and disembarked.

It had been snowing in Tōhoku for almost two months straight, a record snowfall, declared the English newspaper that I had picked up at Morioka station. What Ms. Shizuka had not known and my cursory glance at CNN had not told me that morning was that a bullet train had derailed while at-tempting to cross to Akita. The tracks had been closed, leaving thousands of passengers stranded at points north.

I had phoned Ms. Shizuka from Morioka station, but she hadn't an-swered. It was too early in the morning to call the United States, and any-way, what would Timothy tell me to do? I thought of calling Muryojuji temple but, to be honest, I was nervous about reaching someone who spoke only Japanese. I had learned very quickly how unusual it was to have met someone as proficient in English as Ms. Shizuka.

I decided to play my *gaijin* pass to get to Akita. I found a man in uni-form and through hand gestures and broken Japanese explained my pre-dicament. He sent me to another man in a uniform, who passed me on to yet another man, and so on until I found myself boarding a bus with four strangers. The white-gloved driver snapped his hand, waving to some other suited worker, and we pushed off.

Not long after leaving the outskirts of Morioka, the bus began to climb up a fairly steep mountain. I couldn't see much out of the window, but felt the bus tilt and heard the wheels stolidly churn through gravel and snow. The passengers were mostly quiet. One was a boy around my age, in a cheap, well-pressed suit with a pair of loafers, clutching a briefcase perched on his knees. Behind him was an older man with a horsey, toothy mouth, round spectacles, and shaggy, unruly hair. The pockets in his overcoat had been mended a number of times, and the heels of his shoes were worn down. I guessed he was an academic. He had come prepared for this voyage, carrying a case of beer, which he methodically consumed a sip at a time, every now and then smacking his lips. Two women sat together: a petite older lady with deft hand gestures, a youthful smile, and a short bob, and a young woman I assumed to be her daughter, all shadows and frowns, a person accustomed to expecting life's catastrophes.

The road became windier and steeper, and the engine growled as it contended with the incline and curves of the mountain. I felt the bus nudge around a corner, like a cat prying open a door with its nose. I looked out of the window. An oncoming car lit the side of the road for a precious few seconds. Snowflakes the size of dandelions bloomed in the air, their heavy bodies hurtling over the edge of a precarious cliff just off to the left.

Beside me, the student gasped and hunched over his briefcase, breathing deeply. One of the tires slipped against the ice, and the daughter seated ahead of me gripped the side of her seat.

I told myself that if I concentrated, if I followed absolutely every turn of the road, the bus would arrive safely. But when we rounded the next corner, the bus lurched and slid backward again. The two women in front shrieked. The bus began to spin, the large metallic body whining like an animal downed by a powerful predator. Headlights flashed against the white curtain of snow, and my brain collected snippets of information. I saw trees. Now rock. Now ice. We teetered one way, then back again in the opposite direction, and I pictured the bus toppling down the ravine. The bus gave a great groan and we screamed, sliding, careening to the front door as the driver shouted something unintelligible. I had my cheek pressed against the young student, and the professor had his hands against my back. And then, abruptly, all was still. Eerily quiet. Blood raced from my heart to my toes and back. The air in my lungs was thin. I might as well have been on Everest. Synapses misfired like faulty fuses. Snap. Snap. Then, slowly, the machinery of my body regained control of itself and I strained to look out of the window to see where we were.

The bus driver was screaming that we should take our seats. And we did. After all, we were still on the road. Though the driver tried a few times to urge the bus forward, the wheels whirred in place and refused to move. Between the professor and the driver there was an angry exchange, and then the driver stood up and put on his coat, opened the door, and went outside. Almost instantly, a gust of cold air penetrated the cabin, before the professor pulled the handle and wrenched shut the glass door.

The passengers entertained themselves with the habits of the nervously bored. The daughter breathed on the window, then wiped away the condensation. The college student snapped the handle of his bag back and forth in a rhythmic fashion until the professor told him to stop. The professor conducted a disgruntled monologue, then, putting on his coat, stamped outside. When he came back, the cold had sobered him and he barked out a few short sentences that were followed by a lengthy discussion among the passengers. I sat there, helpless. No robotic voice came to my rescue. No bilingual signs told me which way to go.

The professor turned to me. He seemed perturbed, as though it were either my fault that we were in this predicament, or that I, with my limited language abilities, might as well have been suffering from a mental disorder. "Bus driver. Gone." The latter word was emphasized with a wave of both arms, as though the bus driver had struck out in a game of baseball.

"Gone." I mimicked his exaggerated hand movements. I couldn't help it.

The professor continued barking in short phrases. He had found the bus driver's tracks in the snow and was quite certain that the driver either had gone off to find some help, or had abandoned us. The latter was far more likely, given that the bus driver hadn't told us where he was going. In any case, there was a town nearby. We were going to walk there.

Were they nuts? "*Walk?* Wait a minute!" I protested.

"No waiting," the professor retorted.

The mother turned to me and began to chatter happily in Japanese. She held out two tangerines and a pack of rice crackers. "What are you so happy about?" I asked her. Of course she didn't understand me, but continued yammering away. Then she handed me two plastic bags.

"Snow!" the professor barked again, by way of explanation.

I was to tie the plastic bags around my shoes to keep them dry.

We pared our luggage down to one easily carried bag each, and filed off the bus.

How cold I was that day, the coldest I ever remember being in my life. The mother led us, shining a flashlight on the ground. We followed her, holding on to a rope we'd fashioned by tying together various articles of clothing. Each step was a challenge, for the snow was thick in some places and icy in others. Soon we developed a rhythm, a comfortable pace at which the person in front could secure a safe footing before moving on to find another. Then the person behind would occupy the vacated footprint. I don't know how long we went on like this. It seemed like hours, but then I had no sense of our geography and where we were going.

In the beginning, the mother did most of the talking, adding a cheery *"desu ne"* at the end of each of her sentences, to which the professor responded with a few guttural syllables. Gradually the professor's talk began to take over the group. I realized how clever the mother had been. She had engaged in the old female art of winning over a man by getting him to talk about himself. And so as we walked, his baritone came over us all and though I could not understand him, I imagined him informing us of the university where he taught, the books he had written, the cities he had visited, and the home he longed to see at this very moment.

Once we passed a streetlamp marking a long driveway flanked by a sign with the word *hotel* in roman lettering. There was a brief discussion here as to whether or not we should turn off, but in the end the mother and the professor insisted we continue on.

Eventually the snow stopped falling, and the clouds parted. Moonlight hit the white earth and the air took on a silver quality. Now I could see the outline of trees, the shadow of forests on the snow-covered ground. Sometimes I looked ahead and saw the figures trudging before me and I felt as though I were watching a negative of a film unfold in slow motion: white earth, black sky, blue trees. It was eerily beautiful and foreign.

Like a mirage, a soft glow blossomed in the distance. The glow separated into four little balls of light. Were they headlights, perhaps? The beams didn't move very quickly. In fact, they didn't move as evenly spaced objects at all. I became entranced. We all did. You could hear it in the way we matched our footsteps, as though someone were dangling the proverbial pendulum before our eyes and lulling us to sleep.

I tried to fight the sensation. If in fact it was some kind of mirage, if the snow and stress had addled my mind, then I would need to call on all my conscious faculties to see through this illusion. But we continued to move toward the lights, and they toward us, and I started to believe they were real.

Now the road became easier to cross. It had been freshly plowed, and without even speaking to each other, we let go of the rope, the mother rolling the shirts and socks into a ball, which she shoved into her bag. Soon we were walking in our own separate spaces.

The mother became excited. She started chattering at a pitch that was much higher than her regular speaking voice. I smelled something—smoke. The mother called out urgently to the professor and he replied in a burst of syllables.

All at once the lights were upon us. There were four of them. Then they weren't lights at all, but torches held aloft by four of the ugliest, most frightening creatures I had ever seen. Two had red faces, the other two were blue, and all had oversized heads, as large as my abdomen. Their hair was long and matted and coiled, and their bodies were covered with straw. Prickly, angled teeth studded their mouths. Their eyes, which I could now see clearly, were sharply angled into a V. I began to scream. One of the demons began to chase me with his torch.

Chaos. The mother was running after both the demon and me, while the professor stood in place shouting. The three remaining demons roared and shook their torches. I had to stop to catch my breath and as I did so, I saw something strange. The mother was taking photographs. I heard an odd, garbled sound and it took me a full minute to understand that the others in my party were now laughing.

Everyone was laughing at me. Even the devils were laughing.

The demon who had come after me stopped running, his chest heaving up and down, and he planted his torch in the snow at an angle. With one paw, he tugged at his face, and it came off. Beneath his blue skin was another head, a human head. I'd been chased by a man wearing a mask.

I shouted at them all, at the party of bus riders, at the demon who had chased me, at the snow, and at the missing bus driver.

"So this," I screamed, "is an example of your *unusual* sense of humor?"

The professor mimed my outrage. He pulled off his gloves and used his fingers to stretch his mouth into a shape mirroring my indignation. Everyone laughed. Then he did it again, this time posing for a photo. Everyone continued laughing. I didn't find this indignity funny at all. One moment I'd been in an accident, then mesmerized by a stark landscape, and now this inconsiderate practical joke. I started back to the bus. Who the hell knew where these people were going anyway?

The student ran after me, wheedling in a high-pitched, rat-a-tat voice. Out of the corner of my eye, I could see that he was carrying a bottle of something. *"Dōzo. Dōzo,"* he kept repeating.

I stopped and took a look. It was a bottle of beer. I took a tentative sip, half-afraid it wouldn't be beer at all, but another practical joke. But the liquid tasted so good, I downed half of it in seconds.

Through hand gestures, everyone encouraged me to come back to the fold. Two of the demons handed their torches over to the college student and the professor respectively; the professor made the demon wait while he urinated in the snow. One of the red-faced demons reached into his baggy, ratty robes and pulled out a small cup of what I later learned was a prepacked cup of *sake.* The party started to descend the hill and I lingered behind, still insulted. But the student urged me to follow and, really, I had no other option, so follow I did, keeping a small distance lest there be any more surprises.

At the bottom of the hill the road widened into an avenue. The streets were lined with rows and rows of red paper lanterns, orbs of pulsing light. As we climbed stone stairs, the mother and daughter excitedly exclaimed to each other, and the demons, now back in character, growled and tossed their heads. We passed a one-story wooden structure where two women sat, dressed like creatures from another time in white *kimono* tops and red skirts, their long hair tied in back with garlands of purple flowers. They called out to us and held out small cups of tea, which everyone, including me, accepted.

Soon I could hear the faint beating of drums, and the mother and the daughter began to clap their hands in time to the rhythm. The sound inspired the demons, who waved around their torches with vigor, sending sparks into the air.

Now we were joined by other families, by mothers and fathers carrying their kids, and other demons who, upon seeing the children, tried to pick them up and take them away from their parents. The children cried when this happened, but the mothers and fathers just laughed and laughed— then whipped out cameras to take photos.

Up and up we climbed, every now and then pausing on a landing to admire a stone statue of a dog or a lion, or a row of small igloos that had been carved out of the snow and lit with candles. Finally the steps ended and gave way to a wide landing. Two women, each carrying a tray of roasted rice cakes, greeted us. A large bonfire roared and singed the air with sparks. Several dozen demons lunged from foot to foot around the fire in a dizzying, primal dance. Behind the bonfire was a large shrine and on its steps, half a dozen men dressed in nothing but loincloths and bandannas pounded out a rhythm on drums the size of horses.

I couldn't believe that this was where my fellow travelers had intended to end up. And yet there were the mother and the daughter dancing with a demon. Beside them, an elderly woman scolded another demon, smacking him on the shoulder. The professor and the student had found more cups of *sake* and were drinking them together and nodding to each other in the agreeable manner of men engaged in conversation that has been enlightened by drink. I stood off to the side and wondered what I was supposed to do next. My eyes began to tear.

All of a sudden, the professor was back in front of me with two little girls. They were close in age, perhaps three or four years old, and flushed with excitement and exhaustion from having trudged through the snow in heavy red coats and pink boots. When they were just a few feet away, the professor kneeled down and pushed them toward me in the universal language of an adult urging a child to say hello. I squatted down and smiled. As the girls neared me, their chubby, innocent faces melted in horror. First the older one screamed, then the younger began to cry, and both turned to bury their faces in the professor's legs. When I looked at him, intending to apologize, I saw that he was laughing again.

"*Debiru!*" He pointed at me, his face red with drink. He repeated this word a few more times before I understood what he was trying to say. I was a devil.

Now an older woman came to his side, along with a younger couple. There was also a furtive and embarrassed-looking policeman.

"My family," the professor declared. Then he turned to the policeman and the two of them conferred in Japanese, punctuating the conversation with little bows.

The little girls again turned and stared at me with blatant curiosity. I gathered that it was primarily for the entertainment of the children that the professor was now instructing me that I would pass the night at his home. The hotels were sold out, he continued, and it was too late to call the family in Akita I'd been hoping to meet. Surely they would long since have given up expecting me to arrive by bullet train.

"You cannot sleep in snow," he declared, which was true enough.

Now many people were staring at me—the sole *gaijin* who had inadvertently crashed a demon festival. Should something happen to me— if I were murdered, my paranoid mind thought—dozens of people would remember having seen the strange half-Japanese-looking girl speaking to the professor and the little girls. And so, resigned to be a demon among demons for the evening, I tightened my grip on my bag and followed the strange family back down the stony steps to the parking lot.

Eventually I pieced together what had happened that evening. The bus had slipped and stalled not too far from the center of Shishigane town, and the other riders had known that we wouldn't have too far to go. The professor was on his way to meet his family at Shishigane's demon *matsuri,* or festival. He had originally planned to take the bullet train to Akita, then backtrack to Shishigane.

Rain or shine, snow or avalanche, the people of Shishigane had put the festival together for over five hundred years. Contemporary inhabitants were not about to let a small thing like heavy snow and a blocked bullet train passage stall their efforts. Knowing this, the professor had been quite determined to get to the bonfire in time.

The demon *matsuri* was one of the many snow festivals that take place in the north of Japan during the cold season. Each town in northern Tōhoku had a unique festival that paid tribute to the harsh winter months. Shishigane started its festivities earliest in the sequence. In the meantime, all across the north, little villages were planning to display ice sculptures, build igloos, and hold shrine dances. Adults told children stories about the powerful river god, now sleeping beneath a blanket of snow, and how, come springtime, he'd wake up and his rivers would replenish the land the way veins ignite a body with blood. It was this water, which originated in the mountains of the north, that was famous for giving the rice and the *sake* a clean and pure flavor that the more sophisticated south could never match.

The snow festivals were a manifestation of Shinto, Japan's indigenous religion, which flowered long before Buddhism arrived from China in the sixth century. Shinto involved numerous gods, called *kami,* who could appear anywhere, though objects in nature were the most likely candidates; the Japanese landscape was full of numinous rocks, trees, and caves. If a tree seemed to have a particularly beneficent shape to it, a god was probably residing inside. If a rock in the ocean resembled a turtle, it too must house a god. Because of this somewhat unpredictable nature, it was difficult to come up with a complete list of all the known gods in Shinto; they were numerous and sometimes unruly.

At the very top of the disorganized pantheon was the sun goddess, Amaterasu, from whom all mortals were said to be descended. In the most famous story of all in Shinto lore, Amaterasu had taken a page from Demeter's book and hidden in a cave after a quarrel with her brother, the wind *kami* Susano-ō. The world was soon plunged into darkness after her disappearance, and evil spirits gained the upper hand over the land.

The lesser *kami* tried in vain to convince Amaterasu to return to the world, finally resorting to her vanity to lure her out. First, roosters crowed loudly outside the cave, urging on the dawn of a new day. Then the lesser *kami* covered a large tree with brilliant cloths and jewels and positioned a mirror opposite the mouth of the cave. Uzume, the earthy goddess of mirth, began to dance. She wasn't a particularly attractive goddess, certainly nowhere near as beautiful as Amaterasu, but her good spirits were infectious and the other gods could not help but laugh alongside her. The raucous merriment roused Amaterasu's curiosity, and she crept toward the entrance of the cave.

Amaterasu peeked out and caught her own reflection in the mirror. Astounded, and probably a little bit jealous, the goddess rushed out of the cave to confront her rival. Tajikara-wa, god of strength, caught her, and the other *kami* strung a rice rope across the mouth of the cave so Amaterasu could not hide again. Light returned to the world.

CHAPTER 11

A Forest of Statues

"What will you do at Muryojuji temple?" the professor asked me politely at breakfast the next morning.

We were eating rice, soup, fish, and pickles.

I smiled. "I'm going to see the statues." When he didn't know the word *statue,* I struck a pose. "Buddha," I said.

Evidently this impressed him. Not many tourists, and certainly very few foreigners, made the trek across the north of Japan to see the statues at Muryojuji temple. Most people just went to Nara and Kyoto, if they didn't sequester themselves in Tokyo.

By noon, the professor and I were on the road for what he promised would be a long drive. It had started snowing again, and the roads were still bad. Often I dozed off, only to wake up when the car skidded. I thought back to the evening before and how much the professor had annoyed me.

My first impression of Muryojuji temple came at dusk. We'd been driving along a narrow mountain road just wide enough for two cars. The professor hunched over the steering wheel and peered out of the dusty windshield at the gray road, unruly hair licking at the air like flames while his mouth stayed fixed in a hard frown. The sun was pressed in between the horizon and a layer of heavy cloud, so the light was thin and sharp. Silver trees and bamboo branches huddled over the road, while stubbled rice paddies gleamed with a slick coat of ice and snow. Above us, I could see a foothill on which stood a large building. The professor turned the car off the main road and began to climb toward this structure, driving slowly

214 PICKING BONES FROM ASH

to keep from slipping. The base of the road was lined by rice paddies, but as we climbed, the grounds gave way to tombstones.

Overhead, I saw two figures standing at the entryway of a car park. They were men, one older, one younger, both bald and wearing robes of neutral-colored silk. They were gazing down at us, lips closed, hands resting together in a relaxed clasp. A breeze rushed down the hillside and caught the end of one of their over-robes, which leapt and spread open in the wind. We rounded another corner and I lost sight of them. Now I saw a marvelous wooden gate, flanked on either side by tall wooden statues of the warrior gods. I knew their names from my studies: Ah and Un, so called because their lips were permanently mouthing these exclamations.

The two men were waiting to meet us once we reached the top of the hill, but now there was also a third person. He was very tall and young, maybe around my age, and was just strolling into the parking area as we pulled up. He was wearing elaborate cold-weather gear: a pair of skinny black jeans tucked into a pair of pointy white boots, a slick black jacket left open with a fur-lined hood hanging down his back, and a heavy black sweater with a maze of cables that crept up to his throat like vines hugging a thin but sturdy tree. His long, layered hair framed his beautiful, almost feminine features and hung down over his eyes so that he had to tilt his head a little to actually see me. When he saw me staring at him, he started, then gave me a half smile and turned his gaze away.

The oldest man spoke to the professor in Japanese. He introduced himself to me as Masayoshi Handa, and I bowed to him. The other man in robes was introduced to me as Tomohiro Handa.

"Hello," said the young man in the sweater and the white boots. "Welcome to Muryojuji temple. We are very sorry about your travel problems yesterday." His voice was stilted, almost British, but not quite. I couldn't quite place the accent.

"Oh. Thank you. Who are you?"

He glanced at Masayoshi Handa, then said, "My name is Akira."

"I'm Rumi," I said.

Akira nodded at the two priests, and so I addressed them this time, thanking them for the welcome and apologizing for being so late. In a quiet, even voice, Akira translated my words. My voice sounded oddly twangy and bright against his delicate tone. Then Akira picked up my luggage and nodded toward the house. "Please come inside," he said. Behind me, the professor was resisting an offer of refreshments and climbed back into his car for the long drive home.

I exchanged my shoes for a pair of slippers and the young man known as Akira carried my luggage up two steps and set it down in the entrance to the house.

The age of the building showed in the hallway. Though attempts had been made to modernize it—here and there, a lightbulb covered with a brand-new dust-free paper lantern hung from the ceiling—it was long and narrow, a place built for smaller bodies than mine. It was also excruciatingly cold.

"Where did you learn English?" I asked.

"In Australia," he answered, in a monotone, as though it were perfectly natural for him to know my language. "Here is the bathroom." When I didn't move, he said, "Don't you need to go to the bathroom? Women usually do after a long car drive."

When I came back out, Akira was waiting for me.

"This way," he gestured to another hallway and then a door.

"Who are you?" I whispered as I followed him. "Are you related to the family here?"

Akira ignored my question. "We thought you might like to see the temple while there is still sunlight," he said as we joined the other two men waiting in the hallway.

The four of us made our way through the building, out a door, and across a wooden ramp connecting the house to a side entrance to the temple. The ramp was covered but otherwise exposed to the elements, and the wind and the snow blew in my face, so I was momentarily blinded. Akira took my elbow and hurried me across. Once we reached the other side, he held out two small white packets about the size of portable tissue packs. When Akira saw that I did not know what to do, he shook the little bags vigorously and handed them to me. They were warm to the touch.

"Like this." He showed me the bottom of his foot where a white packet clung to his sock. "Muryojuji temple is very cold in winter," he said to me gently as he knelt down and put one packet on each of my feet. "You must be careful."

Masayoshi pushed open a door and flipped a switch on the inside wall.

Statues three times the size of a man sat on golden lotuses in full bloom. Others stomped on the backs of demons writhing in pain. The altar was a forest of statues, wise faces deep in meditation while they slept. Now roused from rest by our presence, they seemed to come to life. They blinked, parted their lips, and hummed. I heard a low rumbling sound, almost like feedback from a speaker. There were phrases, murmured softly, as though all the objects in the room were practicing meditation. A snatch of prayer here and there, a syllable flying past me, like a bat winging its way through a cave. They were sounds I'd never experienced before.

Bishamonten, guardian of the north, shifted his weight onto one foot and his robes flared in a C shape following the curve of his hips. He hoisted a spear up with his left arm, and grimaced, daring the elements to attack. Over and over again he repeated this bit of drama. And though the howling wind pressed against the northern corner of the temple, pushing up against the sacred space with icy, ill-willed intentions, Bishamonten slew them all, over and over, so the peaceful meditators in the middle would maintain their serenity.

Guanyin, goddess of mercy, had a cool, clean expression, as though I were standing on the bottom of a pool of water and she had broken the surface to gaze down at me. She held a little jar in her left hand, and her long white robes dripped about her ankles. Yakushi Nyorai, Buddha of healing, held out a little container of medicine for me to sample.

The statues seemed intertwined like the gears of a spiritual machine designed to churn out wisdom. At the very center of this arrangement was a large wooden box, perhaps twelve feet high, with doors that would unfold like a cabinet. This was the box I had seen in the pamphlet that Ms. Shizuka had given to me in Tokyo. Akira explained that it was the temple's central treasure, and only on view one day of the year.

The two men opened three smaller rectangular containers, each about three feet high. Masayoshi pulled a flashlight from his pocket and aimed the beam at the contents. All three were *kannons*. The middle box was from the Kamakura era and had the clean, dramatic lines of that period that I have always loved. This *kannon* tilted her hips, and though she only had two arms, her crown was adorned with twelve extra heads. The final box held a very early *kannon*. She had that childishly archaic expression that makes people mistakenly think that ancient people were afraid of far milder terrors than we are today.

Masayoshi stood in front of a fourth crate, similar in size to the others, whose doors remained closed.

"What's in there?" I asked.

"It used to hold a *kannon*," Akira replied. "But it disappeared a long time ago."

I thought of the *kannon* now in the Stillness Center in San Francisco with Timothy Snowden. "I've always loved *kannon*, ever since I was a kid."

"You know about *kannon*?" Masayoshi asked, through Akira.

"Well, yes," I explained, nervously. "My father's an art dealer. So am I."

"You buy and sell statues? Who is interested in such a thing?"

"Wealthy people. Or just people who appreciate art. Buddhism is becoming more popular in the United States."

I studied the men. Masayoshi and Tomohiro were dressed in priestly robes and so at first glance seemed to be of a kind. But now that my eyes had adjusted to them a bit, I saw that they were quite different. Where Masayoshi was grave and elegant, Tomohiro moved like a fighter, taking little jabs at the air. He tugged at his robes with an accusatory sharpness, as though they were being disobedient when they slipped. Akira's hands, for all his relaxed elegance, also danced when he talked.

"Akira," I said, "are you and Tomohiro brothers?"

The question hung in the air and the men all looked at each other. Finally Masayoshi spoke quietly and Akira translated. "Yes. Masayoshi is our father. Our mother, Yoko, is inside the house."

"That makes you my family too, doesn't it?" I asked.

The men were talking to each other again and Akira interrupted me. "Let us go inside and drink some tea to warm up." With that, the strange chorus of men swept through the temple toward the exit. And I, the foreigner, once again had no choice but to follow.

Back in the house, Masayoshi Handa's wife, Yoko, presented me with hot green tea and a tray of sweets. It was cold, she said, using Akira as a translator, and it was important that I eat enough sweets to keep me warm. She floated around the four of us like a small, generous spirit, doling out refreshments, every now and then interrupting our conversation with some point she considered salient. Did I eat red beans in America? Perhaps I'd like a piece of sponge cake instead? Would coffee be more to my liking? She rarely entertained foreigners, she said, blushing, and she was worried that I would go hungry. Finally she left the room and the men and I resumed our business.

"We understand," Akira said to me after we'd gotten the pleasantries out of the way, "that you are looking for your mother."

At last. I pulled an envelope out of my purse and slid it across the table. "I'm trying to find out what happened to her. How she died. If she has any family."

Masayoshi and Tomohiro looked at my birth certificate and several photos that I had received from Timothy before I had left. They turned these over and over, speaking softly and rapidly in Japanese, and I wished, not for the first time, that I could understand what was being said. While Masayoshi held one of the photos up to the light, Tomohiro muttered under his breath, and Masayoshi murmured over and over again. "Hmm. Hmm."

"We would like to know," Akira finally said to me, "how you got these photos."

"From a friend of my mother's. I guess they knew each other in Europe." I paused. "He's a Buddhist priest too."

The men were impassive. "The picture of the statue?"

I hesitated. "I took that myself," I said. "See." I isolated another photo. "The name of your temple is stamped on the foot of this *kannon*."

"But how did you find the statue?"

"My father recently sold it. He said he originally got it from my mother."

"Hmm," the men murmured.

"There's also this." I pulled out the small red box that had been hidden inside the *kannon* at the Stillness Center. "There's a bone inside."

The men exchanged glances as though each held a piece to a puzzle and together they might create a complete picture.

Akira said, "People sometimes come here and claim to be her friend or her relative. Of course, no one has come here with photos like this before."

"I don't understand."

"The woman in your photo is Shinobu Kaneshiro."

"I'm still not following."

Akira said, "She is a *mangaka*. She draws *anime* and *manga*."

"*Manga?*"

"Japanese cartoons." Now he slid his own photo across the table for me to examine. I saw a woman wearing what looked like a fat pink skirt that must have been supported by a hoopskirt or petticoat of some kind, and a short fur coat. She was also wearing bright pink rain boots, and a hat with a wide brim, like a sunbonnet, which was tied under her chin with a piece of white lace. Something had amused her, for she had pulled her hands out of her pockets and was in midclap, the white gloves flashing like little fireflies in the dusky light. "She's very successful. Famous. You must understand that when someone comes here, they mostly ask for money. Or sometimes they want a special favor."

"Wait. You said she is very successful."

"Yes."

"But I thought . . ." I glanced over at the red box with the piece of bone. "Isn't that her in there?"

The men blinked. Tomohiro coughed a smile into his hand. Finally all three men began to laugh. And though the change in mood was a relief from the strained and secretive manner in which they had been treating me, I was also annoyed. "What's so funny?" I asked. "Do you know it's illegal to carry human remains on an airplane like I did? I mean, what if I was caught?"

"What makes you think this is your mother?"

"Because . . ." How to explain my reasoning? A ghost had spoken to me and I had assumed it was my mother asking me to unlock the secrets of her past. "Who else could it be?"

"Where did you find this bag?"

"It was inside the statue in that photo."

After a moment, during which the men regained their composure and conferred with each other, Akira finally said, "That's not her." Then he said the words I needed to hear. "Your mother, Satomi, is alive, Rumi. She goes by the name Shinobu now, but we still call her Satomi."

The air in the room swelled, crested, and broke like a heavy tide. I had to wait for a few moments to breathe again. When I spoke, my voice was very small. "François said that she died. When I was very young."

"No," Akira said. "She is here in Japan." He continued speaking and I tried to listen, but my mind was busy trying to adapt to the new reality that my mother was still alive. "We have never had someone come from America before, although I have heard that she is starting to become well known even over there," Akira was saying.

Masayoshi was holding up my birth certificate and Tomohiro was inspecting my passport.

"I'm sorry," I said. "But I don't understand what's going on. Could you . . . would someone please explain this to me? Because up until a few days ago, I had a completely different life. It wasn't a life with any demons or snow festivals or a mother, even."

"What would you like to know?" Akira asked me.

"Everything!" I was exasperated. "Are we family? Are you my family? Why did my mother leave me? Why did . . ." Tears pooled in my eyes. "Why did my father lie to me and tell me that she was dead?"

Akira gave me a sympathetic look. "Parents do strange things, sometimes," he murmured, "even when they think they are protecting us."

At that moment, Yoko burst back into the room and asked something related to refreshment. Masayoshi and Tomohiro scarcely acknowledged her, just grunting and shrugging as she spoke. Only Akira smiled and bowed his head gently. I felt awkward, wanting to answer her questions—and needing translation to do so—but I also felt that I should behave like everyone else.

Finally, Akira looked at me and asked, "Would you care to stay for dinner? You could stay the night here afterward. It is getting dark outside."

Another night in a strange place, I thought. "Thank you," I said. "I don't really have anywhere else to go."

Yoko ordered *sushi,* which arrived in a series of stacked black lacquer boxes via a delivery van. Tomohiro plied us all with beer, and Akira translated, keeping the conversation light. I only half listened, trying instead to digest what had happened. There was so much information to absorb. My father, a liar. My mother, alive. These strangers, supposedly in possession of the key to it all.

"What do you want to do?" Akira finally asked.

"I want to see her."

"Don't you find it strange that after so many years she has not contacted you? Does that not worry you a little bit?"

To be honest, I had not even thought of this fact. The news that my mother had not died was still so fresh in my mind that I was motivated only by a desire to see her. "She must have had her reasons," I finally said. I thought about the ghost and the strange little statue back in San Francisco. "It's difficult to explain, exactly, but for the past couple of months I've had this feeling that something is not quite right in my life. I've been having . . . bad dreams. I think I'm supposed to find my mother. I think she can help me."

"She might not want to," Akira said.

"I still want to try. I still want the truth."

There was a lull in the conversation, and after a pause Yoko began to ask me questions about America. She wanted to know about San Francisco and if I often saw movie stars, and Akira rolled his eyes and told her that she had confused Los Angeles with San Francisco. Yoko laughed and Tomohiro shook his head. Though I felt tension between them all, I also recognized the dynamics of a family. They were loyal to each other. Protective, even. I wished I could understand the private conversations they shared.

Presently, Akira said, "We can take you to her." He raised his hand when he saw me tighten with excitement. "There is one condition."

"Anything," I said, assuming that I would have to pay for more attorneys, or part with the photos and my birth certificate for the time being.

"My father needs you to convince her to come see him."

I blinked.

"She won't see us," Akira said. "She rarely sees anyone."

"Why?"

Again there was a lag in information while the men discussed matters.

"Satomi," Akira said, "I mean, your mother, has become strange. She's very successful, but she has chosen to cut herself off from her family. It isn't just you that she's abandoned. She has abandoned us, too."

"Then how do you know how to find her?"

"We know her attorney. And we know that she comes to the north every year during the snow festivals because she gets her inspiration from classic Japanese traditions. At least, that's what she says in her interviews."

Yoko began to clear the plates and though I rose to help her, all three men motioned that I should stay seated. Cheerfully, almost too cheerfully it seemed to me, she bustled in and out of the room, carrying boxes and cups, then wiping down the table with a damp cloth and finally reappearing with a plate of sliced apples for dessert. All the while, Masayoshi chewed a toothpick and gazed off in the distance. Tomohiro exhaled and fidgeted while Akira sat patiently, waiting for instruction.

When Yoko finally sat down again, Akira said, "My father says that we should never underestimate the bond between people. Especially a parent and a child."

"And you just . . . want to see her because . . ."

"Because we are her family and we miss her," Akira said.

I looked at the four of them sitting there, waiting to see how I would respond. It seemed like a harmless request. But there was also tension, a neediness in the air and I sensed more to the story. Why, if my mother was alive, would she have avoided her own family for so long?

When he saw my hesitation, Masayoshi began to speak. He sat back on his heels and let his low, musical voice unwind in the room, and after a moment, Akira began to translate.

It was like this, Masayoshi explained. His job as a priest was to usher people on to the next life and he always spent a good deal of time during funerals commanding spirits to leave the bodies of the deceased behind. The most upsetting part of any funeral—for a priest—involved the repetition of the syllable *shin*, which means "heart," and which was used to console the newly departed soul that it was not truly alone, but still needed to depart on its journey.

Problems arose when a soul didn't leave for the north and hook up to the great karmic wheel, which, after completing its rotation in one hundred years, spewed out a newly born soul. A soul who didn't agree to this reprocessing became a ghost, a being who stayed behind to try to finish up something left undone in the previous life or who was too shocked and angered by his newly deceased status to accept it. Most of the time ghosts lingered by the site of an auto accident, on old battlefields, or in hospitals. For a long time Masayoshi had had a working relationship with several construction companies, which had called on him whenever they planned a new apartment building or shopping complex. This was especially true during the late 1970s and early 1980s, when Japan had been busy growing.

At the construction site Masayoshi would wave his horsehair whip and chant *sutras* to any lingering souls. He often saw faces of men in disbelief as their spirits, now released, wound up through the smoke of the incense to the sky. It was exhausting work, but he did it. How could a man who had become a priest not take this kind of work seriously? There was so much suffering in the world.

The work was always problematic. The construction crews were always in a hurry. They hated to wait for the hours it took for Masayoshi to make sure that every last tortured soul had been drained from the landscape. Foremen always wanted to pay him extra money for a rush job, as though a large fee could guarantee that ghosts wouldn't return to haunt the halls of an apartment building or weaken the foundation of a new hospital. It didn't work that way, Masayoshi tried to explain. You couldn't just pay off a bunch of ghosts. Money didn't mean that much to them. What they required was some attention and some respect. The concerns of the dead were always elemental, not material.

There had come a day, perhaps ten years ago, when Masayoshi had been performing his rites with particular intensity. He grew dizzy and closed his eyes once to try to regain his balance. Then he looked down to stabilize himself and saw something unusual about his feet. His priestly white socks looked strangely misshapen, as though stretched. He had blinked, to clear his eyes of tears. Then he saw that his feet really were distorted. Whitish-gray smoke leaked from his toes. His body was melting. Across the field, a long trail of white steam stretched along the grass. It looked like a contrail from an airplane. His body was losing its essence.

Masayoshi had concentrated as hard as he could to finish the chanting and on his way home in the car, he'd broken into a fever. By the time he'd reached the house, he had turned the heat on in the car and was still shivering violently. He had a fever of 103 for three days before his body had returned to normal. When he woke up, he found his wife sitting next to him with deep and sorrowful eyes, and he realized that ushering ghosts out of the soil affected his family too. The next time a construction company called, offering to pay him a million *yen*, he turned down the opportunity. People continued to come by and ask him to pray for their sick children, but he turned them down too.

People could do desperate things, Masayoshi explained. Just this week someone had begged Masayoshi to pray for the recovery of a young girl. Her father and her mother were willing to pay the equivalent of ten thousand dollars. Masayoshi had said "No thank you" to the money, though he had been willing to pray for free. If they wanted to pay him later, when and if the girl recovered, that would be fine. He had prayed and prayed and chanted and blown incense up to the ceiling. When the little girl, who had been hovering so close to the edge of death, woke up in the hospital with clear eyes and the doctor declared her recovery a miracle, the mother and father had paid Masayoshi the equivalent of a hundred dollars.

"My father wonders if you can possibly understand what he is talking about," Akira said.

More than you know, I thought. Out loud, I said, "You worry that my mother is like a living ghost, wandering around, needing an anchor."

When he heard my answer, Masayoshi broke from his controlled look of gravity and seriousness. For a moment, wonder crossed his face. He began to nod. "Yes," he said. "The world of the living can be like that of the dead. It is tragic when we lose ourselves in grief."

"My mother is grieving?"

"She needs her family," Akira repeated.

After dinner, Masayoshi and Tomohiro announced that they would need to retire to a back office to prepare for tomorrow's work. Akira said to me, "Let me show you something."

He led me to a small room adjacent to the greeting room. He snapped on a light, and I saw an ornate gold and black cabinet sitting in a corner. When he opened the doors, I realized that it wasn't a cabinet at all, but a shrine. It was tall, perhaps four feet high, and as I peered inside, I almost had the feeling that I was glimpsing another world in which entwined gold lotuses and *apsaras* flew together in circles. The shrine had a series of levels that rose, like stairs, toward a final stage in the back on which was seated a small Buddha with his eyes calmly half-closed and his hands raised in a benevolent gesture of blessing. Higher up inside the shrine, decorating the walls just below the ceiling, were photographs. All were large black-and-white portraits of men and women.

"This is your family," Akira said. "There is your grandmother, Akiko. And my grandmother, Yuri."

There they were, my Japanese family, gazing down somberly at me. I had the feeling that they were staring at me across a great distance of time, that they had always known everything about me, the totality of what I had done. For a moment, I felt that all my actions had led me now to this place where I might see traces of my smile, my eyes, my high cheekbones.

"Akira," I said, "please tell me what is going on. I know that you know more than you are telling me."

He smiled slightly. "It's difficult to be a traveler. When I lived in Australia, I had the same experience. I couldn't always understand what was happening. Come on." He pulled my shoulder playfully. "Let me show you where you'll be sleeping."

My luggage was already sitting in a room down the hall. In the middle of the *tatami* floor, Yoko was preparing my *futon*. Akira knelt down to help her spread a comforter over the mattress, and the two of them smiled at each other, sliding into an easy intimacy, the first display of open affection I'd seen since arriving here.

When they finished setting up the bedding, Yoko let me know that I was to ask her if I needed anything else and the two of them left. But just before he'd exited the room completely, Akira put his head back in between the sliding doors.

"I'll go with you. I'll tell them that you need a translator."

"You?"

"Well, it's partly for selfish reasons," he shrugged. "I'd like to meet her."

He had tracked Satomi in the news. He'd loved her *anime* and *manga* as a young boy and still read her creations religiously. He even, he whispered to me, had a small side business in Tokyo selling *manga* to the French and a few Americans who couldn't seem to get enough of the stuff. Daily, his apartment received faxed orders for special issues, which he then sent overseas. It had been comforting to think that one of his family had become famous and lived a larger life than he did. It had given him a kind of hope that it would be possible to escape an ordinary life. If Satomi aka Shinobu could do it, then why not him?

"I always thought it was interesting," Akira continued, his voice growing even more gentle, "that she wrote these stories about a young girl visiting a foreign world, or trapped in a strange place."

"She was writing about *herself*," I fumed.

"That's what I used to think about Satomi." Akira nodded. "Then I began to wonder if she was writing about someone else." He paused. "I think she was writing about you. In her mind you were trapped all the way on the other side of the world. She's been imagining the adventures you've been having."

CHAPTER 12

The Edge of the World

I stayed with the Handa family for the next two days and waited for the storms to pass, and for roads leading further north to be cleared. My dreams were cluttered and I slept fitfully in these unfamiliar surroundings. Sometimes I woke up convinced that someone had been watching me, and once I caught the tail end of a silk robe leaving the room.

In the daytime, I sat in the *ima,* or living area, in what I learned was called a *kotatsu,* a low table with a recessed and heated area underneath. From here, I watched tapes of my mother's *anime.* One strange story, titled "Tomobiki," was about a girl named Naho who unwittingly had the ability to unlock parallel worlds. One day she accidentally discovered that an abandoned building on the outskirts of her family town was once a crematorium. She ventured too close to it and was sucked in by a restless fire spirit, who asked her to help him with some unfinished business on earth.

While I watched Naho's descent into the mercurial world of the fire god, the rest of the family floated around me. Yoko was often cooking. When they weren't working, Masayoshi read the paper and Tomohiro watched television or played video games. The only person I really talked to was Akira, who came to the temple for a couple of hours a day, apparently just to see me, since he rarely interacted with anyone else. Yet try as I might to extract information from him, he would not reveal much more about my mother and her family than he already had.

On the third morning, it stopped snowing and the bullet trains and the major expressways reopened. The temperature warmed by a few degrees, and several icicles fell from the eaves. Clouds parted. I felt as though we had been living inside a very cold teapot whose lid had finally been lifted. In came light and new air and the reality that there was a world beyond the one in which I was living now. More importantly, my mother had agreed to see me.

Akira and I were to take a trip north. Because our destination was impossible to reach by train, we would drive. I left my things at the temple, taking only my purse, in which I placed the box with the bone, and a coat I borrowed from Akira. Yoko packed us a lunch box and blankets and several large plastic bottles of tea. "For you," she said to me. "I don't want you to get too hungry."

Masayoshi saw us to the car. "Please bring her back," he said and bowed.

We drove for several hours, the road growing increasingly narrow and serpentine. I saw the Sea of Japan in all its wild and gray glory, so different from the Pacific Ocean on the other side of the island. Here the houses were windswept till they tilted, the landscape harsh as though unjustly scoured by a rough celestial hand. I remembered Ms. Shizuka's warning about the north of Japan. How different was this scenery from the polished city of Tokyo.

It was a long drive, and after half an hour of uncomfortable silence we began to talk. I told Akira most everything that had led up to the discovery that my mother was alive, leaving out the visitation from the ghost.

He was a good listener, asking a question every now and then or empathizing with me when he sensed that I'd reached a particularly distressing part of the story. When I was done, I asked him to tell me about his trip to Australia.

"Oh that," he laughed. "It was because of a girl. She was an exchange student my senior year in high school."

After graduating, Akira had left his priest-training course at university, fled to Australia, supported himself by bartending, and learned to surf on the weekends. Ultimately, as he put it, things hadn't "worked out" with the girl, and I gathered from the sober way he said this that he still regretted the heartbreak. In his absence, his parents had considered him a lost cause, formally disowned him, and groomed Tomohiro to be the next priest. According to Akira, Tomohiro had been all too happy to comply, apparently under the impression that life as a priest would one day make him wealthy and able to afford unlimited electronic gadgets and games.

"My father wouldn't talk to me when I came back from Australia. When he learned you were coming, he realized he would need someone who spoke English. They called me in Tokyo five nights ago."

"I'm glad you came," I said.

"It's tough for my mother." He paused. "They fought a lot over me. They have different attitudes toward life. "

From the town of Mutsu, Akira began to drive along an even narrower road spotted with perilous patches of ice. I began to smell something strange. It was a faint scent at first, reminding me of boiled eggs. As we drove on, the smell grew stronger and my stomach became queasy.

In the distance I could see a tall mountain, shaped like a cone, with a red skirt of clouds.

"Where are we going, Akira?" My voice sounded very small.

"Osorezan." He nodded at the mountain.

It was an inactive volcano and said to be, among other things, the gateway to hell, the entrance to the underworld, the place where little children's souls were trapped, unable to cross to the other side because they hadn't accumulated enough *karma* to be completely worthy of rebirth. Families came here to pray for the journey of the souls of the dead. And once a year, typically during the summer, there was a festival in which blind mediums (or witches, as Akira called them) could be paid a fee to communicate with the dead.

Osorezan was connected to a temple, which was generally closed from October to April. My mother had made a yearly trip here for over a decade. Akira didn't know why, exactly. He suspected that she'd been given special treatment because of her fame. Osorezan was also the kind of place, given her work, from which she would likely find inspiration.

Masayoshi hadn't actually spoken to my mother on the phone to make these plans. He'd talked with her lawyer, who had relayed the somewhat cryptic message that if I wanted to meet her, I should go to Osorezan, pass through the temple, and explore the mountain foothills. Masayoshi and his family had not been sure that this was such a good idea. It was a strange place to meet someone, but the lawyer had been adamant that these were my mother's wishes. I was to come alone, but Akira had insisted on going with me as far as he could.

So it was that we parked outside the temple Bodaiji. Almost immediately I was struck by how much stronger the stench was outside the car. Akira explained that I was mostly smelling sulfur. There were pools of boiling minerals all over the place, and I should take care to stay on well-marked pathways to avoid falling into any of these cracks. If I felt myself getting sick, I should return to the truck and we would go back to Muryojuji temple.

It was just afternoon, but the sun was already past its peak in the sky. Akira and I began to walk across the temple grounds, which spread out over a courtyard covered in ice and snow. Above this, the gray slate tiles of the actual temple formed a roof that flexed like wings. The place was also bleached by the sun, so the entire structure seemed to fade into the snow and the gray sky. Snow and ice had accumulated on the eaves, icicles aiming their teeth at the ground. I heard a soft sound, almost like wind chimes, then realized it was the deceptively gentle sound of ice and steel and slate all groaning from the cold and wind. Aside from this, the only other sound I heard was the voices of crows. Every now and then when I looked up, one of their black bodies was held in sharp relief against the white world around me.

"There's no one here," I said to Akira.

"It's a temple. There has to be someone here to look after things."

Before us stood six statues made of stone. They were all Jizo, the Buddhist deity responsible for helping the souls of children, travelers, and even miscarried or aborted fetuses. They smiled at me in spite of the cold, each seated in a slightly different position, holding instruments, and some arranging their hands in various meditative poses.

We passed through the temple grounds to a path leading from the temple to a lake. Before me was the eeriest, most unsettling and yet strangely beautiful place I had ever seen.

Everything was covered with snow, except for the mineral pools. They had spit up their innards and stained the snow myriad bright colors—yellow, bronze, and cobalt blue—as though a childish hand had laid waste to the environment, dumping brilliant colors on the pristine earth. The hot liquid had melted the snow in some places to reveal a world beneath all the ice. Here were pyramids made from small stones. There was a bright-yellow Pikachu poking out of pile of curry-colored snow. Two Transformers sat side by side, encased in ice. In the distance, a field of pinwheels whirred in the wind, their pink shapes blurring into the white-gray sky.

We climbed to the top of a hill and turned around to take a view of the snow-covered temple below us. Up ahead I could see a lake, the water struggling to lap the shore under its burden of snow and ice. I was freezing.

"Where do we go?" I asked Akira.

"I don't know."

So we continued walking. Mostly we were silent, comforted by each other's presence. But occasionally we spoke.

"I like your parents," I said. "It's not like they ever lied to you or anything."

"You don't have to go back," he said.

"What?"

"Is there something you are in a hurry to go back to?"

I pondered this. "Not exactly."

We walked on.

Presently Akira gestured at the burbling, stained landscape. "Just so you know, this looks weird to me too."

"Everything has been strange so far," I said. "But this might be the strangest."

"That's what I'm trying to tell you. No Japanese person would look at this and think it's normal. You have to be careful when you travel. People can trick you into thinking that something is ordinary when it's not."

The shore of the lake was lined with strange, snowy figures shaped like small pyramids. I stopped to brush the ice off one. It took me a few minutes, but what I found moved me. Someone had arranged numerous small stones around a bottle filled with flowers.

"It's supposed to be a pagoda," Akira said. "The spirits of dead children are stuck here, unable to cross the river to be reborn." This was because they hadn't accumulated enough *karma* in their short lifetimes to repay their parents for the love they received while they were alive. As penance, they built these small stone pagodas. Unfortunately, a demon was always lurking around the grounds of Osorezan and was willing to break apart the pagoda.

"I guess that makes me a demon," I said.

"Foreign devil," he agreed.

We weren't too sure where else to go in this lunar landscape. Every now and then I thought I saw someone. Akira would see the same figure and we'd hurry after it. But whenever Akira and I grew close to the shape, we realized that we had merely seen yet another statue of Jizo or a pagoda.

Once or twice I'd been certain that the figure we had spotted had been moving.

"Look," Akira said solemnly. The clouds had parted overhead. For a moment, the sky was a bloody orange as the sun started her descent to the west, over China. "We have to go back," he said.

"Don't you have any other instructions?"

"No."

I looked out over the strange land, now turning scarlet. "Who does she think she is? Asking us to come to such a strange place and then not even showing up?" I squatted. My feet were tired and, though I knew the ground was wet, I sat down on the snow. Then my fatigue gave way to anger. "This isn't funny!" I screamed. "Do you hear me? If you are out there listening, this isn't funny!"

Akira sat down next to me. "Rumi, even if we don't find your mother, at least you've met us. We are your family too, you know."

"What the hell is the matter with my parents?" My eyes and nose were watering and I tried to wipe the moisture away with my gloved hands. "Why am I the one out here looking for *her,* when she's the one who left *me*? What did *I* do? Are you *afraid*?" I screamed at the snow. "Because I'm not. I'm *right here*!"

"Here," Akira handed me a handkerchief. "Girls are supposed to carry these."

"Then why are you carrying one?" I asked, as I wiped my eyes.

"Well, boys carry them too." He grinned. "You really are a foreign devil."

"It's not me who's the devil!" I shouted back at him.

"That's more like it. You're much cuter when you are angry." He took hold of my hand.

I didn't stop him. I felt like an observer, a third person looking at two other people's hands. Akira removed my glove and put it in his hand. Then he took off one of his gloves. He turned my hand over, massaging the palm, then worked his way up to the inside of my wrist. He stroked my skin and tapped my tendons lightly, and the sensation made me shiver. "Are you okay now?"

"I'm fine," I said.

It wasn't too much later that we kissed.

It wasn't what I expected. The earth didn't open up and swallow me whole. I felt instead as though I regained my balance after slipping. One second I had been standing on one side of the road and the next I had simply shifted over to the other side to find similar scenery.

But then he reached inside my sleeve and stroked my arm, just above my elbow. I felt the contact in my stomach, felt it travel down between my legs. He stroked both arms and then I ran my finger across his right arm. I wanted to be even closer to him. I understood the meaning of a deep kiss after that, a feeling of being suspended in the nadir of a dive in a lake. Silence, danger, peace cushioning all sides of my body. When I came up for a break, the air was filled with the chatter of crows, the throb of the ocean, all running together in a warped burble as though my ears were filled with water.

We began the rocky climb back to the temple. It was hard going. We'd taken a circuitous route, and despite Akira's insistence that we should stay on clearly marked paths, we'd strayed off course and now with the fading light would have to carefully climb our way back to make sure neither of us fell into a pool of boiling minerals.

I felt pressure in the air, and when I looked up, I saw that the clouds had slid back over the horizon. In the distance, over the water, were dark vertical streaks. It was going to snow. "Akira," I said.

How careless we had been! We had the little white heat packs, but no flashlight. "We need to hurry," he urged.

It was then that we saw a glowing point in the distance. Once or twice I nearly fell, but always Akira held my hand firmly. And there before us was a house made of ice, the floor neatly covered with straw. A hand emerged from inside and beckoned.

"I think," Akira said slowly, his face unusually pale, "we are supposed to go inside."

We removed our shoes and climbed into the ice house, whose floor was covered with *tatami*. The inside was surprisingly warm. Akira and I sat down at a small table made from a wooden tree trunk roughly hewn in half. Two women, one young and the other old, were sitting by a small stove on which the girl heated *mochi* and a pot filled with liquid. She ladled the hot drink into cups for us both. The hot liquid brought me back to my senses a little.

The other woman was speaking. She kept her eyes closed most of the time, but every now and then would tilt her head back and I could see the whitish-blue of her irises. Her body was covered with a thick blue-and-white traditional garment so stuffed with insulation that she looked puffed up like some kind of doll. One hand held a dark rosary. The young girl handed us each a piece of *mochi*.

It was the first thing I'd eaten in a number of hours.

"She says there's a bridge near here," Akira said to me solemnly. "It crosses the river Sano, which is like your river Styx."

"That's reassuring."

"The bridge is made of mist."

"Mist?"

He shook his head. "It seems to be some kind of test. The bridge will either fade, or you will see it as something solid."

"What's on the other side?"

Akira shook his head. "These mediums. You know they are trained to be vague."

The medium had fallen silent, letting her head fall against her chest. She appeared to be asleep. The young girl held out her hand, offering to fill my cup with more hot *sake,* and I drank another round.

"I have to stay here, Rumi. I'm sorry. That's what the woman told me. You have to go alone. Of course, if you don't want to . . ."

"Let me get this straight." I smiled, trying to find the humor in my predicament. "I am supposed to look for a hypothetical misty bridge that crosses a river of death."

"Yes." Akira gave me an indulgent smile. "I know it sounds crazy. On the other hand, you didn't come all this way just to go home."

The young girl who had been serving us read the cues in my movements. She stood up in one deft motion and picked up a lantern I hadn't noticed sitting in the corner. Then she went to the front of the ice house and stepped off the straw floor and into a pair of enormous boots made from straw. She hovered around the entrance, waiting for me. I put the cup down on the little table and put on my shoes.

It was snowing only lightly outside, flakes falling against my eyes, the icy cold snapping me awake. The young girl moved sturdily ahead of me, quite clearly more accustomed to the snow than I—I was now half falling and half running to keep up with her. Wherever she was going, the snow was much deeper in this part of the landscape.

Then she stopped and handed the lantern to me. With a blank expression, she pointed off in the distance and nodded that I should keep walking. Behind her, I could see the little igloo glowing in the dark, lit up from the inside. I thought of Akira sitting in there with the old woman.

I felt a powerful surge in my head, blood rushing from the drink and from the sulfur. As I set out, the lantern seemed to glow like a ball of fire in my hand. I held it out, passing by Jizos who nodded and bowed and hummed at me. I passed strange creatures dressed in bibs and pink hats who cooed like little children, and even stranger creatures growling and sniffing at the earth. On I went in the direction I'd been sent.

I heard the sound of running water. I was on the edge of a riverbank. Below my feet, the earth dropped away. There was a mound of coins here, sticking up out of the snow and colored black from years of exposure. Wind brushed through the air and I saw the wet black flow of water running and reflecting a beam of moonlight.

I looked up. The clouds had parted, though only for a moment. I saw more clouds approaching the moon, preparing to shut it out of sight. I looked back down at the water, mist dancing across its edges. And then I saw the bridge.

It was scarlet and seemed so eerily out of place here, so bright it almost glowed in the dark. I went to its edge and watched as mist peeled off its beams. My first step made a resounding thump. I was standing on something solid. And so I walked slowly across the structure. Around me snowflakes had swollen, practically blooming like fat cherry petals. I couldn't resist stopping to stick out my tongue. Sulfurous fumes blended into the snow, and at last I was tasting the terrible chemical smell that had followed me since I'd arrived.

And then I saw her. Standing off to the side, under the protection of a gigantic parasol, mittened hands clasping its handle. I looked into her face. My heart thundered.

She lifted her delicate face toward mine. "Rumi," she said simply.

CHAPTER 13

Disintegration

In photos, my mother takes great pains not to smile. Occasionally there is a candid shot where her lips are parted and you see her teeth, which are strong and white and beautifully shaped, like little pearls. None of the pictures gives you a sense of what could happen when she smiled, because when she did, you immediately had the urge to smile back at her. She would hold you there, until she had had enough, and she would lower her eyes or perhaps shift her attention somewhere else, then back to you, and her eyes would look into you, trying to see how you would react in that moment, while you were left trying to get her to smile at you again.

That night, when she smiled at me, I felt the strength of her charisma. My lungs filled with air, then collapsed. I heard blood whir through the veins in my head, felt juices churn through my stomach. The entire world seemed to concentrate for a moment inside my body, a frail host for the emotions that were possible.

I remember what happened afterward in bits and pieces. I know that I fell and that a group of women picked me up and that we made our way through the snow. I could not get warm and was angry when gentle but insistent hands began peeling off my clothes. Then, a moment of calm. I came to in a cloud of steam. My hands and feet tingled, shaking off the last of the icy cold. I saw a smile through the haze. I was sitting in a bath with my mother and two other women. For a moment, I thought I saw another ghostly face in the fog. I exhaled, my breath chasing the vapor, and the face disappeared. I inhaled and was relieved to smell something other than the foul stench of Osorezan. My breath echoed. I looked up and guessed that I was in some kind of room, but it was difficult to tell how large it was because of the steam.

"You see," my mother was saying to me, "you've visited the gate of hell, but you have survived. Now you are here!" Then she giggled and I wondered what amused her so, if it was some expression on my face, or the entire afternoon, which she had observed in secret.

For nearly three days I was sick and delirious. Mostly I stayed in a room covered with *tatami* mats and enclosed by sliding doors. When I was awake, I lay in a *futon,* staring out of a window, while the women tended me. Outside, the sky alternated between shades of white and gray. It was difficult to tell time. The snow fell hypnotically, and I often passed out while I was watching the flakes. I barely spoke. The only food I ate was a light broth, which I sipped out of a lacquer bowl. I got up solely to use the toilet or, at the insistence of the women, to be bathed.

After a few days I was still weak, but able to sit upright for longer and longer stretches of time. Then I was able to bathe myself and the women showed me how to wash myself properly before crossing the cobblestone floor to the bath, which they informed me was actually a hot spring. I became curious about my surroundings.

"Where am I?" I asked.

"My home," my mother said.

"Where is that?"

"Tochigi. Not *so* far from Osorezan. I'll show you on a map when you are feeling better."

I learned the names of her assistants: Kumi, Keiko, and Megumi. In their presence I felt awkward and foreign and clumsy. Megumi cut my hair and made me sit still while Kumi applied various creams and compresses to my face. Keiko bleached, tweezed, and shaved me. Kumi and Megumi shaped my nails into ovals and painted on a design till my nails were a silvery blue with raised white snowflakes. Keiko threw out my old clothes and the three of them dressed and redressed me according to my mother's whims. One day I wore all white lace. Another day I wore bright red. They made me model my clothes and clapped when I turned around in the center of the room.

"I look like I'm twelve," I protested.

"There is no happier time in a girl's life than when she is twelve," my mother said. She herself was wearing a white lace skirt with a pair of tiered pantaloons and a pink sweater with a Peter Pan collar. She was seated on a square *zabuton* pillow, her back ramrod straight, while she puffed on a cigarette. "After twelve, all our troubles begin. It is a kind of freedom to return to that age."

When I asked after Akira, she merely smiled and narrowed her eyes and said that he was safe, and that I would see him eventually. "He's just a boy. And not terribly interesting from the look of it."

"He was nice to me."

"They're all *nice* at that age. At first." Behind her, out of the window, I could see snow falling against the backdrop of an old, thick forest. I was reminded of those cartoons where a character is lulled into submission by a swinging pendulum. I blinked rapidly to try to force myself awake. I stood up.

"Would you come with me to Muryojuji temple?"

She put her cigarette to her lips and spent a moment inhaling and exhaling. "You aren't well. Of course you'll recover—a doctor came to see you while you were unconscious—but it's not a good idea for you to travel now."

"They made me promise to bring you."

She smiled. "That's Masayoshi. Making someone else promise to do something that he's too afraid to do."

I suddenly felt faint and Kumi and Keiko moved to catch me before I toppled over.

"As I said, you aren't well." My mother looked at me directly. "You inhaled too much gas at Osorezan."

I took a sip of water. "The ice house and that blind woman. Were they some kind of game?"

Thus far, my mother had been sparing in her gestures, as though she moved only when there was a clear reason to do so. Now she began to fidget with the collar of her sweater. "I try sometimes to look at life as a game. It's much less painful that way. You figured out I was alive even when your father lied to you. You're winning the game." She shook her head. "I thought it might be fun to provide you with an adventure. Like one of the heroines in my stories."

"Except I'm not a character," I said.

She brightened. "But travel always does imply adventure. I should know!"

"I didn't ask to play a game with you."

She stopped tugging at her sweater. She drew herself up then, stoically jutting her chin into the air. Her voice sounded oddly formal. "I did not mean for you to become sick, Rumi. I thought that Americans had a stronger constitution. We will all see that you are well cared for, and that you recover."

I watched videos. I watched them while I ate, before I slept, and after every bath. Often my mother watched with me. A couple of days after I had received my makeover from the assistants, my mother slipped a videotape into a player just beneath the television. "My first series," she said. "*The Falberique Forest*. I found a version with subtitles."

This was her earliest *manga*, which had been turned into a cartoon, or *anime*. The main character was a girl named Rose who had grown up orphaned and was adopted by a mysterious man who lived in the town of Falberique. Rose was drawn with a characteristic halo of long blond hair and large, star-spangled eyes. Her true love was a man named Nathaniel, who rode a white horse, and who was also much older than poor Rose, and thus given to alternately treating her as though she were a child (Episode IV, in which Nathaniel gives Rose a puppy) and treating her as though she were older than she really was (scandalous Episode VII, in which Nathaniel gives Rose a velvet dress, then takes her on a horseback ride through a rainstorm, which destroys the dress and leaves her half-naked).

When the tape ended, I turned to my mother to see if she would insert the next one. "That's all, I'm afraid." She smiled.

"But that can only be half the story."

"I know. I sold the rights after that. You wouldn't like what happens next. The new writer killed off Nathaniel and gave Rose a new boyfriend."

"Why did you sell off the rights to the story?"

"I was tired of it," she said. "And I thought it was time for my fans to move on. They were getting spoiled." She stuck a new tape into the machine, a different series altogether. "Everyone said I would fail because I had hurt my fans. But I knew I wouldn't. This *anime* was even more successful."

We watched this new story and the assistants joined us, focusing with rapt attention on the screen. In the next video, *Tsukemono yasha,* an older woman eked out a living in a small kitchen shop on the Old Edo Road where she made and sold pickles imbued with special powers. She worked with the assistance of a beautiful but mute girl named Sasha. A young boy, Tajiro, discovered one day that the purple pickles, when he ate them with an apple, could make him momentarily appear to be a young man, and he became determined to learn the secrets of the shop, particularly when, in his adult form, he was able to get the attention of the lovely Sasha.

So we passed the afternoon, silent before the television, lounging in the bath, eating, and occasionally conversing. Sometimes I wondered to myself what I was doing here, in the company of these strange and playful women. But I was very tired and had little energy to protest my circumstances too much. When I slept, I heard the gentle *twish twish* of snow on the roof, and the sound followed me to sleep and into my dreams where creatures arose from a white landscape and spoke to me in hushed and icy tones.

"What happened with you and my father?" I asked.

She expertly blew a narrow stream of smoke into the air and smiled as it dissolved. "You know, in Japan, when a couple divorces, it's not uncommon for the child to be told that one of her parents has died. We don't have your complicated shared custody system."

"You weren't in Japan."

"I ended up in Japan, didn't I?"

"Come on."

"Look, he loved me more than I loved him. It's not fair how that happens sometimes. I wrote to you a few times, from Japan. But he always returned the letters unopened. That's how angry he was. Eventually I gave up."

"You sent letters?"

"Especially in the first few years."

"You could have come back. Tried to see me."

She considered this. "It's true. And then what?"

"I don't know."

"I don't either. I did think about it." She sighed. "When you are far away from people, when you are in a foreign country, it can be easy to feel that you have a completely different life. That the old one didn't exist and that people are just frozen as you left them."

"*I* didn't exist."

She shook her head. "That's not what I mean. How do you feel now about François, now that you are here?"

"I'm angry."

"Does he know where you are?"

"I left a note saying that I was coming to Japan to find out what happened to you."

"And have you imagined what has happened to him since then? He's probably trying to find you. He's probably worried, Rumi. And he has no idea that you found me alive."

"Let him worry for a while, then," I said.

"You see? You think he's the same old François, at home, still reading your letter. I'm sure many things have happened while you have been gone."

I did not want to think about this. I did not want to feel sorry for my father.

"I wonder," she said, "how did you find me?"

"I can . . . hear objects. They speak to me. They led me to you."

Now she grinned. "I have never heard of such a talent. How does it work, exactly?"

"I don't know. It just started happening to me one day. François was trying to teach me how to be an antique dealer and then I started hearing what objects had to say about their age."

She mulled this over, then turned and barked out an order to Kumi, who nodded and backed out of the room.

I continued, "I started seeing things. A ghost—I thought it was you, and that you were dead."

"Not much of a talent, considering you turned out to be wrong."

I got up from the *zabuton* pillow on which I had been sitting, then went over to the small bag I had carried with me to Osorezan. I pulled out the little red box with the bone and set it on the floor in front of her. "I found this."

She eyed the box for a time, then inhaled sharply so the air whistled through her nose. "Where?"

"It was inside a statue of a *kannon*. My father had hidden it in the floor-boards of the house in San Francisco. There's a bone inside."

"You should put that away and put it back where you found it," she said ominously. "Such a thing should not be out in public."

"At first, I thought the bone belonged to you."

She tapped her throat. "Mine is right here."

"Then, whose is this?"

She shook her head. "It's illegal, isn't it, to transport human remains as you have?"

"If this is originally from Japan, then someone else once traveled with it too."

She nodded at me, and smiled, almost proudly. "Yes," she said, "this is true." Before I could ask her more questions, Kumi had returned to the room carrying a wooden box about the size of a large watermelon. She kneeled and placed the box on the table and the assistants huddled around it with my mother, who looked expectantly at me. "Open it."

I was tired by now of the toying way she talked to me and irritated by her gamesmanship. "Why?"

"Please," she wheedled, "I'd like to share something with you. Open it."

The box did intrigue me. I knew what it was for; I'd seen plenty growing up with François. So I crossed the room to the table and lifted the lid off the box. Inside, I found a layer of old newspaper, then a yellowed sheet of Styrofoam. And below this, a Korean melon pot. I pulled it out and set it down where it glowed, a pale, icy green against the polished cherrywood of the table.

"Does something like this speak to you?" my mother asked.

"Usually," I said, and began to concentrate. The floor creaked as my mother sat back to watch me.

I picked up the pot and looked at its base, then set it back down again and leaned forward. Then I took off its lid. The melon pot opened its mouth and began to sing. It told me how it had been created in the twelfth century as part of a wedding dowry for a wealthy princess and had barely been used. The pot had survived for over seven hundred years before it was bought by a Japanese textile merchant and taken to Japan, where it had languished in the care of connoisseurs. I turned the pot around and around and as I did so, it began to ring louder and its voice became clearer and clearer.

It had been abandoned once, like the many things in this home, but had kept its beauty intact. There had been a time recently in its long history when it had feared for its future, but now it was back with its rightful owner. It did not like being shut away in a box, though this was how so many of its sisters spent their time protecting their value. The melon pot missed warm hands and fresh air and being admired in the sun.

"Koryo," I said. "It wasn't made for export, but it ended up here anyway."

"Yes."

"And you don't take it out very often."

"Anything else?" She smiled sweetly.

"Most people just want to know if something is real or a copy and this is not a copy."

"You aren't curious about its history?"

I reflected on the other things the melon pot had said to me. "Where did you find it?"

"It was part of my mother's collection. My stepsisters sold it without telling me. It took a number of years for me to find it, and it cost me a great deal of money, but I am happy to have it back." She picked up the pot, cradling it, then petted its skin.

"Your mother was a collector?"

"Porcelain. You see, our childhoods are not completely different." She drummed the table once. "What does it feel like to hear an object speak?"

"Most of the time it feels good to hear something clearly."

"Like the precise notes of a song."

"Exactly."

"It must be a powerful feeling."

"Sometimes. Maybe. I don't know." I told her then how for most of my life I'd believed that I had a special ability to hear the truth of things and yet as it turned out, I'd missed the most important truth of all, which was my father's relationship to me and my mother's disappearance. I went on to recount everything about the past few months: Timothy's reappearance in our lives, the ghost and the statue that seemed to speak, and how all this had driven me to Japan.

Then I told her another story. François and I had once discovered a beautiful painting of a *geisha* holding a parasol in the snow, but the silk on which it was mounted was badly damaged, and the painting rippled in places. Soon the painting would crack. It had been up for auction in the

East Bay, and we'd had little competition for it because of its condition. Together we had removed the fine paper off the backing, cleaned it, then matched it to new silks from a pile of scraps François kept just for this purpose. Slowly, we had lowered the painting back on to the new mounting, and once it was in place, flat and clean, it had been a sight to behold, the chilly beauty in the frigid snow, on a search for warmth.

"Ah," she said. "It matters how things are framed."

"Yes."

"But this is impossible, Rumi. We can't ever understand everything. I know Americans have this fascination with going over and over something that happened in the past, but sometimes the best thing to do is to simply create your own life. That's what I have done."

"Then we are different," I said.

She nodded. "That is true."

"And you won't help me."

"I didn't say that. I only mean that you should be careful in the kind of help you expect to receive."

In the evening, we had another bath and then settled down to watch more of the *Tsukemono yasha* video series. After a little while, Kumi and Keiko brought our dinner on black lacquer trays each of which had a small *hibachi* burner to cook three fine slices of fish meat. My mother lit the flame beneath my burner with a match, exclaiming, "Aren't we having a good time? When I was a little girl, I wanted nothing more than to spend time in a hot spring with my own mother and eat a nice dinner."

"It's been kind of a long time since I was a little girl."

"It's winter," she observed. "Time stands still during winter. It's easy for us to imagine that you are a little girl." She signaled to Kumi to rewind the tape to the beginning. "I love this part." She sighed as the opening credits rolled and then she sat back, smiling as the world she'd created flashed across the screen in shades of pink and gold.

Not for the first time, I felt how helpless I was here. I didn't really know where I was, couldn't communicate with most people, couldn't call Akira on my own because someone had removed the Muryojuji pamphlet from my purse. I was completely dependent on yet another group of strangers.

My mother picked through the dishes, leaving the leftovers to her assistants. She insisted that I eat everything that arrived on my plates.

"When I lived abroad, I did not eat, and I became very weak," she said. "Don't let that happen to you." She looked at the television again, and fell silent for a moment. "My mother used to starve herself just so I could eat. It's very important to me that all my girls are well fed.

"You're still doing things because of your mother?"

"Of course." She paused. "Everything she said would come to pass in my life has happened, Rumi. There were times when I thought it would be nice to be free of that influence."

I couldn't imagine what that would feel like and I said as much. But if I hoped to prick her ego a little bit, I failed. "Yes, how interesting," she mused. "Here we are. A girl without a mother and a girl with too much of a mother. Which, I wonder, would most people rather be? One inherits history. The other is free to create it herself."

"It must be nice to know where you are from."

She shrugged. "No one knows everything. It's silly to think that we can, or should even spend our time trying."

After a week and a half, I began to feel like myself. I began sleeping regularly at night and became restless during the day. I went for walks from the room to the bath and back. I opened the window to blast my face with cold air. "I think," my mother said, "that you are feeling well enough to see the rest of my home. Shall we go for a walk?"

I was in a house, or rather a large complex, light and airy in feel, with plenty of windows and smelling of wood and paper. The hot spring and the room where I had been staying were in an outer wing, and when the snow stopped, as it did for half an hour the day I finally decided to inspect my surroundings, I could see that the bath was on the edge of a cliff with a view of a town and rice paddies below. A hallway connected this wing to the main house, which I began to explore with my mother, Kumi, Keiko, and Megumi following close behind.

In the hallways I encountered more young girls dressed as French maids with little aprons and white lace caps, and they curtsied to me and giggled as I passed. Music streamed out of loudspeakers, a piano composition that sounded vaguely familiar to me, but that I couldn't identify specifically.

The hallway formed a square, with doors along the perimeter. Along the corridors, I saw cases of *manga* and *anime* and posters on the wall—all tributes to my mother's universe. Here and there were pictures of her posing with Japanese dignitaries whose faces I did not recognize, but whose tense and expectant expressions telegraphed their importance. Around a corner I saw a case filled with wooden Japanese *kokeshi* dolls, and another that contained plastic robots frozen in salute. And beyond this, Peter Rabbit, Hello Kitty, and Snoopy. Then the toys were everywhere, on the floor, on chairs, high up on top of cases.

I climbed a staircase to the second story, the women following closely behind. An army of stuffed teddy bears lined the stairs and I had to be careful not to knock them over as I walked. Upstairs I was greeted by the hush of girls concentrating in a pale room that would have felt completely utilitarian what with the stark lighting and silver paint had it not been for the rows of toys lining a high shelf on each of the walls. Three girls were bent over a table using paints and pens, and the room smelled of ink. When the girls saw me they smiled but did not get up to speak.

"They are the youngest assistants," my mother said. "They do line drawings and fill in the ink. These girls," she gestured to the trio dressed as French maids, "hope to graduate from housework to artwork one day."

Back downstairs, I followed the hallway to the main entrance of the house, whose heavy double wood doors gave way to a courtyard, now covered in snow. I put on a pair of boots, abandoned by the door, and went outside. We were living behind a white wall, smooth and seamless like an egg, that circled the small estate in a neighborhood populated by tall trees. We were also on a hill and I had to stand on my toes to see the rooftops of buildings below us. With the heavy snow, it was possible to feel entirely isolated. Abruptly, a portion of the wall slid away. A car drove into the driveway, and the wall was sucked seamlessly back into place.

"That is Shinobu," my mother said. "Back from the store. She does all the cooking."

"I thought *your* name was Shinobu."

"She is the real Shinobu. We just use her name, for fun. As I said, life is more manageable if you think of it as a game. Shinobu," she said, "is like my sister. And that makes her like your aunt."

Shinobu was paler than my mother, with graying hair pinned to her head like a ballerina and smiling eyes. She alone among the women dressed as an adult, in a shapeless brown dress and nylon stockings. She smiled when she saw me and her eyes smiled harder as though to squeeze out excess light buried deep within her body so her face shimmered. She bowed to me repeatedly and asked me numerous questions through my mother. She wanted to know how I was feeling, if I was well enough to eat in the dining hall this evening, and if I had liked the food so far.

I said that I was feeling much better and wondered if I could help her. There was something likable and uncomplicated about this woman; she was more in keeping with what I had anticipated a mother would be. Shinobu laughed and, through my mother, explained that she was not used to too much assistance. But I insisted. Communicating mostly through pantomime and the few expressions I knew, I tried to help her prepare a meal while my mother hovered around the edge of the kitchen, frowning, smoking, and interrupting us every now and then. When it became clear to me that Shinobu really was accustomed to working alone, I parked myself by the sink and began to wash pots and pans. Observing this, Shinobu rattled off approving sounds that I recognized as thanks.

In the dining room, girls were allowed to eat together based on rank; those who had been with my mother the longest, like Shinobu and Kumi, sat with us while the others were relegated to sitting elsewhere, rising to bring us tea or water as my mother needed it. My chair was initially occupied by an enormous white teddy bear. My mother expressed her irritation and the girls giggled and Keiko moved him into a corner.

"You can sit now," my mother said.

"There are no men here," I observed.

"Men complicate everything. If one of the girls developed feelings for the man, how would we get any work done?"

"People get work done with men around."

"When you were a girl growing up in San Francisco, did you hear the mothers of your classmates begin their sentences with 'My husband thinks?' I hear that all the time. 'My husband thinks.' I want to ask these women, what do *you* think? So many times, they don't even know. In this house, no one ever needs to worry about what a husband thinks. That is what it means to be talented." She took a bite of her dinner. "Isn't the chicken good?"

"Yes."

"We grow the bamboo shoots ourselves. Out there," she waved at the garden in the inner courtyard, which was, like so much else, covered in snow. I peered through the glass to see the tips of a bamboo grove waving down at us from the shadows. "Do you like Chopin?" My mother tilted her head in the general direction of the stereo.

"It's nice."

"Rubinstein is the best."

I continued eating my chicken.

"Have you ever played the piano?"

"No."

"Would you like to learn?"

"I don't know."

"What do you want to do when you have fully recovered?"

"I don't know."

"Can you do something other than identify antiques?"

"Not really."

"I'm sure you have other talents," she said. "You have my blood, after all. Perhaps you just don't know yet."

"I don't think so."

"How about a piano lesson after dinner?"

"No thank you."

"Aren't you interested in discovering your talents? That's why everyone else comes here."

"I'm not everyone else," I said. "I'm your daughter."

I was going to be sleeping on my own, in a small private chamber located not too far from the quarters of the other girls. My mother's room was upstairs, and I gathered from the vague way that she talked about it—"Oh, up there"—that few were allowed to see it. In my room, a *futon* with a pink-and-white cover lay spread out on the *tatami* floor, with an elephant and a lamb tucked inside the cover.

"Rolo and Rami," my mother said. Behind her, the assistants struggled to pronounce the r's and the l's.

There was an armoire in one corner and a small couch in another, and the latter was covered with blue-glass-eyed blond dolls wearing pinafores. On top of a dresser, Japanese dolls of various heights wore *kimonos* in shades of red and navy blue.

"It's a small room," my mother said, "but quiet." She picked a few dolls up off the couch and held them to her lap, then sat down on the couch. With her petticoats and lace blouse she looked like a doll herself, albeit an oversized one. "Shinobu's children were taken from her."

The admission startled me. "Why? When?"

"A long time ago. She hasn't seen them in years. When we were in college together, a man seduced her and she became his mistress. She thought he was going to keep her. It turned out he was looking for someone *like* her—a gifted musician—so he could produce children with talent. His wife is wealthy but not talented, you see. *Their* children all became bankers and he wanted some who would become artists."

"That's . . . awful."

"She discovered she could cook. So she stays here and cooks for everyone and occasionally gives piano lessons when one of the girls is interested. Everyone, you see, does something."

"I'm not asking to stay here for free. I just wanted to meet you." I picked up the little red box with the bone in it and held it on my lap. "I'm feeling a lot better now. You could just take me back to the temple."

This was not the response she expected. She smoothed the hair on the head of one of the dolls. Then she picked up another to hold along with the others. "What do adult mothers and daughters do in America?"

"They talk on the phone. They have lunch and they go shopping. I think sometimes they fight."

My mother winced.

"Do you have friends?" I asked.

"Everyone here is my friend. Shinobu has always been my best friend."

"I mean, outside of here."

"Not really. Do you have friends?"

I thought about François and Akira. "Not that many. Most people at home think that what I do is strange."

"Well, it is."

I shrugged.

She sighed and stood up suddenly, then placed the dolls back on the couch. "I will keep thinking."

"About?"

"What you can do." She nodded. Then she wished me goodnight, reminding me that I knew where the bath was, and that someone was always awake and keeping guard in the dining room if I needed anything in the middle of the night.

When I went to sleep, I kept the elephant and the lamb on the floor beside me. Once I woke up to see their plastic eyes gazing at me sadly. Then I went back to sleep and dreamed about a girl—or was it a woman—dressed in white and clutching two teddy bears on her lap as she sat on the couch. She gazed right at me, as though it were the most natural thing in the world that we should be looking at each other.

"How did you get in here?" I asked, but she didn't answer. Then she smiled and closed her eyes and seemed to sway back into the sea of toy animals and dolls and they passed through her skin. "Oh," I said, not completely disappointed. "It's you."

She smiled in salutation and then her dress and finally her face dissolved into mist. When I woke, I heard the space heater clatter to attention. The room looked completely normal and, slowly, I fell back to sleep.

I helped Shinobu with the housework in the morning, and separated the laundry, and helped her to cut vegetables. She was precise in everything that she did, and I felt clumsy by comparison. I could not cut the carrots into uniform pieces and she laughed when she saw my oddly shaped pellets in the glass bowl. I did not know how to slice a green onion finely enough. But still, we tried to work together. Later, she took me into the study, which was connected to the dining room, and seated me at the piano. She lifted the cover, placed a book on the stand, and pointed to the keys. "She," she said.

"She," I said.

She shook her head. "A, B, She."

"C," I said.

She nodded and pointed to a figure on the book. "She."

"That's C," I said.

She struck a white key beside C and said, "D." Then she pointed to a spot on the notebook again. Taking my unwieldy hands, she tried to guide me through a scale. My fingers felt fat. I imagined toddlers taking their first steps, or the one time I'd tried to climb a ladder onto the roof. "No," I said to Shinobu. "I don't think so."

Shinobu nodded with encouragement. "She. D." I tried to send my graceless fingers up and down the piano. And I really did try. Shinobu was a good sport, laughing at my mistakes and patiently trying to fix my fingers as I wobbled through a version of "Twinkle, Twinkle, Little Star."

Finally, I'd had enough of playing the piano, and though I was glad to see Shinobu smiling, I wanted to give my fingers a rest. "Shinobu," I said to get her attention. Then I pointed at her. "You have children. Babies." I cradled an imaginary child in my arms.

She grew sad then and nodded and held up two fingers as her eyes moistened.

"Satomi?" I asked. "Does she have any other children?" I pointed to myself and held up one finger. "Just one?"

It took her a moment to understand but then she nodded. "One," she said, her voice hesitant in trying to speak my language. Then she pointed at me.

"Just me."

Shinobu placed her hand on her heart. "Satomi," she said, patting her heart a few times. Then she put her two fists together and separated them, as though to break an invisible object in the air. "Mother."

"What happened?"

Between the two of us we did not have enough vocabulary to flesh out the story, but I understood the gist of what Shinobu had wanted to tell me. Between my mother and her mother, something had been broken. Then Shinobu pointed at me and put her hands together again. "You want me to fix something? Or the fact that I'm here means I've fixed something?" Shinobu laughed and shook her head regretfully and the two of us sat quietly for a time, and I was sorry that our language abilities made it almost impossible to discuss these difficult things that pained us both.

At dinner, I asked Satomi, "What happened to your mother?"

It took a moment for her to answer. "She became sick and she died."

"How long ago?"

"This isn't dinner conversation." She smiled at me with her full, glamorous smile, the one that was supposed to keep me pinned in place, unable to press her further.

"Well, do you know where she was from? I mean, do you have brothers and sisters? Do I have more family I can see?"

"No."

"No, there isn't any more family for me to meet, or no you don't know where she was from?"

My mother set her chopsticks down on the table and took a deep breath. She lit a cigarette and began to inhale and exhale fiercely. One by one, everyone around us stopped eating. I hated this feeling, that one person's mood was responsible for everyone else's, and I tried to fight her influence and to keep chewing and swallowing. Finally, she said, "I don't know anything about her family, or where she was from."

"Have you ever tried to find out?"

"No."

"Why not?"

"Because I accept the life that I have here, Rumi."

"Wouldn't it be good to find out?"

"Why?"

"So . . . you would know?"

She smashed the cigarette in the ashtray. Her face became blank. It was the strangest thing. It was as though a curtain had simply closed across her heart and her face would no longer betray any emotion at all. I'd noticed versions of this behavior during my stay in Japan: how the professor had acted with propriety on our drive to Muryojuji as though he hadn't teased me with the demon festival, and how Akira had retreated into a neutral pose in front of his family. It was a kind of disappearing act and I found it frustrating and almost alarming

"Satomi . . . ?"

"Please enjoy the rest of your food," she said with exaggerated decorum as she stood up from the table. "I have work to do."

"Wait a minute," I said, but my mother had already disappeared from the room.

I turned to Shinobu, who had watched all this with an increasingly sorrowful expression. She, too, stood up from the table and retreated from the room in the direction Satomi had gone. The other girls would not meet my eyes. One by one, they ceased eating and left, and finally I, too, finished my dinner and made a hasty retreat to my room.

At breakfast the next morning, Satomi said to me, "I know you want to return to Muryojuji, Rumi. If you'd like, we can arrange for you to go today."

"Today?"

"You are feeling better, aren't you? And you've been asking to return."

So, this was to be my idea.

She went on to explain, somewhat stiffly, that I was always welcome for visits, but there was now a great deal of work for everyone to do and if I was not going to be able to help her in some way, then it was best for everyone that I return to the temple. She spoke in vague terms, something about how nice it had been to meet me and that she was happy I was healthy. I only half listened.

Then I went to the room where I had been sleeping and changed into the clothes I'd worn on Osorezan, now cleaned and pressed. When I came back to the dining room, I found my mother, Shinobu, and a few of the assistants waiting. Shinobu was arguing about something with my mother, and Kumi and Keiko were hesitantly chiming in, clearly torn between the two women.

"Shinobu thinks I should take the day and go with you."

I shrugged. I didn't see how traveling together would change things between us. "It's up to you. I mean, I know Masayoshi wants to see you. But I know you're busy."

My mother exhaled roughly. "He could come here if he wanted to see me so badly." Shinobu began to insist on something again and Satomi rattled off a response. I stood and listened, feeling uncomfortable, until my mother again sighed harshly. "It's true. I should thank him in person. I suppose we can use the driving time to do some work." Then she walked briskly out of the room, calling back to us over her shoulder that she needed to get her coat.

My mother, Kumi, Keiko, Megumi, and I all left together in a small minivan, painted pink and white and made to look like a cat, with the headlights as eyes and special attachments to the side mirrors to look like ears. Kumi took the wheel, wearing white gloves and a little black conductor's cap, while Shinobu waved good-bye to us, smiling and nodding, I thought, with particular intensity to me. The minivan was outfitted with a video screen, and as we drove to Muryojuji temple, my mother played tapes of her favorite cartoons for me, commenting on the characters and the settings and how her travels had inspired both. Now that I was in the thrall of her world again, her mood improved considerably. If she had really intended to do any real work on that trip, I never saw her lift a pencil.

It was a long drive, perhaps four hours, and it became clear to me that my mother did not at all live "near Osorezan" as she had told me the first day I'd woken up in her house recovering from the gas. We stopped just once at a rest area to use the toilet and to buy some tea, and then we were on our way again. Eventually, Kumi turned off the expressway and began to take a series of increasingly narrow roads. I started to recognize my surroundings.

Muryojuji temple came into view as it had before, with the two priests standing on the cliff watching our van approach. We parked and climbed out of the van, stretched our legs, and bowed in greeting. Later, we drank tea and made small talk. Masayoshi sat like a man in his palace, while his twitchy Tomohiro eyed us all, ready to protect his father if need be. Satomi, the assistants, and I crammed all together on the other end, and Akira was by himself. I looked to him for some hint that he would acknowledge what had happened to us on the mountain, but he had retreated to a characteristic aloofness, nodding at me only once.

Masayoshi seemed almost amused to see my mother, as though she were a child entertaining him with her antics. For the first time since I'd met him, he shed his somber, grave demeanor to smile broadly. He interrupted her every now and then as she spoke, and then she would chastise him and he would blush.

I felt as though the two of them were bound together by invisible thread and between them was suspended a precious object. Pull one string too tightly and I imagined that the treasure would shatter. It had grown windy outside, and gusts of air battered the windows and ceiling. Meanwhile, Satomi and Masayoshi continued their game, maintaining a delicate balance, pulling against each other so hard over the course of the next hour, they seemed to have lifted one another into a room of their own, while around them, the wind seemed to whirl like a cyclone.

About an hour after we had arrived, Tomohiro went out of the room, returning with an envelope, which he handed to my mother. The tense atmosphere in the room took a turn. My mother became aware of the rest of us seated around her. Glancing at us all first, she briskly undid the clasp and pulled out two photographs. Her fingers trembled slightly while

Masayoshi spoke to her. Then Akira said something to her in Japanese and, after a moment, she slid the pictures across the table to me.

"Your grandmother," Satomi said to me curtly. The invisible thread binding her to Masayoshi began to fray.

I saw a young woman standing outside a building with a sloped roof. She was very small and very serious, yet with a little bit of mischief playing in her eyes and at the corners of her mouth.

The other picture was a similar portrait of my grandmother taken by the same building, but at a slightly different angle. In this photo my grandmother was not posing alone. Another young woman stood next to her with a cautious, almost suspicious expression on her face.

"We don't know who that is," Akira explained, suddenly sitting beside me. "We think it's your grandmother's servant."

The rest of the envelope contained documents, papers, and a small piece of wood, flat and five-sided, not like a pentagon but like a square house with a triangular roof on top. Traces of paint and writing clung to the surface. Akira explained to me that this was an old *emma*, or Shinto charm. Shrines made these tablets and sold them to the public, and most came with a little picture of the zodiac animal corresponding to the year in which it was painted. This *emma* had a monkey. Most of the time people wrote wishes or hopes on the *emma*, then left it at a designated place at the shrine where it would be blessed and burned, the smoke delivering the prayers to the gods. In this case, though, my grandmother had kept the *emma*, along with these two photos and the other documents my mother was looking at now.

"Kashihara." Satomi turned to me. "It's the name of a shrine." Outside, the wind howled.

When my grandmother had died, Satomi had been led to believe that there was nothing for her to inherit. My mother had skipped out of Japan after the memorial service and gone off to America, as we now all knew, coming home only much later to Japan to reinvent herself. Satomi's relationship with her stepsisters had always been strained, and in a moment of spite, Mineko hadn't told my mother about the envelope. Somewhere in the intervening years, Mineko had relented and, according to Akira, become less bitter. "Apparently, her children are fans of your work," he told Satomi, who laughed. Mineko had given the papers to Masayoshi for safekeeping with the hope that he would be able to turn everything over to my mother one day. Though he'd tried repeatedly to contact my mother, her staff and attorneys never allowed him to send her anything.

Much later, Akira told me how my mother had responded to this information. Gone was the happy, toying way they had related to each other. "So, the only reason you wanted to see me was to give me these papers so you wouldn't have to feel guilty about hanging on to them anymore," my mother said.

"That isn't the only reason." Masayoshi responded. "We are family and it hasn't been right to be apart all these years." My mother switched off the alluring beam of her smile, almost a physical thing in its intensity. With her smile snipped clean out of the air like that, the room had instantly felt colder.

"There were plenty of ways for you to get this information to me."

"You wouldn't see us."

"I don't like cowards." She paused. "You have always been such a headache. Ruining our nice reunion. Never able to say what you really feel. Talking in circles around the things that really matter."

"*I'm* a headache? Do you have any idea what kind of trouble you've caused for me? The temple? My family?"

"This has nothing to do with your family!"

"Maybe you were just trying to get back at me when . . ."

"Oh, don't flatter yourself. You're not important enough to me for me to want to hurt you!"

"I know I caused you pain . . ."

"Any pain you've caused is for yourself, Masayoshi, and this weird life you've created . . ."

"Stop yelling at me! This shouldn't be about us anymore but about our children. Your own daughter came all the way from America to look for you and . . ."

"How convenient. I say something that gets too close to the truth and the little priest hides himself by acting all enlightened, as though he has no feelings of his own and only cares about other people!"

"Satomi!" he thundered, and we were all startled. This angry man roused into a passion was not the gentle, slightly absentminded person I'd come to know. "Where is the statue? And where are the bones? Where are your mother's bones? I know you took them!"

She looked stunned for a moment at the escalation in his temper. Then she licked her lips and smiled a small, triumphant smile. "You see. I knew you weren't really interested in me."

He was beside himself. "I don't want to talk about our lives right now! I want to talk about your mother and your obligations to her!"

She waved her hand. "This is all becoming so uninteresting. I haven't done anything wrong. My mother has been dead for a long time." But I could see that she was nervous, for her breathing had become shallow and quick and her gaze darted around, unable to find anything on which to rest.

Masayoshi too could see that she was nervous. Seizing the moment, he began to talk rapidly and urgently. "I know what you have done," he said. "And I am trying to help you fix it."

A number of years ago a relatively powerful quake had struck the north of Japan, decapitating tombstones and disturbing the Handa family plot. Masayoshi had saved up money for a replacement and a few months ago before the winter season had set in, he had finally set about replacing the tombstone. To do this, he needed to temporarily remove, then rebury all the bones. In a very private moment, Masayoshi and Tomohiro had chanted together before disinterring the family remains; anytime a grave is disturbed, a priest must make the appropriate prayers. When they went to put the old urns into the new grave, which had been reinforced with concrete, they found that Satomi's mother's bones were missing.

It is natural, of course, for bones to disintegrate. Even after two years, an urn filled with bones is going to absorb moisture and fill up with water. When they opened the urn belonging to Akiko, however, they had been disturbed to find that it was filled with tiny stones. This could only mean one thing: Akiko's bones had never been buried.

What had happened? They recalled a period after Akiko's memorial service when her bones had been placed in a hidden room at the very back of the temple. The family had not buried the bones immediately because Akiko's death had been unexpected and her family plot not yet ready to receive her. A year later, in the spring, they had buried the bones. Or so they thought.

So what had happened to the remains and where had they gone? Had there been some sort of mix-up in the bone room? Had someone perhaps inadvertently buried the wrong urn? But no. All the urns were clearly marked. Someone had intentionally taken the bones from the temple, replaced them with a false urn containing stones, and sent the bones off somewhere else.

But who?

Grudgingly, they'd all come to agree on the same culprit.

There had been a few hours during Akiko's funeral when my mother had been left unattended while she slept in the house, working off a hangover. No one saw Satomi leave that day. She had simply disappeared. It was possible that she had snuck into the back room to swap the bones with stones. Scandalous, offensive, but possible.

This would also be the ultimate revenge against the Horie family for hoarding Akiko's affection. The bones had been taken somewhere only my mother knew. For Masayoshi, this was a terrible discovery. It was his job to usher souls to the next life, and my mother had committed a terrible transgression. Was she not worried that her mother, Akiko, would be unable to continue her peaceful progress to rebirth?

"You have had great sadness," Masayoshi said. "It is because you did not properly take care of your mother when she died. And now you must tell me where the bones are so we can try to fix things."

When he had finished speaking, my mother sat with her gaze off to the side, her body tilted and slightly limp, like a once stiff balloon gone a little soft. If I touched her, she might roll over. Her mouth flitted in and out of a small smile, searching for the appropriate reaction on which to settle. When she jerked her head up to look at all of us, her eyes cleared, irises whirling. To me she said, "I hope this has been interesting for you." She nodded at her assistants, and then as one they all stood up, petticoats and ruffles fluttering. Then they hurried toward the entrance.

"Wait a minute!" I called out. "Are you leaving?"

"Yes," my mother replied primly. She said something to Kumi, who helped my mother into her coat and began to fasten the large pink buttons.

"You're just going to run off again?" I screamed at her.

She stepped off the landing with one foot and began to put on her boots. "I don't appreciate that you and Masayoshi tricked me and made me come to this place," she snapped.

"Tricked *you*? You were the one who insisted on meeting at that hellhole of a mountain. Anyway, he didn't tell me what he planned to do."

Now she had both feet on the ground and was nesting her discarded slippers together.

"So, that's just it?" I looked back at the Handa family, watching us with solemn horror. "What am I supposed to do now?"

Satomi's lips tensed as though she were fighting a tiny monster inside her mouth. "You should do what you want. I always have." She paused just outside the door. "You could come back with me. You don't have to stay here with these people." Beside her, Kumi made ready to close the door.

"Why should I go with you?"

My mother gave a deep sigh. The black night sky framed her wiry figure, as though she were a bolt of lightning. "To find out about your grandmother. Obviously *I'm* not the ghost you saw."

I stared at her.

"Come on," she urged me. "We're letting in too much cold air. And it has started to snow again."

"Wait one minute," I said and ran back down the hallway to the room where we had been sitting, with Akira close behind me. Inside the room, I grabbed my purse off the floor. "Why didn't you tell me about the bones?" I asked Akira.

"They asked me not to. We weren't even sure if you were really Satomi's daughter. Only she would know for sure."

I scowled at him.

"I'm sorry, Rumi. I wasn't even speaking to my parents a few weeks ago. I was trying to do what they wanted."

"Did that include . . . ?"

"I kissed you."

"And not just once."

He nodded, and turned his gaze down at his feet. "That was impulsive. I've been thinking that maybe I took advantage of a delicate situation. You didn't come to Japan for me, after all."

"Well, it was unexpected," I agreed.

"After you left with your mother, I spent the night in the temple. The priests found me outside their door."

Dazed and feverish all night, he had woken in the morning feeling more or less like himself. He'd driven back to Muryojuji temple to tell his parents that I'd been reunited with my mother. Then he'd stayed with a friend nearby, waiting for my return.

It had all been more responsibility than he was used to or than he had expected when his parents had called him and asked for his help. He'd been ambivalent about continuing that feeling of liability for someone whose emotions he didn't know. He stretched, suddenly thrusting both arms into the air. "Honestly, the whole experience was very strange. I've been thinking the last few days that you are a very strange person to have taken me to such a place."

"Strange? I'm not the one who reads cartoons."

"On the other hand, it was also kind of . . . fun." He gave me one of his half smiles. "Call me here if you need anything." He gave me a another temple brochure. "Don't lose it this time."

I put the pamphlet into my purse. "Thanks," I said.

"You should go with her." He nodded at the door. "She's who you came to see. Come on. I'll get your coat."

We spent the night in a *ryokan* while a storm raged outside, and I was grateful that the Japanese inn included a *yukata* to sleep in and free tooth-brushes. In the morning, we were on the road again. Kashihara was a good three-hour drive away. We passed through hills and valleys to reach it, small towns poking their heads up through the snow. But the shrine was located to the south, in a valley where it was warmer, and where there were signs of spring. Plum trees had pushed forward a few pink blossoms. Bright yellow shoots crept out of the ice. By the time we'd reached the shrine, the snow had thinned to a crusty, icy layer.

The shrine grounds, which snaked up a hillside, were composed of a se-ries of smaller buildings spaced around open courtyards and little intri-cate gardens, which we admired on our walk from the parking lot to the shrine's main complex. Along the way, we met an elderly woman cleaning fallen and rotted apples off another part of the walkway. A sign next to the walkway displayed an apple falling off a tree and hitting an unsuspecting passerby on the head. Below this, text implored visitors to "Beware of fall-ing apples."

The elderly woman's back was hunched over like the crook of a finger. No doubt she was a legacy of Japan's many years of malnutrition during and after the war. She had few remaining teeth, and treated them as though they were a nuisance, sucking in her cheeks and pushing her lips out of the way of her teeth to speak. *"Ohaiyo gozaimasu."* Good morning.

"We are here to see Mrs. Sakurai," my mother explained in Japanese.

The elderly woman gestured toward a two-story structure set apart from the shrine grounds, and we followed a path that twisted around a small azalea garden to a wooden gate and then on to the front door, which slid open easily.

"*Gomenkudasai,*" my mother called out. She motioned for me to follow her into the house.

"*Hai!*" a bright female voice called back to us from another room. I heard a light shuffling and a few minutes later, a woman around my mother's age and dressed in a neutral-colored dress and a faded blue apron came around the corner and fell to her knees. "Welcome." She placed her hands on her knees and bowed low to the ground, her forehead nearly touching the wood floor.

I followed the gist of the conversation. My mother was sorry to disturb Mrs. Sakurai, who, in turn, was always pleased to have visitors. When we'd finished bowing, Mrs. Sakurai invited us to come inside. My mother and I removed our shoes and changed into slippers. Mine were made of pink terry cloth and embroidered with a small cat and the caption, "Today is happy day. Think peace and be pink with laugh."

Mrs. Sakurai giggled, apparently embarrassed that she had forgotten to take off her apron. Her laughter was engaging, and soon my mother and I were laughing with her in an effort to assure her that we were not at all offended by her choice of dress. Mrs. Sakurai peeled off the apron, folded it, and left it on a shelf by the front door before ushering us around the corner. Outside a sliding door, we removed our slippers and then stepped onto the *tatami* mat floor.

My mother and Mrs. Sakurai wrestled politely over whether or not it was necessary to drink tea. Eventually Mrs. Sakurai won out and began to fill the teapot with fresh, loose leaves, while I struggled to sit on my knees in the same position as the other two women.

Later, my mother told me everything they talked about that afternoon. She had mentioned to Mrs. Sakurai how lovely the shrine was and asked about its age.

"Well, I'm not completely sure." Mrs. Sakurai squinted. "Maybe three hundred years."

"Please forgive me for asking, but has the shrine always been in your husband's family?"

"Oh, no. My husband was originally a schoolteacher from Osaka. As for Kashihara, well, it did belong to one family. But after the war . . ." She bowed her head sorrowfully. "It was not a good time to be Shinto."

"No," my mother agreed.

"My husband believes that Shinto is at the core of every Japanese." Mrs. Sakurai brightened again. "He wants little children to all know about their culture. That's why he became a priest. We were very excited when he was given this post."

My mother pulled the photographs out of her bag. She wondered if Mrs. Sakurai could identify either of the two women in the photo.

Mrs. Sakurai put on glasses to see the picture clearly. She turned it over a few times. "I think this photograph was taken on the south side of the main complex. The family used to live in a small house closer to the shrine. When we took over, we bought this small house here. The girl in the photo looks familiar. I think she's from the original family; we have found some of their belongings over the years." Mrs. Sakurai pushed the photograph back across the table.

My mother hesitated. And then she explained. The woman in the photo was her mother. Satomi had never known where her mother had come from. She had recently come across this photo, and now she wondered if there was anyone Mrs. Sakurai could think of who would be able to provide us with more insight.

Mrs. Sakurai bent her head, then forced a smile as though to say she had always suspected it would come to this one day. She stood and asked us to follow her.

We climbed up a stone path to a landing on the hill. The main building of the shrine was here, though its door was shut. A couple of townspeople stood outside and tossed money into a wooden box before praying. Mrs. Sakurai unlocked a side door and led us inside. The interior was dark, and smelled of mold. At the far end of the shrine I could see the main altar displaying the sacred mirror. It looked like the mirror my father and I had at home: a circular disk made of silver, hiding behind a curtain of bamboo the way the moon crouches behind the clouds. "If you wouldn't mind waiting here," Mrs. Sakurai said, gesturing to a few pillows around an old, scarred table. A few shrine maidens, wearing red-and-white robes, brought us tea, then departed.

I heard a noise. A hesitant scuffle. Out came the elderly woman we had seen on the temple grounds when we had arrived. One eye was cloudy from a cataract and I wondered how much she could really see. But she blinked furiously at us as if to pull us into focus.

"Why don't you sit here, *obaasan*." Mrs. Sakurai pulled the elderly woman toward a pillow.

"I can sit by myself," the old lady scolded. "Hello." She smiled at me. She began to prattle. My mother told me later that the old woman, named Tomomi, had been born before Japan had decided on a standard way of speaking. Consequently she spoke with a thick regional accent and was difficult to understand.

"Yes, that's right," Mrs. Sakurai shouted at the old woman. "Rumi-san is a pretty girl. Very pretty."

"I was also pretty," Tomomi said.

"Yes," Mrs. Sakurai shouted. To us, she explained that *obaasan,* or Granny, had been the caretaker at Kashihara for almost seventy years, since she was a small girl. When Mrs. Sakurai and her husband had accepted the position at Kashihara, they could not just let Tomomi go. "She helps with the children sometimes. Looks after the garden."

"What?" Tomomi shouted.

"I said we are very lucky that you are here to help us," Mrs. Sakurai barked. Then, quietly, "Why don't you give her the photo?"

Tomomi held the picture close to her face and inspected it. Then she picked up the *emma* and placed it in her palm gently, as though it were the wing of a bird recently recovered from an injury. *"Heh,"* she intoned. She gazed at the photo again.

"Do you recognize her?" Mrs. Sakurai shouted.

Tomomi sat back on her heels and held the *emma* reverentially up to the light. I could see her pupils dilate, and knew from the focused expression on her face that she could see the object clearly. She waved her free hand back and forth as if recalling the steps of a dance.

Mrs. Sakurai looked at us anxiously. *"Obaasan* has told us many stories about the shrine. In one story . . ."

Tomomi interrupted. "Why, it's Akiko! And me."

We all stared at her. In an old, creaking voice, Tomomi continued. "Akiko never said who it was. But when her parents found out, well, they did the only thing they could do. They cast her out, to the street. It was terrible, sending a girl out into the city at a time like that! Oh, I worried about her so much. It was even worse after the war when there was not enough food to eat."

"A hundred sisters," my mother said.

Before I could ask her what she meant, Tomomi peered into my mother's face and said, "You've finally come back."

"Me?"

"To take care of your mother."

"My mother is dead."

"I know that," Tomomi snapped. "I was talking about your mother's bones. Poor thing," Tomomi continued. "You probably gave her some kind of depressing Buddhist funeral."

"I don't have her bones."

"Why not?" Tomomi barked. "Didn't you realize? She has no business being buried where she is. She's not a Buddhist. She's Shinto. She needs you to bury her here, at home."

Unlike Buddhist temples, Shinto shrines were not physically connected to a cemetery. Death, in Shinto, was considered a kind of infectious disease. If you got too close to it, you ran the risk of catching it. In the case of Kashihara, the founding family—whom I was still having difficulty accepting as my family—had bought a small plot in a cemetery belonging to a neighboring Buddhist temple.

Tomomi, whose legs had suddenly become sturdy, led us along a concrete path that zigzagged up a hillside. It was evening, the long day still bracketed by high-flying pink clouds to the east and a pale blue sky now ripening with gold to the west. The pathway was lined with glossy black tombstones, engraved with the names of the deceased, whose shiny surfaces reflected the sky like a field of irregularly shaped mirrors. Nearly every plot was accompanied by a small flower vase in the shape of a bamboo stalk. In the distance, I saw a woman solemnly ladle water out of a bucket and over a tombstone. At one point, we reached a small patch of bamboo where a side path veered off to the left and down toward a rivulet.

"Our cemetery is down there." Mrs. Sakurai pointed. Then she gripped the railing and began to take the stairs one by one down toward a small shady patch of earth. I followed.

It was darker here, the remaining sunlight obscured by the shelter of bamboo leaves. I heard water burbling below, and I was reminded, briefly, of the small brook I had crossed at Osorezan.

We wended our way down to a rough field of what I thought were stone lanterns. Mrs. Sakurai explained to me that we were really looking at Shinto tombstones. "They are a different shape than Buddhist stones," she explained.

Then Tomomi led us off onto an earth trail, and we followed her. I had the grim awareness that here, beneath the earth, lay the remains of people who had once been as alive as I was now.

"Here," Tomomi said.

Five stones, each a slightly different shape, nestled against a hillside. Their faces were worn from the elements, but I could still make out the original embellishments that had decorated the lanternlike tops.

"These are old," I said.

"This is your family," Tomomi said to my mother.

Mrs. Sakurai shifted uneasily from foot to foot. "I'm sorry. My husband and I haven't been here as much as we should have been." She knelt down on the ground and picked a few weeds that had sprouted in between two of the smaller tombstones. She made a pile of these weeds, root side up, so they would die and not be able to reseed.

"There's no name," I observed.

"They didn't need a name," my mother explained.

"Only priests can have tombstones in this shape." Mrs. Sakurai lovingly traced the outline of one of the tombstones as if it were the face of someone dear to her. "When my husband dies, his tombstone will look like this."

Below us, the water of a small creek rushed enthusiastically toward a distant destination. Somewhere in the sky, a crow cawed. My eyes welled up. I couldn't help it. Never mind that my ancestors asleep beneath these lantern-shaped stone columns were people I neither knew nor would ever know. It was as my mother had said: examining the past had complicated my view of my life, not simplified it. And yet, I was right too; my life now had a frame, and was colored with a history that stretched far, far back.

For every thought I had ever had, every preference or burst of temperament had originated with these beings. So many stories I had never learned, those moments when my ancestors would have rolled their eyes and said, "Well. It runs in the family." I wished—no, I hungered—to know what those little idiosyncratic characteristics would have been. I felt as though someone had looped an invisible cord from my gut to my mother to the ground in front of us. An unseen hand jerked on the connection, and we lurched to our knees.

I looked at my mother. I knew there was something we were supposed to be doing in this situation. But there were so many rules in this country. It would be so easy to do the wrong thing accidentally. I needed her to help me.

Overhead Tomomi's voice cackled, "Would you like some incense?" She reached in between us, her gnarled fist wrapped around two dark-red sticks.

"Rumi," my mother touched my arm. I started. She had not touched me before. "Say thank you."

"Thank you," I said immediately. Then I turned to look at her. My mother was praying and so I sat back on my heels and prayed too. We sat there for a long time. The earth underneath my knees grew cool, and my legs cramped, unused to being in this position.

PART FIVE

CHAPTER 14

From the River to the Sea

Satomi
Muryojuji temple, Japan, 1992

I had initially been amused when Rumi had come looking for me, wondering if she might provide me with the kind of entertainment I needed to soothe my restless nature. I had forgotten the impression I'd had of her when she was growing inside me, that she would be such a serious person who might not like to play games at all. Also, I had not expected that her arrival would involve my own mother. And how could Rumi, who was born in America, have been the one to see my mother's ghost? I was the Japanese one. We Japanese are sensitive to our environment in a way that the Western mind cannot be. Our world is alive, populated by ghosts and *kami*, little gods who can inhabit anything from a tree to a rock to a cup. This is why we take such pains to design the perfect tape dispenser, the most charming toilet.

Then again, I suppose it was typical of my mother's stubborn and slippery nature to find an indirect means to get her point across to me. I thought to myself how predictable it was that she would still be trying, after all this time, to have the upper hand in my affairs.

"I'm glad you decided to be sensible and come back," Masayoshi said. "So. For the last time. Where did you put the bones?" We were sitting in the front room of his house, sipping tea.

"Oh," I shrugged. "Inside a statue."

"A *statue?*"

"Most large statues of the Buddha have a space for relics," I said. "They are always trying to tell us that the Buddha's rib is in Burma, or that his tooth is in Sri Lanka."

"Which Buddha, Satomi?" Masayoshi asked, spacing out his words as he fought his rising anger.

I reminded Masayoshi that after my mother died, Chieko and Mineko had essentially cut me out of my mother's will and taken all her treasures without consulting me. Bit by bit, I said, I'd been replaced by *them,* and I was not about to let my life's path become completely decided by two girls who were too scared to ever leave Hachinohe.

"I put most of the bones inside the main statue in your temple. The one you keep closed with a padlock," I said.

Then I sat back to watch the drama unfold, as everyone around me came to terms with what I had done.

Masayoshi was not willing to unlock the Buddha case just to get my mother's bones. He said it was bad enough that I'd violated the rules once already by opening the box on the wrong day of the year. Even though I tried to apologize, Masayoshi insisted we would have to wait until April 8 to unfasten the case. This was the historical Buddha's birthday, and the one day of the year when the cabinet could be unlatched, allowing the Buddha to gaze out at the world. Locals would no doubt come and take a look, and there might even be a few tourists, middle-aged women or couples on holiday interested in taking a peek at the work of a master. Until then, Masayoshi said, we were all going to have to wait.

"Well, I'm not going to wait. I'm going back to Tochigi," I said.

"You do what you want," Masayoshi said. "But the offer stands for you to stay here with us. I think it is important. When parents and children can accept each other—no matter what that means—their relationships with everyone else will change."

Masayoshi went on to say that April really wasn't that far away. It was almost the end of February now, and then we'd just have to go through March. He had many duties to perform until then, including Ohigan, the twice-yearly ritual that fell on the equinoxes during which the souls of the dead returned to visit the living.

Rumi would remain at the temple and Akira would continue visiting her. And if I stayed, I could also spend some time with Rumi, which he thought I should consider since Rumi had come from so far away to find me. Plus, he added, a little nervously, we could spend time with each other. Almost as an afterthought, we agreed that one of us ought to contact François to let him know that Rumi was all right.

Rumi called her father the next day. I watched her through a small hole poked in the rice paper that otherwise covered the *shoji* door. Masayoshi had one of those old Showa-era phones in the hallway. It was a made of dull pink plastic, and the handle looked oversized even in Rumi's American-sized fist. It was cold out in the hallway and she was pacing back and forth while she talked on the phone, explaining her situation. Abruptly, she turned and looked straight at me and I backed away from the *shoji* door, startled to have been so easily found out. "Satomi," she called out after she had hung up. "He wants to talk to you next time." Then she hurried off in the direction of the temple.

I thought back to the years that had passed since I'd left Rumi alone in San Francisco. At first I had been deeply relieved not to have to worry about her every need. There had been the adventure of going back to Japan and climbing out of my obscure little position as an art student to become the *mangaka* I am today. I was very busy during all that time, as my mother had promised me a talented person always was.

The stories and pictures I'd created had come out of me almost in a rage. I suppose this was natural since I'd been holding back my talents for the years in San Francisco after my mother had died. The success had felt wonderful and I could not shake the feeling that my mother was watching from somewhere, approving as I lived out her wishes. It had felt right, as critics and fans one by one lauded my work. It was as though I'd resumed the story of my life as it was meant to be, before I'd been sidetracked.

Of course, there had been a few moments here and there when I'd thought about Rumi. After a few years, when I was earning some money and I was no longer so tired or sad all the time, I had thought to myself that I might have had the energy to care for her after all. Occasionally Shinobu had encouraged me to try to find my daughter, but I'd always shrugged off her prodding. Wasn't she confusing her predicament with mine?

"No," she'd always told me. She wasn't confused at all. I was simply afraid.

I told her that this was impossible. *I* was never scared of anything. Anyway, I am quite good at putting things in their place and not indulging in too much reflection, a skill I learned once I came to accept that my mother intended to stay married to Mr. Horie. Likewise, in time, I had convinced myself that my daughter was better off without me.

When Rumi first arrived, I thought she might want to join me like all the other girls. Shinobu tried to explain to me that things were probably not going to work out this way. She said that Rumi could be my future, but in a very different way from Kumi and Keiko. It was intriguing, this idea that my child could give me a sense of what was to come, so unlike the one I imagined in my head when I was writing stories. I still didn't understand how Rumi was unable to see the benefit of what I had to offer; life can be cruel to a girl of limited talent. But Shinobu has been right about things before.

I went to look for Rumi in the *hondo*. It was very cold because Masayoshi couldn't afford to heat the entire structure. I handed her my handkerchief. "The woods were my friends when I was small. I always had my privacy there."

She dabbed her eyes and stared at the statues and I looked at them too, wondering how she saw them and how they appeared to her Western eyes. Then I remembered. Because of François, she had grown up with similar objects and the altar would be familiar to her. It might even be comforting. The idea startled me a little bit, that someone so foreign could have something in common with me.

Presently she told me about her conversation with her father. François had tried to insist on flying to Japan, but she had told him that she was not ready to see him. Even just speaking to him, she said, made her feel a bit ill.

"When he told me you were dead," she said, "he was talking about himself. You were dead to him and he wanted me to feel about you the same way that he did. It never occurred to him that maybe I would want to see you anyway."

"He has always had too much longing for things. And he never understood how to use his own talents to get what he wanted. It's a weakness in people."

She thought about this for a while, and I watched the surface of her face shift, just as clouds lighten and darken a landscape, altering its mood. She had and has no *shirankao,* no *I don't know* face. Finally, she said, "He told me about the *kannon.* He said you were the one who originally stole it." She turned to look at me. "*You* could get it back. Buy it from Snowden-roshi."

I rolled my eyes. "That's probably what Snowden-roshi planned all along. He gave me back my daughter, and now he wants my money," I growled.

"He might just give it to you," she said.

I thought about this. I wondered if I could charm Timothy again, now that so many years had passed. Rumi could come with me, though I would have to find something suitable for her to wear. It might even be fun to appeal to Timothy's so-called Buddha nature, and test just how enlightened he really was. I settled back on my heels and looked up at the altar, imagining and dreaming. It could even be as it had been with my mother so many years ago, I presenting my younger, more attractive self—Rumi—to the world, the two of us making our way through life and forcing it to pause in its frenetic activity to make a path just for the two of us.

Throughout March, the men of Muryojuji were often occupied with funerals and exorcisms. Still, Masayoshi was able to make time for us; he and I spent a few hours a day recounting tales of our earlier lives to Rumi so she gradually became familiar with the cast of characters of her family in Japan. She, in turn, told us about her childhood with François. When Masayoshi worked, I sat in the main room sketching, or went to the *ryokan* where I was staying to call my assistants with instructions; they ferried clothing and supplies back and forth as I needed them.

Yoko was constantly busy. She made and returned phone calls, arranged her husband's and her son's calendars, organized meals and banquets, kept a flower arrangement in the entry, cleaned the family altar, did the laundry. Around all of this, she had to find the time to shop and prepare the family's meals and baths.

During the day, she listened to the gossip of unexpected guests, pouring them tea, bringing them treats, and accepting gifts, which piled up in a spare room. She had an endless supply of tissues and fruit boxes, which she sorted and ordered so we would eat things before they spoiled. Some things she arranged to donate to charity or to send to friends, always making sure that the giver wouldn't find out that the gift hadn't been consumed at the temple.

Observing Yoko, I wondered if I could possibly have adjusted to so much work had Masayoshi and I ever married. How different was this relationship from the one Masayoshi and I had had! The two of them were always working. From the outside, it seemed much like the relationship François had tried to have with me in San Francisco, where we dedicated ourselves to his business. I wondered if it was as my mother had said, that my talents could not have flourished with him.

By the end of March, the temple had become even busier. Masayoshi, Tomohiro, Yoko, and Rumi pitched in to clean up the house. Groundskeepers came to organize the garden, clearing out fallen leaves and branches and encouraging the few optimistic plum blossoms, which had started to sprout some buds, to bloom. The tension in the scenery moved me and I felt deeply nostalgic. This, after all, was the landscape of my childhood.

Around the twenty-first of March, people began to come to the temple in even larger numbers. Yoko booked back-to-back time slots for the Ohigan memorial services. Day after day, Masayoshi and Tomohiro trekked out to the graveyard to give prayers and light incense.

On the eighth of April, Masayoshi unveiled the statue. It was the first clear blue sky at Muryojuji temple since I'd arrived. The last of the snow was melting so feverishly, you could hear it. The courtyard and the garden were filled with the sound of water dripping and ice cracking.

Masayoshi had told us that we would all need to gather at the temple very early that morning to open the box. He wanted to retrieve my mother's bones before any of the tourists came. So, at five o'clock in the morning, I dressed in every bit of warm clothing that I had and entered the temple. We were all there: Masayoshi, Tomohiro, Yoko, Akira, Rumi, my assistants, and Shinobu, who had arrived the day before. I had thought there would be some ceremony about opening the box, but instead things were very matter-of-fact. Tomohiro undid the padlock, and he and Akira struggled with the knots on the rope. Then, very carefully, they opened the box, one door at a time.

Light poured out from the interior of the box and we had to cover our eyes. When my eyes adjusted, I could see a man dressed in gold, holding a box of medicine.

"He's beautiful," Rumi said. She told me later what she had seen: a man moving just slightly, undulating, like a wisp of grass caught in a tide. His nimbus radiated light, the beams reaching out into the farthest reaches of the temple, merging with the rays of sun, which were only now starting to steal in between the cracks of the windows and the doors.

When we'd all adjusted to this bright, brilliant shape, Masayoshi asked me to help him remove the panel from the back of the statue to get at the relics. To do this, both of us had to slide in around the side of the statue; the box was that big. We were covered from view, only our feet sticking out from either side of the statue, while our torsos and hands were occupied with the panel. I looked at Masayoshi's handsome face and thought to myself how it would only be in moments like this that we would now ever have any privacy. He turned and looked at me too, and I saw his eyes soften. "Do you remember how to open the panel?" he asked.

It took some time. I fiddled with the wood behind the Buddha's head and eventually heard the groan of wood giving way. I let Masayoshi reach inside the statue's brain and retrieve the parcel with one hand. For a moment, I could see through the Buddha's glass eyes to the little group gathered at his feet. Then we closed the panel and came out to rejoin our little family. Masayoshi held out a white cloth bag. At last, the bones.

It was a busy day. Tourists came from across Japan to see the statue. Most were older enthusiasts who had decided to spend their retired years visiting some of Japan's beautiful but less popular and lesser-known treasures. Masayoshi even relaxed some of his rules and allowed a few amateur photographers to take pictures, as long as they didn't use a flash.

I spent most of the day in a corner, drawing some sketches. The assistants and Shinobu went for walks. I drew Rumi and Akira like little birds nestled on a branch. François was an old rangy horse peering over the fence of his grazing ground. Timothy a proud old cat. I amused myself by making Masayoshi look like an old badger on a pilgrimage.

Toward the end of the day, I saw Masayoshi heading for a stroll. I stood up immediately and went to accompany him.

He was quiet for a long time while we climbed up to the highest point in the cemetery. Here the wind whipped through the bamboo around us and birds of prey surveyed the valley floor. Finally Masayoshi said, "Your mother told me that I'd never be able to make you happy. And I decided that she was probably right."

"I was always happy with you," I protested.

"Look at my life, Satomi. Could you have done everything that Yoko does? Working all day like she does and raising two children?"

"Has this life made you happy? I mean, really and truly?" I asked.

"I can't imagine my life without Akira and Tomohiro."

"But beyond that? You have no regrets?" When he did not answer, I said, "Anyway, all this time has passed and here we are again."

"Unless you disappear."

I shrugged. "I'm going to get the *kannon* back for you."

"That would be helpful," he said. "It would be much easier to be friends if you did that." After a moment, he added, "Yoko will accept you if I do. I just ask that you are nice to her."

Below, so absorbed in each other that they did not notice us, Rumi and Akira were walking hand in hand and talking together. "If I were going to put Rumi in a story, what kind of tale would it be? A girl who reaches out to find her mother. It's like Demeter and Persephone, except in reverse. Such a girl, I think, must be very brave."

"What happens when she finds the mother?" Masayoshi asked.

"Well, the mother isn't what she hoped. That would make the story boring."

"Maybe at some point the mother would at least be a little bit grateful or happy that the daughter showed up," Masayoshi suggested.

I shrugged. "Probably."

"They might," Masayoshi continued, retrieving the now soggy hand-kerchief, "become friends."

"Friendship," I laughed ruefully. "I used to think that was such a weak emotion. Not as powerful as love."

"You can love your friends too. In fact you should."

He looked at me, and I saw his hand twitch. For a moment, I thought he was going to reach up and touch my face. Then he turned to look out at the valley, and after a while, I did the same, and the two of us were silent.

A few days later, we were back at Kashihara shrine. The Sakurais had insisted on overseeing the funeral.

While the outside of the shrine was painted a vibrant scarlet, the inside was quite plain, just a *tatami* floor and an altar barely visible behind a curtain. At the far end of the room, a little table supported a bowl filled with water and a display of green branches with slick oval leaves. Behind this was the urn filled with my mother's bones. Mr. Sakurai stood just off to the side and came to greet us as we entered, smiling and dignified, putting us all into a relaxed mood.

We sat on a row of small chairs. After a few minutes, Mr. Sakurai gestured to me, and I stood up and walked gingerly over to the little table. Then I picked up a green branch that had a white piece of paper tied around it, placed this gently on the altar, and bowed. I raised my hands and clapped twice. I bowed low and walked back to my seat.

One by one we all stood up and went through the same motions. I could tell that Rumi was nervous when her turn came. When she returned to her seat after a final bow, I leaned over and whispered into her ear, "That was better than most Japanese people."

We buried all the bones together, including the Adam's apple in the red box. Now that spring had come, the nearby river all but roared as it raced by the cemetery grounds.

"Your grandmother's soul needs to travel to the ocean," I explained to Rumi. "All this time she hasn't been near any water. She was caught."

Mr. Sakurai said more prayers, and my mother and I placed branches on top of the grave. A quiet wind stirred the bamboo overhead and I looked up to see the leaves undulating under the invisible pressure.

I thought to myself that there are always unseen things in this world. Love blooms in unlikely places, and though we long to pass this blossom back and forth between us, circumstances don't always make this possible. A girl inherits the invisible pressure of guilt from her parents and she might not know exactly what she is feeling or why she knows it. A man might feel the loss of a lover so keenly it's as if she's there, mocking him every day with her paradoxical absence.

Then I imagined the invisible soul of my mother drinking water for the first time in over twenty years. Imagined her floating through streams filled with *koi*, past wooden riverboats where fishermen speared eel, out into the great harbor of Yokohama or perhaps Kobe, where unsuspecting freight ships had just been launched on trips to California. Out there in the water, she would feel purified. The salt and the water would strip off the injustice of death, and a false burial. And the essential part of her personality, that aspect of her that had arrived on the earth so many years before, would go back to the gods of Japan, waiting, just waiting for another chance to taste the earthly pleasures of love, longing for another chance to feel the heat of summer.

We had a luncheon back at the shrine and everyone became very drunk. I was talking with Rumi about the possibility of visiting San Francisco.

"I like the feeling of being far away," she said to me.

"Ah." I smiled. "You are like one of the heroines in my stories who doesn't want to leave her magical kingdom because it makes her feel powerful." Then I shook my head. "François will worry. He does love you."

"How do you know?"

"Because," I said, "you look like a loved person. It always shows on people's faces. The ones who discover love when they are much older always look startled. The loved ones expect it from other people." Softly, now, I said, "Let us see how we feel in a few months, Rumi. Perhaps by then you will be interested in returning to San Francisco. At least to rescue a misplaced statue?"

She lifted her head and met my gaze and the directness unsettled me. Still, I said, "You won't have to go alone. And anyway, what is there to be afraid of? There aren't many more secrets."

Abruptly Tomomi appeared at my side. She tugged at my sleeve, insisting that she had something important to show me. Grudgingly, I stood up and followed her outside. I was still standing in the doorway wrestling with a pesky heel when Rumi came to stand beside me. "What is it?" she asked, as Tomomi reached the foothills bordering the shrine grounds and disappeared in between two trees.

"According to Tomomi, your grandmother used to meet her lover up there," I nodded.

"You mean," Rumi laughed, "that's where you were conceived?"

"Shall we go look?" Akira, Masayoshi, Shinobu, and the others came out to join us.

So we climbed, a drunken party of funeralgoers dressed in black and scaling a steeply inclined hillside. The terrain altered, now bamboo, now trees, now bamboo. Tomomi led the way, apparently convinced that she knew the proper direction to take. Occasionally I paused to catch my breath and to take in the sight of the bamboo. Tall stalks reached up almost as high as any tree. All the greenery buffered us from sound, and the slight hum of traffic from the nearby expressway faded. Soon all I heard were the sounds of the woods and of all of us crashing through the hillside.

Suddenly Tomomi yelped. When I came beside her, I found her standing next to a large stone, shaped like a mushroom. We turned around to the front and saw that it was a carving, very old and weather-beaten, but there was no mistaking the general shape of a *kannon* gazing out at us, beautifully dressed and smiling at us through the surface of the rock.

I felt the earth shake. I thought I must be drunk, but then I realized that the earth really was trembling. Everyone screamed, and I grabbed Rumi's hand, pulling her into a nearby bamboo grove. I held onto the stalk while the earth roared. And when it was over, the only sound I heard was running water.

Picture two equally matched *sumo* wrestlers leaning against each other in a ring deep below the earth's surface, and you have an idea of the forces that have shaped Japan. The silent and insistent pushing of the earth's Pacific and Asian plates forced the earth's crust up through the ocean floor where it pooled, hardened, and then rose ever upward in a geological elevator until it punctured the waters of the Pacific like a breaching whale. The resulting structure, the island of Japan, isn't completely steady, and is a frequent victim of earthquakes as the two wrestlers deep beneath the land's surface struggle to gain advantage. It's no wonder, then, that Japanese mythology is full of dragons and monsters wriggling beneath the skin of the earth, disrupting carefully planted rice paddies and upending the foundations of homes.

But there is one good thing about all this geological indigestion: Japan is dotted with hot springs. It couldn't have taken long for the first Japanese to discover the pleasures of sitting in a hot spring, and of spending time in the company of people who had recently cleaned themselves. For inspiration, they didn't have to look much farther than the Japanese monkey, who to this day adroitly dips in and out of mountain springs whenever the air grows too cold in the winter months.

Some of the springs are filled with sulfur and smell like boiled eggs. Others are rich with lime or magnesium, coloring the water shades of green or blue, inkpots in which a celestial hand has carefully cleaned her brushes. Some hot springs cluster together—one red, one white, one green.

Each of these pools is assigned a healing property, and Japanese healers work out the permutation of how these pools can be combined to heal a variety of old-age ailments (pool one plus pool two to cure arthritis in the hands and feet, pool three and pool five for the heart, and so on).

Naturally, there is a mythology about these hot springs. According to legend, most are the result of a beneficent *kami*, or god, who decided to give villagers their very own communal place to play, Nintendo not having yet been invented. Others are credited to the legendary Buddhist priest Dōgen striking his staff against a rock to start the magical flow of water. Whatever the mythical origin, many hot springs are associated with a shrine, and it's not difficult for a Japanese person, chin-deep in green-tinted water, to imagine that he has dipped himself, tempura-like, into a marinade of the gods' own creation.

That afternoon, after the funeral and after the earthquake had scared us silly for a time, the plates near Kashihara shrine shifted, releasing the pent-up pressure of mineral water. We crept out of the bamboo grove and, when all seemed safe, walked over to the earth near the stone *kannon*, now completely wet. I knelt down and tested the water.

"It's warm," I said. I left my hand under the stream, which had grown stronger over the past few minutes. "Hot," I corrected myself. Then I looked at Mrs. Sakurai and laughed. "You're going to have to build a bath."

Acknowledgments

Thank you to my parents for demonstrating the deepest and truest kind of love. Through my American grandmother, I discovered books and the magic of storytelling and that one could become this thing called a "writer." My Japanese grandmother, so whimsical and elegant, helped me look at the details of her world, and was delighted when I learned to share her secret vision. My Japanese grandfather, still alive at ninety-six, has shown me how the soul continues to become tempered and wise over time.

Thank you to my agent, Irene Skolnick, who battled plenty of *onis* to find the perfect home for this book. Rose, Erin, Julie, and the staff continue to be a wonderful support. I must thank Fiona McCrae at Graywolf for superb chiseling; you helped this hunk of unfinished marble become more of what it was supposed to be. Would that all first-time novelists could be so lucky. Thank you Polly, Katie, Erin, and everyone else at Graywolf. Many thanks to the *South Dakota Review,* where the sixth chapter appeared in slightly different form as "True Nature."

Special thanks to JauntyQ and Brian, who know why, or should. Jeffrey Lependorf, I'm grateful that fate seated us next to each other on that plane. William Clark, I will always appreciate your early belief in me. Thank you to Laurence Hobgood for piano lessons over Brazilian food, and the rest of the band, old and new, for the music. Thank you to the daemon for provoking me when I needed it most; the shadow is a powerful thing. Very special thanks to Maud Newton for more than anyone will ever know.

Ellis Avery and Juliet Grames assured me that all would end well. Alexi Zentner, Kaytie Lee, Lisa Gluskin Stonestreet, and Vanessa Hutchinson were early readers who insisted I should "have some f*cking confidence."

Thank you to everyone at Empukuji, but especially Shizuko, Sempō, and Ryōko. Also Akemi and Nobata, all the Ogawas, everyone at Tsū-Hachiman, the Kurasakis, Phil for lessons in jade and porcelain, Debbie, Nono, and Isao, and all the other Americans, Japanese, and Scots.

To my in-laws, Ian and Sarah: when I first set foot in your lovely house, I knew that I was home. And finally, to my husband, Gordon, who taught me how to slow time down so ideas and characters have room to breathe and are able to spring to life with richness and complexity. The book lives because of your faith in me, and thus I have learned something of what it means to have faith at all.

PICKING BONES FROM ASH

A Novel by

Marie Mutsuki Mockett

The Bone Room

There was a mysterious room behind the main altar of the Buddhist temple where I stayed when I visited Japan with my mother. Visitors to the temple went in and out of the room speaking in hushed tones, and it took me several years to summon up the courage take a peek. Before that, the adults always steered me away from the room in the subtle, discouraging way that grown-ups have when they want to prevent you from doing something, but don't want to tell you why. I was probably around twelve when I got my first look. Alone, I snuck into the temple's main room, then slid past the immense, theater-like altar with its gold chandelier and brocade tapestries and the large Buddha seated at the very back surveying his offerings of melon and peaches. Just off to the right was a nondescript door, so artfully hidden behind the altar one might miss it altogether. Beyond this door was the strange room.

The space inside was dark and I left the light off, afraid I'd get caught. I could see that the room was narrow, and that it followed the width of the temple's back wall from left to right. To the left were dozens of pinwheels, children's toys, and bottles of Yakult yogurt milk. The rest of the walls were covered with boxes, plaques, and Japanese Buddhist statuary. Serious, adult stuff. But what was with the toys? I struggled to understand what these playful, brightly colored things were doing in a place that was otherwise so somber. In the years that followed, I asked for an explanation, but no one ever gave me one. It would be up to persistence and adulthood for me to find the answer.

My parents—and my American grandmother—were very committed to my Japanese education. Every summer my mother and I boarded the plane in San Francisco, bidding farewell to my American father, who could not speak Japanese. Once on the plane my mother refused to communicate with me in English. In those days there was no fax, no internet, and no Skype. International phone calls were expensive and reserved for emergencies. I had to rely on blue aerogramme letters to learn what was happening with my father and my parakeet, Cheerful. Once on the ground in Japan, I felt isolated, transported to another world whose rules became increasingly complex as I grew older and more was expected of me.

We nearly always began our visits to Japan at the temple because my mother's aunt, who ran the complex, welcomed us. My grandparents had been deeply upset by my mother's marriage to a foreigner and we visited them only briefly and always with trepidation. At the temple in the north, tucked into a hillside and surrounded by rice paddies, I would shake off my jet lag and struggle to re-attune my ear to the Japanese language, and try to mold my body to the shape and space of Japanese life: sit on knees and not Indian style, squat over the toilet, leave shoes at the door, wear one set of slippers in wood hallways and another in the toilet, wear no slippers on *tatami*, sit and sleep on the floor, bathe in extremely hot water, watch everything but save the questions for later, do not gesture too broadly. Accept that people will stare.

If I was often confused and homesick on those trips, I was also increasingly bewitched. At the festivals I wore a *yukata* (summer kimono) and admired fireflies and fireworks against the dark night sky. Streets were lit with paper lanterns and young men sang twangy folk tunes. The occasional wedding featured a bride dressed in bright red instead of white. Bamboo forests rattled and beckoned in the rain and cicadas sang me to sleep. Northern California is dry and gold in the summer; in Japan, the vegetation was lush and ripe. At home we were always on the verge of a water shortage; in Japan, we bathed in hot springs morning and evening to rid ourselves of sweat. In time, my mother reported that I was speaking in Japanese in my sleep. When we'd return to California, I would long for Japanese breakfasts with fish and seaweed and rice. By the time I was an adult, Japan had taken a permanent hold of my psyche.

Now I know that the mysterious room was the bone room. The boxes were filled with ash and bone, as the Japanese don't cremate human remains at as high a temperature as we do in the West; the bone is intentionally left behind. Sometimes grieving families don't have enough money for a burial plot. Sometimes, as was the case with my grandmother's remains a few years ago, the ground is too cold and frozen and the burial can't take place immediately after the funeral. In the meantime, the bones need a place to go. The toys were offerings to the spirits of dead children and aborted fetuses. Children, in general, haven't amassed enough karma to automatically begin the journey toward reincarnation; they need the help of a bodhisattva (an enlightened and compassionate being) to help them get started. The toys and clothes and candy were offerings, desperate gestures, bribes: the saddest and most personal acts of people deeply immersed in grief.

The bone room, that tragic yet clinical space, gets at the heart of what Buddhism is and does in Japan, which is to oversee all aspects of the afterlife. We like to think of Buddhism in the West as being a kind of philosophy, and of course, it can be. But in practice, Buddhism in Japan gives followers a window into the afterlife and very clear guidance at the moment of death and thereafter. A temple is not really a child's plaything, and knowing this, my mother's aunt and my mother had tried hard to make my early visits to Japan as devoid of any reference to Buddhism as possible. We focused on festivals, castles, animated television shows, food, and travel. The philosophy, and the grieving of dead relatives and friends, were all in the future.

Travel to Japan

When I started writing *Picking Bones from Ash*, I had a fairly simple premise: what if a girl was haunted by a ghost and readers thought they knew who the ghost was, but turned out to be wrong? And what if the key to understanding what the ghost wanted hinged on understanding another culture?

I knew that most of my characters would be women, but they would be modeled on the Japanese women I knew, and not the flimsy, suffering-but-beautiful stock characters I'd run into in so many historical novels written by Western authors. I would not write armchair-travel fiction. I thought about the lives of women in my family. My grandmother, who was born into an aristocratic family only to see its wealth and reputation vastly diminished during the early twentieth century and after the war. Despite this, she instilled a firm sense of aesthetics in her children. My mother, who was brave enough to leave her country and her parents to enthusiastically seek out a new life in the US. My aunt, who staunchly ran the temple, seeing it through some very financially troubling times, until she finally persuaded her brother's illegitimate son to cut ties with his mother and take over. And I thought about the marriages I'd observed since childhood and the quiet way in which men and women formed alliances and relationships—even when not married to each other.

As I thought about all these women, I began to think about the folk tales and children's tales my mother had read to me and those animated television shows I'd been allowed to watch in Japan as a child. It occurred to me that unlike Disney cartoons, Japanese fairy tales often feature preternaturally powerful women who are not in search of a man. Growing up, my favorite story had been about the Moon Princess, found inside a fat stalk of bamboo and raised by a poor bamboo cutter and his wife. The princess is wooed by princes from the far corners of Japan and by the emperor himself, but spurns them all, eventually breaking the hearts of her would-be suitors and her adoptive parents (who promptly die) when she returns to the kingdom of the moon. No Disney fairy tale ended this way.

What was more, most of these Japanese stories developed in surprising and unexpected ways. Nature was often a powerful character, adding a quality of chaos to the universe. Evil characters were slippery, and sometimes become forces of goodness and wisdom. Structure, I realized as an adult, did not need to adhere to strict and symmetrical rules to be beautiful. My own characters thus came to life, with all the challenges, pleasures, and difficulties that come from being a girl who truly believes that the most important thing in life is, like the Moon Princess, to be talented and special.

Finally, I wanted to begin to share with readers some of what I believe makes Japan so unique, tantalizing, and rich. For a few years, I wrote for the blog *Japundit,* whose mission, according to its founder, was to show the world all that was Japanese and yet was not "tea and temples." I've been going to Japan for a long time—over thirty years. In my efforts to learn "how to behave correctly," I've listened to what people say and find funny and like to eat and do in their spare time. The tea and the temples are of course bulwarks of Japanese culture and are fascinating, as are the objects of current Western obsessions: love hotels, *Akihabara,* and other marginal cultural establishments. But there is much, much more to Japan—there has to be, with a culture that is over a thousand years old—and in *Picking Bones from Ash,* I wanted to try to unfold some of that mystery for curious readers.

Questions and Topics for Discussion

1) At the beginning of the book, Satomi says: "My mother always told me there is only one way a woman can be truly safe in this world. And that is to be fiercely, inarguably, and masterfully talented." Is Satomi safe in the end? At what cost? And what about the other female characters, particularly Akiko and Rumi? What does it mean for a woman to be safe?

2) Satomi seeks out Western music in Paris, Timothy yearns for spiritual enlightenment through Buddhism, and François reinvents himself in San Francisco. Discuss the ways in which these and other characters—and perhaps you yourself—find freedom through other cultures, and comfort in what is native.

3) On page 246, Satomi tells Rumi, "Here we are. A girl without a mother and a girl with too much of a mother. Which, I wonder, would most people rather be? One inherits history. The other is free to create it herself." Do you think it is better to inherit history or to create a history for yourself?

4) François teaches Rumi the importance of seeing beauty out of context. How does this skill help her later on? How does it relate to the Buddhist notion of seeing through illusion?

5) Why do you think the ghost of Akiko revealed itself to Rumi and not to Satomi?

6) Masayoshi says: "When parents and children can accept each other—no matter what that means—their relationships with everyone else will change" (page 272). How do you feel about this statement?

7) How did Mockett's use of interlocking stories and voices affect your reading experience?

8) Mockett has said: "I felt it was important that any supernatural elements in my novel would be grounded in psychological truths, because that's the 'reality' of true supernatural experiences." How does the supernatural function within her story? Does it add atmosphere? Did it detract from the story?

9) On page 224, Akira says: "The world of the living can be like that of the dead. It is tragic when we lose ourselves in grief." What do you think about this statement? Is it something that you or someone close to you has experienced?

10) At the end of the novel, Akiko says to Satomi: "You look like a loved person. It always shows on people's faces. The ones who discover love when they are much older always look startled." Do you agree?

MARIE MUTSUKI MOCKETT was born in Carmel, California, to a Japanese mother and an American father. She is a graduate of Columbia University with a degree in East Asian studies. Mockett's essay "Letter from a Japanese Crematorium" was cited as a notable in *Best American Essays 2008*. She has been a Bernard O'Keefe Scholar for Nonfiction at the Bread Loaf Writers' Conference. *Picking Bones from Ash* was shortlisted for the Saroyan International Prize, a finalist for the Paterson Prize, and longlisted for the Asian American Literary Awards. She lives with her Scottish husband and son in New York City. This is her first novel.

This book was designed by Rachel Holscher. It is set in Minion Pro type by BookMobile Design and Publishing Services and manufactured by Versa Press on acid-free paper.